Anger in the Wind

Other Books By Logan Forster

Proud Land
Desert Storm
Mountain Stallion
Tamarlane
Revenge
Run Fast, Run Far

Anger in the Wind

by

Logan Forster

David McKay Company, Inc.
New York

ANGER IN THE WIND

LIBRARY OF CONGRESS CATALOG CARD NUMBER 74-80503

ISBN 0-679-50464-8

MANUFACTURED IN THE UNITED STATES OF AMERICA

For Eunice, with gratitude

1

He traveled steadily westward through an emptiness of grass and sky; distance and openness were all around him. He crossed rivers running bank-full with the spring burden of icy water, and at night he slept in wind-brushed grass or in long-abandoned ruins, as the pungent sage shivered in the winds. Through the night came the faint, far-away pulse of an antelope band running, or the thin, long cry of the coyote calling across the canyons of the night, like an echo of his longing.

One day he glimpsed the mountains as a blue shadow a hundred miles away, and as he traveled he watched them grow until they towered high above him. He entered a canyon. Near sundown he looked behind him and saw that the yellow and green and open plain was gone.

The arms of the mountains enfolded him; the wild hills reared up, rough, old, and hugely somber. A river roared through its confining cliffs beside the road, and in the narrow defile a constant cool wind carried a chill of high peaks as twilight cast its shadow across the lower hills. The bellowing river echoed against the deeper canyon walls.

For a moment he sat deliberately taking in the smells and sounds, which were wholly different from what he had known, and watching the play of shadows along the canyon walls; then he shrugged away a forming doubt and rode on, noting the caution with which his two giant dogs scouted this shadowy newness, the feeling of tension in the grey stallion under him, and the way the two mares and the foal closed up and followed uneasily on the stallion's heels.

Suddenly he saw the stallion's pricked ears swivel back, and an instant later he caught the sound of wheels and running hoofs approaching from behind. The canyon wall fell back slightly from the river here, and he reined to one side to let the vehicle pass. The grey's curiosity mounted as the strange horses drew near. Without warning, it wheeled and danced along sideways, warily eyeing the oncoming four-horse coach. When the rider's hand firmly straightened it, it slugged its head resentfully, squatted on powerful hindquarters, then flirted sideways again as the double team galloped past.

The rider gave the high-wheeled coach his surprised attention, for this region was serviced by no stage line; then he recognized it for what it was—a sleek, light, private carriage, steel-sprung and fashioned for comfort and speed.

Through the dusty glass of the window he caught a brief glimpse of gilt fittings, red plush upholstery, and the shadowy silhouette of a woman—a flash and it was past. Then he caught the driver's shouted, "Whoa!" and saw the vehicle come to a halt a hundred feet ahead.

At once he drew rein and sat closely watching, not liking his position here in this narrow defile. His whistle sliced the river-troubled air, and in response the two giant dogs wheeled in their tracks far ahead of the halted coach and came racing back, their wolf-like appearance and savage mein creating brief pandemonium among the four mettlesome coach horses as they approached. Reaching the stallion, they flattened themselves in the dust and lay rapidly panting, their pale amber eyes riveted on the strange vehicle.

Except for the inquiring flick of its ears, the stallion stood rooted in its tracks. But when the coach door swung open and a woman alighted with a sudden and violent billowing of emerald skirts, it loosed a shattering snort and skittered backward in alarm.

The woman had taken three steps before she realized that she herself was the cause of the stallion's fright. At once she moved into the lee of the coach, holding her skirts from the pull of the wind. She stood quite still then, gathering the folds of green material close against her sides while she waited for the stallion to calm down. Her voice came down to the rider, barely heard above the river's roar.

"May I speak with you, please?"

For a thoughtful moment the rider considered the request, glancing from her to the lone man on the high driver's seat. Arrived at his decision, he laid a reassuring hand against the grey's rigidly bowed neck and walked it forward.

"Magnificent!"

It came as a cry of sheer delight, and she stood there openly reveling in the imposing reach and bulk of the towering grey as he swung broadside a dozen feet away and again adopted a rock-like stance. For a full minute she studied the stallion with appraising eyes, then as carefully assessed the merits of the two mares and the foal. Satisfied, she made her decision.

"I will buy them . . . all four."

It was a statement of fact. She had no doubt at all that her desire would become reality, and she was pleased by this stroke of fortune.

"No."

The flat refusal drew a faint line of displeasure across her brow, and for the first time she lifted her eyes to the man. For an instant only, as she caught the striking sun against the high planes of the coppery face and read the Indian breeding there, she betrayed surprise. It registered in the barest widening of her violet eyes;

3

then her heavy lashes shuttered her gaze. "But you haven't heard my offer."

"You can make it; I still won't sell."

The coach rocked slightly as the driver turned on the seat. "Listen, feller—" he began, but the woman cut in, swiftly, smoothly.

"That will do, Henry."

If the rider had entertained any doubts about the woman's authority, they evaporated at once as the driver turned back without a word, staring over the backs of his horses.

Deliberately the rider eased himself in the saddle, assuming an air of utter indifference. Nothing showed on his boldly carved features, but his dislike for this chance encounter was obvious. From the concealing shadow of the hatbrim, he surveyed the aristocratic figure before him, his black eyes boring down at her with an intensity wholly at variance with his relaxed attitude.

She was a tall, fair woman with a wealth of auburn hair. Her features, her statuesque figure, and her regal bearing were striking. Yet it was not so much her beauty that riveted his gaze as her utter unawareness of it, or, he corrected himself, her calm acceptance of it as a quality rightfully hers. He had a sudden conviction that she was a woman who belonged to herself alone.

And this puzzled him, for the simple reason that she was so obviously female. By the sheer force of her inherent sensuality, without giving any sign of awareness of him as a man, she touched his maleness in a way that aroused him alarmingly, so that he suddenly averted his gaze. In that same instant, the instinct that had halted him a mile back and warned him against these unfamiliar hills brushed his thoughts anew. Without knowing why, he was certain that the woman before him represented a danger to him.

"You're headed west?"

Her question made him start; then some perversity prompted him deliberately to misinterpret her meaning. He glanced up at the lowering sun. "No, I'd say I'm headed pretty much northerly just now."

Again that faint line of irritation creased her brow. "I meant that you have apparently mistaken this road for the main route westward."

"No. There was no mistake."

His words wiped all trace of politeness from her expression and blunted her speech. "California?"

He answered in kind. "I'd have sworn this was still Colorado Territory."

"Are you *bound* for California?"

"Not necessarily."

Suddenly out of patience with him, she fired her words back at him. "Is this necessary?"

"I don't follow."

"You follow me perfectly, sir. My object in stopping was to make you an offer for those four animals—a generous and fair offer. May we not, at least, discuss the matter like two sensible adults?"

His leather-clad shoulders lifted in a noncommittal shrug.

"Naturally," she went on, choosing to interpret the gesture as assent, "I wouldn't expect to put you afoot. If you will deliver the horses to Star, I will give you four horses from my personal stable . . . in addition to paying you the price you name, of course."

"And which star would that be, ma'am?" he drawled.

Color tinged her neck but she checked her temper. "Star," she stated with monumental patience, "is a ranch some thirty miles north of here. I own it. I am Fresno Star Taggert."

His head inclined; his right hand went up to touch the brim of his hat in a courtly gesture. "Your servant, ma'am."

For one brief instant she was deceived by the apparent sincerity with which he acknowledged her introduction. On the point of nodding in answer, she caught the glint of sardonic amusement in his dark eyes. She stiffened, her classic features turning cold. "Good day," she said curtly, and turned around the coach, her shoulders rigid.

In leaving the protection of the coach, she unthinkingly released her skirts to the quick rush of air that filled the canyon. The effect on the stallion could not have been more startling had she fired a gun in its face. It loosed a gusty snort and reared into

5

the air. Only the rider's automatic reaction prevented the horse from crashing backward. Just before it lost its balance, an iron-like fist smashed squarely between its flattened ears, driving it back to all fours.

Startled, the woman whirled, took in the sight, and at once divined the cause of the animal's terror. For a moment she was openly amused at the rider's discomfiture; but her inherent sense of fair play would not allow her to avenge herself in so petty a fashion. "I apologize for that," she said through the drifting dust kicked up by the flurry of hoofs. When no answer was forthcoming from the dark-faced rider, she caught up her offending skirts and placed a foot on the step. But in the act of entering the coach she hesitated: "You will not sell your horses . . . at any price?"

"No, ma'am."

For a moment their eyes locked. In no way did she betray her disappointment. But when she spoke her displeasure was evident in the frigid voice. "That being the case, you would be well-advised to retrace your way to the western route. You will accomplish nothing at all by following this road further."

"I'm a curious man."

"You are a curious man," she stated, smoothly shading his own words to give them quite a different meaning. At once she regretted having done so. She said abruptly, "Good day to you, sir," and entered the coach and closed the door.

The driver's whip cracked, sending the four horses lunging into their collars. The coach rocked far back on its springs, and then the wheels began lifting streamers of dust into the air as the horses hit their tireless running stride along the narrow defile.

The rider sat watching the coach until it was out of sight. When it was gone, he smiled a slow, speculative smile, shrugged his wide shoulders, and followed the twin tracks that already were dimming as darkness spread through the river canyon.

2

Dawn filled the sky in changing sheets of color as Aaron Lord rolled over in his blankets and sat up. One instant he had been sound asleep. The next, he was wide awake. Four feet away, the huge dogs, who had slept the night through curled into tight knots, lifted their heads, rose to their feet, and stretched with prodigious yawns.

Some distance away, the three horses and the foal graze steadily, their movements rendered clumsy by their hobbles. At Lord's piercing whistle they lifted their heads and slowly moved toward him. He waited, letting his gaze travel around Star Valley.

From the moment of his entrance into the valley, he had been acutely conscious of its overpowering solitude—a silent, brooding quality that emanated from the surrounding hills and flowed out over the grassland with an almost tangible force. This silence worked more and more strongly in him until it absorbed him completely. Then, suddenly, a mountain thrush sent out its song from far away; his eye caught the flash of a band of antelope streaming over a low swell half a mile away. The region, then, was no longer empty, but warm and comforting. The warmth touched his innermost soul with a force that caused him actual pain.

For a long time he stood there, filled with an emotion he would never have allowed another to suspect—a lean, dark man with an air of solitude as complete and untouchable as that which dominated this high wilderness. He had a head of thick, black hair that reached to his shoulders, and a pair of deep-set eyes utterly devoid of light. His nose was narrow and straight, his mouth full. High, prominent cheekbones and skin the color of smooth copper proclaimed the blood of his Cheyenne mother. His single concession to vanity was a full mustache, shaped in a wide downward curve around his mouth, that reached almost to his jaw.

He was a man taller than the average, wider of shoulder and chest. Life had given him a lean trimness; constant riding and hard work had built within him a vast supply of vitality. Never in his life had he known absolute safety or enduring comfort, and therefore he had a habit of accepting the brief moments of ease, whenever they came, as a means of fortifying himself against the stress, danger, and humiliation that, he knew, lay always in wait.

He stood now in the attire he had worn for months—a buckskin shirt worn with the tail outside and belted about the waist, and fringed leather pants that molded his long legs like an outer layer of skin. Knee-high fringed moccasins encased his legs, and when he knelt to rekindle the fire, he moved with the silent, easy grace of an animal.

Because the horses were incapable of ignoring the lush grass, but must stop every few feet to snatch a mouthful, Lord had finished his hurried breakfast and had the supplies neatly stored away in the rawhide paniers by the time they finally came in. He carried his gear to the grey stallion and saddled up. Twice the animal reached its head around and nudged him affectionately, then stood quietly by while Lord lashed the packs on the chestnut mare.

Kicking sand over the dying fire, he swung up on the stallion and moved down the valley, heading for a tiny patch of green at the point of a hill some five miles away.

All the way from St. Louis, Lord had studied his surroundings with an eye for detail that would have permitted him to draw a map showing each river and creek he had crossed, each hill and valley, each town and isolated way station. He could describe the quality of grass along the trail, the crops that grew in any given area, the condition of summer water and winter shelter, the differing qualities of the people who claimed this more and more sparsely populated land. Now, studying the valley, he realized that it was in reality a feudal retreat. The vegetation was lush, the water supply inexhaustible, and the surrounding hills formed both a natural barrier against livestock's straying and an impregnable defense in all quarters.

With rising confidence he found himself approaching a triangular green meadow whose base lay against the tumbled wall of a benchland, the valley's boundary at this southeastern point. The path he had been following now all but vanished in rank undergrowth, but the big dogs, ranging far ahead, held to their course, making for a stand of cottonwoods a quarter mile to the east. He lifted the stallion to a trot.

His excitement transmitted itself to the other horses. The filly shot past, her short brush curled up over her swiveling rump as she raced into the grove, whirled, and came streaking back. When even with the stallion, she aimed a spirited kick at its shoulder, missed, skidded to a halt, and erupted into a fit of bucking that caused her dam to draw up and regard her in amazement, and Lord to laugh with pleasure. He gave the stallion a slap on the shoulder that sent it toward the trees at a run. A moment later, he pulled up in the grove. A steady, muted roar assailed his ears, and he caught the gleam of water falling over the sheer hillside into a wide pool. Nearby stood a stone house.

It was apparent that the place had been long abandoned.

Lord rode slowly forward. To the left of the house, two corrals, with poles tiredly sagging, flanked a roofless stable. Midway between stable and house a wagon stood with its front wheels sharply cramped in an attitude of arrested motion, its tongue broken.

On the wagon he glimpsed the top of a warped dresser and a set of rusted bedsprings—mute evidence of a hasty evacuation never completed.

He swung down in front of the house, and with difficulty shoved the door back on its badly sprung hinges. Stepping inside, he stopped, appalled. Everything in this main room bespoke deliberate, savage destruction. A legless sofa lay on its back, its upholstery ripped away. A table and three chairs were crumpled in their own ruins.

His lips thinned to a grim line as he stepped through this wreckage and peered into the two small bedrooms on his right, and to the left the kitchen. Here, too, the same wholesale destruction was evident. In the kitchen shards of crockery crunched underfoot, and battered utensils lay buried in wind-drifted sand on the floor and around the stove, canted drunkenly on two legs against the wall. He shook his head, the picture growing clearer and more disturbing, as he crossed to the back door.

Once outside he surveyed the homestead with the eyes of a potential owner. Both house and stable were of sandstone and were of admirable construction. With a new roof, the latter would be as weathertight as the day it was built. Clearly the corrals would have to be rebuilt.

Impatient to be exploring, he rounded the house, caught up the stallion's reins, and led it over to the larger of the two enclosures. He fished a hammer from his saddlebags and made a quick circle of the corral, shoring up the weathered poles in a fashion that would delude the two mares into thinking them unassailable, for the time being at least. Then he whistled the mares and foal through the gate and divested the chestnut of her pack before wrestling the gate shut. This accomplished, he mounted the stallion and reined away across the yard, heading for the far end of the grove.

He was halfway across the yard when the gaunt dogs rounded the corner of the house, water spiraling off their shaggy coats. They angled to intercept him, but he drew up. "No," he ordered. "You'll stay here and keep an eye on the girls." Their ears drooped, but they turned and headed for the corral as Lord rode into the trees. They would remain on guard until he returned, be it a day or a week hence.

Once out of the grove, he headed east, paralleling the line of hills that rose in a series of steep benches off to his left. The stretch of valley he was traversing formed the base of a Y and an hour of leisurely travel brought him to the division of the two arms—one approximately two miles wide, the other less than a mile. He elected to explore this smaller valley first and rode up its center at a canter. He spied a cabin set flush against the hill on his left and angled toward it. But even from a distance he could see the crudely built structure crumbling on its foundation, and so passed on without stopping. Further on, where the hills widened out into a large oval, he came across a second abandoned homestead, and this time he paused for a thoughtful look at the sagging cabin.

He rode slowly around it, all the while pondering the mystery of these three deserted claims. That the act of relinquishment had been no voluntary thing, he was certain. No man, having once stamped a plot of earth such as this for his own, would willingly surrender it. Yet there it lay—at least twenty-five square miles of prime range land, unclaimed and ungrazed.

Giving over the puzzle, he put his mount to the steep hill behind the cabin, gained the timbered benchland, and struck straight north toward the other arm of the Y. Here he entered a cooler world of resinous pine and cedar and juniper, ragged outcroppings of granite and sandstone, and long green meadows, crystalline streams and unexpected canyons. He passed through it, riding in and out of shadows and across long reaches of sunlight. Once a shout came faintly to him from some far distant place, and once a rifle bounced its long-echoing sound across the maze of rampart-guarded glens while the belling notes of several bloodhounds rang hollowly down to him from some high place he could not ascertain; and he realized that these hills were not empty after all. The knowledge afforded him little pleasure.

He had gone what he estimated to be three quarters of the distance separating the two side valleys when the stallion pricked its ears and tensed under him. A laugh sounded on the still afternoon air, amplified and rendered directionless by the walls of this rocky defile he was traversing, and he drew up and sat closely listening to the muffled drumming of a running horse somewhere in the timber above.

A moment later a sorrel flashed out of the trees, took the steep decline at a buck-jumping, twisting rush, and raced along the narrow game trail between two sheer walls. The trail bent sharply just ahead of him, shutting off his view of the oncoming horse and rider. The sorrel shot around that bend, spied the big stallion barring its way, and pulled to a gravel-spraying stop. The rider, twisted around in the saddle, was watching the backtrail as the sorrel's sudden halt sent it skidding into the stallion, which reared and lunged aside against the confining wall.

Lord spoke sharply to the plunging stallion, then stared in open-mouthed surprise at the woman strongly handling her own rearing mount as she fought to bring it down to all fours. As abruptly as it had flared up, the confusion subsided, and the two riders sat less than ten feet apart, exchanging incredulous looks.

The woman was the first to find her voice. "Sorry. I'd no idea there was another soul within ten miles, except Lewt."

Lord's brows lifted. "Lewt?"

"Lewt Shadley—the bastard." She had a long mane of sun-bleached brown hair, and now she whipped it back over her shoulders with a quick toss of her head. "Know him?"

"No," said Lord. "I wouldn't know him."

"Well, don't cry about it. It's to your credit." She had the most startlingly direct green eyes Lord had ever seen. They crawled up and down his length and over the grey stallion, like live things, missing nothing. When she returned them to his face, her expression tightened. "My God!" she said wonderingly. "Damned if you're not a breed!"

The words slapped Lord like a rude hand. He put the full weight of his aroused stare on her and examined her with a deliberate and personal care that was a studied insult. "Among my mother's people," he told her, "a woman with your manners would be horsewhipped."

If he had thought to embarrass her, he fell short of the mark. She threw back her head, her teeth flashing in the darkness of her face as she loosed a gusty laugh that died as abruptly as it had erupted. "That's been tried," she admitted. She studied him once again with that bright, measuring gaze, and suddenly grinned. "As a matter of fact, I'm almost a half-breed, myself."

"Almost?"

"My stepmother's a Comanche. My father bought her for eight horses and a pouch of gunpowder when I was two." Her explanation effected no change in Lord's stony look. His utter impassivity posed a challenge she could not ignore. She was a creature of swift, forever-shifting emotions, with an inner restlessness keeping her constantly on guard and lightly poised for combat. Her lithe body appeared wholly relaxed, thus lending an air of carelessness at variance with her sharp probing gaze. She added, then, as an afterthought, "I'm Lila MacKay. Who are you? What are you doing ramming around these hills?"

"Aaron Lord. And it's none of your business."

Her quick, explosive laugh came again, but the surface of her eyes remained flat and unreadable. "Friendly bastard, aren't you?" she drawled. When he did not reply, she cocked her head to one side and became openly curious. "I named you. You told me off. I'm not put out. Why should you be?"

She paused, waiting for him to respond to this clumsy overture of peace, and when he merely glowered at her she shrugged. "By God, you *are* sour!"

Lord's head moved in the briefest of nods. "That could be."

Lila could detect no faintest dent in the invisible armor encasing that impassive figure. For a long moment her eyes bored into him, and then her shoulders again rose and fell. "Hell!" she said disgustedly. "You act like I called you something dirty. If you're a breed, you're a breed. I wasn't *blaming* you; just *naming* you. What's wrong with that?"

Lord's eyes narrowed to thin slits and his nostrils flared whitely against his coppery skin. "There's dirt on the word when you say it."

Lila MacKay's swearing was clearly an integral part of her vocabulary. "Well, God damn you for a touchy bastard!" she burst out, genuinely stung by the remark. "I did nothing of the kind! If there was any dirt in what I said, *you* put it there. I sure as hell didn't!" Her flash of anger died as swiftly as it had flared, and she shook her head from side to side. "Man," she said quietly, "you've got one hell of a sore inside you. If you don't take some damned good medicine for it mighty soon, you'll up and die of blood poison, sure as sin's black."

Lord's head snapped up and pinpoints of light glittered in his black eyes. "All right! Leave it alone!" He faced her with his anger beating through his eyes, trying to glare her down. But there was no give to her. His voice came out on a lower note. "Maybe I was wrong about the dirt," he admitted sullenly. "Just maybe."

She let the grudging admission lie unnoticed for a moment, then accepted it with growing interest. It was one of the surprising things about her, the way her features mirrored her changing moods without visibly altering—as if the whole of her character lay quite near the surface, always on the verge of exposing itself. But her starkly naked gaze she used like multi-faceted reflectors, one instant letting her quicksilver thoughts lie unabashedly revealed, the next, showing only a glassy surface.

Now a frankly appraising glint shone in her eyes as they made a leisurely examination of his torso. It was done with such unmistakable purposefulness and with such painstaking care to detail that Lord had the sensation of being slowly undressed. In acute embarrassment he shifted in his saddle and glanced away, not knowing what to do or say.

Never before had he encountered such blatant desire in a woman's gaze, and his body's immediate and purely automatic response to the baldly apparent invitation in the green eyes rendered him helpless and increasingly embarrassed.

Out of the corner of his eye he saw her knee her mount closer until she was almost stirrup to stirrup with him. The blood rushed into his groin, struck up an expansion there, and pounded upward to spread a suffocating heat all through him so that he could scarcely breathe. When the hotness flooded into his face he quickly bent and fumbled at the latigo under his left knee in a vain attempt to mask his agitation. The leather turned to iron under his futilely groping fingers, the simple knot into a complicated problem beyond all solving. When at long last he reluctantly straightened, her disconcerting green eyes were still fixed on him, knowingly amused. He said in sudden accusing anger, "Damn a woman who'll play with a man that way!" and saw the words strike up an answering fire in her.

"And damn a man that'll sit under a tree and starve for want of guts to make the climb!" she shot back.

"Who's starving?"

She was then openly amused. "Now, you just tell me about all the nice, juicy apples you've picked lately, Mister. Go on, tell me!"

She was facing him squarely, ready to make a quarrel of it. Her mind was as quick as his, her temper hotter. Now, with her invitation rejected, she was determined to salvage her pride in the only way she knew, by humiliating him still further.

But he would not rise to the bait. With the ease of long practice he willed himself away from her, showing her an inscrutable mask that was pure Indian.

The silence that followed on the heels of the sharp exchange ran on and on. "I thought as much," Lila drawled finally. "There haven't been all that many apples for you, my friend. Not lately, and I suspect not ever."

She backed her horse clear, then moved past him. She said over her shoulder, "If you're smart, which I doubt, you'll make yourself scarce around here. If you're dumb and stubborn, which I don't doubt at all, I'll see you again," and was gone at a hard run down the narrow trail.

When the receding drumming of hooves had faded away, Lord put the grey into motion, more disturbed by the long-maned girl than he liked to admit.

In an altered frame of mind he climbed the slope and resumed his northerly course. Another hour of this up-and-down riding brought him out onto the timbered slope overlooking the upper arm of the Y. Directly below, he saw yet another roofless cabin sagging weakly in upon itself, and he made his way down to it and on past without halting. Having reached the eastern limits of the range, he pointed the stallion down the valley, more and more satisfied with what he had found this day.

When he rode into the clearing behind the screen of cottonwoods at sundown, the mares left off grazing and trotted over to the fence, loudly answering the stallion's whistling summons. The dogs left their post near the gate, their tails gravely wagging a welcome, and all this gave Lord a sense of having come home after a long, long journey. He drew up at the corral and for a while sat there savoring this strange and warming sensation. His eyes lost focus, and he stared unseeingly at what lay in store. His head slowly inclined. "All right," he said aloud to the oncoming dusk, "here I stop, and here I stay. This is the place."

He unsaddled, and turned the stallion into the corral with the mares and foal. On the point of lugging his gear to the house, he decided against it. Memory of the depressing rooms had made him delay moving in until the place had been set to rights. And so he made his camp beside the roofless stable, eating his supper as full night came on. Afterward, staring into the flickering flames, he became aware of the unremitting noise of the waterfall fifty yards away. It was a thing that beckoned to him, and he undressed, anxious to rid himself of the accumulated grime of the day.

An early moon climbed above the cottonwoods. In its luminous glow he crossed to the pool, hesitating a moment on the edge as the surprising chill touched his reaching foot. Taking a quick breath, he flung himself forward and gasped as the water closed over him. He surfaced midway across, and in wild abandon circled the pool, driving himself to his uttermost.

After a final pass under the plummeting falls, he waded out and returned to his fire. In the warmth of the flames, with the night wind steadily stroking his nakedness, he recalled the challenging invitation of Lila MacKay, and his remembering brought him to an acute awareness of his sensual longings. He whirled away from the fire and made off around the yard in long-striding agitation. But even in action, he found his thoughts repeatedly darting out of control to fasten on the girl, and at last he halted in his tracks and stared up at the blue-white moon making its slow way through a field of scudding clouds. He muttered in savage self-contempt, "What a slow-witted, stupid son of a bitch!" and trudged back to his blankets, made lonely and morose by a hunger that would not let him alone.

3

Aaron Lord woke in chill dawn, saddled up, and rode out without bothering to eat, anxious to reach town ten miles away. The dogs, determined to accompany him, sprang past to take their customary positions out in front. On the point of ordering them to remain on guard, he sensed how disappointed they would be, and so left the order unspoken. There could be no risk in leaving the mares and foal alone here during his absence.

He struck straight south, following the trace that had brought him yesterday. Under him the stallion's impatience was contagious, and he let it stretch out in a full, reaching run along the stream.

Something over an hour later he forded the river above Valley Junction and entered the waking town. It was still too early to transact his business, and since he was acutely hungry after the ride, he racked the stallion before the town's lone restaurant and entered, not without misgivings. Two days ago he had eaten his noonday meal here, bearing in stony-eyed silence the unspoken hostility of the other diners. It was an old and familiar scene, and one that never changed. Each time it happened he sought to steel himself against the animosity in the eyes turned on him—to convince himself that it did not really matter, that the time would come when the very air would not burn bitter in his mouth, and his eyes would not blur with helpless rage and humiliation. But, in some way not yet clear to him, the incident here two days ago had marked the end of that phase of his life. Precisely when the decision came, he did not know. He knew only that he would not again remain passive in the face of insult. It was all very well to pretend that it was enough for a man to know himself to be a man: unless he planted his feet and asserted his rights, he would be overridden and trampled into the ground.

So resolved, he passed down the room between the empty

tables and took his seat at the one farthest from the door. Because of the early hour he was the only customer in the place. Even the harassed girl who had waited on him two days ago was nowhere in sight. But sounds of someone moving about in the kitchen off to his right indicated that at least one other person was up and about, and he removed his hat and dropped it on the floor beside his chair.

Shortly, the thin, stringy-haired girl of his previous visit came hurrying in from the kitchen, spied him, and started forward. A dozen feet short of his table, she recognized him and came to a sudden stop, embarrassment coloring her pallid features. She caught at her dingy apron and wadded it into a limp ball in front of her in an agony of indecision. Her glance flew nervously around the room, and she seemed incapable of speech for the moment. Despite himself, Lord felt sorry for the distracted creature, and he inclined his head in a courteous bow. "Good morning, ma'am," he said. "I'll have some bacon and eggs, please."

The girl started. She turned as if to flee, then cast another wild glance toward the kitchen. Her first attempt at speaking produced a choked, gurgling noise that she tried to turn into a cough. She swallowed, took a firmer grip on the apron, and fixed her eyes on a point just above Lord's head. Her words came out in a jumbled rush, almost indistinguishable. "Sam told me that if you come in here again, I wasn't to give you nothin' to eat."

Lord's dark face showed no emotion at all. "I see," he said in the same courteous voice. "And where is this Sam, ma'am?"

"Probably still drunk. Leastwise he ain't come in yet."

"Could you tell me where I might find him?"

The girl shook her head. "Wouldn't do you no good, anyways." She whirled and made for the kitchen, but halfway there she stopped and stood staring straight in front of her for the space of a dozen heartbeats. "I don't care!" she said defiantly, whirling around and glaring at Lord. "I'm gonna git you your grub, and if Sam don't like it, he can just go jump in the horse trough! Besides," she added, as if that eventuality justified the act, "he

18

could sure use the bath!" She disappeared through the doorway, and an instant later the sound of an iron skillet being banged down onto the stove lid reached Lord.

He was finishing his second cup of coffee when the door crashed back on its hinges to admit a lanky figure. At first, the man did not spy Lord. When he did, he slammed the door shut behind him and shambled slowly down the room. Pale blue eyes glared at Lord out of an unshaven face, and when the man halted at the table, the stench of sweat and cheap whiskey hit Lord like a blow in the face.

"I don't know who you are, or where you come from, or what you think you're tryin' to pull off around here," he said harshly. "But I sure as hell know *what* you are, and that's all I care about. Now you git up outa that chair and git the hell out of here, and be quick about it."

The strident outburst seemingly fell on deaf ears as Lord took another leisurely sip of coffee. He set the cup down and glanced up at the livid man from behind thick, shadowing lashes. "Would you be Sam?"

"Never you mind who—"

"Shut up," Lord said softly.

If he had reached out and slapped the man, the effect could not have been more startling. The slack jaw dropped, and Sam stood there staring at him out of disbelieving eyes. His Adam's apple leaped convulsively in his scrawny neck as he struggled to get his voice out. It came at last on a high, strangled note of purest outrage. "Why, you dirty, stinkin' half—"

"I told you to shut up," Lord said in the same unruffled voice, and rose with an easy, uncoiling motion. He lifted his head and looked Sam full in the face, his eyes cold. He spoke softly, but every word struck the astonished restaurant owner like ice. "You run a public eating place here. If you ever put your filthy tongue to me again, as you just now did, I'll make you wish to God you'd never learned how to talk." He bent, caught up his hat, and reached into his pocket. Taking out a silver dollar, he dropped it on the table. "The meal was fifty cents," he said. "The rest of the dollar is for the young lady who brought it to me. *All* of it, understand?" On the point of leaving, he had a last thought. "Another thing: the young lady told me about your little rule. I told her if she didn't serve me I'd wreck the damned place. Say one word to her about this, and I'll do it." He moved away from the table. "Now get out of my way. Smelling you makes me sick to my stomach; and damned if I want to lose a meal I just paid for."

He went past the still-speechless Sam, deliberately letting the point of his shoulder strike the man and spin him halfway around as he strode toward the door.

On the walk outside he halted and stood staring unseeingly across the street, so shaken by the scene he could hardly breathe. It was the first time he had ever allowed his iron control to slip, and the experience left him weak. Whether he had acted wisely or foolishly, he was incapable of judging. He only knew that had the man uttered another word or moved to stop him, he would have destroyed him in that instant. And the realization of what he was capable of doing to another human being filled him with dismay.

How long he stood there, Lord did not know; when he again became aware of his surroundings it was to realize that the town was wide awake and going about its business. Directly across from him was the Federal Land Office, and, judging the hour to be eight, or thereabouts, he dropped into the dust of the street and crossed toward it.

He arrived just as the roan-haired clerk was inserting his key in the lock. Their meeting two days before had been anything but congenial, and at Lord's approach, the man turned unwelcoming eyes on him. "You again," he growled and opened the door just wide enough to slip through. He would have shut it in Lord's face, but in the instant before the latch caught, Lord reached out and casually shoved the door open and stepped in after him. Lord crossed to the counter and stood waiting while the clearly upset man made a show of setting the office to rights. When the man reached for the broom, to sweep a floor already clean, Lord straightened from his easy slouch and laid his voice against the unfriendly silence. "I'll see that map again."

The other gave no sign of having heard. Engrossed in his sweeping, he jumped as if stung when Lord reached out and tore the broom out of his hands. The handle cracked like a gunshot as Lord brought it down across the edge of the counter, then let the two sections clatter to the floor. He turned to the white-faced clerk. "I'm getting tired of this," he stated. "Now, either you get that map for me, or I snap your goddamned spine like that broom handle. You hear me?"

For a long, uncertain moment the man faced Lord in tight-lipped fury while he waged a silent battle with himself, but when Lord shifted his feet, his tenuous resolve broke; he leaped around the end of the counter and pulled the map from its pigeonhole. He was not a coward by nature, and he had had his orders; but he was also utterly incapable of withstanding the pressure of those un-winking black eyes.

Lord took the map to the far end of the counter and unrolled it. He appeared to be wholly engrossed in spreading it flat, but when the clerk started for the door, he spoke without looking up. "Stay right there."

The man turned agonized eyes on him. "I was just going—"

"Nowhere at all," Lord cut in quietly. When the man did not move from the door, he tapped the surface of the counter with a long forefinger. "Mind me, now."

With a final, despairing glance at the door, the clerk turned back across the room, his narrow shoulders bent under their burden of humiliation.

Lord made a second perusal of the map to fix the boundaries indelibly in his mind. That done, he unbuckled his belt, lifted his tunic, and unfastened the money belt from around his narrow waist. With the heavy belt on the counter, he crooked a finger at the clerk, and when the man was directly across from him, indicated the lower scallop of Star Valley and its eastward-fluttering sections.

"How many acres here?"

The clerk gave the designated area a single, quick glance and stepped back, his face closing like a trap.

"I couldn't say."

"It's in your files. Find it."

The man would not meet his gaze. He stared fixedly at the window behind Lord, his hands clenched at his sides.

"That's all preempted land," he said tonelessly. "I just haven't bothered to mark it yet."

"You're a liar. It's government land. Now, let's have the description and the deed."

The clerk's voice climbed shakingly above his fear of the big half-breed.

"Listen here! This is government property you're on, and I'm a government official. You can't come in here and threaten me like this. In case you don't know it, there's laws about Indians—"

Lord's patience snapped. Without warning he reached out, grasped the man's shirt front, and with a convulsive heave, dragged him over the counter. In one continuing move, he pulled him close, then whirled and slammed him against the wall with a violence that shook the frame building. The man's head cracked against the boards behind him, and he hung spread-eagled there. Lord stepped close and crouched over him, like a great cat.

"Never talk to me like that again," he said thickly. "Understand?"

The man's terror burst from him in a choked sob as he stared up into the furious eyes above him. He nodded numbly.

"All right, then." Lord reached down and hauled the man erect. "Let's have those papers."

With the documents assembled in front of him, he briefly studied them and glanced up. "Twenty-five cents an acre?" he asked. At the other's nod, he opened the belt and began counting out double eagles. At a thousand dollars he paused and looked up again.

"The name's Aaron Lord," he said. "Double 'a.' You can fill out the papers while I finish counting up here."

No other word was spoken throughout the transaction. Fin-

22

ished with his chore, Lord pushed the three stacks of gold across the counter, tucked the papers into his belt, and strapped it around his waist. With the heavy gunbelt buckled over his tunic, he gave the clerk a final, knowing look.

"Tell your friends their plan didn't work," he said, and turned and strode out of the office.

He crossed to the stallion and the waiting dogs, led the horse three doors down the street, and tied it to the rack in front of the town's single mercantile. With the saddlebags looped over his arm he entered the store and gave his order to a surly clerk who, after a glance, silently filled it.

He lugged the filled bags out to his horse. Down the street he saw the land office clerk standing in the sunlight talking with another man. They watched him as he tossed the bags into place behind the cantle, tied them, and slipped the reins free. Going into the saddle, he reined away from the rack, the two dogs rising silent as shadows from the ground and drifting ahead of horse and rider. As he passed the two men, Lord doffed his hat in mock salute and rode off up the street, conscious of their gaze on him, like angry hands pushing him on his way.

Despite his bravado in town, his mood was black as he recrossed the river and rode through a profusion of apple and peach trees ripening in the July sun; it was not until he reached his own land that his depression lifted.

Then putting the stallion into motion, Lord breasted that sea of grass, savoring the taste of the wind, reveling in the feel of it, because it, too, belonged to him, as did the timbered hills and grassland over which it blew.

He had the strongest conviction that were he to turn onto the holdings marked "Taggert" on the map, this same wind would lack strength and would taste flat and unexciting because it blew over land not his.

He was brought back from his fanciful flight by the odd behavior of the dogs. Both were standing motionless, their heads turned back to Lord, alerting him to an unfamiliar scent. He was at once on guard, knowing they never erred.

He had bought them as pups from one of his father's trappers who had mated a mastif bitch and a timber wolf. The litter of four murky-colored whelps combined the massive bone structure of their mother with the ferocious attributes of their sire. All had inherited the latter's amber eyes; in addition, two were duplicates of the sire, except in size. In that they had far exceeded him before the end of their first year.

It was this pair that Lord had chosen for his own, and he had bestowed on them the inappropriate but resounding titles of King Leopold and Empress Elizabeth, after the mad monarch of Bavaria and his only slightly more normal cousin, the Empress of Austria.

In these two the wolf blood was all-predominant. Their ability to pick up a scent and follow it was uncanny. From puppyhood on, they had seemed to require the friendship of no living creature; and if they entertained any affection for Lord, they gave little sign of it, beyond an almost imperceptible wagging of the tail when he returned after an absence or called them by name. But their loyalty was unflagging. Now they waited until he had come to within a dozen paces of them, then sprang forward along the trail they had found, Elizabeth in the lead, her muzzle dipping and lifting at regular intervals in a manner characteristic of her when on a hot scent.

Looking down, Lord detected unfamiliar tracks leading in his direction—fresh tracks—not over an hour old. There was no confusing them with those of his own horses. The latter were as well known to him as the prints of his own moccasins. Instinctively, he felt the tracks concerned him.

He threw the stallion into a hard run after the dogs. But even with the big horse moving out at near top speed, the dogs drew steadily ahead, having now fixed the scent so well that the faintest trace of it rising from the grass was sufficient to hold them on course.

Lather showed white along the grey's neck and shoulders, and it was reaching deeply for wind as it ran through the grove and sank to a plunging halt at the edge of the yard. Lord's curse exploded in the sudden stillness, and he stared in stunned disbelief at the gate yawning wide on the empty corral.

Unwilling to accept the evidence of his eyes, he rode slowly forward. Already the dogs had finished their swift examination of the vacant enclosure, and at Lord's approach they turned, their eyes fixed on him in waiting readiness.

"Elizabeth," Lord singled her out for her ability to pick up a cold trail. "Find the horses. Hurry up."

Now she dropped her muzzle to within an inch of the ground and began casting back and forth over the trampled earth in front of the gate. She moved out, working in a series of ever-widening circles. Suddenly she stopped, and in deepest concentration she examined the hoofmark with her nose, left it, and three feet beyond studied a second with the same minute care. Her great frame stiffened: her head came up and around, and her eyes telegraphed their signal to the waiting man. The instant Lord started forward, she sprang out along the discovered trail at full speed, her muzzle again dipping and lifting with flawless precision.

Dust spurted under the stallion's hoofs as it pounded across the yard. A dozen strides onward, Leopold flashed past and fell in directly behind the speeding Elizabeth. Across the yard and through the grove he held that position, the up-and-down rhythm of his head now duplicating that of his mate's as he picked up the quarry's scent. When they burst from the trees he forged into the lead.

A mile sped past, with both dogs streaking along in utter silence, and then Elizabeth began to lose ground. Lord saw no need for her to expend her strength further, now that Leopold had assumed charge. He went alongside and caught her attention with a low word. When she looked up he made a palm-down canceling motion with his hand.

"That's enough," he told her. "Rest."

She flashed him a grateful look and at once dropped back. Drawing rapidly away from her, Lord threw a glance over his shoulder and saw her stop and sink to all fours and knew she would wait only until she had regained her wind before resuming the chase.

Another mile dropped behind, and though Leopold still held to his hard run, he had begun to slow. Close ahead, the hill jutted sharply out into the plain, and when the dog reached that point he suddenly flattened against the ground, staring at something beyond.

Lord was following so closely that he almost overran the dog. He dragged the stallion to a stop and saw, less than a quarter mile ahead, three horses and the foal jogging up the valley. The chestnut was being led by a man astride a leggy roan.

That one glance was sufficient for Lord. He wheeled the grey and sent it lunging up the hill and into the timber of a long bench. Once into this screen, he ran straight east, the dog drifting soundlessly in his wake.

A cathedral-like stillness hung over this timbered benchland of diffused sunlight and dense shade—a quiet so complete and enduring that the dull sound of the horse running heavily through it sank into nothingness in the yielding mat of needles. The plaintive song of a mountain thrush seemed surprising in that impenetrable quiet.

It was Lord's intent to outflank the man on the roan, and in this he was aided by the contour of the hill, which fell back in a long arc at this point. Making a wide half-circle around the little cavalcade below, he swung down toward his quarry.

His luck held, for here another irregularity in the hill's outline afforded concealment. Reining in behind a screen of scrub cedars, he sat the hard-blowing stallion and waited.

Long minutes went by. Ghostlike, the dog drifted down through the screening brush and rocks and sank into the grass just ahead of the horse, its gaze fixed on the broken headland around which the stranger must come.

Another stretch of silent waiting, and then Lord saw the dog's hackles lift. Without a sound the massive brute rose to a half-crouch, stole forward a dozen feet, and again sank into the grass.

A moment later, the beat of trotting hoofs came to Lord's ears. Reaching down, he drew the heavy saddlegun from its scabbard

26

and rode out past the screening cedars and rocks to halt squarely in the path of the astonished rider.

Trained to respond to the lightest signal, the grey sank back on its haunches and with all the seemingly effortless grace of a master dancer executed a smooth half-turn in response to the pressure of Lord's left knee. By the time the oncoming rider had checked the forward motion of his mount, Lord's rifle was negligently pointing across the saddlebows at the rider's chest. In hard-eyed silence Lord watched the man dart a look at the stallion and swiftly read that animal's relationship to the mares and the foal.

He was a slim, blond young man. Shocked and stiffly erect in the saddle, he remained silent, clearly alert for a way out of his unexpected dilemma. And then the look of alarm that had come into his face at sight of Lord changed to one of contempt as he belatedly realized that no possible danger to himself could reside in a man of Lord's breeding. The taut line of his shoulders eased, and he emitted a mirthless laugh.

On the point of speaking, he detected a movement beyond the stallion and fixed his gaze in sudden consternation on the murky apparition noiselessly rising from the grass and advancing on him. He was staring transfixed at the stalking Leopold when a faint sound jerked his attention to his right. The ruddy color left his face at sight of Elizabeth circling up from his rear. Within striking distance on either side of him, the two dogs sank to the ground, hindquarters bunched for the spring. Their upper lips curled away from their gleaming fangs in the blood-chilling wolf grin.

Into that silence Lord dropped three quiet words.

"Drop that rope."

The very softness of the voice whipped the rider's gaze around. Lord's black eyes should have warned him. But with brash confidence in his superiority over men of Lord's heritage, he eased himself back in the saddle.

"In this country, unbranded stock belongs to whoever dabs a rope onto it."

"If you'd bothered to look, you'd have found an A.L. branded under the mane of each of those animals."

"That's your story."

"You'd do well to believe it."

The blond man looked Lord up and down, eyes brightly glinting. Doubt touched him; but he lifted his voice loudly against it. "You really expect me to believe that a breed would own hotbloods like these here?" He gave a laugh of derision. "Man," he said warningly, "you'd be wise to get your red ass back to whatever reservation it belongs on. You keep on runnin' around this country accusin' white men of bein' thieves, you're apt to git your hide shot full of holes, don't you know that?"

Lord jiggled the saddlegun. "Drop the rope and move out," he ordered. When the other did not comply, he added more urgently, "Better go. I want no trouble. Just my horses."

The man on the roan was tragically incapable of gauging the full depths of the danger confronting him.

"Once more," Lord said tonelessly. "I'm telling you just once more. I don't want—" He caught the slight tightening of the younger man's frame and as the right hand snapped down toward the gun at his hip, Lord squeezed the trigger.

The big saddlegun bucked in his hands, its furious bellow shattering the sun-drenched stillness of the afternoon. The echoes beat themselves into a thousand fragments among the upper crags and canyons and sank at last into nothingness far away.

Through drifting smoke Lord saw the big slug's impact twist the blond man halfway around and rock him back in the saddle. The man flung up a hand and futilely pressed it against the blood pouring from his chest. He said in a breathless, falling voice of deepest dismay, "Oh, my Christ Almighty!" and looked down at his chest with an expression of pure horror. For a moment he held that pose, and then with a faint sigh he went limp and slumped sideways. He was flung loosely to the ground as his horse suddenly lunged out from under him.

The scent of blood set the roan wild, and with a shattering blast from its flared nostrils it bolted straight past Lord before he could stop it.

Knowing the animal must not escape, Lord wheeled the stallion and threw it into thundering pursuit. But from the outset, it was all too apparent that the chase was a hopeless one. Formidable racer though it was, the grey had already run more than five miles; and while it managed to stay almost within striking distance of the speeding roan, it could not close that distance. Acknowledging the futility of the chase, Lord pulled the stallion down from its hard run and swung back to do what must be done with the dead man.

He dismounted beside the lifeless body and for a long time stood looking down into the young face. The features were serene, unbelievably innocent.

A wave of sickness rolled over Lord. Wanting to turn away, he forced himself to look at the result of his handiwork, as if by doing so he might somehow be rid of the dismal feeling that it need not have happened at all. It was . . . so utterly pointless. He forced his thoughts back to the present. What was he to do now?

His gaze lifted to the timbered hills, then focused on a point where a bare reach of cliff protruded above the tops of the trees. With the solution to his problem decided on, he went over to the chestnut mare and brought her close, reassuring her with murmured words and gentle hands when she tried to wheel away from the scent of fresh blood.

He tied the slack form onto the mare's back, then said to the dogs, "Stay here with Cassy and the baby," and mounted the stallion. With the mare scrambling upward in his wake, he set off through the trees in the direction of the high overhang. Beneath it, he loosed the rope and eased the body to the ground, afterward leading both horses well back into the trees and tying them. Returning to the overhang, he searched along its base until he found a way up, and began climbing.

It was a tortuous ascent through brush-choked boulders and scrub cedar, but he did not pause for breath until he clambered over the crest. Even then, he waited only until the stitch in his side eased before setting to work. Distaste for what he was doing drove him. A moment's indecision now would, he knew, result in his abandoning the project altogether.

A swift examination of the area showed him that the ledge of rock on which he was standing ended some distance short of the rim. The rest was clay deeply cracked and crumbling. Fully aware that he was courting disaster, he lifted a rock the size of a bushel basket and carried it to the edge. He lifted it chest-high and brought it crashing down on the crumbling rim. The shock broke off a great section, and he flung himself backward to avoid being carried away with it as it plummeted downward and exploded in a cloud of dust a hundred feet below.

Returning to the rock ledge for another boulder, he repeated the process with the same result. At the end of a dozen such trips a great mound of earth lay banked along the base of the cliff.

Dragging air into his burning lungs, he wiped his forehead and made his way along the rim on legs that threatened to buckle at every step. He descended by the same route he had climbed up and went over to the waiting horses. Mounted, he made one final survey of the place and nodded, satisfied. To even the most observant eye, there was nothing to indicate that the collapse of the rim of the cliff was anything other than a natural occurrence.

He returned then to where he had left the dogs on guard over the freckled mare and her foal and slowly led off along the way he had come so swiftly a short time ago, sinking deeper and deeper into gloom.

4

In a black mood, Lord prepared his supper and ate. After he had set the camp to rights again, he undressed and started for the pool, carrying his belt and handgun. Behind him the moon lifted over the cottonwoods. In its light, the corrals and buildings stood out in sharp relief, and he paused and sent his possessive glance around the secluded setting, once again savoring his ownership. Reacting to this upswing of the spirit, he sprinted across the yard, dropped his gunbelt at the edge of the pool, and hit the water in a long, clean dive that carried him to the far side. He surfaced, blowing lustily and flailing the water with both arms in a wild burst of energy, then launched himself forward to circle the pool.

Several minutes of this frenzied activity served to work off the day's tension, and after a last pass under the battering fall of water, he was wading through the shallows when a low laugh sounded directly in front of him. He jerked his head up like a wild animal and saw a figure on the edge of the pool, blackly outlined against the moonlight. In mid-stride he froze, one arm unconsciously extended toward the holstered gun lying so impossibly out of reach a dozen feet away.

The laugh came again, and he backed into deeper water with his recognition of that short, explosive sound. "What the hell are you up to, prowling around a man's place in the dead of night?" A thought stopped him. "How did you get past the dogs?"

Lila MacKay's answer was amused. "I'm not prowling around; it's not the dead of night; and I have a way with dogs." She moved closer to the water's edge and peered through the gloom. "I'm curious about something," she said in her blunt way. "How has a damned fool like you managed to stay alive this long?"

Anger still rode Lord. "What am I supposed to make out of that?"

"Somebody shot Lewt Shadley off his horse this afternoon," Lila stated, and the way she said it gave Lord the feeling that her strange green eyes were easily reading him, even in the near-darkness. "I ran across his roan with blood all over the saddle. Now, let's hear what you've got to say about that, mister."

A chill touched Lord. "Never heard of the man."

"You've heard of him," Lila contradicted him. "A yellow-haired bastard riding a roan. He never could tell the difference between his own horses and somebody else's; so mostly he rode somebody else's." When Lord merely stared back at her, she went on. "He went to town last night; but he never came home. My guess is he probably happened by here, and I'd guess that if he spotted those two mares and that foal of yours, the temptation would've been more than Lewt could stand. And then I'd guess that a certain somebody with a pair of good tracking dogs took out on his trail and ended that trail pretty damned sudden."

"You ought to be writing tall stories."

"I can read sign like a Comanche."

"So?"

"So, the sign I read right now is of one dumb breed that's let himself in for one hell of a mess."

"Go on."

But Lila's never-still brain was following another tangent. "What'd you do with the body?"

Lord was suddenly through pretending. "It won't be easy to find."

"You're sure about that?"

Picturing the tons of dirt and rock dumped onto the tangle of brush and dead trees, Lord nodded. "I'm sure."

She seemed relieved. "I buried his saddle and turned the roan loose. It'll drift back to whoever Lewt stole it from; so that gives you a headstart. When're you leaving?"

"Leaving?"

"Well, good God, man," Lila said disgustedly, "you don't figure on staying here, do you? Sooner or later, the Shadleys will do a little sign-reading of their own. When they do, you'll last just about long enough to wish you'd gone." She gestured toward the distant corrals. "If you've the sense God gave a goose, you'll fork your horse and hightail it to hell out of here."

He shook his head. "My clothes are over by the fire."

"The hell!" Her quick laugh broke the night with a throaty vibrance. "Come on. I'll shut my eyes."

But he folded his arms over his chest with rocklike immobility, clearly putting no faith in her promise.

When it became apparent that he had no intention of leaving

the water, Lila folded her legs and sank to the sand in an attitude of relaxed waiting. "You're apt to get mighty cold before morning," she observed idly, and lapsed into silence. But a moment later her voice burst out impatiently. "My God! Haven't you ever been naked with a woman before?"

"That's no concern of yours."

She cocked her head and with knowing eyes took in the broad sweep of the wet gleaming torso visible above the water. "Of course you have," she decided. "So why so bashful now? What are you waiting for, anyhow?"

It was said so matter-of-factly that for an instant Lord thought he had misunderstood her. Before he could frame a reply he saw her rise and start to undress. In growing disbelief he watched her slip the leather tunic over her head and toss it aside, then unbuckle her belt and let her doeskin skirt drop to the sand. Lastly, she bent and removed her knee-high moccasins. And then she was wading out to him.

She grasped his arms and pushed them aside and came firmly against him. "Damn you," she said hoarsely. "Just how plain do I have to make it?" When he remained dumbly unresponsive, she encircled his narrow waist in both arms and leaned the upper part of her body back, her hips pressing against him. Her voice came out in a throaty rush. "I saw you yesterday and wanted you and told you and you turned me down. Now, I'll go no place until I've had what I want from you." She broke off, drew a long, shuddering breath and moved her hips demandingly against him. "You want it, too, don't you?" she demanded roughly. "Don't you?"

Lord heard his voice come out, thick and unsteady. "Yes. Of course I do."

"Then show it, damn you!"

He bent, slipped an arm behind her knees and lifted her. Wading out of the pool, he knelt and laid her on the sand that was still warm from the heat of the day. She was staring up at him with the dull, fixed expression of the hypnotized, and when he stretched out beside her, she uttered a low moan and turned to meet him, her hands fluttering up and down his damp torso, like the seeking hands of the blind.

Her unloosed hunger rendered him momentarily impotent, and this failure of his body to respond to the opportunity thus afforded filled him with mortification. In him was the leaping fear that he would utterly fail. He tightened his arms around her. "Just wait awhile," he muttered thickly, "I—"

"My God!" she moaned. "All last night . . . all day today . . . I've seen you and felt you inside me." Her hands moved along his ribcage. They were at his narrow flanks, then lower, finding his lax member and encircling it.

Her touch burned his flesh, striking an answering fire that brought him throbbingly erect in her grip; and with that involuntary awakening, all doubt vanished. He was seized with an excitement that left him trembling and constricted his chest until he thought he would suffocate. Born beyond constraint, he lifted himself above her and positioned himself between her thighs, his actions sudden and heedless and increasingly rough.

Willing himself to contain his well-nigh insupportable eagerness, he touched the moist opening and began the first slow inward thrust. He was dimly aware of the woman's shuddering cry, but he was in the grip of an urgency such as he had never known. It robbed the moment of its magic and left him devoid of all emotion, save a reckless resolve to have his way with her. Grimly, inexorably he continued his advance, while his senses strayed ever further from their moorings. The darkness of night came thickly down. Cool air streamed down from the black timbered hills to wash over his damp and rigid body, and this chill breath, contrasting with the heat within, drove him onward. Wholly caught up in the sensations trembling through his indriving shafts, he instinctively slowed his advance to greater prolong the ecstasy. Without warning, Lila cried out and thrust upward to envelope his entire length and was then a wildly sobbing creature of the night, writhing and plunging beneath him. Her hands slid around his waist, gripped hard, and strained him even more tightly against her.

He was helpless to suppress the unending moan that rose in his throat with every thrust. A miracle of awareness burned inside him like a glaring light, and he was for the first time free of uncertainty. Dimly he heard her say, "Aaron, kiss me," and still he did not comprehend until she drew his head down. It had not occurred to him that she would want him to kiss her. The animal joining of their bodies he had taken as her sole reason for coming here tonight. Now, at her signal, he gave himself over to her with an ardor that roused her to still higher passion. On the instant, he felt himself enveloped in a sheet of writhing, leaping flame that ignited his every nerve and tissue.

With shocking suddenness he realized that he had unwittingly rushed to the brink of fulfillment, and abruptly stopped his frenzied thrusting. Too late. A curse of dismay burst from him and became a choked cry as he clamped the wildly sobbing woman to him and let the flood pour out of him with a violence that rendered him dazed and spent.

Over in the corral a horse stamped, and Lord clearly felt the faint tremor running through the ground, and from a still further distance the hoot of an owl drifted down the night wind, lonely and empty. And then his body was floating free above the earth with only a slender sheath of warmth to support it, and he dimly wondered at his inability to think clearly, or even to care that he could not.

Long afterward, he roused from his torpor and lifted himself on his elbows. "I'm too heavy for you," he said, and would have withdrawn; but she reached up and held him motionless.

"Not yet," she whispered. "Don't end it so soon."

His low laugh came and he enfolded her in his arms again, letting his contentment come out in a long sigh. "I was hoping you'd say that," he murmured, and was amazed and pleased to discover that he was still fully distended inside her, for all the violent completeness of the act just accomplished.

Lila reached up and ran her fingers through the dense mass of black waves over his temples. The feel of his head between her hands and the nearness of his shadowy face produced a change in

35

her. It softened her expression and turned her thoughtful. "You're only you while you're like this." Her lips lengthened in a slow smile. "Did you know that?"

"And what am I?" he asked, half amused, half serious.

She did not reply at once, but continued absently to stroke his heavy hair. "I think," she said finally, "you're not really so all-fired tough . . . not inside. I suspect you're really all soft and warm, way down deep. But you wear that hard face to keep people away, because you don't want them to see or touch the real you."

He flexed his hips, implanting himself more deeply. "*That's* the real me. I'm letting you feel it."

She gave a low laugh, and when he again flexed his hips she tensed briefly against the obvious resurgence of his desire, as well as her own mounting passion. His mouth found hers, its knowing touch sending tendrils of flame all through her. Yet, even with her senses reeling under this second onslaught of lust, she was troubled by the discovery that he could so easily draw her after him wherever he chose to lead.

For Lila lived in the wilderness of the senses. In her indiscriminate quest for gratification she had ranged from disappointment to ecstasy; but none of her considerable company of partners had ever given her anything to equal the passion engendered by this copper-skinned giant. She felt herself rushing again toward that highest pinnacle in the arms of this violent, unknown man, and she moved with him, timing her actions with instinctive precision.

Then her climax again seized her; she cried out. With the moment upon them both, they were locked together in a straining embrace that thundered in their ears and gradually subsided, leaving them numb and spent.

Later, with the night wind running chill fingers across her damp skin, Lila struggled up from languor and stirred in Lord's arms. "I'm going now."

His hold tightened immediately. "Not yet."

She did not argue with him, nor did she struggle; but when he slid a cramped arm from under her, she disengaged herself with a sudden contraction of her body and went to her feet. She waded out into the pool, circled it once with long, even strokes, and came back to the shore, wringing water from her streaming hair. In silence she dressed, and in silence she would have left then; but he rose and stopped her with a hand on her shoulder. Again she refused to pit her strength against his; but she remained half turned away, passively waiting for him to release her.

They stood thus in an awkward silence broken only by the steady beat of water in the dark pool. Lord reached up and laid his hand against the wetness of her hair and gently turned her face up to him. When she did not resist, he drew her close. "No," she said, and turned out of his encircling arms.

She was gone, then, moving swiftly across the yard and into the blackness at the far end of the house. A moment later she reappeared astride her horse, angling toward the upper end of the grove, and there was then only the muffled beat of her running horse drifting back through the night.

5

Lila MacKay rode steadily through the night, quartering toward the point of the hills dividing the arms of the Y. Once a distant shout came down to her from the wall of blackness off to her left, and she drew up, listening, but the sound was not repeated; after a time she rode on at a reaching gallop.

This country she knew as few others knew it. All her life she had ranged the length and breadth of this region, watching, hearing, feeling it, smelling it in all its moods and seasons, until she had become one with it. The dim and seldom-traveled trails she knew as well as the interior of the cabin she shared with her parents; and those few who followed these trails were known to her also, far better than any of them suspected. Trusting no one, asking nothing of anyone, she was completely self-reliant, free of any sense of obligation to anyone except herself. Her greatest enjoyment came from knowing that she had triumphed over the less adept and bent them to her will. It was a game with her, always challenging. The ultimate result never concerned her. Each day brought its own novelties, its own pleasures.

But, riding now through the night, she found her thoughts traversing unfamiliar terrain. Ordinarily, having had her way with a man, she would have forgotten the incident with the ease known only to the utterly self-centered. But the memory of Lord worked at her with rebellious persistence. *Except at the first, I wasn't in control at all. He made me follow him.* She brought her horse to a halt, all at once angry at the turn of events back there. She was within a quarter mile of the hill now and she sat staring up at the black-timbered benchland, re-enacting the scene to discover what had gone wrong. Was it his overpowering male-ness that had proved her undoing? Or was it some unsuspected need in her leaping up in response to a like need in him?

But as soon as she was aware of her physical need for him, she rebelled against it, sensing in it a threat. It would not do to relinquish control now. Yet even as she reprimanded herself, she knew her own strong hungers would draw her back to the valley and to the sullen giant who swam naked at night in the pool of the abandoned ranch.

It was late when she threaded a final canyon and sent her horse scrambling up the narrow trail onto a wide shelf that lay like a jagged scar on the mountain face. Fifty yards away, a cabin crouched in the blackness. At her approach a half-dozen gaunt hounds came lumbering to meet her, whining happily at her return. She spoke her low greeting to them and watched them turn and gravely escort her to the corral some fifty feet from the cabin. She turned her horse into the corral, dumped a measure of grain into its box, and made her way to the cabin.

The open door apprised her of the fact that her father was

away, his Comanche wife at home. None but the severest weather could induce Carla MacKay to bolt a door or close a window. Halfway across the main room, Lila became aware that she was being watched, and she spoke to her stepmother. "Go back to sleep, Carla. It's only me."

The woman would speak English only to her husband, and now she addressed her stepdaughter in Comanche. "You think I need to be told who enters my house?" she demanded; then shoved a second question at the girl, before the first had been answered. "Whose blanket were you sharing this night?"

Lila knelt on the hearth and helped herself to the boiled venison, still warm from the banked coals. She spoke Comanche as fluently as the woman, and habitually fell into that dialect when conversing with her. But some perversity prompted her to respond now in English, well aware that this would irritate Carla. "Why do you always ask the same question?" she said around a mouthful of meat. "If I didn't know better, I'd think you didn't trust me."

Her sarcasm was not lost on the woman in the bedroom doorway. "You're always so smart. One day you won't be smart enough, maybe. One day you will wait for the blood to show, and when it doesn't, you'll wonder how a smart girl stops the seed from sprouting. Have you thought about that?"

"Lots of times."

"And what will you do if that happens?"

"Why," said Lila matter-of-factly, "I'll come to you, of course. You'll use one of your Comanche cures on me and the seed'll stop sprouting."

Carla's voice thickened with anger. "So? You think it's as easy as that, do you?"

"Well, won't you?"

Carla came deeper into the room. She was a tall, full-bodied woman, still handsome and still careful of her appearance. At one corner of the fireplace she stooped and laid a handful of twigs on the coals and stirred the fire to new life. She straightened slowly and put the point of her shoulder against the mantle, looking steadfastly down at the kneeling girl. Lighted thus from below, the dark, ungiving cast of her features was wholly Indian. In silence she watched Lila for a time, a lonely woman turned angry by something she felt powerless to handle. Her voice fell heavily into the room. "You care about nothing but yourself."

Lila glanced up from under heavy lashes. "That's not true. I care about you."

"Not much."

"Not much." Lila echoed the thought. "I can't say. I've never thought very much about it." Suddenly she said: "Do you love Douglas MacKay, Carla?" and caught the faint movement of the Indian woman's strong shoulders. "Did you ever love him?"

"Where he walks, I follow," Carla said in the flat, noncommittal tone she employed whenever her feelings threatened to unmask themselves before another. "I am his woman. It is the only way I know."

All at once Lila felt a need to understand something. "Tell me how it is between a man and a woman, Carla. I want to know."

But Carla shook her head in slow denial. "No one can tell you that. With each two people it is different. With your father and me it is not the same now as it was at first. Nothing stays the same."

Lila nodded slowly. She knew the talk was ending here but she was unwilling to have it end. With sudden insight she sensed that this withdrawn woman held the key to what she needed. "Do you think I'm bad, Carla?" she said, and saw the dark woman's impatient shrug.

"Why do you want me to answer, 'yes'?"

The evasive reply brought a slow smile to Lila's lips. "Tell me."

But Carla refused to be thus cornered. "You want me to tell you something but I will not. Something happened to you tonight . . . something different from the other times. And you think maybe I can explain it to you." She stopped and studied the girl out of unwinking eyes, knowing that she had read her right. She moved her shoulders again with vague impatience and turned her gaze to the fire. "Maybe I could do that," she said gently. "But words are not enough. I could only tell you what I think, and that is no good because I am not you. But I will say this: lying under a man is not the same as standing beside him. I will tell you one more thing: every man wants a woman under him in the darkness, but not every man wants that same woman at his side in the daylight."

It was the closest thing to a warning she would utter, and Lila knew that further pursuit in that direction was fruitless. She said in a musing tone, "This man is not like the others," and waited for some sign of interest from the woman.

Carla shot her a skeptical glance. "A cottonwood is tall and a piñon is short. Each is only a tree."

"But different," Lila pointed out.

"In some ways, yes," Carla admitted, then paused, wanting to rouse this willful girl to an awareness of the risk she so heedlessly ran.

"How different?"

"He's a half-breed."

"Ah!" It came out in a breathy rush, and Carla was no longer leaning against the mantle.

But Lila moved her head from side to side. "That's not the only difference—not the real one. It's something else; but I'm not sure what." She raised troubled eyes to the woman. "He changed something in me. He keeps bothering me."

Carla said again, "Ah!" but this time it was a prolonged, questioning sound. "And because he keeps bothering you, you will go back to him." She leaned down and sent her words at the girl in a rush. "You will say it is to find out how he made this change in you, and you will keep going back; but you may never find the answer. And when he has had enough of you, he will turn away, and what will you have then? An empty heart and a big belly, maybe! What then?"

Lila placed her hands against the floor and pushed herself to her feet. She was almost as tall as the older woman and she looked straight into the black eyes. "Would you stay away if you were me?"

Carla made a refusing motion with both hands. "Don't ask me

41

that!" she said harshly. "How can I say what I would do in your place? But this is a bitter taste in my mouth. That I will say."

"Why, Carla? Why shouldn't I go back?"

"You know why!"

Lila shook her head. "Tell me."

"You have said it. He is a half-breed."

"But you're a Comanche. My father married you; so what's wrong with my—"

"It is not the same. I am a woman."

Lila rejected this with an impatient toss of her head. "What the hell kind of sense does that make?" she demanded. "Are you saying it's all right for a white man to sleep with an Indian woman, but wrong for a white woman to sleep with an Indian man . . . or a half-breed?"

"I didn't make the law!" Carla shouted. "Ask your father! It is men like him who make such laws! I only know that a bad thing will happen if it becomes known that you are lying with this half-breed."

"To hell with them!" Lila flared. "I answer to nobody."

Carla shook her head. "You may think that. You will find out differently, my daughter."

Lila's anger subsided as quickly as it had risen. "What if I want to go back, Carla?" she asked quietly.

In the silence that came down between them Carla's inscrutable eyes reached deep into the girl. After a long time she moved her hands in a slow, palms-out gesture of defeat. "Then you will go," she said heavily. "I would help you if I could, but you have gone beyond my help."

She fell silent again, still holding Lila with her immutable gaze.

She did then what was for her a curious thing. She reached out and laid her hand against Lila's cheek. "You never cried when you were a girl," she said. "I think that one day you will find all those tears inside you, waiting to come out. I think it will be hard to bear, but a good thing, too, when it happens. Maybe you will not be so alone then, my daughter."

The shadows grew thicker and heavier in the room, separating them as they stood there, closer than they had ever been before. Lila's faint nod was a part of this shadowy movement. She said then, "It's late," and crossed the room to her own door. She turned and gave the woman a slow, half smile. "Good night, Carla," she murmured, and stepped into the darkness, closing the door behind her.

There was no response from the figure near the dying fire. Long after she was alone, Carla continued to stand there, a high, unmoving shape, soon indistinguishable as the growing darkness claimed her.

6

Aaron Lord woke to his third day of corral-building and lay taking painful soundings of his abused body. Restoring the corrals had been the first task he had assigned himself, and sunset of this day should see it finished.

A year of little beyond riding had well nigh let him forget what it was like to use his muscles, and when he reluctantly rose he found them so cramped and sore that he remained half-bent for a long moment, wondering whether he had been set upon by some agonizing malady during the night. It was altogether unnatural for any one body to be so beset with pain. When at length he straightened with a groan, he glared accusingly at the newly erected pole fences beyond the stable and grimly asked himself what fool vanity had made him think he could accomplish the task in one day.

That first day had been spent trimming the slender lodgepole pines, cutting them into the desired lengths and snaking them down off the hill behind the house. After that there had followed the setting of new posts, and then the levering of the poles into place and securing them to the posts.

It was hard, hot, tiring work; but he was forced to admit now that the results were worthwhile. Four of the fences were as stoutly set and truly aligned as the most critical eye could require. After today, with the dividing barrier down the center replaced, he would be able to congratulate himself on a job well done.

After a hurried breakfast he saddled the stallion and rode off with the axe over his shoulder. Arrived at the site of his morning work, he once again found cause to be grateful to the winter storms which had felled great numbers of the slender trees along the bench. He had only to trim the dead branches away before topping them and dragging them down the steep trail.

Within an hour he had a dozen ready; he looped the lariat around the butts of three, mounted and snaked them out of the timber and along the trail that was beginning to take on the appearance of a heavily traveled thoroughfare.

At noon he broke off long enough to reheat the leftover coffee and eat his cold biscuits and beans.

He was halfway across the yard, with the poles gouging a shallow furrow in the sand behind him on his second trip of the afternoon, when the stallion's ears shot forward simultaneously with the dogs' sudden uproar over by the house. He looked up to see the pair of shaggy brutes streaking into the grove and heard a moment later in those distant trees the telltale sounds of frightened horses being sternly handled. A moment later two riders trotted into the clearing, slowed at sight of the figure atop the grey stallion, then came on at a walk. Halfway to him, one of them lifted a hand in careless salute.

Lord ignored the salutation and watched the men approach, his face empty and cold. His chest swelled as he drew wind deep into his lungs and braced himself for the dismal scene that was sure to follow. Knowing what would happen, he felt no surprise at all when he saw the first rider's smile vanish. The man checked his horse as though he had come up against a fence, and his face closed against Lord like a door slamming shut. He was a big man, only slightly shorter than Lord and perhaps twenty pounds heavier. On his arrestingly handsome face was a look of quiet arrogance known only to one wholly sure of himself and of his position.

A long moment he sat and surveyed Lord out of tawny eyes, reading the Indian blood in the other and making his measured estimate. His big bay moved forward again a dozen paces and again halted. In the silence the man let his gaze travel over Lord with a deliberateness that was blatantly insulting, then thumbed back his hat to reveal a shock of tightly curling sandy hair.

"And just what in hell do you think you're up to?"

Lord inclined his head in a mock salute. "Welcome to you, too, neighbor."

The sandy-haired man's lips tightened. "Star names its own neighbors. You're not among them."

"And you're Star?"

"I'm Dave Moline. I represent it. Who are you?"

"Aaron Lord."

Moline eased back in his saddle. "Well, *Mister* Lord," he said, his emphasis on the title conveying his contempt, "you seem to have strayed off the reservation, looks like."

"I did no straying," Lord stated. "I traveled in a straight line, for the most part, from St. Louis."

Moline maintained his easy pose, but the skin at the corners of his eyes tightened ever so slightly, narrowing his gaze. "That being so, you'll likely have no trouble following that same straight line right back out of here."

"I'm going no place."

"I'd think that over, was I you."

"But you aren't."

Swift anger beat upward into Moline's face. The heat that emanated from his strangely tawny eyes was something Lord distinctly felt. "You're on preempted land. This is Star—"

"No," Lord contradicted gently. "This range belongs to me. All legally bought and paid for three days ago."

The handsome man's amazement for the moment overrode his anger. "Why, you blind son of a bitch!" he exclaimed. "Do you think a breed like you—"

45

Lord pointed a big forefinger straight at the man. "Don't put that name on me again," he said, his voice as hard as iron. "Don't even think of it."

Moline spurred straight at him as if to overrun him. At the last instant he dragged his horse down squarely in front of the grey and pinned Lord with his aroused stare, too overcome by his sudden rage to speak for a moment. He swallowed and hurled his voice into Lord's face. "If you hope to see today's sunset, you'll undally that rope and make long tracks away from here. I mean that."

Lord laid a flat order on the man. "Ride out of here unless you mean to fight."

"Why God damn you, I've buried better men than you," Moline shouted chokingly. "I'll ride out when I'm damned good and ready."

"Better go," Lord warned, his voice never wavering. "You're on my land. I won't tell you again."

Moline was all at once unsure of himself. He had the kind of mind that settled on a goal and never veered aside. Yet twice during this scene he had found himself stalled by this half-breed. Now he surveyed Lord from a new, disconcerting angle and was not pleased with what he saw. Lord's face was bone-hard and his eyes were narrow and wicked. The danger in him struck Moline fully for the first time, turning him for an instant more curious than angry.

"Well, God damn!" he said in sincere disbelief. "You really think you can make this stick, don't you? You actually believe you can stand against Star, don't you?" The idea was so patently preposterous that he could not digest it. The half-breed's ignorance of his position here was so abysmal that it threw this confrontation all out of kilter, leaving Moline without familiar guideposts. He said in a calmer tone, "I'm almost sorry for you," and backed his horse a half-dozen yards.

Lord watched him with infinite care. "Don't ever come onto my land again, and don't ever let any of your men come here. If you do, I'll come to you."

"No," Moline said. "You'll never come. Not after this."

"Remember I told you," Lord ordered. "Now that you've delivered your little welcome speech, there's nothing for you to do but ride out."

Moline sized up the situation, holding himself in check only with the greatest difficulty. No man who knew him would have dared speak to him as this man had done, and the knowledge that one of his men was witnessing this unprecedented challenge to himself and to Star's authority was wormwood in his mouth. Wanting to destroy the still-faced man in front of him, he clamped an iron control over his impulses. A coldness touched the back of his neck, and then a thin wave of heat washed over him, so intense and so unexpected that his mouth involuntarily opened to admit more air. He clamped his jaws together until the muscles stood out in hard, white ridges, and he put both hands on the horn and pressed all his strength into them in an effort to steady his nerves. "I think you'd like me to try it," he said thinly.

It was the sound of his voice, coming out distinctly and evenly, that served to restore his habitual self-assurance. He jerked his head to his companion. "What do you think, Frank?"

The man thus addressed briefly glanced at Moline; then he shrugged indifferently and shot a stream of amber juice from between his bearded lips.

"Hell, Dave, I dunno. It's fer you to say."

It came to Lord suddenly, like a shouted warning, that this was the one to watch, with his loose-knit frame, the careless garb and unshaven face. The air of nonchalance was a trifle too well managed—too pat. And when the slovenly rider lazily lifted his glance to him, the man's eyes were devoid of expression, his features as blank and cold as marble.

"Maybe," Moline suggested, "we'd better get back to Star and find out about this."

Frank nodded, his grey eyes never leaving Lord's face. "That might be best," he agreed gravely.

With one accord they wheeled off. They were perhaps thirty feet away when the lank rider said something to Moline, too low

47

for Lord to catch. It brought a negative response. But Frank, without warning, threw his horse back on its haunches and pulled it around in a smooth pivot. In the same instant his right hand lifted as swiftly as a striking snake, the gun in it glinting dully in the sun as it swung up.

To Lord, the entire scene seemed to transpire with agonizing slowness, even as he reacted with automatic, lightning speed. He saw Moline haul his horse around, heard him yell, "No, Frank!" and drive his big bay into the hindquarters of Frank's wheeling mount, futilely reaching across an impossible distance in an effort to strike down the gunman's lifting arm. And then that arm halted its upward arc as Lord drew and fired across the front of his saddle.

The crashing report of the heavy Navy pistol echoed back and forth through the hills before falling finally into a complete and dead silence. A look of pure shock settled over the rider's face as he stared wordlessly across the intervening space at Lord. His gun fell from nerveless fingers and he clamped both hands on the horn in a reflexive attempt to hold his dying body erect in the saddle. And then his right spur struck deeply into the horse's flank. Hard-held by the death-grip on the reins, the horse reared, and the slack body was flung suddenly to the sand.

Moline had pulled his horse about and was sitting the trembling bay, looking dazedly from the dead Frank to Lord, and back at Frank again.

He said in a tight, thin voice, "That was a mistake, mister," and showed Lord a grey and frozen look. His frustration at having let matters get out of hand prodded him to further violence; but with an effort of will he mastered it. "That was a mistake," he said again and nodded, as if agreeing with his own statement.

"The mistake was his," Lord stated flatly. "Now get him off my land."

In silence Moline stepped down, caught the dead man under the arms, and heaved him across the saddle of the nervously blowing horse. He took the rope from the horn and secured the man's feet and hands under the horse's belly, then remounted. He picked up his reins and laid his bright gaze on Lord. "Your land?" he said softly. "Redskin, this is not your land. It never will be. The only part of it you'll ever hold will be the hole where Star buries you."

Lord watched him out of sight under the trees. He replaced his gun in its holster with a hand that trembled uncontrollably. In the backwash of emotion, nausea roiled up inside him, and he dismounted and bent over and was suddenly and retchingly sick.

The seizure subsided, and he sagged heavily against the stallion's shoulder. He said in a whisper of deepest despair: "God damn them! Will they never leave a man alone?" and stared unseeing at the towering cloud of fluttering leaves of the cottonwoods, knowing the answer and numbly accepting it. In the westering sun bright prisms glittered in the tears that streamed unheeded down his convulsed face.

7

These hills and the valley, Lord now knew, comprised a vast, listening gallery in which the acts of men seldom went unnoticed, however carefully guarded. It was a place of great openness and unnumbered retreats, large enough for an army to march through and so small that one man, thinking himself unseen, might be closely watched by a dozen pairs of eyes.

The wilderness was complete. It was a region of endless bounty: where the strong grew inexorably stronger, feeding on that bounty, while the weak and the dispossessed looked on in envy and waited and schemed for their fall. There was a restlessness here—a constant movement of elusive shapes through shadowy glens and across open expanses—and an unquiet that pervaded the very air.

Lord felt this restless stirring and knew that he stood in the center of a gathering storm. He knew he should not tarry here —knew that the sense of well-being that had come to him with his purchase of the abandoned ranch had been false, an outgrowth of his need. The two grisly incidents had proved this.

But the unfed hunger of a lifetime would not let him go. It colored all his thinking and turned him deaf to reason. It rose, a constant pressure, inside him. In the end it made him all the more determined to stay.

In this hard-set frame of mind he turned the mares and the foal out of the corral and leaned against the gate to do some practical planning.

The season was too far advanced to stock his range this year. There remained then only to prepare for his first winter here—a winter which, he well knew, would be definitely more severe than those to which he was accustomed.

The stable roof must be replaced and a supply of grain hauled in from the basin below Valley Junction. After that, it would be time to cut hay and stack it near the stable, for he could not conceive of leaving his blooded horses to forage during the worst of the winter, as ranchers were wont to do in this country.

But he was suddenly impatient to make the house habitable. Now that he was a landowner, it was somehow unfitting that he should continue to camp out like a transient, especially with a house available to him.

For a moment he allowed his thoughts to drift and pictured himself coming to the door to welcome some caller inside. And then he was thinking of Lila MacKay, remembering her wildness and her gusty humor, the quicksilver play of emotion across her high-planed features, and, most vividly, the disconcerting directness of her strange green eyes. She had emptied him completely that night; and memory of it returned full force to become a turgid swelling in his groin so that he abruptly shoved away from the gate and sought relief in rapid movement.

Having settled on a definite course of action, he entered the house and set to work. At this altitude of 4,000 feet, decay made infinitesimal progress, and the contents of the house that had escaped destruction at the hands of the long-ago marauders had remained in a state of near-perfect preservation.

Broken sticks of furniture he piled in the backyard and set afire. In the larger of the two bedrooms he examined the springs and found them undamaged except for a coating of rust. He leaned them against the wall and bent to examine the battered bedstead and rails. At first glance they presented a sorry spectacle but closer inspection showed the bed could be made serviceable again. The dresser was beyond all hope of repair, and he dragged it outside and added it to the fire.

The second bedroom was devoid of furniture, but he remembered the set of springs outside in the wagon and realized that he could even put up a guest overnight, if the occasion warranted it.

Back in the kitchen, he ran across one lone cup still intact and two chipped plates which he placed on the work counter with infinite care before again delving into the jumble of battered pots and pans buried under fine drift sand. Two cast-iron kettles and a skillet had survived intact, and with increasing satisfaction he set them alongside the cup and plates. A tin dishpan had suffered a severe beating, but he knocked out the deepest dents with the stove poker and added it to his collection.

He next righted the drunkenly leaning stove, substituting a rock for the broken front leg, straightened the battered sections of pipe, and set them back in place, and lastly kindled a fire. From the debris, he dragged a crumpled tin bucket, beat it back into a semblance of roundness, and made a half-dozen trips to the pool to fill the big dishpan. With the water heating, he cleared out the wreckage and swept the kitchen clean with the remnant of a broom also found buried under the sand.

For the next two hours he labored with water, broom, and an improvised mop, and at the end of that time stepped to the doorway and proudly surveyed the results. The room fairly gleamed with cleanliness.

It occurred to him that he was ravenously hungry, and he hurried to bring his store of provisions in from the stable and put them neatly in the cupboard. Afterward, he cooked his dinner and ate, pausing a dozen times to run his gaze around the cheery room and congratulate himself on a job well done.

Finished with eating, he took paper and pencil from his saddlebags and began to compile a list of needed supplies. Now committed to establishing himself in his own home, he was determined to do it properly. It would be a home again—his personal haven. So resolved, he wrote: "red curtain material, also blue; green." He looked at this, then added: "Needles and thread," and wondered how one went about making curtains, and decided it probably was no more complicated than sewing patches on clothing.

He left the list on the worktable to be added to as other items occurred to him and set about swamping out the main room. He was in the backyard, dumping his third armload of refuse onto the fire, when he looked up at the dogs' sudden outburst and saw with pleasure Lila MacKay ride in under the trees.

"What in the name of hell are you still hanging around here for?"

"Cleaning house."

"Well, don't waste your time," she said tartly. "Whatever housecleaning is due will be done soon enough, if not by the Shadleys then by a certain Fresno Star Taggert. It'll take her just about five minutes, and, mister, you've no idea how clean and neat she can make a place, once she starts in on the trash."

"Would that be the lady who came in from the south in a private coach a few days ago?"

That surprised her. "It would," she admitted. "But she probably doesn't know yet you're here."

"I suspect she's gotten the word by now."

"What's that supposed to mean?"

"Two Star men came down to run me off. I sent one of them home dead."

In the act of crossing her forearms on the horn Lila reared bolt upright, her green eyes shocked. "You *what?*" she almost shouted.

"Christ's bloody wounds!" she said, more to herself than to him. "What happened?" she asked. "Who was it?"

"The one who identified himself as Star's representative was called Moline. The other was named Frank, I think."

Lila opened her lips but no sound came. She gave her head a quick shake and forced words past her frozen lips. "Which one . . . is dead?"

"The one called Frank."

"Ah!" It came out as a sigh, and Lila put both hands to her heavy mane and raked it back against her head with a strength that tilted her head up so that the full beat of the sun poured warmth and color back into her chilled features. It required only that movement for her to regain mastery of herself. "How did it happen?"

Lord rolled his heavy shoulders, reluctant to go back over it. "The two of them rode up while I was working on the corral. Moline ordered me off the place. I told him I'd bought it, and he said maybe they'd better go home and see what the boss had to say. Then the one called Frank tried a sneak draw."

"And?"

"That's all," Lord stated. "He didn't quite make it."

But it was not enough to suit Lila. "How close did he come?" she asked quietly.

"He made his move before he'd really set himself."

"That's not like Frank Wheeler," she said musingly. "Now, why in hell would he let himself get in a hurry?"

"It was my mother," Lord explained quietly.

"Your *mother*? What the hell—"

"She painted me the wrong color. At least, I gather neither one of them cared for it, from a few stray remarks they dropped."

"You mean to say," Lila asked, slowly looking down on Lord from her place atop the tall gelding, "that you figure Dave and Frank tried to run you off just because you're a breed? Mister, if you *really* think that, then you *have* stayed out in the sun too long! *Way* too long!"

"Moline saw me and named me," Lord stated flatly. "That I know."

"Well, so did I! Where's the difference?"

"The difference is *you* were only *surprised*," Lord explained impatiently. "Moline wanted to see me *dead*."

"Because you're a breed?" Lila asked incredulously. "That's hogwash, and you know it." But even as she spoke, she read the truth in his face and sensed something in him that bothered her because she could not understand it. "No," she said, "you *don't* know it. You really believe that the color of your skin was back of the whole thing, don't you?"

"And you," Lord said in a voice heavy with sarcasm, "really think my being what I am had nothing at all to do with it. Don't make me laugh!"

"Mister," Lila replied softly, "you listen here. If your skin had been shining white with a holy light, it would have been the same. You'd better believe that, because it's God's bitter truth. You are on forbidden ground. *Star* ground. And Star will put you off."

Lord rejected both points with a slow shake of the head. "You could not be more wrong."

"Take a ride with me," she invited. "I'll introduce you to . . . oh, say about ten men. And after I've introduced you, I'll leave it to you to ask each of those ten men where they used to live. And then, after you've heard each and every one of them say, 'Star Valley,' I'll have *my* little laugh. And by the way," she added, "there's not a single breed among them. They're as white as can be." She sat there watching doubt touch him. "Come on, Mister Lord," she prodded gently. "Come on."

It was the challenge in her green eyes, as much as her complete sincerity, that rendered Lord less and less sure of himself. Wanting to retain his conviction that his personal stigmata accounted for the wholesale resistance he had experienced in these mountains, he found himself cornered by this unpredictable, self-assured hill girl. All unwittingly she had called to mind certain irrefutable facts—the stately red-haired woman's pointed suggestion that he retrace his steps southward, the poorly erased

54

section of Star Valley on the map in the land office, the abandoned cabins in the arms of the Y, the methodical destruction of the interior of the house behind him—all of which added up to one truth: he was unknowingly thwarting a powerful woman's claim to a cattle empire such as few men had ever dreamed of. With a sensation bordering on relief he gave voice to his decision.

"I hold title to this section of Star Valley. I've bought it with gold coin, all of it."

"You've bought nothing but grief," Lila retorted bluntly. "Oh, I know . . . the Government claimed it was open graze. Hell! For over thirty years every damned blade of grass in this valley has belonged to Star and will go right on belonging to Star 'til hell freezes over! A few years ago, some men—my old man among them—decided to try grabbing off shares of this section of the valley. Fresno Taggert ran them out faster 'n they could blink. You'll learn that once Fresno Star Taggert sets her sights on something, it's as good as hers."

"She stopped me on my way in here and tried to buy my horses."

Lila's gaze widened ever so little. "Did she, now?" she drawled, making no attempt to mask her amusement. "Well, in that case, you'd best enjoy them while you can, sonny."

"Meaning?"

"Meaning they're as good as wearing her Star brand already."

"We'll see."

"Hunh unh," Lila contradicted him. "*I'll* see. What *you'll* see is the yonder side of the fartherest hill you can find."

The memory of the aristocratic woman as she halted beside the travel-stained coach and sent her summons drifting down to him on the canyon wind swept over Lord: the natural pride and grace of her bearing, her rapture as she had watched the grey stallion's prancing, wary approach, and finally, the unmistakable gentility of her speech. Unthinkingly he gave voice to the suspicion in his mind. "You really dislike her, don't you?"

Lila's denial was abrupt. "Nothing of the sort. As a matter of fact, I've only actually met her face-to-face maybe a dozen times.

I happen to *like* her. Not only that, I *admire* her. Make no mistake, mister, she's hard as nails, for all her fine ways. What she wants, she takes: and what she takes, she *keeps*. For that I admire her."

"That being so, then all I can say is you've a strange way of airing your admiration."

She straightened in the saddle, picked up the reins, and nodded down at him. "I've wasted all the breath I'm going to waste on you. I'm off for town; can I fetch you anything *for your trip south?*"

Lord seemed not to have heard her. In fact, he seemed not to be really seeing her. Knowing, from her long association with Carla, the Indian trick of withdrawing into himself at will, she recognized the familiar blank look now on Lord's face, and reined her sorrel around the fire. She was almost past him when he came to with a start and took two swift steps that put him directly in the sorrel's path.

Frightened, the horse shied, but Lord's long arm reached out and his fingers closed on the bit shank, bringing the sorrel to a nervous stand. "Wait," Lord said, and looked up into the deadliest pair of eyes he had ever seen.

"Take your hand off that bit," Lila said, her tone as dangerous as her gaze. "Now."

"Not until I apologize."

"For what?"

"Misjudging you."

"In what way?"

"More than one, I think."

There was no softening of her stony stare. "All right, you've said it. Now take your hand off that bit."

He loosed his grip and let his hand drop.

"Then I'll be on my way," she said shortly, and lifted her reins.

"Wait. I've a favor to ask."

She halted her horse in mid-turn. "Well?"

"I need a team and harness."

That brought her back around. "A team?" Clearly she thought she had misunderstood him. When he nodded, she gave it a moment's thought. "All right. Lige Evans runs the livery. He generally has some decent stock around. Where's the money?"

"I'll give it to you in a minute," Lord told her. "I've also got a list in the kitchen. Would it be too much trouble for you to tie my packsaddle behind you and bring the stuff back? You could use the team to pack."

"Where's the trouble?"

Lord stepped onto the porch. "Come on in. I'd like you to see what I've been up to."

Her eyes sharpened suspiciously. "I'll wait here."

"I promise not to corner you in the bedroom."

His easy, open manner brought a laugh from her and she swung down. "You're a horny bastard," she told him. "I'll have a quick look and be on my way. I don't fancy dragging a team of dead-headed plow horses ten miles from town after dark."

He motioned her ahead of him and was pleased when she halted in the door and in frank surprise surveyed the kitchen. She made a low approving sound in her throat and crossed to the main room. "Damned if you *haven't* been house-cleaning!" she said. "Looks like a different place."

He came up behind her, placed his hands on the doorframe on either side of her head and leaned forward. "Care to see my bedroom?"

She made a quick half-turn and stepped deeper into the room. Her face showed him nothing at all, but there was a noticeable sharpness to her voice as she put out a hand and waggled her fingers. "The list."

He held to his position, seemingly at ease but there was a visible tension in his hands and the half smile on his lips did nothing to relieve the waiting soberness of his expression. They continued to face each other in this way, neither speaking, neither moving, while the silence built up between them, higher and thicker.

He was watching her carefully for some slight break, and

when he caught the quickening tempo of her breathing and glimpsed the faint, swift pulse at the base of her throat he knew that he had roused her. He could have her now in this ruined room simply by reaching out.

It was a thing she clearly wanted and clearly expected. It showed in the loosening of her mouth and in the blankness of her wide-set eyes, and in the way her whole body seemed to be waiting. He had instigated this little play to test his effect on her—to reassure himself that her stopping by here had been prompted by something quite aside from the reason she had given. Knowing this to be so, he felt excitement start to build in him. On the point of going to her, he all at once pushed himself away from the doorway and swung back into the kitchen. He caught up the note, folded it, and held it out. "If you see anything else you think I could use, just toss it in."

Lila tucked the square of paper into a pocket of her deerskin tunic and held out her hand. "The money," she reminded him.

He lifted his shirttail, reached into the money belt, and counted out five double eagles into her palm. "That's a hundred. How much will you need?"

"A decent team and harness will cost probably a hundred. I don't know what all you've got on your list."

Lord counted out three more coins. "That's another sixty. Should be enough."

He closed the flap of his belt, then slipped his shirt over his head in one swift movement. When he looked at her again he noted the wariness in her eyes, and the tightness that had come back into her face.

She was in full control of herself again, and increasingly certain that she disliked the way this had turned out. Definitely she disliked having to admit that she had again failed to handle him as she handled other men. Her nerves were still on edge from his nearness, and on the instant she made up her mind that she would not play his game.

She went past him without speaking, crossed the porch, and

was in the saddle when he reached the door. He gave her horse a swift, approving appraisal. "You're well mounted."

That pleased her. She reached down and gave the tall gelding a fond slap alongside the neck. "He's a Star horse, sired by Fresno Taggert's stud," she informed him. "I got him off Moline as a weanling. He's beat everything in the country that's ever come up against him."

Lord nodded, once again running his admiring gaze over the tall, powerfully muscled sorrel. "I can believe it," he admitted, and then could not let her boast pass unchallenged. "Might be interesting to see what he could do against a *real* horse."

"Such as that grey stud of yours over in the corral?"

Lord grinned at her eager acceptance of the challenge. "Like to try it?"

"Anytime," Lila replied. "Any old time at all. You name the day, the distance, and the stakes. Ridgerunner and I'll be on hand."

"The place will be that stretch of flat tableland just below the grove," Lord told her. "The distance, two miles. The time will be one of these days before long; and the stakes I'll name about fifteen minutes after my stud runs your gelding straight into the ground."

Lila's lips quirked. "I like to know the size of the purse I'm gunning for."

"That," Lord grinned, "you already know."

Her ribald mirth exploded in a lusty shout. "Hell," she said. "Why should I ask Ridgerunner to work for something I can have for free?"

Before he could frame a reply, she lifted the reins, leaned slightly forward, and left the yard at a climbing run.

For the next hour Lord worked steadily, all the while thinking of Lila and what her return might occasion.

He was bent over, sweeping the last of the scourings of the main room's floor into the fireplace when the dogs' warning clamor again caused him to straighten and go to the front door.

59

He arrived there just as two riders ran into the yard and bore down on the house, loudly cursing the roaring dogs. He stepped to the edge of the porch, his whistle at once bringing the dogs back to him.

The pair pulled up a dozen feet away, and sudden tension gripped Lord. Below the brim of both battered hats gleamed a ragged fringe of brightest blond hair. He returned their hostile gaze with no show of emotion. Nor did he speak.

"Who are you? And what the hell are you doing here?"

It came from the older man, and so closely resembled Dave Moline's earlier greeting that Lord almost smiled in spite of his anger. "You've an odd way of greeting strangers in this country."

"I don't make it a habit to waste no polite 'hello's' on no damned breeds," the spokesman for the pair snapped. "I asked you who you was an' what you was doin' here. You better answer me."

Lord took a step that placed him on the edge of the porch. "I'm Aaron Lord," he said with deceptive mildness. "I've bought this place, and if you've a decent set of manners about you, I suggest you put them to work right now, or ride out of here."

The younger man's jaw dropped in outright astonishment. "You hear what he said, Paw?" he exclaimed. He glanced over at Lord, then back at his father. "You gonna take that off'n him, Paw?"

"Shut up, Newt," said the elder one. On Lord he bent an aroused stare. "You say you *bought* this here place?"

Lord nodded.

"Who from?"

"The Government, naturally."

For some reason, the man was hugely pleased. "Well, now!" he murmured. "An' what did Fresno Taggert have to say about that, pray tell?"

"I've not discussed it with her."

The man reared back and loosed a shout of laughter at the sky.

"Well, you *will*," he promised Lord. "You can bet your red ass on that."

Lord's lips thinned. "State your business. I'm busy."

"Don't go gettin' mouthy with me, feller," the man warned; but his voice lacked force. Something about the big man on the porch bothered him. He did not run true to form. It was no imagined thing, but a quality that showed as clearly as the man's very size, and the way he stood easily balanced on wide-planted legs, his right hand carelessly brushing the butt of the long Navy pistol belted about his narrow hips. It caused the ruddy-faced blond man to ease himself carefully in the saddle and speak in an altered tone. "I'm Balaam Shadley, and this here is my boy, Newt. We're lookin' fer his twin brother. Don't s'pose you've seen him?"

Lord kept his face impassive. "No," he said, detesting the lie, "I've only just —" He broke off as the dogs again erupted into violent outcry directly underfoot. His low command held them where they were, and as he turned to look in the direction they were facing, he caught the sounds of horses coming through the grove. A moment later six riders filed out of the cottonwoods and came steadily toward the house. Before they were halfway across the yard he recognized the figure of Moline.

And then he forgot Moline as his gaze fastened on another rider. The auburn-haired woman on the tall chestnut mare could be none other than Fresno Taggert, owner of the all-powerful Star.

A chill touched him and held him motionless there on the porch as he watched the woman come on. But even with tension drawing his nerves tight, he could not but marvel at the superb way she sat her big mare. Unlike Lila MacKay, Fresno Taggert rode the customary sidesaddle, and though she was dressed in worn, scarred leather, she still contrived to appear altogether feminine, altogether cool.

She walked the mare straight up to the porch and drew in. Lord was suddenly aware of being naked to the waist, but his

61

concern for his personal appearance was wholly wasted. The woman seemed as unaware of him as though he did not exist. She was facing the two Shadleys, and in this scene Lord watched her wield her power with all the lofty disdain of a vexed ruler.

Her voice cut the elder Shadley with the clean precision of a finely honed knife. "You have been warned about showing your face in this valley, Mr. Shadley. I am not in the habit of repeating such warnings."

Shadley dipped his head, and the careful way he used his voice revealed his awareness of the ticklish situation in which he found himself. "We was jest askin' this breed, here, if he'd seen Lewt, Mrs. Taggert. That's the only reason we was here—lookin' fer Lewt."

"The reason is not good enough," Fresno Taggert told him. "I suggest you look elsewhere . . . *now.*"

The last word was spoken in the unalterable tone of a displeased adult addressing a recalcitrant child, and the woman waited there on her mare, her head slightly tilted back, so that she gave the impression of looking down on Shadley.

Observing her at this range, Lord could discern no hint of softness in her. Below the hem of her leather skirt, her left boot was firm in the stirrup. Her flat-crowned hat sat squarely on her mass of red hair, and a heavy quirt swung from her right wrist. In the shade cast by her hatbrim the planes of her cleanly etched features were perfectly composed and wholly cold.

All this Lord noted while the woman faced the two Shadleys in a manner so overbearing that he actually felt a momentary twinge of sympathy for the luckless pair. What was going on here now had nothing to do with him, and he had the strangest conviction that even were he to step forward and confess to having killed Lewt Shadley it would make not the slightest difference. Not to the woman. Her sole concern was the presence of the two hill riders in Star Valley.

In this tense silence Balaam Shadley's voice sounded unnaturally loud, although the man held it to a carefully respectful pitch. "We're goin', Mrs. Taggert. But I'd mightily appreciate havin' your word that Star had nothin' to do with Lewt's not showin' up t'home."

"You have it. Now get out."

"Yes, Ma'am." Shadley ducked his head, masking his impotent hatred of the woman behind this outward show of respect. He reined his horse half around, then stopped, unable to bear his dismal foreboding. "I jest cain't figger it out. It ain't a' tall like Lewt to light out 'thout tellin' me where he aimed to go."

Fresno Taggert fingered her reins, drawing them to a precise tension in her left hand. "I'll have my men check the horse herd," she said drily. "It's quite likely they'll come up with the usual reason for Lewt's absence."

The inference was not lost on Shadley. "No," he said in a definite way. "It wasn't no horses that tolled Lewt away this time. He'd of said so, if'n he was of a mind to run stock south. He's allus been right good about tellin' me whenever he meant t'do that."

"A considerate son, indeed," the woman answered. "You must be very proud of him."

"Why," Shadley replied, "I am that, ma'am. Any man would be."

Fresno Taggert was suddenly impatient with this protracted charade. She said curtly, "Go find him, then," and held herself in that high, alert position until the two men wheeled and galloped back the way they had come.

When they had disappeared in the grove she swung around to face Lord, and looked down at him with the same cold disapproval she had shown Shadley.

"You killed one of my men yesterday. I want to know why."

Lord was obliged to tilt his head back to meet the violet eyes boring into him. In the time it took him to frame his reply he dismissed all thought of trying to placate her, knowing she would interpret any gentleness on his part as weakness. "Didn't your foreman tell you how it was, ma'am?" he asked.

"*You* will tell me."

It was a command issued by one accustomed to being obeyed.

Lord's glance flicked past her and touched Moline, who sat his horse a dozen feet to the rear, and saw the look of enjoyment on that handsome face. He said, "Let's hear his version, ma'am," and continued to watch Moline.

"All right," Fresno Taggert agreed. "Dave, tell what happened." When the man did not immediately move, she turned in the saddle and used her voice more roughly on him. "Come on! Come on!"

Her impatience with him in front of the men at once angered Moline. His mouth thinned, and his whole face narrowed and hardened. But he rode forward and stopped near her. "I've already gone over it three times for—" he began, and clamped his jaws tight as the woman's chill voice struck him.

"If I ask you to repeat it fifty times, you'll do it."

Moline closed his eyes and the hissing outrush of his breath was an audible sound. "All right, Mrs. Taggert," he said tightly. "Frank and I came by here yesterday afternoon and found this breed making out like the place belonged to him. When I suggested he pull out, he got smart. We argued awhile and I said to Frank that maybe we'd best go back to Star and see what you had to say about it. We started away, and this breed shot Frank in the back." He paused, then added, with his bright gaze unwinkingly on Lord, "And that's what happened, just like I told you."

Fresno Taggert had been watching Lord all this while. When Moline's account ended, she continued to sit there studying his reaction. "Is that true?" she asked, her voice surprisingly mild.

"Up to a point," Lord murmured.

"What point?"

Lord gave Moline another knowing look. He said in the same soft voice, "Ask him."

"I am asking *you*."

"All right, then. The point where he says I put a bullet in his back."

Moline gripped the horn until his arms shook. "He's a damned liar," he said hoarsely.

The woman gave him a long, thoughtful look, then slowly

swung back to Lord. "He says you're a liar. You say he's one. Now, which of you is right, I wonder?"

Whether she was acting, or honestly puzzled, Lord could not tell. She apparently had come here to order him out of the valley, or to kill him, as was evidenced by the five riders she had brought with her. But now she was unexpectedly diverted by this disparity in the two versions of Frank Wheeler's death. In the brief, uneasy silence that followed, it struck Lord as strange that she who clearly had no need at all to weigh the right and the wrong of a question would do so at possible cost to herself. Sensing her dilemma, he elected to prompt her. "Did you examine the bullet hole in your man's chest, ma'am?"

There was a quick narrowing of the violet eyes. "His *chest*?"

"That's where I put it."

Without taking her eyes off him, she spoke to one of the men ranged behind her. "Hod, come up here, please." When the rider complied, she put her question to him in quiet tones. "All right now, Hod: watch what you say. I want only the truth. I didn't examine Frank when Dave brought him in, but you helped change his clothes for burying." She paused to let that sink in, then continued in the same businesslike way. "If necessary, I'll have Frank's grave opened. But you can clear up at least one part of this mess now by telling me where he was shot. Was it in the back, or in the chest?"

Hod's expression was that of a man in torment. His loyalty to the ranch was on the line. He was being required to choose between that loyalty and the life of a man whose presence here constituted a threat to the very person who was forcing the choice upon him.

He wiped his forehead and shot a look of pure distress at Moline, whose instructions in this matter had been unmistakably clear. He started to answer, choked, and said in a barely audible monotone, "He was shot just under the heart, ma'am," and sat there miserably enduring the combined gaze of all who heard.

Fresno Taggert said gently, "Well, now," and turned her head by slow degrees until she was looking at Moline once more.

When she spoke again it was in a studiously calm, inquiring tone, but under the brim of her flat-crowned hat a vein appeared as a faint blue mark against the fairness of her skin. It swelled and lengthened until it reached from the outer edge of her left eyebrow to the hairline, and Lord realized then that she was possessed of an almost overpowering rage. "Hod says the bullet caught Frank in the chest, Dave. Not the back. Why would he say that?"

Moline's violent outburst was wholly unexpected. "Just whose word is good with you, Mrs. Taggert?" he demanded in a strident shout. "Just who in hell is boss at Star, anyhow—Hod or me?"

The man's fury was real. It pushed him beyond the bounds of reason. His right hand flashed down, grasped the pistol at his hip, and was sliding it free when Fresno Taggert moved with blinding swiftness. In one continuing move she reined her mare about, rammed it shoulder-on into Moline's mount, and slashed Moline across the forearm with her heavy quirt. The blow brought a yell from Moline, and he dragged his horse aside, trying to get into the clear where he could bring the gun to bear on the tall half-breed who had brought this humiliating thing to pass. But the mare lunged again, knocking Moline's mount off balance. Dust boiled thickly around the two wheeling horses, and then, as quickly as it had broken out, all this confused activity ceased, and Fresno backed her mare out of the dust and leaned forward to speak directly to Moline. "Get out of Star Valley, Dave," she said in a coldly wicked voice. "You are an insult to the Star brand. You know the rules here, and they do not include lying. I will not have a man on the ranch whose word I cannot trust."

She straightened and sat there staring unwinkingly at the man, seeing the ruin her actions had wrought in him and letting none of it touch her. "Don't go back to the ranch for your gear," she added. "If you ever set foot in the valley again, you're a dead man. Now go."

Moline held his horse in place with a shaking hand. He bent

66

over the horn and sucked air in through his open mouth with fixed intensity.

He had ruled these men for five hard years, and at times had even influenced the woman, to a degree. All his thoughts and loyalties had belonged to Star and to its autocratic owner. A single error in judgment and he was a man with no dignity left him.

His face was grey when he painfully straightened. His eyes were blank as he swung his horse around and looked across the distance separating him from Fresno Taggert. At the last he could not meet her condemning gaze, and he closed his eyes and let his head fall back, so that he seemed to be silently praying. He said in a strangled whisper, "All right, Mrs. Taggert. But I promise you, this isn't all of it."

Fresno seemed not to have heard him. "Better go," she said, her voice unnaturally quiet. Its very gentleness jerked Moline's head straight and sent his glance darting to the four riders sitting off to one side with such steady watchfulness. He started to say something more, than clamped his lips shut, and left the yard at a surging run.

In the backwash of silence Fresno reined over to Lord, freed her right leg of the curved rest of the sidesaddle, and jumped down. She drew Hod to her with a look and tossed him her reins. "You're foreman, now," she told the man. "Take the boys over to the pool and water the horses. Stay there until I call you." She stepped past Lord, saying, "I'll have a word with you," and went into the house without bothering to see whether he followed.

Her incredible self-possession was a thing Lord had never before encountered in a woman. It was a prominence from which she looked down on everything and everyone and which rendered her wholly untouchable. It bestowed on her an air of overlordship wherever she went, so that by the very act of entering the room she summarily reversed their respective roles, leaving him to play the part of the unwelcome caller.

She crossed to the fireplace with long, measured strides and turned there, her right arm coming up in a graceful gesture to rest on the mantle. The braided quirt gently swung from her wrist by its looped thong.

Lord stepped through the door and halted, his attention settling closely on her. In the brief time before he spoke he noted that she was taller than he had at first thought, with a strong, athletic reach to her slimness that further emphasized the impression of height. In her delicately drawn features there was a curious stillness. Only her violet, thick-lashed eyes betrayed the fact that she was not completely at ease.

Lord in that fleeting moment discerned this air of utter concentration in her and recognized the glaring paradox she represented: she was one of those rare women who could take on a man's responsibilities without becoming in any way mannish. She was her own law and her own strength.

And she was undeniably beautiful. Even in her rough riding attire, and with her wealth of glowing hair cascading down her back in careless disorder, she made a picture that would stay with him a long time. He gestured toward the backless rocker he had resurrected from the room's wreckage. "Would you care to sit, ma'am?"

She did not bother to acknowledge his courtesy but continued to study him with that cold, impersonal intensity that seemed a part of her personality, taking his measure without regard for propriety. She had a task to perform; that alone concerned her.

"I took Dave's word on blind faith," she said in that direct way of hers. "I apologize for him on behalf of Star."

Lord sensed what that cost her. "Perhaps he had his reasons, ma'am. Or thought he had."

"No," Fresno contradicted him. "He had none at all. I will not tolerate dishonesty, well-intentioned or not."

The flat, unequivocal statement afforded Lord a glimpse into the woman's character, whether she had intended it to or not. She was so sure of herself that she could not conceive of stooping to subterfuge for any reason.

68

He dipped his head in a curt nod, realizing that the words called for no reply on his part. A waiting, uneasy silence came between them. It deepened and pushed them farther and farther apart until all recollection of their ever having spoken to each other was lost. They were then come face to face for the first time in a present that had no past leading to it.

In this stillness the woman reacted to something that made itself known suddenly and sharply to her alone. It laid a faint color across her cheeks and made her alter the direct line of her gaze to a point somewhere beyond Lord's left shoulder. She straightened slowly and swung the quirt up across her waist, catching the lash in her left hand and exerting a steady pull on it.

"You can't stay here, you know," she said finally, and though she spoke quietly, the very unexpectedness of her words gave them an abrupt, harsh quality in all that stillness. "It's quite out of the question."

"I have bought this range," Lord replied. "That fact puts it beyond any question, ma'am."

She shrugged it aside with a graceful movement of her shoulders. "No matter. The land office will refund your money."

"I don't want the money. I want this land."

Her eyes fastened on his, narrowly speculative. "And that is bound to pose a question in a good many minds around here, you must realize—the source of that much money."

Points of light flared in Lord's black eyes. "It's clean money. At least, as clean as conscience money ever is."

Her brows lifted. "*Conscience* money?"

"I inherited it from my father—my *white* father, Mrs. Taggert. He owned quite a good fur business in St. Louis." He paused, then added, "My Indian blood comes from my mother. She was a Northern Cheyenne."

Color again touched Fresno's face, and she lowered her gaze. "I see," she said awkwardly. It was a moment before she could collect herself, and even then she found it difficult to meet his sardonic gaze.

She lifted her head, and her cool demeanor came back to her. "Since she once lived in this area, I wonder she didn't return with you."

"She's here."

Fresno started slightly and glanced around. "Oh. I didn't realize—"

"Not right *here*," Lord said. "At Sand Creek. She's buried there, along with some four hundred other women and children." He paused, then said with cutting sarcasm, "You *have* heard of the Sand Creek Massacre, haven't you, Mrs. Taggert?" and watched the insult bring a wave of crimson to her face.

"I have heard of it, Mr. Lord," she replied stiffly. "I am not proud of what Colonel Chivington did there. The man ought to have been hanged."

Surprise altered Lord's expression. "You're the first white person I've ever heard say that. I wonder if you mean it."

Her head snapped back. "You go out of your way to be insulting, Mr. Lord. For your information, I never say what I do not mean."

"Nor do I. Now I'll say I've no intention of tearing up the deed to this land."

The shift in topics could have disconcerted a less agile brain than Fresno's. But she parried with the easy grace of a fencer.

"I'm curious about your sudden appearance here, Mr. Lord, and about your determination to stay. For almost thirty years this has been Star range. Now you appear out of nowhere, making wide tracks, so to speak. Why? What is here"—she lifted a booted foot and tapped it against the hearth—"right *here*, that makes it so important to you?" She waited for his answer, and when it did not come, said very quietly, "It's not a wise decision you're holding to, Mr. Lord. Nor a safe one."

A glint of amusement showed in Lord's gaze. "Fools rush in where angels fear to tread," he quoted.

She rejected this with a slow shake of her head. "You have rushed in, but you're no fool, Mr. Lord. That is why you will not stay."

Lord leaned the point of his shoulder against the doorframe. "I'm going no place at all."

"You're tougher than I thought," she said frankly. She gave the quirt a quick, hard pull. "It's a bit uncommon for a man of your background to take such a stand."

"I can back it up."

"With what?"

"Myself."

The flat statement jolted her. She said in a thoughtful voice, "Under different circumstances I'd admire you for that. As it is, I'm sorry for you."

"Don't feel sorry for me," Lord replied sharply. "I want none of your sympathy."

"Be that as it may, you have it," she told him, and added meaningly, "Not that it alters matters, of course."

She was calm and she was unshakable, and the realization that this talk was leading nowhere put Lord out of patience. He straightened. "If you've nothing more to say—"

She brought the quirt down against her leather skirt with a popping sound, cutting him off. "But I have," she said sternly, thoroughly displeased with his manner. "I want you gone from here by noon tomorrow. I am not concerned with the legality of your claim. My father held this valley by right of prior claim. He was the first white man in this basin country. He drove the Indians—"

Her outburst was cut off as though a hand had been clamped over her mouth. Flushing to the roots of her hair, she stood there staring at him, knowing there was no way to cover the mortifying slip of the tongue.

Lord crossed the room and halted directly in front of her, near enough to reach out and touch her—near enough to take in the faint, indefinable woman smell of her. It filled his nostrils and he recognized it with an awareness that shocked him. It threw his relationship to her completely out of balance, and dismay rose in him, stopping his breath in his throat. The words that had been forming on his lips died between his hard-clamped jaws. The

71

emotion rioting through him was wholly concealed behind the noncommittal expression that settled over his face. On wide-planted legs he loomed over her, his gaze locked with hers. Almost imperceptibly the look on her face altered, leaving it curiously devoid of expression.

The violet eyes flicked glancingly down across his chest and fell to the hearth between her booted feet. She made as if to step back, but the fireplace barred her retreat.

To Lord's watchful eyes these little signals betrayed her, and their meaning he interpreted with the unerring instinct of a predator closely watching its prey for some sign of panic. His proximity to her had shattered her composure as no spoken words of his would have done.

"You were saying, ma'am?" he prompted.

Fresno forced herself to look up into that dark face. "I didn't mean—" she began, and could not go on.

"To embarrass me? Don't let it trouble you; you didn't." He took his time before continuing. Knowing what he was going to do, he yet could feel something akin to pity for this beautiful woman in front of him. It was a feeling that came to him, unbidden and unwanted, and it made no sense at all. But it was there, all the same. He took a slow breath, wanting to make the thing quite clear to her.

"As you were saying, your father drove the Indians out of this valley. This time, an Indian will do the driving out, if any driving is done. I researched the law pretty thoroughly before I paid out good coin for this property. My title is watertight."

He paused to let that sink in, then went on in the same deliberate way. "As to the legality of *your* claim; it does not exist. The Homestead Act gave your father three sections—one for himself, one for your mother, and later a third for you, when you came of age. In round figures, then, that means you own two thousand acres. I own the deed to every square foot of ground east of Star River—in the same round figures, some twenty thousand acres."

Fresno met his downbearing gaze with the same air of assurance she had maintained throughout this meeting. "Ten years ago," she said evenly, "a man named Bland built this house. He was a good builder, but a poor judge of character. He didn't stay long."

"So, it was you who wrecked this place!"

"No, it was not I. I was nineteen at the time, and away at school."

Lord felt like a fool. "I apologize. Of course it couldn't have been your doing."

"And there," she informed him, "you are quite mistaken. It not only could have; it most surely would have been my doing, had I been in charge. My father was a hard taskmaster, Mr. Lord. I learned my lessons well."

"You apparently overlooked one," Lord told her. "The one having to do with safeguarding your rights to this part of the valley."

The statement raked through her like a jagged blade. "That," she said, closer to betraying anger than Lord had yet seen her, "was Farley Taggert's contribution to the cause of peace in this valley. He thought that he could purchase peace with Star land."

Hearing the contempt in her voice, Lord wondered what sort of man Taggert was to engender such loathing in his mate. "Perhaps your husband merely errs on the side of justice," he drily suggested. "Could it be that his chief sin consisted of a belief in the limited rights of Star's claim to open land?"

She was faintly amused. "This is clearly your hour for error, Mr. Lord. I hold title to some fifty thousand acres—or all the land west of the river. No," she said and pinpoints of light flared in her eyes. "He wanted nothing! He thought that if he backed up far enough, they would stop grabbing."

"They?"

"The riffraff who came here after my father had stamped this valley as his own—the thieving scum who always follow the trailblazers, thinking the strong should feed the weak—the Shadleys and the Matlocks and all the others like them who creep through the hills around here." She lifted a hand in a gesture that took in the hills to the east. "My father chased them up there. My husband let them slip back down. I chased them back again after he died, and that's where they stay."

"I see," Lord murmured. "Still, I wonder that you never bought this range. It would only be common sense, with all the land-hungry settlers coming out here now."

"A month ago I sent a herd east to raise the money to buy this range. That money should be here within a week."

Lord nodded his understanding. "Unfortunately, I'm a few days ahead of you."

The vein again showed blue under the fair skin of her temple. "That is of no importance. You are not staying."

"We go in an endless circle," Lord said tiredly.

The finality of the words lifted her voice to a warning note. "I want no trouble over this thing, Mr. Lord. Truly I don't."

"Nor do I, Mrs. Taggert."

Whether by choice or accident she misread his meaning. She put a hand to her throat, her expression lightening. "Then, you'll go?"

Lord sighed. "No, ma'am. I won't."

The change in her then was shocking to see. All her monumental dignity deserted her. Her head jerked back and she glared up at him out of eyes gone dark with rage. "I don't want to see you killed over this!" she said harshly. "I'll pay you double the price you paid for this land. *But you will not stay.*"

"I am staying."

Her fury burst forth in a strangled shout. "Damn you for a stubborn fool!" She shoved away from the fireplace, her right hand lifting to strike him.

As swiftly, Lord reached out and imprisoned her wrist in his long fingers. For a moment frozen in time they maintained that grotesque pose, their eyes locked, their bodies ungiving. "I've never before laid a hand on a woman," Lord said in a voice that shook, "but if you ever try that again, I'll beat you. Do you understand?"

In the stricken silence that swirled in around them Fresno

closed her eyes, unable to bear the sight of the primitive rage her actions had called to life in him. All color drained from her face, and she moved her head from side to side in unbearable humiliation.

It remained for Lord to end the painful scene. He released her wrist and stepped back. "I think you had better go now, Mrs. Taggert," he said heavily.

She was free of his grasp, but not of his presence. She turned half away from him, her eyes still shut, her right hand going up to grip the edge of the mantle. Her breasts rose with her slow, indrawn breath. "Yes," she whispered. "Yes, I'll go."

She released her hold on the mantle and made her way blindly down the room, her face still averted, her movements stiff and jerky. In the kitchen doorway she paused as if reluctant to display her defeat before the eyes of her waiting crew. She smoothed her hair in a swift, gesture that was purely feminine and purely automatic, stepped through the kitchen, and left the house by the back door.

A moment later her voice sounded from the backyard, summoning her men from the pool.

Rendered numb by the scene's harrowing climax, Lord was only dimly conscious of the sounds outside as the Star Riders came up—the faint squeaking of saddle leather, the metallic jangle of bit chains, and the dull thud of hoofs in the sand. And then he heard the woman say, "All right, boys, let's go home."

He was shocked at the effect that changed voice had on him. He started and turned to the door to catch another glimpse of her as she led her crew around the house at a surging run.

Her big mare was faster than the other horses, and she pulled quickly away from them, racing for the trees. She was halfway across the yard when the grey stallion's piercing neigh rang out on the afternoon air. Halted in the doorway, Lord watched her drag the tall mare to a skidding stop and swing to face the source of that arresting sound.

Heedless of the dust billowing over her as her riders overshot her and came to a milling halt beyond, the woman stared intently at the grey. She bent sharply forward as it raced the length of its corral, wheeled, and came racing back. It moved with that peculiar high, floating action known only to the aroused stallion, and came to a sudden stop midway down the fence. Frozen into immobility, it stood with head and tail upflung, its eyes glaring fixedly out at the intruders from behind its wind-tossed forelock. A shattering blast exploded from its belled nostrils, and it launched itself into movement again with the swift, effortless grace of a great cat. It circled the corral at a full run, wheeled in mid-stride and went to the corral's exact center, there again to freeze into sudden immobility.

Lord was only vaguely aware of the stallion's actions. All his attention was centered on the woman and her utter absorption in the picture the animal presented. For a moment she held that forward-bent attitude, oblivious to everything around her. At long last her voice came to Lord, the words indistinguishable at that distance. She was answered by one of the men, and only then did she move. Her head dipped once, as if in agreement with what was said. She cast a quick glance in the direction of the house, saw Lord watching her from the doorway, and abruptly straightened. In that same instant she threw her mare into a sudden run and raced out of sight under the trees.

The picture that stayed with Lord long after she was gone was of her leaning low over the neck of her running horse, her great mass of hair lifting straight out behind her, like a bright banner riding the wind.

8

Jesse Whitehead drifted down through the timber with a constant wary regard for his surroundings. His head turned unceasingly from side to side as his eyes darted about, and this constant jerking whipped his unkempt mane of grey-yellow hair about his shoulders so that he had the look of a man afflicted with some nervous disorder. He was old and gaunt and slyly suspicious of almost everything and everybody, and with very little prompting he could have become a hermit.

In an earlier day he had been a bona fide "mountain man," and he still considered himself such, for all the breed was well-nigh extinct. He kept the illusion alive by continuing to run his line of traps in winter and collecting bounty on the pelts of the various predators he killed in his role of defender of the area's herds. For this last, he received the sum of twenty-five cents per animal.

During his twenty-five years in the region he had come to know it as a farmer knows his barnyard. On the darkest night he could set his course and arrive at a given point at a specified time. There was little he did not know about the goings-on around him, and even less that he chose to tell, for whereas he had a boundless respect for the wild creatures he hunted down and killed, he had almost none for the humans who preyed on each other. He lived a monastic life; yet paradoxically the only two people with whom he would pass more than the time of day were women: Fresno Taggert and Lila MacKay. To everyone else he was an enigma, a spectral shape always on the move, always fading out of sight at the approach of the uninvited intruder.

This was Jesse Whitehead. Twice within the past week his nocturnal wanderings had disclosed the red eye of a campfire winking at him from the old Bland place. At first he had put it down to some Star hand stopping off there overnight. But today he had noted a thick spiral of smoke rising from the place for a good three hours and knew that somebody had moved in. He was curious about the identity of this ill-advised stranger.

That it was a stranger, he had no doubt. No one else would commit such a blunder.

Another half hour's travel brought him out of the trees on the bench directly above the Bland place, and here he slowed down. All in one continuing movement he halted his pony and sent it scrambling backward as his gaze took in what was going on down there. He dropped to the ground and crawled to the edge of the bench and from this prone position again studied the scene.

Thus it was he witnessed the encounter between the Star contingent and the two Shadleys, Moline's punishment and banishment, and the far more puzzling meeting between Fresno Taggert and the big stranger that took place within the privacy of the house.

When they disappeared indoors, he scowled as if at a personal affront. "Now, that right there I don't figger a'tall," he murmured to himself.

Jesse Whitehead held to his place with the stolid patience of an Indian while the minutes eased past. When Fresno Taggert suddenly reappeared, his lips drew back in an expectant smile, and he hitched himself forward on his elbows and peered around the base of the scrub juniper. "Now, by God," he murmured, "we'll see how the cow eats the cabbage!" But to his amazement, the woman swung up on her mares and exited from the scene at a dead run, with her escort pounding along in her dust.

"Well, now," he said, pushing to his feet and returning to his pony, "I guess I'll jest mosey down an' have a look at this feller."

He stepped into the saddle and put the pony to the sharp descent. Moments later he trotted out of the trees and drew up at sight of the pair of mammoth dogs streaking toward him. He knew an instant of actual fear as he took in their size and read their mastiff-wolf breeding in their shaggy coats and their bone structure, and then a shrill whistle sliced the air and the dogs' drive ceased as abruptly as if they had run into a wall. They wheeled and trotted back toward the house, and Jesse Whitehead looked beyond them toward the tall man standing in the back-yard.

The figure remained motionless throughout the remainder of Jesse Whitehead's jogging advance, giving no sign of greeting, showing no welcome on his sun-polished face. Jesse Whitehead thumbed his battered hat off his forehead, had his brief, surprised look, and folded his arms across his chest. He said, as if to a third party, "Well, good God Almighty! Shit if he ain't a breed."

Aaron Lord endured the bony man's appraising look with no betrayal of the fury swirling through him. He said coldly, "I'm a breed, but you're still shit," and watched surprise deepen and spread across the other's craggy features.

"Well, now," Jesse Whitehead said in a chiding tone, "you've no call to get mouthy with me, boy."

"Old man," Lord replied quietly, "don't call me 'boy' again."

Jesse Whitehead's downbearing gaze was hard and bright and strangely pleased. "All right," he murmured. "All right, son." He dipped his head sideways. "Do I git invited down? Or do we stay here all afternoon, like a couple of bulls with their horns locked?"

"Suit yourself," Lord said shortly and turned back to the house. At the porch he picked up the battered tin bucket and made for the pool. He said in the same terse way, "I'm busy," and went on without looking around.

Jesse had caught a glimpse of the kitchen through the open door. Now, following on Lord's heels, he noted the bedding on the line and the newly repaired corrals. "That's a fact," he stated. At the pool he held the pony away from the water until Lord had filled the bucket, then dropped the reins and squatted back on his stringy hunkers. "Rest a spell," he suggested, when Lord would have left. "I hear tell whippin' a house into shape can be pretty tirin'. Not that I ever tried it."

"Don't," Lord advised. "It's too much work for anybody but a woman."

"Don't aim to," Jesse admitted, and repeated the nodding motion. "Set a spell, son."

Lord lowered the bucket to the ground and squatted on his heels. He picked up a flat stone and skipped it across the surface of the pool, idly watching it jump high on the outermost ripple, then drop from sight in the froth boiling up at the foot of the waterfall. Acutely aware that he was the object of his visitor's frankly curious stare, he stolidly held his silence.

"Whitehead. Jesse Whitehead."

Lord said, "What?" and turned to find the man's right hand extended toward him. "Oh," he said, and hesitated briefly before returning the handshake. "Aaron Lord."

"Figgered as much," Jesse stated. His bright gaze missed none of Lord's puzzlement, and he was drily amused. "Goes without sayin' you taken your coloring and your eyes from your mamma's people, but they ain't no mistakin' old Angus' stamp on the rest of you."

"You knew my father?"

"Trapped fer him twelve-fifteen year. Reckon you could say I knowed 'im. Knowed yer mamma, too. As pretty a little gal as ever walked. Dirty shame, the way she was done."

Lord nodded, not saying anything. They resumed their former positions, and Lord sent another pebble across the pool.

Jesse Whitehead drew a black lump from a cavernous pocket of his leather tunic, palmed his knife, and shaved off a chew. "Had many visitors?"

Lord turned and showed him a slow grin. He said, "If you hadn't known, you wouldn't have asked," and watched approval and amusement run in swift succession across the weathered features.

"They was eight of 'em an' only one of you," Jesse Whitehead musingly observed. "Then they was six of 'em an' one of you. An' that's somethin' new for Star."

"It's something new for me, too," Lord admitted. "But I plan on getting used to it."

Jesse Whitehead's eyes were fully as effective at close range as they were at great distances. They remained on Lord, busy and sharp. He was a thoroughly skeptical old man who let his sight and his instincts ferret things out, and right now he was receiving all manner of signals from them—signals which made it downright difficult to go on squatting there and pretend the mildest kind of interest. Nothing of this inner tension showed. "Plans can go haywire," he offered, and kept on with his careful prowling.

Lord's head slowly inclined and slowly lifted. "On one side or the other, or both," he elaborated in his turn. "In the end, it's all owing pretty much to luck."

"Which same can change with most every deal of the cards, I've observed."

Lord glanced down, selected another stone, and absently shook it around inside his closed fist. "I'll play the hand dealt me," he said, and sent the stone dancing across the sunlit water.

Jesse Whitehead's rusty voice barely lifted his words above the unending beat of the heavy water.

"You got no choice."

"No?"

"No, by God, you ain't!" Jesse said violently. He stopped, deeply shocked by the thing he felt. He had spent a lifetime watching others—always from a careful distance that precluded personal involvement. His was an altogether private nature, and his outburst just now had been prompted by the unnerving suspicion that his seclusion was being threatened by this dark-faced giant who crouched by the pool. Suddenly uneasy, he pushed to his feet. "T'hell with this!" he muttered and stepped over to his pony. He flipped the reins over the little dun's head, went into the saddle, and was turning away, when a last thought brought him back around. He nodded in the direction of the far-running valley. "You ort to of studied the game awhile before askin' to be dealt in," he said in the querulous way of an old man.

Lord bent and picked up the bucket of water. He straightened and showed Jesse a slow smile. "Why," he murmured, "I didn't ask. I just pulled up a chair and sat in."

"Jest so," Jesse Whitehead grumbled. He gave Lord a dour, measuring look from his elevated position and made his blunt assessment. "From the heft of you, an' that mean look in your eye, it goes without sayin' you'll hang an' rattle 'til the chips run out, either yours or the other feller's—or both. Well—" He picked up the reins and put his tough little mount into motion. "I'll likely be around, time to time," he said over his shoulder, and went loosely joggling along the hill's steep shoulder toward an overgrown trail which only his eye could have spied out amid the tangle of brush and undernourished trees blanketing the slope.

Lord watched the horse bear its forward-bent rider up the steepness of the climb and afterward top out on the timbered bench a hundred yards above. When horse and rider dropped from sight behind the rim, he shrugged and returned to the house and his thrice-interrupted cleaning.

He decided to be moved in before nightfall. His ownership was regarded as of no import by Star, and, despite the fact that the woman had called off her dogs for the time being, there was little assurance that she would hold them in check for long. He resolved to be standing in his own doorway when that time came, mounting guard over his home.

Of more immediate importance to him was the matter of Lila MacKay's imminent return from Valley Junction. With this quick passage of the girl through his musings, he at once closed his thoughts on her. Remembering the moment that saw her wading through the water toward him, he experienced again the electrifying shock that had gone through him at that first coming together of their nakedness. And then all the rest of it flowed hotly back, acutely felt by every remembering nerve and sinew and tissue of his body. In swelling discomfort he broke off his examination of the battered bedstead and went in search of wire and nails with which to repair it. Afterward he would have to stuff a mattress with clean wild hay. In the bottom of his pack, carried from St. Louis and never used for a year, were sheets.

Some time later, he turned and walked slowly through the house, more and more satisfied with what he had accomplished this day. A feeling of possessiveness settled in him as he paused in the kitchen doorway and surveyed that room, now softening under the mantle of oncoming dusk, and he spoke his determination aloud, making of it a blinding oath. "This is my home. I'll not give it up." He heard the silence-magnified words fill the rooms and settle there like a tangible presence, and nodded his definite support of the statement.

He kindled a fire in the stove and put water on for coffee. With the bacon sizzling in the reclaimed iron skillet, he went outside to whistle the two mares and the foal in for the night. The light was almost gone now, but the warmth of day still lay close over the land. Remembering that he was without candle or lamp, he gathered an armload of broken corral poles and took them to the house, afterward kindling a fire in the fireplace and eating his supper by its light. And all this while, and later while washing the utensils and putting them away in the darkened kitchen, he was conscious of doing these things in his own house on his own land, and for the first time in his life felt himself at one with his surroundings and surely approaching a peace of mind that had until now been such an illusive thing.

In the light from the fire he rummaged in his packs for towel and soap, then undressed and made for the pool and his nightly bath.

He dropped the towel to the sand and waded out to lather himself from head to knees. He tossed the soap onto the towel and had barely surfaced after his first plunge when the stallion's piercing neigh rang out on the evening air, followed immediately by the mares' concerted call. And then the dogs joined in to sound the warning of someone's approach, and he emerged from the pool and started for the house, wrapping the towel about his hips as he went.

He reached the back porch simultaneously with Lila MacKay. "I was about to come looking for you," he said quietly.

She swung down and turned to take in his naked silhouette against the diffused light of the sky. Her throaty laugh came up. "Like that?"

She was within arm's reach of him and her husky voice was like a hand provocatively brushing him. "Why not?" he asked, and was reaching for her when she turned and busied herself with the pack lashings.

"I swear, there's a ton of this stuff," she announced. When he stepped close to lend a hand, she threw him a suspicious glance and retreated around the horse's rump to work on the knots on the other side. A moment later her voice struck at him out of the gloom. "Why don't you go put some clothes on, for God's sake?"

His enjoyment of her uneasiness turned his voice light. "I'm fine. Not in the least cold."

Lila jerked a rope free, tossed it across the top of the pack, and glared at him. "Neither am I," she said. "And you're not helping the situation, standing around like that."

"Like what?"

"Like a damned stud, all primed and waiting for a mare to show up!"

She was sincerely angry, albeit with herself rather than with him. It was vitally important to her that she dictate the nature of things happening. Now, for the first time in her life, she was finding her control threatened, not by anything this dark man said or did, but rather by what he was—a mystifying force she could neither handle nor define.

It turned her sullen and it made her determined to be rid of his troublesome presence as soon as she could effect a retreat without leading him to suspect she was in any way unsure of herself around him.

"There's a lantern and a lamp and a can of coal oil in that panier on your side," she said. "Why don't you dig them out and get at least one of them lit, so we can see what we're doing?"

Lord found the carefully wrapped articles and took them inside. When he had the lantern going, he hung it from a nail on one of the porch supports and rejoined Lila in unslinging the heavy paniers and lugging them into the kitchen. He said, "You can light the lamp while I take care of the horses," and stepped outside.

At the corral he turned the new team and Lila's gelding in with the mares and foal. Slipping the bridle from the gelding, he gave the horse a pat on the rump. "Have yourself some supper," he said. "You won't be going anywhere for some time." He shut the gate and turned toward the house where a rectangle of light now showed, his strides growing longer and swifter.

He entered the kitchen soundlessly to find Lila on her knees busily unpacking the second of the paniers. "Looks like you bought out the town," he grinned, and indicated the bulging packs. "Did you have enough money?"

"More than enough." She took two eagles from a pocket of her tunic and tossed them to him, then went on with her work without again looking at him. Her awareness of his near-nude state worked at her ever more strongly, and memory was a never-lessening warmth inside her, turning her movements hurried and jerky. She spoke quickly to relieve the tension growing in her. "I bought a lot of stuff that you didn't have on your list. I figured you'd be needing it."

"I'm beholden to you."

Lord reached down, wrested a heavy sack of food staples from the panier nearest him, and heaved it up onto the work shelf. He was directly behind her, and on a sudden impulse, he bent over, caught her upper arms, and brought her up and around. She was a slender sheath of heat held flat against him by his encircling arms, and his voice came out breathy and unsteady. "Lila . . . ever since the other night I've been waiting for this again. I want—"

She wrenched away from him with a hard, twisting motion that swung her halfway around and took her to the other side of the narrow room. Her volatile temper flared with shocking violence. "*You want!* I know what you want!"

He stared at her, utterly confounded by her unexpected reaction. And then his own answering anger rose and he lashed back, his voice flat and wicked. "Let's get one thing cleared up right here and now. Just who started this thing, anyhow?"

"All right!" she shouted. "I was curious. I'm not denying I got as much as I gave; but if you think I'm going to haul my skirt up around my neck every time you get a hard-on, you've a thing or two to learn about me!

His anger died. "What's got into you?" he asked, sincerely baffled. "Why the sudden change?"

Lila shook her tangled hair out of her face and placed her hands on her hips, braced and ready to quarrel. "I'll tell you what's got into me, mister. Something about you bothers me like hell, and I don't like being bothered. It's the way I am."

"But why?" Lord persisted. "I thought you liked me."

She made a swift, dismissing gesture, and again threw her head back in that hard, jerking way of hers. "What the hell has liking got to do with it?" she demanded. "It's something you either want or don't want. Well, I don't happen to want it right now. That's all there is to it."

Lord's low question barely carried to her. "Is it, Lila? Is that really all there is to it?"

But she would not be drawn in. She put up a hand and impatiently pushed her heavy mane back over her shoulder. "Quit pulling at me, dammit! Just leave me alone!"

"Am I pulling at you?"

"Hell yes, you are. She raked him with her aroused eyes. "And I don't like it!"

"And so," Lord said quietly, "you've got to pull away."

She reached deeply for air. "Yes," she said in a ragged voice. "Yes, I've got to pull away." She shifted her feet so that she was standing quartered away from him. Outlined against the light of the lantern on the back porch, she reminded Lord of a wild creature on the verge of flight, held there by some force she did not understand. Her breasts strained against the soft leather of her tunic with her audible intake of air, and her words came out low and unsteady, and strangely sad. "I can't explain it, because I don't understand it myself. But something's gone wrong. I wish—"

Lord's bare feet made no sound as he skirted the empty paniers and halted in front of her. His towering bulk blocked her single avenue of escape.

He did not touch her then. There was no need. "Nothing's gone wrong, Lila," he said finally, and his voice was very gentle.

For a long moment she stared up into his face, making no attempt to mask her naked desire for him. And then in some inexplicable way she changed. She did not move any part of her body, but her brilliant eyes barred any advance on his part. By some unaccountable shifting of her will she went away from him as completely as if she had gone into the next room. Across the vast emptiness yawning between them her voice came faintly to him. "I'm going now."

His head moved in negation. "No."

Her unpredictable temper exploded a second time. "Nobody tells me what to do! Nobody! Least of all some goddamned—"

She caught herself and stopped, and Lord smiled coldly down at her. "Half-breed?" he asked. "Is that the word you wanted?"

She gave back a step and stood glaring at him, her anger momentarily checked by something she did not fully comprehend. "Now, *you* make it sound like something dirty," she said, low-voiced. For another moment she faced him, trying to reach beyond the impenetrable mask he showed her. Her mouth turned down. She said disgustedly, "To hell with you," and was moving around him toward the door when he reached out and seized her by the shoulders.

"Not yet," he said tightly. "You're not going yet."

She swung around and without warning brought her right hand up in a looping, backhanded blow that had all the weight and leverage of her turning body behind it. It caught him squarely on the side of the face with a force that rocked him on his feet. "God damn you!" she swore in a shaking voice. "Don't ever lay your hand on me without my say-so! Now get the hell out of my way!"

The impulse to hurt her was a shocking thing in Lord. With his balled fist lifting, he caught himself. He closed his eyes and drew a long, shaking breath. He dipped his head in a curt nod and stepped back to let her pass.

Halfway to the door she paused, glanced back over her shoulder, then swung fully around. "There's no sense in talking to you," she told him. "That thing you've got about your Indian blood's clamped so tight around your brain, a crowbar couldn't pry it loose. It's nothing to me, but it's everything to you. So, to hell with you, mister."

She was turning to leave, but a final thought came to her and brought her back around. When she spoke again there was no trace of animosity in her voice. "You know what's wrong with you?" she asked. "You spend too damned much time looking at yourself. Not to admire yourself, but just to make damned sure you're really a dirty half-breed instead of just some ordinary *man*." She paused to let that sink in, then went on. "And I'll toss in one more thing, for whatever the hell good it might be. When I look at you, I don't see *color*. All I see is a *man*." Her shoulders lifted and fell. "But then, I'm not very bright, I guess."

Lord's lips twisted. "Thanks for the compliment," he said with heavy sarcasm. "It explains why you can't stand for me to touch you."

"I don't want you to touch me," Lila admitted, "but it's got nothing to do with the color of your skin, my friend."

"Then what is it?"

Again Lila gave that quick shrug. "I can't explain it because I don't understand it myself. The best I can do is to tell you I don't feel safe around you."

Lord looked in puzzlement. "Safe? Why? What have I done to make you feel afraid?"

She did not try to hide her confusion behind womanly guile which, at best, she possessed in scant measure. "Nothing," she stated frankly. "Like you said, that thing the other night was all my doing. I put no blame on you."

"Then why are you afraid of me?"

Lila stood there trying to think of an answer to give him, wanting to be honest, but unable to understand her behavior. But her thoughts milled about in wild disorder, and in the end she again shrugged, the gesture looking oddly girlish and helpless in one customarily given to such forthright behavior. "You don't know me," she said with a rueful little smile. "But then, I guess I don't know myself very well. I've always come and gone as I pleased. What I want, I take, with no questions asked and no answers given. I never gave much thought to the why's of what I do, and I don't intend to start now. That's why I'm backing off."

Lord was studying her with a determination to see what lay behind her words, but the sheen of her eyes shut him out. "That doesn't explain why you're afraid of me, Lila."

"No," she admitted slowly, "it doesn't. But then, it's not you I'm afraid of."

"What, then?"

She tried to smile. But it did not reach to her eyes. Her gaze remained on him, intense and unfathomable, and, for one fleeting instant, disturbingly unguarded.

Lord started toward her, but suddenly the doorway was empty. He heard her footsteps fading swiftly in the outer darkness, and halted in the place she had so recently occupied in the doorway. He was still standing there when her horse wheeled away from the corral a few minutes later and ran across the yard just beyond the lantern's feeble light.

After a long time he sighed, took the lantern from its nail, extinguished the flame, and returned to the kitchen. Setting the lantern down inside the door, he picked up the lamp and made his way to the bedroom. On the threshold he paused and eyed the bed which short hours ago had afforded him such a sense of accomplishment.

Crossing to the trunk under the window, he put the lamp down and blew out the light. He unwrapped the towel from about his hips, let it drop to the floor, and slipped in between the cool sheets. It had been months since he had slept in a bed, and when he felt the grass-filled mattress give to his weight he gave a long sigh of sheer delight.

For a long time he lay staring up into the darkness while quiet flowed around him and laid its soothing touch over his frayed nerves.

The scene in the kitchen came back to him and he relived it in its entirety and found nothing to tell him what had gone wrong. In the end he could not but believe that Lila MacKay had turned away from him in sudden aversion to his blood. She had been jerked out of her short-lived infatuation by that remorseless force called racial heritage, for all her hotly voiced denial.

This he believed. It was an old and all too familiar pattern, and it would never change—not even here on this far frontier of limitless horizons and untouched beauty. He thought hopelessly, *I was a fool to think it would be different here. It will never change*, and lay there, rigid, staring into nothingness.

From deep in the lower regions of sleep, he was dimly aware of Elizabeth's fretful barking, and of Leopold's deeper echoing complaint. But there was no note of urgency in the sounds, and he slept on until Lila said from directly above him, "Aaron? Where are you?"

He roused and rolled onto his back, not certain that the voice was not of his imagining. "What?" he asked drowsily. "Who is it?"

A hand reached down, touched his neck, and slid across his chest, and Lila's low laugh was a warm and intimate sound in the suddenly vibrating silence of the room. "Exactly how many women come creeping into your bedroom in the middle of the night, anyhow?"

He was then wide awake. "What are you doing here?"

Her laugh came again. "Nothing . . . yet," she replied, and slid under the covers.

His arms went around her, drawing her close, and this contact laid its burning touch over his nakedness and roused him so quickly and so strongly that his breath stopped in his throat. Her hands were on him, urgently seeking and finding.

On the verge of lifting himself above her, Lord willed down his wild impatience. "I thought you had gone for good. You said—"

"Hush. It doesn't matter. Nothing does . . . except this."

Her unpredictability was something beyond his understanding. "What brought you back?"

She withheld her answer, losing herself in her deepening awareness of him. Her breathing quickened, so that she seemed to be moving restlessly against him, even though she was motionless in his tight embrace. Her desire equalled his; but his question required an answer. "Myself," she said. "I wanted to, so I did. Don't ask me anything more." Suddenly she moaned under her punishing desire and seized him by the shoulders. "Come on!" she urged.

He rose over her at once, moved his pelvis seekingly, and was then gliding strongly into her. A sigh came from her as he penetrated to his full length, and she locked her hands in the small of his back and strained herself against him with a mindless abandon.

Their joining was wholly unlike that other time, for all that the same animal need again obsessed them. For now, with Lila holding him quiescent inside her, Lord dared for the first time to believe himself desired for himself and was numb with the wonder of it. He experienced in that long-running time of motionlessness the wild tumultuous ecstasy of the exhausted wanderer come all unexpectedly upon the region of his longing.

In coming thus to him, out of her self-acknowledged need, this woman who lay beneath him now, so oblivious to all but the oneness of their meeting, had all unknowingly wrought this miracle of pride in him. By her own admission, she was one who had always taken without giving. Now she had brought herself to him, and through her body was returning to him a vital part of himself that she had heedlessly robbed him of so shortly before.

Time moved unmeasured down the corridor of the night, pausing now and then, as if closely listening to the husky run of the man's voice meaninglessly murmuring to the moaning woman. Then again, and ever again, it resumed its onward flow toward memory with the reawakening to movement of the two figures on the grass-filled mattress.

Another time of respite—the last and the longest—and the metallic squeaking of the springs sounded an unmistakable warning as the movements quickened. A sense of urgency trembled the air of the room as the movements rose in tempo. It changed to blind panic as time raced ever faster; then rose on a convulsing wave of raw, unheeding violence with a last, long-driving thrust of the dark pelvis.

The agonizing spasms climaxed on a straining note of sheer incredulity, endured endlessly, then slowly eased. And they emerged, shocked and spent, into the reality of their separate selves.

9

Those miles to Valley Junction were the longest Dave Moline ever rode. The treatment he had suffered at Fresno Taggert's hands had destroyed all but one last thread of self-control. But for it he would have turned back and tried to kill the tall half-breed and anyone else who stood in his way. He was that close to absolute despair.

His was a singularly uncomplicated nature, with an incredibly firm-rooted fixedness of purpose. Once committed to a cause, he was immediately and wholly dedicated. Nothing was permitted to interfere. Nothing else concerned him.

Until this afternoon, Star had been the sole recipient of this dedication, for to a certain extent he considered himself Star. A mere suggestion offered by Star's owner he interpreted as an imperial decree. Little in his life had afforded him as much pleasure as driving the night-riding land-grabbers back into the hills, immediately Farley Taggert had ridden off to war.

That his heavy-handedness had alienated him not only from those directly under his authority but from the inhabitants of the lower Basin as well, he had known without being bothered by it. Intent solely on the task at hand, he had neither offered anything of himself to others nor accepted any individual's proffered friendship. Even the rapport he had enjoyed with Fresno Taggert had been born of necessity rather than from any wish for personal involvement on his part. She was Star; he served Star. It was that simple.

It was this blind loyalty that had prompted his lie about the manner of Frank Wheeler's death. That Star's owner would stop short in her march to empire while she weighed the right and the wrong of the manner in which her empire was to be saved had never occurred to him, especially when the threat was comprised of so negligible a thing as a half-breed.

Always before, she had summarily ordered all such obstacles removed. Let her hear that a stranger had entered the valley, and a dozen riders were immediately dispatched to escort him on his way. The most innocent wayfarer, overtaken by darkness inside the constantly patrolled limits of the hallowed valley, invariably looked up from his campfire to find himself hemmed in by a ring of grim-faced Star riders. One and all, they either left voluntarily or remained to occupy only enough Star ground as would accommodate their lifeless bodies. The rule was unshakable.

Now it seemed that Fresno Taggert had suddenly and unaccountably chosen to flout her own law on behalf of a contemptible half-breed. Even worse, she had turned on Moline with the unreasoning fury of a paranoid lashing a faithful watchdog, and in so doing she had on the instant become a mystery to Dave Moline and, in his eyes, no longer worthy of the heritage left her by the empire-builder, Ewing Star.

In a blacker frame of mind than he had ever experienced, Moline held his big bay to a straining run down the valley long after common sense should have prompted him to draw in and allow the horse a chance to regain its wind. And this was wholly unlike him.

A knowledgeable and sensitive horseman, he accorded horses that consideration and respect he consistently withheld from his fellow man. It was the gauge of the depths into which his dark temper had flung him, therefore, that he was now completely oblivious to the state of the horse under him.

In an area widely known for the equality of its horseflesh, the big bay was famed for its phenomenal endurance and blazing speed. Only Fresno Taggert's blaze-faced mare and Lila Mac-Kay's long-striding sorrel had ever been known to best it at any distance. On this mad run down the valley it had covered the first three miles with the effortless, flowing stride of the racer bred to go long distances without running itself out. Had it been allowed to slow up and gain its second wind, it would have been good for another run of equal distance. But when it sought to shorten stride, sharp points of steel raked streaks of crimson across its lathered barrel and drove it into headlong flight once more.

For another mile it sustained that punishing drive; but the great lungs were rapidly emptying, the rocklike muscles becoming flaccid. Imperceptibly but surely the ground-devouring strides began to shorten, the lifting glide went out of the pistoning legs, and the out-flung head began the ponderous up-and-down movement bespeaking exhaustion.

Once again the spurs bit deep, and the bay broke and began to labor. It was running heavily now, the air whistling in and out of its distended nostrils with the harsh, stertorous sound of a blacksmith's bellows. The chiseled head dropped lower. The legs reached and folded with a mechanical, jarring action, and the game animal was then running on heart alone.

Had Moline been even mildly aware of what was happening to the big horse under him, he could not have failed to note the danger posed by the high creek bank suddenly cutting across his line of travel. The dim trace he followed curved with the stream's horseshoe bend and thereafter straightened for its run for the river a mile away.

The curve was caused by one of several upthrust ledges of sandstone which dotted the valley floor. Directly ahead of him the protrusion that had forced the stream to cut through a low hillock had become a bare expanse of broken sandstone on the stream's far side.

At no point was the bank more than five feet above the stream. Thus it did not in itself present a formidable barrier to a horse negotiating the drop at a sensible speed. But a descending jump onto that expanse of broken stone would ordinarily have been considered by Moline the height of folly.

In his present frame of mind, however, the curving road that by-passed the danger existed only as a needless waste of time. When the bay veered to follow it, he straightened it with a jerk and drove it ruthlessly at the jump.

Too late his glance speared forward and down to the naked

expanse of broken stone. His reaction was wholly automatic. With the horse launching itself into space in an impossible attempt to clear the fifty feet of dangerous footing, he threw himself to the left and hauled on the reins with all his strength in a vain effort to drag it back onto the bank.

He could not have made a more fatal mistake. The sudden shift of weight occurred at the instant when the force of the jump was at its greatest and produced precisely the same result as that of an obstruction flung suddenly up before an arm arcing forward to throw a stone.

The shortened rein cramped the bay's head around; the rider's weight hauling back and to one side destroyed all impetus. With the helplessness of a bird struck down in flight, the big horse turned half over in midair and crashed down into the rocks in a writhing, skidding fall that took it across the ledge, a juggernaut out of control. Rocks, gravel, and dust exploded above the stream, and the air was driven out of the horse's lungs in a loud grunt.

From first to last the whole thing took place in nightmarish slow motion. Trying to shove himself away from the horse as it rolled sideways in the air, Moline glimpsed the panoramic sweep of the entire upper valley with the distant stand of cottonwoods and the glint of sunlight on the little stream, and the grass rippling in the breeze. And then, twisting around and throwing out his arms in an instinctive attempt to break his fall, he saw the rock bed lift to meet him. There was then only a blurred glimpse of gravel and rocks and red sandstone rushing past, and the searing agony of his left leg being twisted in the hip socket; his lower leg snapped like a matchstick under the horse's downcrashing weight, and a sharp blow sent him spiraling into blackness.

The sky was awash with crimson to the west when Lila MacKay put her horse down the bank of the ford above Valley Junction. Just over the edge she was hauled half out of her saddle by the two packhorses hanging back on the lead ropes. She reined around on the shelving bank and gave the ropes an impatient jerk, then spurred out of the way barely in time to avoid being overrun by the team of heavy footed draught animals who suddenly heeded the tug on their halters and plunged down.

In the ensuing melee at the water's edge she was so concerned with getting the team straightened out that she did not see the big bay making its painful way through the shallows towards her. When she reined around, she almost collided with Dave Moline.

Automatically she gave to the left in the exact instant Moline turned the bay in the same direction. For a moment, then, they were stalemated, each trying to decide which way to turn.

Not until then, with Moline raising his head to order her out of the way, did Lila recognize him. They had maintained a sporadic and wholly sexual relationship for five years; but in his present state, she had mistaken him for a complete stranger. Now she half rose in her stirrups and stared at him in consternation. "Well, for Christ's sake!" she burst out. "If it isn't Dave!" She leaned forward and peered at him with a show of uncertainty. "It *is* Dave Moline there, isn't it?"

Moline's indistinguishable growl drew a short laugh from her. Ignorant of the full extent of his injuries, she was openly curious about the condition of the erstwhile handsome face. "What the hell did you tangle with, anyhow?" she demanded. "A meat grinder?"

He glared balefully out at her from between puffy lids. "My horse fell. Any fool can see that."

Lila nodded. "That's for damn sure." She was about to let it go at that, but the suspicious side of her nature warned her that there was more to it than this. She and Moline were by no means strangers, yet clearly he was anxious to be quit of her. She examined him more closely and this time noted the odd way he was sitting his saddle, with all his weight shifted to his right stirrup, and the right forearm thrust inside his shirt. "Where?" she asked, letting him see nothing of the genuine concern she felt for him. "Where'd he fall?"

"A couple miles north of the pass."

"Why?" She was genuinely puzzled. She knew the road; she knew the horse and the rider. Moreover, the bloody slashes on them both bespoke rocks, not the powdery dust of the river roadbed.

She sat back in the saddle and indicated the bay with a nod. "There's just three things that horse of yours can't do," she said pointedly. "He can't talk; he can't outrun Fresno Taggert's chestnut mare or Ridgerunner, here; and he can't fall down on a string-straight, floor-flat road, not even with a damn fool like you handling the reins." She paused to let that sink in, then asked very quietly, "Now, just where did this little tumble take place again, Dave?"

A chill touched Moline, and he inwardly cursed the foul luck that had brought him face to face with her this day. She was, he thought glumly, like one of her damned bloodhounds, forever working out some new scent. Her green eyes missed nothing; her ears heard things never meant for them; and her tongue was like an open razor in the hands of a child.

"Get the hell out of my way, Lila," he said in surly frustration, and tried to pass.

She cut him off, her gaze stabbing into him. "Why the big rush, Dave?" she queried. "Your horse was run out before he ever took that spill. How come? Where were you headed for, or from, in such an all-fired hurry?"

"None of your damned business!"

Lila pursed her lips and cocked her head. "I wouldn't take any bets on that, if I was you," she warned him gently. "You ought to know better than that by now."

Moline lowered his gaze, his mind darting frantically about in search of something that would throw her off the track. If he told her the truth, it would be all over the valley and the hills by tomorrow night, and he would never be able to hold his head up again. If he tried to outwit her with a falsehood, she would know it instantly. Nor could he buy her silence.

His only hope was to stall, to buy a measure of time with his own silence. In that swift condemning judgment of the girl he erred as badly as he had in judging Fresno Taggert. Had he but known it, a single plea for help on his part would have brought Lila MacKay to his side on the instant and guaranteed him a protector and champion without peer.

But the idea never crossed his mind. A completely self-centered nature prompted him to judge others solely by surface reactions. Never in the five years he had known this unpredictable girl had he once reflected on the underlying reason for her making herself available to him whenever he sought her out. Had he done so, he would have been surprised.

Now he suddenly reined to one side and spurred up the bank, choking back a scream as the violent action brought pain crashing in on him in a solid wave that made him grab the horn to keep from falling. Once safely atop the bank he glanced down and caught a fleeting glimpse of her half turned in the saddle watching him. He had the most depressing conviction that she would have the entire story at her fingertips before the dawn of another day.

On the point of heading into town he drew up and looked around in hopeless indecision. It needed no deep insight into the workings of the minds of an isolated community such as Valley Junction to tell him what would happen the instant it was discovered that a Star rider had come seeking medical attention. The news would spread like wildfire throughout the entire Basin. The dismal ending of the story he knew all too well. He would be identified at once, the nature of his injuries ascertained, and immediately a dozen curious noses would be sniffing along his backtrail.

He groaned aloud at the humiliating prospect and knew that he could not endure it. In deepest despair he stared dully at the ground, and then, quite suddenly glimpsed a ray of hope.

A half mile down the river Martha's Mission nestled safely off the road under its giant canopy of cottonwoods. It was the region's only brothel, and Moline had long been one of its most regular customers. Now he felt an almost overpowering urge to lash his faltering horse into a run as he pictured that isolated haven.

In the red wash of sunset he made his slow way down the dusty road and turned at last into the side yard. In an age that saw such establishments striving for anonymity Martha's Mission was as unabashedly demonstrative of its charms as a successful courtesan flaunting her finery at a church social. In all the Basin it was the only house boasting a coat of paint. Whitely gleaming in the last rays of daylight, it looked strangely out of place in its rustic setting under the cottonwoods. Carefully tended flower beds surrounded it, and the yard, stable, corrals, and chicken house had an air of scrupulous neatness unexpected in an establishment of its kind.

As he turned into the yard and drew up at the back porch, the door opened and a woman backed through it dragging a mop pail. Turning to dump the water into the flower bed bordering the steps, she caught sight of Moline and jumped, dropping the bucket with a clatter. "Good heavens!" she exclaimed. "What a start you handed—" Her words died in her throat as she took in the sight of the battered rider and horse. She put a hand to her throat and came to the edge of the porch. "Do I know you?"

Moline's head swung slowly around. "Martha," he whispered through broken lips, "I need help."

"God in heaven!" Martha gasped. "Dave Moline!" She whirled to the door and sent her call through the darkened interior of the house. "Laurine! Get Ruby and Viola and come out here quick!"

She turned and crossed back to Moline. Putting a hand on his leg, she looked up at him. "How bad is it, David? Is anything broken?"

"My left leg and my right arm," Moline mumbled. "I don't know if I can get down."

"Never mind. We'll manage."

For a moment Moline stared down at her through the fading light, as if trying to think of what he wanted to say. "I oughtn't to of come here like this," he said finally. "But I didn't want to be seen in town."

The woman's answer was very gentle. "It's all right, David. You've always been welcome here. You are now. I mean that."

"One more thing," Moline went on doggedly. "You didn't ask how I got in this fix."

"Your business, David. Not mine."

Moline's single-mindedness was unshakable, even now. "There was some trouble with a feller that's took over your old homeplace," he said. "Fresno ordered me out of the valley, and I run my horse off a ridge into some boulders."

Swiftly shifting emotions briefly showed in Martha's face. She said in the same unruffled voice, "I see." She gave him a reassuring pat and turned swiftly across the porch and disappeared into the kitchen. A moment later a dark-haired girl rushed out, came to a dead stop in the middle of the porch, and stared in disbelief at Moline slumped over the saddlehorn. She said, "I'll be a sonofabitch if it *ain't* Moline!" and with that jumped off the porch and went racing across the yard toward the stable. Shortly thereafter a horse ran past, dodged onto the path behind the house, and raced for town by that back route.

Just as the rattle of hoofs faded away, Martha reappeared on the porch with two more girls closely following. At sight of Moline their agitated questioning abruptly ceased. As calmly as if she were dealing with an everyday occurrence, the owner of Martha's Mission set about executing her plan.

"Ruby," she said to the tall, flame-haired girl on her right, "turn his horse around so we can get him off without jarring his left leg any more than necessary. Never mind the Sweet Williams: they'll survive."

When the bay was positioned alongside the porch, she motioned for Ruby to rejoin her. "All right now, David," she instructed Moline. "Ruby will steady your leg while Viola and I support you. Just let yourself go limp. We'll not let you fall. Everybody ready?"

In tight-lipped silence they set about the tricky operation. With Ruby bending to support Moline's left leg at the knee, Martha grasped him about the waist and Viola anchored his left arm about her neck with a tight grip on his wrist.

"Let yourself fall, David," Martha commanded. "It's bound to hurt some, but it won't kill you."

He was halfway out of the saddle when Ruby tripped on the hem of her dress and was jerked to her knees. Instinctively she tightened her grip on the broken leg to steady herself. Her "Oh, Christ!" was blotted out by Moline's loud yell. He fainted then, and all the dead weight of his big frame descended suddenly upon Viola and Martha, driving them to their knees.

"Christ!" Ruby wailed. "The bastard's fainted!"

"Fine!" Martha panted. "He won't feel anything. Get around here and take his other arm and help lift."

Swearing steadily under her breath, Ruby hastened to comply. But when she grasped Moline's right arm and saw the broken forearm slip free of his shirtfront, she averted her face. "I'm gonna throw up!" she whispered.

"Do, and I'll kill you!" Martha snapped. "Together now . . . lift!"

How to maneuver their sagging burden onto the bed in the small bedroom nearby held them momentarily nonplussed until Ruby solved the problem. Hoisting up her skirts, she clambered onto the bed. "You two steady him," she directed. "I'll drag him up and try to hold that damned busted arm of his out of the way."

The plan worked—too well and too quickly. When Moline sank onto his back, there was no sign of Ruby.

Martha and Viola exchanged puzzled looks. "Ruby," Martha said. "Where are you?"

The answer came in a muffled shout. "Goddammit! Get him off of me! I'm smothering!"

At sight of the yellow skirts billowing out on either side of Moline's hips, Viola burst out giggling. "Wouldn't you know it! Old Ruby's so used to having him on top of her, she just automatically got into position!"

"Stop it!" Martha ordered sharply. "Help me roll him. Ruby, get out of there!"

Cursing and panting, the hapless Ruby clawed her way free of

Moline's weight and rolled off the bed. She got to her feet and sagged back against the wall, looking like the looser in a hotly contested wrestling match. "I think he busted my ribs!" she gasped.

Martha shot her a look of disgust, then whirled on the still-giggling Viola. "Straighten up or I'll slap you!" she commanded. "Go get some towels and water so we can get him cleaned up before Doc Bolter comes." Bending to unbutton Moline's tattered shirt, she glared across the bed at Ruby. "Stop carrying on about your silly ribs," she commanded, "and bring some whiskey. He's going to need it when he comes around."

By the time the two girls returned, she had Moline undressed and under the quilts. She took a towel, dipped it in the basin of water, and wrung it out.

"Viola," she directed, "you stay and help me. Ruby, go get that horse out of sight. It could do with some doctoring too, if I'm not mistaken." She bent to lay the damp cloth over Moline's blood-encrusted face, but broke off her work to hurry to the door after Ruby. "Go tell Zelda and Hester they'll have to take care of any customers who show up," she instructed the girl. "And tell them I want not one word said about this. Understand? *Not one word*!"

With Viola's help she proceeded to cleanse Moline's wounds, thankful for the man's state of unconsciousness. Twice she straightened to listen to some sound from outside. The second time, she crossed to the window and lifted the curtain aside to peer out at the darkened yard. "Plague take that man!" she muttered. "What's taking him so long?"

"Maybe he wasn't home," Viola suggested, and was startled by the angry look thrown at her by the older woman. "Or maybe he had trouble catching up his horse," she amended quickly.

"Don't talk drivel!" Martha said impatiently. "You know perfectly well he keeps his horse stabled." She brushed a tendril of hair back, looking distractedly at the motionless figure on the bed. "If somebody's called him—" she began, then broke off and hurried back to the window at the sound of a buggy wheeling up to the porch. "He's here!"

She was out of the room and halfway across the kitchen when a bearded man entered. "Thank God you're here!" she said feelingly, and indicated the bedroom behind her. "He's in there . . . unconscious."

Doc Bolter nodded imperturbably and crossed to the table. Setting his leather bag down, he proceeded to remove his hat and coat. After fourteen years of answering imperative summonses such as this he was beyond surprise or haste. "The only thing Laurine was clear about was that Moline had been hurt," he said. "Just how bad is he?"

"Frightful! His left leg and his right arm are broken, and he's got cuts and bruises all over him."

The doctor folded his coat across the back of a chair. "Did he say how it happened?"

"His horse fell."

For all his seemingly casual attitude, Bolter was a man who seldom missed anything. Picking up his bag, he started for the bedroom, but paused to lay a hand on the woman's rigid shoulder. "I don't want you around in your jittery condition," he stated bluntly. "Knit a shawl, bake a cake, or go talk to yourself . . . I don't care. Just stay out of my way."

Two interminable hours later he re-entered the kitchen, snapping his bag shut with an air of tired finality. He crossed to the table where Martha sat bolt upright, and slacked into the chair opposite her. "Got any of that black thunder Ruby insists on calling coffee?"

Martha rose, took a cup from the cupboard beside the stove, and filled it from the big pot. She placed it before him and resumed her seat. "How bad is he, Dan?"

Bolter took a sip of the bitter concoction, grimaced, and shook his mane of white hair. "With a broken arm and leg, he's worrying about the cuts on his face. That damned fool is as vain as a woman." He took another sip, grimaced again, and sat back. "He'll live."

"Will he be crippled?"

Bolter's medical skill was his single vanity. "You think you're talking to some Army sawbones? Of course he won't be crippled!"

"Thank God! You know, I always thought him a nail-hard man. But when I was putting him to bed, it suddenly struck me that he's really nothing but a very, very frightened boy." Her compassion turned her features soft and vulnerable. She gave a little sigh and moved her hands in a palms-up gesture. "What will he do now, Dan? I gather Fresno has run him out of the valley. Nobody in the Basin would dare hire him."

"It's a pretty big world," Bolter said. "He'll likely find some corner he can fit into, sooner or later."

"I suppose so." Seeing Bolter lift the cup, she put out a hand and halted the movement. "You need something to cut that stuff. How about a shot of my private stock?"

"Well, now you're talking!" Bolter grinned, and watched her rise and go to the cupboard for the bottle. She was, he thought, one of the most comfortable women he had ever known, and one of the most capable.

When she returned to the table and leaned over to pour a generous measure of whiskey into his cup, he was struck by the strength of her features. She was, he knew, in her mid-forties; but even in the unkind light of the bracket lamp she appeared little changed from the erect, strong-bodied young farm wife who had come into the region with her husband twelve years before. Laying no claim to traditional beauty, she was blessed with an inner calm extraordinary to her position, and for the thousandth time he found himself inwardly damning a society which callously ordained that the victim of a crime be judged more harshly than its perpetrators. It was one of life's bitterest ironies.

He spoke gruffly to divert his thoughts from their unwelcome path. "Sure you can afford this?"

Her eyes laughed at him as she put the bottle on the table and sat down. "Who better? You know perfectly well I'm one of the richest people in the area."

Bolter chuckled and for a moment continued to enjoy the sight of her, warmly lighted by the soft glow from the lamp. He had known her for a long time, now. "You ought to get richer," he told her. "You've a monopoly on the trade here. With your reputation you could ask five dollars a trick and get it."

Martha laughed low in her throat and shook her head, the pale gold of her hair catching the light and reflecting it. "I'm not a greedy person."

Bolter was closely studying her. When she fell silent, he took a long drink, set his cup down, and leaned back. "How is it with you, Martha?" he asked, serious now. "And I'm not talking about business."

She made a wholly feminine gesture with her hands, reaching up to test the firmness of the bun on the back of her neck. "All right," she replied, her tone making it plain that she had no wish to talk about it. "Time passes . . . and regret. I'm fine."

But he wanted to know one more thing. "Is it very lonely for you, Martha?"

She lowered her hands to her lap and looked levelly at him. "A lonely person," she started, "is one who's always wanting something he's never going to get. Feeling sorry for yourself is the only truly unforgivable sin I know of, because it's committed against something that was put here for a better purpose than simple self-indulgence." She sipped from her cup, her fine eyes meeting Bolter's over the rim. Placing the cup on the table, she revolved it in her long, tapering fingers, the suggestion of a smile playing about her lips. "It's true, you know. Self-pity shuts you off from everything worthwhile, and pretty soon you find yourself going around and around in a meaningless circle, tripping over the same untidy little thoughts, bruising yourself and cutting yourself on the same sharp little regrets, and all the time the circle's getting smaller and smaller, until finally, without ever knowing how it happened, you look around and see that your untidy little world has shrunk to nothing at all, and you're standing right in the middle of all that nothingness. Then, my friend, is when you discover that you have exactly nowhere to go. Your self-allowed loneliness has led you all the way down the path, straight into the hedge of thorns at the end."

She gave a short laugh, pushed her empty cup aside, and sat back. "And that's my profound sermon for the day, Doctor Bolter."

Bolter's eyes were twinkling. "I ought to have written it down," he chuckled. "I could have copies made and pass them out to about three-fourths of my patients, in place of sugar pills." He nodded, sincerely appreciating the idea the woman had expounded. He grew serious then. "Do you mean to say you've never indulged in self-pity, Martha?"

She made a swift gesture of denial. "I didn't say that. Like everyone else, I knelt in my own personal Gethsemane, once. Just once. But I realized that if I didn't get up—and pretty quick—I might not ever make it at all. So"—her hands moved expressively—"I got up."

As if to demonstrate her statement, she rose and turned to the stove for the coffee pot. But Bolter shook his head and got up. "No more of Ruby's lye water tonight. My stomach's not lined with enamel." He lifted his bag and walked heavily to the door. "Better keep some wet towels on your patient's face," he suggested. "It'll help reduce the swelling. I'll look in on him tomorrow sometime."

He had his hand on the knob when Martha spoke. "Had you heard that someone's taken over my old homeplace?"

"It was all over town the day he took over. Big, mean-looking half-breed by the name of Lord."

Martha's face registered her surprise. "A *half-breed*, did you say? I don't believe it!"

"You will when you see him," Bolter assured her. "I caught a glimpse of him talking to the sheriff the day he came in. He paid for your old place in solid gold coin. He's half Indian, all right."

"And he bought it, you say? He isn't just squatting?"

Bolter chuckled. "He's squatting, all right; but yes, he bought it, all nice and legal."

Martha's brows came down to a point. "You're amused by this whole thing," she accused. "Why? What sort of man is this half-breed? What has he done, besides buy the place?"

"Quite a lot, it seems. To start with, he informed old Sam that he'd wreck his beanery if Sam tried to keep him from eating there. Next, he discussed the finer points of Government land law with Harold. A day or so later he killed Frank Wheeler and ran Moline off. That's the kind of man he is, and that's why I'm amused." Bolter finished his recital and chuckled again. "Wouldn't you say it's something to be amused about?"

But Martha was shaking her head. Her knowledge of the country was too complete to allow her to put too much faith in the stranger's ability to hold his winning hand to the end. "What will happen now?" she asked. "You don't think Fresno is going to sit still for this, do you? I feel sorry for the poor fellow."

"Don't go burying him yet," Bolter advised. He shifted his bag to the other hand and jiggled it absently. "It just might turn out that he can chew what he bites off. I haven't met him yet, but I think I'm beginning to take to him already."

Martha's gaze went past Bolter to the darkened yard beyond.

"Then, perhaps I should have said, 'poor Fresno,' " she murmured.

It was Bolter's turn to be surprised. "You can say that after what Star did to you?" he demanded. "Woman, you'll be sprouting wings, first thing you know!"

"That was none of Fresno's doing, and you know it."

"She's been heard to say it wouldn't have turned out any different if she'd been in charge at the time," Bolter pointed out. "Doesn't that tell you anything about her?"

Martha's tone was disapproving. "Ah, Dan! Of course it does! It tells me she's so tragically aware of being a woman among men that she must talk rougher and act tougher than any of them in order to convince them she's in charge. I pity her."

"Well, by God, you constitute a minority!"

"That may well be," Martha admitted drolly. "But then, I travel in rather exclusive company, don't I?"

Bolter reached out and laid a hand on her shoulder. "Martha, get out of this sorry neck of the woods. This is no kind of business for you to be in, and you know it."

She shook her head. "I can't."

"Why not?"

She shrugged. "It's hard to explain, but I've always had the feeling I can't leave . . . not until it's settled, this thing between Star and the hill people. I know it sounds silly, but I once was part of it. I still am, in a way. I've got to see it out to the end."

"The end of Star, you mean?"

"I'm not one to make predictions, but I've always believed that everything happens for a reason. Sooner or later the pattern becomes clear. It's not clear to me yet, because it's not finished. I've got to know why so many things have happened the way they have . . . to me, to Fresno, to Lila, to Moline . . . to so many people. It seems utterly senseless, utterly without rhyme or reason. But it's not. There *is* a reason behind it, and sooner or later it'll come out. And something tells me it's going to happen sooner than anyone expects. That's why I can't leave."

Bolter dropped his hand tiredly. "You're a stubborn woman."

"Why," Martha said with a smile, "that's hardly news, is it? As a matter of fact, I've long since designed my gravestone. I'm having a bulldog carved atop the stone, and underneath, in big, bold letters, the legend, 'Here lies Martha—a stubborn woman.' "

They stood there laughing together, two old friends with few illusions left. Bolter took Martha's hand and squeezed it. "Go put some wet towels on your boy's face," he said gruffly, and crossed the porch and stepped into his buggy.

Entering Moline's room with a basin of water, Martha set it on the table and nodded to Ruby, who had assisted the doctor and now sat steadily watching the sleeping Moline. "You can go now. I'll stay with him."

"Ain't he a sight?" Ruby whispered. "I've seen dogs come out of a free-for-all lookin' prettier!" She shook her head dolefully and moved to the door. "Just give a yell if you want me to spell you," she offered. "Probably won't be any customers tonight, anyhow. Late as it is."

Martha closed the door and turned her attention to Moline. In the turned-down light his head and shoulders loomed dark against the white pillow, and she stood looking down at his battered, swollen face, wanting to cry. She bent and gently smoothed the tangled hair off the flushed forehead. "David," she murmured, "is there anything I can bring you? Water? Something to eat?"

He made a slight motion of refusal with his head. "Thanks anyway."

Martha dipped a towel in the water, wrung it out, and laid it over the discolored face. Moline gasped and started up. "It's all right," she said. "It will draw the fever."

He subsided onto the pillow with a grateful moan as the cool dampness laid its soothing touch over his burning skin. His voice came up to her, muffled by the towel. "Anybody ever tell you you're a damned fine woman, Martha?"

She did not answer at once, but there was a swift run of feeling across her face. She drew a chair close and sat down, exchanging the first damp poultice for a new one. "Yes," she said finally. "But it was a long time ago." She was silent, then, staring unseeingly at the wall. The minutes passed, and again she changed towels. "It's nice to hear it again, after so long a time," she said, and laid her strong hand on Moline's limply upturned palm.

His fingers curled up and closed. "Your husband, you mean?"

"Never mind," she said quietly. "The story ended. I closed the book."

His grip tightened. "I've heard that story. I'm sorry."

"Sleep now."

"Will you stay awhile?"

"I'll be right here."

He gave her hand another squeeze. "Thanks," he mumbled,

and was almost instantly asleep. She remained sitting there, watching the slow rise and fall of his chest under the quilts, her hand gradually growing cramped in his calloused grip. She was still there when the oil in the lamp gave out and the low flame flickered and died.

Long after, Ruby stole down the backstairs and tiptoed across the kitchen to the closed door. Easing it open, she peered into the darkened room and saw the woman silhouetted against the faint light from the window beyond. The steady rise and fall of the room's two sleeping occupants was the only sound in the night.

"Well, I'll be a sonofabitch!" she muttered. "Anybody'd take her for his mother!"

Swallowing the lump that rose in her throat, she turned and crept back upstairs as soundlessly as she had come.

10

It was long after midnight when Jesse Whitehead put the little dun down the brush-clogged shoulder of the hill east of the old Bland place and invaded the wind-ruffled grass. He was but a short distance into that whispering expanse when he caught the faint beat of a horse running down to him from the black line of cottonwoods a quarter mile away. Immediately he swung around to face that direction. The fading moon shed only a suggestion of light onto the plain, but his ears told him he was directly in the path of the oncoming horse. He murmured to the alertly listening dun, "Make up your own mind about which way to jump if they go to run you down," and glimpsed a shape emerge from the gloom a hundred feet away and bear squarely down on him.

At the last instant the running horse sensed the obstacle in its path, altered stride, and bore out. Simultaneously Lila MacKay spied the same obstacle and called, "Who's that?" and threw her mount back on its haunches. She was a forward-leaning shape in the sickly diffusion of light as she walked her horse forward. "Who is it?"

"Who d'you think?"

Lila's swift laugh exploded and dissolved on the wind. "Jesse! Who else would be ramming around this time of night?"

"Well, now," Jesse observed pointedly, "I ain't exactly talkin' to myself, don't look like." He sat loosely in the saddle, at once curious at the presence of the girl. "Hear tell somebody's took over the old Bland place," he observed. "You by any chance run into him yet?"

Lila's breathy laugh sounded again. "Why don't you come right out and ask what you really want to know: have I got him undressed yet?"

"The thought," Jesse stated innocently, "never even crossed my mind."

"Like hell it didn't! It was the first thing you thought of, you dried-up old he-wolf!"

"Well, have you?"

"Why, hell yes!"

Jesse could not suppress a chuckle at the girl's blatant honesty. "From the heft o' him, I'd guess you'd likely know you'd been rode by a top hand. That right?"

Lila caught him up at once. "So, you've met him, then?"

"Didn't say I hadn't."

"You didn't say you had, either."

"S'afternoon," Jesse admitted. "And how long you been blanket-rasslin' him, girl? From the day he showed up, I don't doubt."

"I was a little slow this time," Lila laughed. "It was the second day."

Jesse's whispery answering laugh sounded as a part of the wind. "You're slippin', girl. What made you so slow?"

"I didn't know where he was holed up at first. It wasn't until I'd back-tracked Lewt Shadley's roan that I—" She broke off, knowing she had blundered. She said quickly then, "But once I flushed him out, things went along right smart," but she knew the old mountain man had caught the slip.

Jesse made a thin humming sound in his throat. "Soooo, that explains what Balaam an' Newt was doin', nosin' around down here t'day." He threw a quick glance to either side out of long habit, ascertained that no foreign ears were present to overhear, and bent forward. "This Lord feller done Lewt in; that right?"

Lila made a belated attempt to cover up. "Who said anything about Lewt being done in? What are you talking about?"

But he would have none of that. "Don't play dumb with me, girl! The day ain't dawned that seen you out-foxin' me. Now talk up. How come Lewt got hisself killed by this Lord feller?"

He waited for her answer, and when she remained silent, he hit her with his voice, harder and sharper. "Are your brains addled, girl? You thought about what's apt t' happen t' him if them Shadleys find Lewt an' do some hard thinkin' on their own? If'n they come up with the right answer an' go mouthin' off t' them Matlocks an' Rob Haller, how long you figger your new friend's goin' t' last around here?" He leaned farther toward her. "Now, where's Lewt's carcass hid?"

"I don't know, dammit!" Lila snapped. "He didn't tell me."

"Don't give me none o' that!"

"I'm telling it straight, Jesse! All I know is that he tracked Lewt down while Lewt was trying to run off his two blooded mares and a filly, and shot him out of the saddle. I asked him, but all he told me was that Lewt was where he'd not be found. I suspect it's true, else he'd not have said it."

"An' that's all they is to the story?"

"I turned Lewt's roan loose and dumped his saddle and bridle down a crack that a mouse couldn't find the bottom of, and dragged a juniper along his backtrail 'till the tracks played out in the grass."

"How come you go to all that bother, 'fore you knowed he'd done Lewt in?" Jesse demanded suspiciously. "Don't seem the natural thing for you to do."

Lila resented having her actions held up for questioning by her old friend. "Who says I didn't know? Hell! I knew who'd shot Lewt the minute I found his roan! I met him, Lord, that is, the day before when he was poking around the neck between upper and lower valley. Running across Lewt's bloody saddle that way, and knowing Lewt's fondness for other folks' horses, it wasn't too hard to figure out who fixed his wagon for him."

Jesse nodded and slowly eased back in his saddle. "I'd not want you on my trail if'n I'd reason to hide it," he said with grudging admiration. "I swear you could give a damned timber wolf a headstart an' still beat him back to his own den, the way that damned brain o' yours works."

Lila shrugged the compliment aside "A kid could have figured it out. Lewt was too damned cagey to get caught by any Star hand. He always worked on Star stock at night; you know that. And this happened in broad daylight. Besides, his tracks led straight down the valley to where the shooting took place. The whole thing was pretty easy to read."

"Fer the right pair o'eyes, anyways," Jesse agreed, and grinned at her in the murky light.

This was the way it was with them. Their paths had crossed high in the far-rolling hills; they had nodded once in mutually suspicious greeting, and had then fallen into an easy association that had steadily become a bond of respect stronger than either of them realized.

It was due solely to a factor each of them possessed to a high degree: a total disregard for the opinions of others, which, in turn, engendered a complete withholding of moral judgment.

Now Jesse Whitehead dug a plug from the depths of one of the cavernous pockets of his tunic and busied himself trimming off a substantial chaw.

"Where you off to, Jesse?"

He licked the last morsel of tobacco from his palm, slid the skinning knife back into its sheath, and tipped his head toward the south. "Perce Downing's been ketchin' hell from the cats lately. Ast me t' come down an' see could I maybe grab me a few of 'em by the tail."

"That's what I figured," Lila said, and dispatched that matter with one more question. "Has Charity dropped her latest, yet?"

"Three . . . four days ago. 'Nother girl."

"That makes six," Lila laughed. "Poor old Perce is never going to get his free crew if he doesn't change his recipe."

Jesse's answering chuckle had the sound of dry cornstalks rubbing together. He leaned over and sent a stream of juice into the grass and grew too idle with his talk. "Seen Dave Moline lately?"

She was instantly on guard. "This evening early. The bastard nearly ran over me at the ford. Damn! He looked like he'd just tangled with one of those cats you mentioned. Who cleaned his plow, anyhow?"

But Jesse's curiosity equaled hers. "What d'you mean? Last time I seen him—an' that was along in the middle o' the afternoon over at the old Bland place—he was all in one piece, 'cept fer his pride. What was wrong with him?"

"His face looked like it'd been run through a sausage-grinder," Lila reported. "He was riding with one stirrup, and he had his right arm shoved inside his shirt, like maybe it was broken." The meaning of Jesse's words hit her belatedly. "What do you mean, you saw him at the old Bland place?" she demanded. "What the hell's going on around here, anyhow?"

"Ain't sure," Jesse admitted. "But whatever it is, it's got underway mighty sudden-like, what with this Lord killin' a feller the minute he hits the valley, an'—"

"Two," Lila corrected him. "Two men."

"What's that you say, girl? Who was the t'other'n?"

"Frank Wheeler."

The idea of questioning the girl's veracity did not even cross Jesse's mind. The facts alone concerned him. "How'd that come about?"

"Frank came down with Moline to run Lord off yesterday. He

tried a sneak draw, only he wasn't only not sneaky enough; he wasn't quick enough either." Lila's quick laugh reflected another of her swift-changing moods. "Can't you just see Fresno chewing nails over that little setback? I warned Lord he'd better real quick grow a pair of eyes in the back of his head if he planned on staying around these parts."

"Well, she was some put out, all right," Jesse agreed. "But it don't make no sense . . . what she done s'afternoon."

"What was that?"

"Clouted Moline with her quirt, then ordered him out'n the valley."

"The hell!" Lila exclaimed incredulously.

"Seen her do it. I was scrooched down behind a scrub juniper up on the rim above the old Bland place. Seen the whole thing."

Lila stiffened, her gaze going past Jesse to the grove of cottonwoods that showed only as a faint shadow in the night. "You mean," she asked slowly, "that Fresno was over there this afternoon?"

Jesse Whitehead was as adept at reading voices as he was at reading long-cold trails. Now Lila's unexpected quietness turned him sly. "Y'mean your big playmate didn't say nothing to you about it?"

"No," Lila replied in that same slow, thoughtful way. "No, he didn't."

Her tone engendered a similar curiosity in her companion. "Now, I wonder why?" he mused. He spat again, and wiped his mouth on the back of his sleeve. "Didn't say ary a word?"

Confusion laid a rough edge over Lila's voice. "I said he didn't!" she snapped. "Now stop acting like a snoopy old maid and tell me what happened!"

Jesse related the incident he had witnessed, including the part having to do with Lord and Fresno Taggert's brief sojourn indoors. Throughout the recital he was acutely aware of his listener's close attention.

"She went *inside* with him, you say?"

"You heard me."

"How long were they in there?"

Jesse's bony shoulders rose and dropped. "Hell, I got no timepiece. Likely ten–fifteen minutes."

"And then what?"

Jesse was wryly amused. He ejected another stream of juice earthward, savoring his role. "What you want to know is did she send her boys on home, then go back inside with your friend, right?"

Lila was not amused. "You're a sly old fart, aren't you?" she replied scathingly. "Well, did she?"

"Did she what?"

"Ride out, dammit!"

Jesse found it necessary to spit yet again. "Yeah," he said then, "she rode out."

A vague resentment stirred in Lila at finding herself shut out by Lord in this fashion. With her long mane blowing around her face in the strengthening night wind she considered the puzzle and could find no answer. Could it be . . . ? She fastened her thoughts on Fresno Taggert and at once regretted having done so; for in the aloof beauty she recognized such an obvious threat to her own relationship with Lord as to fill her with dismay. It was her first acquaintance with jealousy, and she was for the moment wholly incapable of dealing with it.

"Jesse, tell me something. We were together a long time tonight: and I'd talked about Fresno for about an hour this morning. Now, how come he said not one damned word about that visit of hers?"

Jesse remembered his swift assessment of the man as he had squatted beside him near the pool that afternoon. "Did he say he *hadn't* met her?"

"He told me this morning that she'd stopped him down in South Canyon the day he was heading in here and tried to buy his horses off him, but he never opened his mouth about her visit this afternoon. Now why?"

Jesse ejected another stream of amber juice. " 'Pears like the only thing you've learned about men is how to trip 'em and pull 'em down on top o' you," he observed bluntly. "Otherwise, you'd of seen that that big half-breed ain't what you'd call exactly mouthy. Doubt it ever crossed his mind to mention it."

"He could have at least mentioned it, couldn't he?"

"He *could* of sang 'Rock of Ages' fer you, too," Jesse said drily. "But I don't reckon singin' was on his mind any more than knittin' was on yours. Listen—" He straightened sternly. "If'n you're thinkin' this Lord feller is jest another big hard-on fer you to fiddle around with whenever the notion hits you, you'd best think again, fer he ain't. The way I figger him, you'll either play by his rules, or you play alone. He ain't one o' your trashy Matlocks, y'know."

Lila's thoughts never remained long on any one subject. Now, the mere mention of the hill family was enough to divert them into a new channel. "What have they been up to lately?" she asked. "Anything new?"

"Luke run off eight–nine head o' saddle stock last week. Taken 'em south."

This was ancient news to Lila. "I cut his trail before he was an hour on his way," she reported smugly. "Anything else?"

"Well, Bob Willis shot hisself in the left foot four days ago. Heard about that, had you?"

"No!" Lila was delighted. "Too bad he didn't aim about six feet higher." With characteristic abruptness she changed the subject. "Have you ever noticed how much that whole tribe of Matlocks smell like a herd of goats?"

"Why? You smell one of 'em jest now?"

Lila laughed again. "No. It just crossed my mind, is all. Funny that anybody as well set up as they are—the whole damned shooting match—wouldn't take a little pride in their looks."

"Looks they got, all right enough," Jesse admitted. "Pride they ain't." He broke off, half angry at the unexpected concern he felt for this restless girl's welfare. Fatherly solicitude was strange to him, and his awkwardness made him rough with his words. "Ner you neither, fer that matter. You orta have yer damned butt blistered fer lettin' that passle o' trashy bulls hump ye whenever the notion strikes 'em. It's yer own business, who ye spread yer legs fer, but damned if I kin see how you kin look yerself in the face after bein' serviced by such scruffy stock as that. God *damn* if I kin!"

For one surprised second Lila sat there utterly astonished by the unexpected calling down. Then she threw her head back and whooped. It erupted from her open mouth in a prolonged shout that overrode the rushing wind and bounced back from the black wall of the hill behind her. She choked down a second burst and dropped her head forward to fix her unsmiling comrade with an amused stare. "Well, thank you for the sermon, Reverend Whitehead," she drawled. "I'll never do those naughty things again." She suppressed another laugh, then feigned an air of wronged innocence. "Instead of cussing me out, though, you should be thanking me on behalf of your nose."

"What the hell are you talkin' about?"

Lila tossed her hair back with a circling movement of her head. "You really ought to be thanking me for cleaning them up," she told him. "Sometime back, I passed a law that says I don't climb down off my horse until after they've washed down . . . with soap."

Jesse had never caught her out in a lie, but this was too fantastic to be believed. "Do you expect me to swaller a fool story like that?" he demanded. "Jest how the hell do you go about enforcin' your law?"

"Easy. Whenever I run into one of them and they make a grab for me, I just reach down in my saddlebag, take out a bar of soap, and say, 'Let's go find some water, then we'll take care of what's bothering you.' Works like a charm." She nodded to give emphasis to her words, then heaved a doleful sigh. "Being a refined, high-toned lady is such a trial at times."

It was Jesse's turn to be amused, though on a less ribald scale than Lila. His bony shoulders jiggled with his dry chuckling, and he shook his unkempt mane from side to side in admission of defeat. "If you ain't the damndest!" he sputtered. "I'd give a prime beaver pelt to ketch one o' that bunch soapin' hisself down."

"It's a little trickier in the winter," Lila admitted. "But I finally got tired of their excuses and told them they'd just have to get in the habit of bathing before coming to look for me. They generally cooperate."

She then became mindful of the lateness of the hour and gathered up her reins. "Well, don't get swallowed by one of those cats," she instructed him, and reined away.

"Hold on a minute, Lila."

The tone, more than the words, stopped her, and she swung around again to face him. "Yes?"

Jesse put his dun close alongside. He said, "Somethin' I'd like to say t'you, fer whatever it might be worth," and stopped, clearly at a loss as to how to proceed.

Lila peered sharply at him, knowing immediately that his trouble was genuine. "All right, Jesse," she said quietly. "I'm listening."

He crossed his arms over his chest and stared straight ahead through the gloom. "You do as you think best," he said. "But was I you, I'd think twice't about spendin' too much time with this breed feller."

Lila was instantly back in the sparsely furnished bedroom hearing the dark man's long-suppressed agony faltering into the night. She said in a stricken voice, "Oh, my God, Jesse! Not you too!" and felt as if she were witnessing the death of a loved one. She shook her head in vehement refusal. "Not you too!"

Her reaction completely mystified the old man. "What do you mean . . . not me *too*?"

But Lila had already closed him out. "Never mind. Let it go, Jesse. It's just that I didn't expect you to be like everybody else."

"Shit!" Jesse said disgustedly. "Don't talk in damned riddles. I'm about as much like everybody else as a Lobo's like a lapdog, an' you know it!"

"Then why did you bring it up?" Lila demanded hotly.

"Fer yer own goddamned good! Yer business with Lord is yer own affair. But yer old man is apt to turn all holy-pure righteous, if'n he finds out you been lettin' a breed hump you. Douglas MacKay's about as no-good an excuse fer a human bein' as God ever let set foot on green ground; but it's jest his kind of mongrel son of a bitch that confuses hisself with God almighty when it comes to tellin' others how they got to handle themselves."

"To hell with Douglas!" Lila flared. "I answer to him for nothing! I never have! I never will!"

Jesse slowly straightened, his head moving from side to side in a gesture of defeat. He could not shake her. "That won't do it, girl," he said quietly. "Not in a case like this. You think you're able to ride the wind, same as allus. But you'll find you've straddled a whirlwind this time, sure as God's blind to the stinkin' sins o' man."

Lila's anger slowly ebbed. "You've met Lord, Jesse. What do you think of him?"

"I think he's a man, jest like any other, except he stands a heap taller in my book. But then, I'm me, an' I never did have the sense God gave a goose."

Lila held him with her gaze. "Did the color of his skin bother you?"

"His *skin*?" Jesse echoed disgustedly. "Why, hell no, its color didn't bother me none! Looked jest like plain old human skin t' me, 'cept maybe a mite darker than most. But then, I allus been color blind, where skins was concerned."

The smile Lila showed him then was one of startlingly girlish sweetness. She was in that brief moment wholly without guile and wholly vulnerable, warm with the glow of complete trust. "Jesse," she said huskily, "if I ever come to a river I can't cross on my own, I hope to God you're around to give me a hand to the other side."

He was profoundly moved. In his sixty-eight years no one had ever before spoken so to him. He bent his head and hacked loudly to cover his embarrassment, then leaned over to expel the played-out chaw from his jaws. He said noncommitally, "Could be such a thing was t'happen, we'd both go down, girl," and caught the shadowy denying movement of her head.

"Not us," she stated with a swift return of her old assurance. "The river doesn't run that could pull the two of us down."

"Well, now," Jesse observed skeptically, "they's rivers, an' then they's rivers."

"True, but sooner or later they all run down to level ground and smooth out. When that happens I've a hunch old Lila and old Jesse will still be treading water to beat old Billy Hell."

Jesse chuckled. "Allus said they was two things I never wanted no truck with," he observed. "One was hangin', t'other was drownin'. But if you hit that river, girl, jest sing out, loud an' clear. I'll see what I kin do to give you a hand across."

Again that strangely sweet smile briefly showed in Lila's face. She reached out and touched Jesse's time-ravaged cheek with slender fingers. She said so softly, "Aaron Lord is at that river now, Jesse, and he can't swim it alone." All at once her voice betrayed her. It thickened and sank back into her throat, and then quite without warning tears were running down her face. She said in a shaking whisper, "Give him a hand, Jesse. Nobody else ever has," and wheeled her horse and went away from him at a sudden run.

He held the little dun where it was long after the muffled drum of hoofs had faded far up the valley. The wind was stronger now. It threw his long hair forward around his face and streamed through the grass with a ceaseless hissing noise. It set up a wilder, lonelier song in the yonder hills and turned the night increasingly uneasy. It was a thing that worked steadily at him, going deep into his bones, making them hurt with a pain he had never felt before. He thought with a faint flush of fear: *I've no place in this. Why don't I stay out of it altogether?* and knew it to be a vain and hopeless wish. He was already in it, like an antelope whose curiosity will not let it rest until it sees for itself that the strange object on the hilltop was only a colored rag. And, like an antelope, he might well find too late that a black stick that killed without touching was concealed near that same colored rag.

There was evil in the night around him—an anger in the wind such as he had never known. He could feel it working at him, driving into him and all through him until he was cold, and filled with a nameless dread. He thought: *Leave it alone, dammit! Leave it flat alone!* and knew that he could not. Lila's words came back to him, unbidden and unwanted, and when he would have rejected them, they darted in past the guard he raised against them.

"No!" he said violently. "He's got no business here, by damn! This ain't no kind of country for him to come to, and he'd orta know it!"

It was the sound of his own voice, so angrily stating an incontrovertible fact that brought him up short. He said in astonishment then, "Why, that's true enough, as fer as it goes. But jest what country *is* the right one fer a man like him?" Having come to grips with an unsavory truth, he found that he could not free himself from it. He thought: *I should have let it lie*, and groaned aloud in his distress.

He turned in the saddle and gave the cottonwood grove a long, accusing look, then stared in the direction Lila MacKay had gone. He drew a long, slow breath and let the wind take it away, and afterward he spat into the streaming grass. He picked up the reins and sat there, deliberately testing the strength of his grip with a tightening and loosening motion of his hand on the worn leather. He said with the air of a man with things to do, "Better be movin' on," and rode out onto the empty sweep of plain where the grass rolled and heaved before him and all around him, like an uneasy sea under the angry wind.

11

Ewing Star had been a man above men, with a sense of history narrowly limited by purely personal interests. He had possessed a knack for conquest that bordered on genius. The scion of a wealthy New England shipping family, he had turned his back on the sea as a young man and fixed his hungry gaze inland. Just where and how he would discover his destiny, he had no idea, until an equally hungry-eyed friend unwittingly furnished him the means to attain it.

In the year 1842—a year which saw long lines of wagons invading the British-claimed Northwest Territory to turn that rain-washed Eden into an American stronghold—John Frémont pointed his independent self toward Spanish-held California. With him went Ewing Star, close boyhood friend and staunch supporter, in what would prove to be Frémont's successful bid for immortality. On a midsummer day of that same year, while riding at the head of a wide-ranging detachment of the expedition, young Star had quite accidentally stumbled across the great Basin, and above it the valley that was to become his own personal Eden.

Fully as impulsive as his commanding officer (and definitely possessed of more foresight, insofar as his own future was concerned), Ewing Star had resigned his commission on the spot and hied himself south to Santa Fe. An hour after his arrival in that Spanish settlement, his letter was on its way East, ordering his wife and their year-old daughter to join him. And long before a long-suffering Alexandra Star had dismounted from the box of the high-wheeled wagon that had brought her all those hundreds of miles to the western edge of the "Unorganized Territory," Star Valley had resounded to the hammer-strokes of his house building.

It was a monument Star built in a sheltered scallop of the leaf-shaped valley three hundred miles north of Santa Fe—a great monument of stone and hand-hewn timbers that would stand for all time as a symbol of his empire.

It was night now, and Ewing Star's sole heir restlessly prowled the confines of her great stone cage like a wild animal. She passed down the long hall on the second floor, opening doors and peering into dark and empty rooms, and going on again to repeat the process over and over in a kind of absentminded frustration.

The stairway was before her finally, and she stood staring down into the black well of the foyer. On a sudden impulse she caught up the folds of her robe and made her winding descent into that blackness. First one and then another of the three heavy oak doors leading off from this focal point swung wide before her, and she snatched up a handful of matches from a silver box on the table near the stairway and proceeded from room to room, lighting lamps, until the night was driven from the surrounding yard by myriad yellow shafts lancing out of the deeply recessed windows.

But even this did not help, and in increasing frustration she went outdoors and made a wide circle of the house, passing from shadow to lightness to shadow again, like a prowler furtively questing the night. She stopped to let the coolness of the wind play over her. She opened her robe and held it wide to catch as much of the wind as possible; but that too afforded only a transient relief, and in sudden desperation, she let the robe fall to the ground, pulled her gown off over her head, and stood in the biting chill, waiting dumbly for that coldness to conquer the inner hotness. But it proved to be a vain hope, and she turned, shivering in the wind, but inwardly suffocating from the heat of a desire that would not let her alone.

A hundred yards away the crew's quarters bulked irregularly against the skyline and she faced that way for a time, staring at the several lights of the ranch village glowing in the darkness. She pictured the people inside settling down for the night and was gripped by a feeling of total isolation from her kind.

She asked herself why she so suddenly felt a need for the warmth to be found in a closer relationship with others.

It was no easy thing she willed herself to do, for the mores of a puritanical society stood close-ranked between her and the object of her thoughts, like stern-faced guards warning her away from the forbidden territory. She retrieved her gown and robe from the ground and slipped them on. Making her slow way back to the house, she reluctantly but remorselessly kept her thoughts firmly fixed on the half-breed Aaron Lord.

When all was said and done, she knew almost nothing about the man. True, his relationship to Angus Lord, the St. Louis fur merchant, explained his money; it in no wise explained his determination. And it was this which most deeply concerned her. In his glittering eyes it was a hunger bordering on savagery. It lent a contradictory hardness to his sensual lips that made of his occasional slow smile an astonishing revelation, and exerted a constant tension in him oddly at variance with the easy grace of his tall frame.

But most of all it was apparent in the implacable voice that seemed to emanate from deep inside the hidden recesses of the man. And then her thoughts turned to herself, and she became again uncomfortably warm and hampered in her thinking, as sensuality assumed dominance over her mind. She tried to tell herself that she was acting like a wool-gathering idiot, that such daydreaming had no place in her life, that it was not only foolish but indecent to regard a half-breed in such a light. She said sternly to herself, "Stop this right now!" and for an instant managed to believe that she was revolted by her response to the man's remembered maleness. But she found herself unable to expunge these desire-inspired images from her mind and was more and more dominated by the remorseless pull of that maleness, until the wish to let it have its way with her was an obsession, laying waste her drought-ridden body and rioting through her senses.

125

In this state of devastation she staggered into the foyer. She put her hands to her face and felt the heat like a living presence under her palms. She pressed them flat against the door and was conscious of the immediate coolness there. She was a strong, carefully composed woman who seldom admitted doubt. But an unnerving, alien thing was inside her now, dragging at her so that she was for a time incapable of pushing herself upright. She whispered hoarsely, "No! I will not! I *cannot!*" and in the next instant was thinking, *Why shouldn't I? Who's to know?* Panic seized her as she recognized in the thought an ever-strengthening wish to surrender, and she whispered protestingly, "But what if someone found out?" and replied with a readiness that appalled her, "I am Fresno Star Taggert. Nothing can touch me."

It was not the first time she had admitted that her status rendered her immune from the penalties imposed on lesser beings. She had from birth been aware of the wide gulf separating her from others. But until now she had restricted the exercise of her power wholly to the welfare of the ranch. Her personal conduct she had always guarded carefully, knowing all too well how mercilessly people judge those whom they regard as their betters.

But now her position offered her an immunity to public censure, and she seized on it before her habitual iron discipline could assert itself. She was free to do as she wished *because* she was Ewing Star's daughter. She needed no other vindication.

On the point of crossing the foyer to extinguish the lamps in the distant rooms, she glimpsed herself in the huge gilt mirror on the wall and abruptly stopped to stare at her reflection.

It was a face she had never seen before, and she studied it narrowly in an effort to pierce the surface of the violet eyes. But they presented a cool and glassy sheen that would not be penetrated, and this failure to break through to her own self filled her with resentment. She said coldly, "So, we are to be strangers, then," and saw the full lips repeating the dictum. "Perhaps it will be easier so," she murmured then, and caught that aloof person's slow nod.

For another long moment she continued to stand there, her

eyes no longer focusing on the alien image but instead seeing beyond it a darker countenance that slowly emerged and hung suspended in the near-darkness of the foyer. She said in a harsh, accusing voice, "You have done this to me! You have divided me and changed me, and I no longer know which is myself!"

Ever so slowly the long lips thinned in a knowing smile, and the black eyes took on a glittering hotness that speared deep into her and turned her half mad with their regenerating heat. A wordless cry broke from her and she flung herself away from the door and across the foyer, in a terror to have the lights extinguished and blackness come concealingly in.

But there was no comfort to be had, even in the dark, high-ceilinged library to which she fled. The thickness of the walls rendered the house impervious to heat and cold alike, and in summer the rooms were always shadowy havens of coolness. But a stifling heat enveloped her as she slumped over the desk and waited for relief to come. With rising panic she realized that this torment was fired and fed by an insidious demon from within.

The collar of her dressing gown choked her, and she tore the garment off and, naked, began once more to pace the confines of her luxurious prison. Yet, not even this swift, determined movement could assuage the suffocating sensation that possessed her. It was a tangible palpitation—an unremitting, offbeat tempo centered in her groin, steadily mounting in intensity until she slowed her steps and finally stopped and surrendered herself to it.

And again, through the darkness, the coppery features emerged and hung suspended before her with that knowing expression. The nakedness of the half-breed's body was a tangible thing, its turgid maleness impaling her and setting up its own counter-tempo of invasion and withdrawal within that most flamingly aroused region of her body. It was an undulating heat inside her, more real than any reality she had ever known.

"This is what I want from you!" she whispered harshly. "This! Nothing more! I saw it in your eyes when you looked at me. Damn you! God damn you!"

Her raw, gusting voice thinned to a protesting wail. The sound of it penetrated her riven senses and brought her up short, and she stood there panting, aghast at what had happened to her. She moaned like an animal in pain. Her muscles went slack, her legs buckled, and she sprawled loosely across the deep-piled rug and lay sobbing uncontrollably in an agony of shame.

Long afterward, she got painfully to her feet and made her way upstairs to bed, there to doze fitfully and wake and turn while the night wore leadenly away toward dawn.

She rose in a state of mind as grey as the mist-shrouded day, dressed listlessly, and descended to the kitchen. Mary Gilstrap, who was cook and housekeeper for her, was not due for another hour, so Fresno kindled a fire in the range and put the coffee pot on to heat.

Later, at the sight of Mary hurrying along the path to the back door, she rose quickly and retreated to her room, reluctant to have even that gentle soul see her in her present state of mind.

From her high window, which afforded her an unobstructed view of the home valley, she saw the sun flood the bowl and knew that it would be another hot day. She looked eastward to where a trail climbed up over the encircling wall of the high peninsula that closed this side of the valley in, and thought with sudden longing of the cabin situated on the edge of the little lake over there.

It was her private refuge, discovered by her as a child and immediately claimed by her. It comprised a haven to which she had all her adult life retreated to regroup her forces whenever the pressures of holding her far-flung empire together became too burdensome. At her request, it had been placed off-limits to everyone in Star Valley, and after her father's death, she had kept the rule in force. No Star hand ventured near it without her express permission, and even the hill people respected the taboo. Nestled in the pines, its doorway commanded a view of the entire southern quarter of Star Valley, and she reflected that were she now standing in that doorway, she could look straight across the restless grassy ocean and see, five miles away, the sharp point of the hills where they broke back upon themselves in a curving eastward swing. In that curve, hidden from view by the jutting shoulder of the hills, lay the old Bland spread.

For the first time in its existence, Star had been balked in its attempt to expand its conquest of this untamed wilderness. Awareness of this defeat was a galling thing to Fresno—a personal affront which she was loathe to accept as final. It turned her at once bitterly angry, and she balled her hands into fists and brought them down hard on the window sill. Tendrils of pain shot up her arms and brought her back to her senses, but almost immediately she was thinking of Aaron Lord and recalling the details of his face and body with a clarity which shocked her.

She thought: *Hiding from it is no good. Perhaps if I see him again, I will admit how disgusting this whole thing is,* and knew that she was deliberately deceiving herself. But with a manipulation of the mind wholly unlike her, she closed it down against further thought and turned swiftly from the window to dress.

Fifteen minutes later she again descended to the kitchen, now attired in a tight-waisted blue linen riding habit whose great overskirt trailed four feet behind her until caught up and hooked to her waist by its carrying loop.

After a hurried breakfast, she made her way to the corrals, where five of the crew were snaking out mounts from the milling remuda. She called to Doyle Patton, "How about catching up Nut Maid for me?" and, seeing the man's answering nod, went into the barn for her saddle and bridle.

With the blazed-face mare brought up, she took the rope from Patton, slipped the bridle on, and with the mare ground-anchored, saddled up. She ascended the mounting block, stepped into the saddle, and reined away in the direction of the peninsula a mile distant, letting the big mare rise to a run when she was well out of the yard.

At the bottom of the steep trail, she drew up to let the mare catch her wind, then went up at a scrambling rush that sent a shower of gravel rattling back down the hill. They topped out on the narrow ridge, then plunged downward into the coolness of the pines. Reaching the cabin, she hesitated for a time, undecided whether to prolong her game of self-deception. But the ridiculousness of this pretense struck her and took her out of the trees and around the lake before she had fully resolved the matter in her mind. Determinedly she pointed the mare straight south.

At a swinging canter she navigated the tawny sea and in due time reached the point of land that speared out into the valley, swung around it, and splashed across the stream that marked the edge of the green triangular sward below the Bland place. She reached the grove, rode through it, and at once stopped as the two giant dogs came hurtling toward her from the stable. Looking that way, she saw Aaron Lord step through the doorway and whistle the dogs back. He gave no sign of welcome as she rode over to him and halted.

Expecting him to tender some sort of greeting, she realized too late that he had no intention of doing so, and covered her embarrassment with a show of cordiality. "Neighbors are too few and far between around here for us to start off on the wrong foot."

His response was bone-dry. "That's kind of you. But from the looks of this place, a person might get the idea that your way of welcoming neighbors could be a bit rough."

She rejected the calculated affront with a swift show of temper. "What happened here took place a long time ago. It's best forgotten."

"I doubt Bland would agree with you," Lord stated. "And it's certain Martha Bland wouldn't see it that way at all."

"She's forgotten it long since," Fresno retorted, and stopped, realizing too late that she had blundered.

Lord's eyes struck at her like twin daggers. "How would you know that, ma'am?"

"Women can't hate as well as men," she stated defiantly, knowing she was making a bad thing of it. It was a lamentably poor defense, and she saw that Lord was not deceived. With actual dread she watched him step forward until he was almost at her stirrup. He was holding her with his eyes, and for all that his voice was seemingly unperturbed, it laid a chill on the morning and turned her increasingly uneasy.

"What became of Martha Bland, Mrs. Taggert?" he asked quietly. "She didn't leave the country, after all, did she? You know where she is, don't you?"

For an instant Fresno hesitated, but Lord's quiet self-assurance touched off a spark of anger in her. Her voice struck down at him, rough and heavy. "Yes, I know where she is! She has a . . . house, not far out of town. She's a—" She hesitated, at a loss how to put it delicately. A flush tinged her cheeks and she dropped her gaze to her hands. She said in a lower key, "She has something of a reputation in the Territory," and would not look at him.

"You mean she's a whore?" Lord asked, deliberately choosing the vulgar term. "Is that what you're trying to keep from saying, Mrs. Taggert?"

Her face went dead white. "Must you be so crude, Mr. Lord?"

He stepped back and raked her with unkind eyes. "I'm not at all sure I'm the cruder of the two of us," he told her. "I wasn't the one who made a whore of a decent woman."

"Nor did I! I told you yesterday that I had nothing at all to do with it . . . any of it. I was in school in Baltimore when it happened."

"You also told me you might very well have done it, had you been in charge," Lord reminded her.

"The point is, I didn't."

He shook his head. "The point is, you can't admit it was a wrong thing Star did."

"That is a lie!" Fresno denied hotly. "I tried to make amends. Later, when I took charge, I went to Martha Bland's . . . well, house . . . and offered to do everything in my power to make it up to her. Money . . . this place—"

"But she turned you down," Lord said. "I wonder why?"

Fresno again dropped her gaze to her hands. "It was too late," she said miserably, and again her sense of delicacy turned her awkward. "It wasn't until I talked to her that I learned the whole sordid story. The six Star hands who staged the raid were not . . . gentlemen, if you understand my meaning. I could hardly believe what she told me about that night. They—"

She broke off, unable to cloak the thing in decency, yet equally unable to reveal it in its true guise. Lord said with calm bluntness, "You mean they raped her? Is that what you're not able to say out loud?" and watched her again blanch at the choice of words.

"All six of them," she admitted in a barely audible voice. "But even worse, they went into town afterwards and got drunk. I guess it gave them the courage to spread the story that she had been . . . entertaining them . . . when her husband came home unexpectedly. No one believed them but it ruined Martha Bland as surely as if they had stripped her in the town square."

"And are those men still at Star?"

Her head came up and her eyes struck into him like points of steel. "Are you always so insulting, Mr. Lord?" she asked coldly. "If those men were at Star would I be telling you this unspeakably foul story?" She watched this register on him, and added in the same cold voice, "I am no saint, Mr. Lord. But neither am I a monster."

He made a short, stiff bow. "I apologize, ma'am. The question was completely out of order."

"It was," Fresno agreed icily, and shortened her reins. In the act of turning her mare, she paused, not quite through with him. "I had not expected this kind of reception when I rode over here," she told him. "I had thought to correct the impression I undoubtedly left with you the other day. I see now how ill-advised that notion was." She said without looking around, "Good day to you, sir," and shot away with a suddenness that threw stinging sand into his face.

He watched her out of sight, miserable at his rough handling of her, and shaken by the effect of her presence on him.

12

Lord was peeling poles for the stable rafters three days later when Fresno Taggert again rode in under the trees. She was attired in the same vivid blue habit she had worn on her previous visit, and he was struck anew by her incredible beauty. In the same instant he became aware that this marked the second time she had caught him naked from the waist up.

In a kind of frustrated rage, he dodged inside the stable in search of the shirt he had discarded at the start of his labors. He saw it hanging from a peg near the door, snatched it down, and hastily slipped it over his head. Lacking a comb, he raked his fingers through his tangled hair, gave the leather shirt a final tug, and stepped outside to greet his visitor with a heartiness wholly out of keeping with his actual frame of mind.

"You're a surprising lady, Mrs. Taggert. And I'm a surprised man, and an honored one. Good morning to you."

She was a woman with a warm smile and a quick wit, and today she turned an old-world charm on him. "Then, good morrow to you, honored sir," she responded. "I'm perhaps surprising, as you said. I'm also very stubborn, as you can see."

His brows described a puzzled arc. "Stubborn, ma'am?"

"As a bulldog," Fresno stated. "I refuse to believe neighbors have got to quarrel every time they meet. Sooo," she paused and smiled, "I came over to refuse to quarrel with you, Mr. Lord."

His answering smile lent a fleeting warmth to his features. "I've no wish to quarrel with Star," he told her. "Nor with its owner: I apologize for the other day."

"Least said, soonest mended," Fresno quoted. "We'll forget it. I came to invite you to take a ride with me—for two reasons."

"Two reasons, ma'am?"

Fresno inclined her head. "Correct. Will you saddle up? Or must I convince you of the honesty of my motives beforehand?"

His slow smile once more altered the stern cast of his face. "I'm new to the ways of the country," he admitted. "Maybe you'd better convince me first."

"I'm really trying to toll you away from here so my men can burn the place down without risking getting shot in the back," Fresno said straight-faced, and watched for another break in his expression before going on. "I'll show you the boundaries of your land, and then I would like to discuss certain matters with you."

For a moment he stood gravely studying her, then finally nodded. "All right." He went for his horse, saddled quickly and swung up. "Where to now, ma'am?"

She indicated the upper valley, which was blocked off by the neck of the hill to the west. "I'll show you your northern boundary first," she said, and headed for the grove.

Before they had reached the point of the hill she was convinced that he was either a born horseman or had been schooled by a master. With his feet lightly resting in the stirrups, he sat a reaching trot, the roughest of all gaits, as smoothly as if the long-striding stallion were moving at a leisurely walk. Her admiration was evident in her voice. "Where did you learn to sit the trot like that?"

He gave her a surprised look. "Angus Lord was a mighty particular man where his hot-bloods were concerned—and the men who rode them. He well-nigh killed me off before I sat a saddle to suit him."

"He knew his business."

Lord said nothing for a while. The stallion broke stride in order to stay with the powerfully moving mare as they rounded the hill. A dozen cantering strides onward, he brought it back down to the trot with unconscious ease. He said then, above the rhythmic thud of hoofs, "He knew all there was to know about almost everything, I guess," and in that simple statement revealed his profound respect for his late father.

"What a beautiful thing to have said about one!" Fresno exclaimed. "I hope you told him."

"No," Lord replied. "We never talked much."

"Was he a hard man?"

Lord nodded. "Yes. I was always afraid of him."

Fresno gave him a measuring glance. She said quietly, "I can understand that," and continued to watch him, even when he turned his brooding eyes on her.

"I doubt it."

"I admired my father," Fresno replied. "But I never felt he knew who I was, or cared. That can make a person afraid, too."

It was the first time she had ever put into words the emptiness she had felt as the only child of the autocratic Ewing Star, whose chief accomplishment had been an uncanny ability to take from others without giving anything of himself in return. It was this quality in him which had engendered a feeling of admiration in her and had repelled her to an equal degree. In the end, it had alienated her so completely that she had buried him with a total absence of emotion.

"I take it you weren't too fond of him."

Lord's voice jerked her back to the present. "I spent twenty-one years trying to find the father inside the man," she said, "and failed. When he died, I felt as if a crushing weight had been lifted from my shoulders. Nothing more." She broke off, embarrassed at having shown him this intimate glimpse of herself and surprised that she had felt prompted to do so. "So, you see, I *can* understand the fear you mentioned. I carried it around inside me a long, long time."

He had never ceased to watch her. He said enigmatically, "A strange woman," and was more personal with his voice than before.

There was a faint deepening of color at the base of her throat. "I suppose I am," she confessed. "But aren't we all strange in one way or another? Depending upon the angle from which we're viewed, of course!" She gave a little laugh. "Looked at head-on, as we see ourselves, we usually appear quite ordinary. It's the little, crooked angles that reveal our little, crooked quirks."

He permitted his droll humor to surface briefly. "Then we'd be better off with the head-on view, wouldn't we?"

"It's generally the most reassuring," Fresno agreed, and laughed again. Suddenly the irony of this personal exchange struck her and turned her sober. It had happened so naturally that she had been unaware of it, as if they had, by common consent, dropped their rapiers, and come close to engage in conversation.

He was facing front now, watching the grassland wave under the pressure of the wind that breathed across this upland plain. On a mutual impulse the horses broke into a measured canter, carrying them deeper and deeper into the tawny sea, and all this while she watched him. At first she permitted herself only darting glances but as he became more and more engrossed in his thoughts, she held her eyes fixed on him, studying him from boot to hairline. And thus openly examining the superb reach of his body, she felt herself responding to the pull of an animal magnetism stronger than any she had ever felt. It emanated from him in a series of heavy pulsations, like the numbing beat of a giant drum.

In this state of increasing arousal she saw him pull up without warning and lay his intense gaze on her. A dozen yards onward, she brought her mare to a stand and swung about, wondering at his actions. For the space of a dozen heartbeats he sat there regarding her in thoughtful silence, and there was that in his manner that told her as plainly as spoken words that he had not at any time been unaware of her steady watching. It lent the merest suggestion of amusement to his lips, and she realized all at once that it was something he definitely wanted her to see. He made a sweeping motion, indicating the surrounding terrain.

"Isn't this my northern range?"

She hitched around in the saddle to trace the eastern line of hills with an extended arm. "Your line follows the hills. The river marks your western boundary. There's no better graze in Star Valley, which is one of the things I wanted to talk to you about."

He said, without ceasing to study the designated boundaries, "Talk away, ma'am."

"This has always been used by Star for winter range. The storms glance across here, leaving it wonderfully open all winter. Then, too, the lay of the hills makes ideal hunting for Jesse Whitehead."

Lord glanced around. "Whitehead? Is he your hunter?"

"The best in the world," Fresno said, and meant it. "If you were to ride through those hills over there, you'd find them carpeted with skeletons of cougar, wolf, bear, coyote, wildcat, and lynx . . . all Jesse's doing."

Remembering the gaunt old man's quick eyes and steady hands, Lord nodded. "And you'd like to go on using this section of range during the winter months. Is that it?"

"Only until you get your own herd," Fresno corrected him. "I'm not asking you to make me a gift of it, of course. I'll pay you whatever you ask, either in seed stock, beef, or cash."

He considered the proposal briefly. "I see nothing wrong with it."

"And what sort of payment do you prefer?"

He gave her a long, thoughtful look. "Seed stock," he said finally. "Yearling heifers. What percentage did you have in mind?"

"Does one to one hundred sound fair?"

"Fair enough. How many head will you winter here?"

"Close to six thousand."

Lord gave a low whistle. He ran a skeptical look around the territory under discussion. "I'd not think it would hold that many."

"They range south and east on your property, depending on the snow and the trouble we catch from the cats and such like. Jesse sets the boundaries. This is merely the main holding ground, so to speak."

He nodded, at once grasping the general outline of the operation. And then his brows drew down to a sharp V as he voiced a last stipulation. "I'll have to have a bonus."

It was her turn to be surprised. "A *bonus*, Mr. Lord? What did you have in mind?"

He maintained his scowling expression. "Pelts."

"*Pelts?*"

He nodded. "Unless I get a bearskin and a wolfhide, the deal's off."

"Oh, for heaven's sake!" Fresno exclaimed. She saw him grinning at her and realized that he had been deliberately baiting her. "You can have a dozen of each," she laughed. "With another round dozen wildcat and lynx as a bonus to the bonus. There's no fur quite so beautiful as prime lynx, by the way. I've a magnificent coat made out of pelts Jesse gave me two years ago. I feel like the Empress of Austria every time I wear it."

"And look the part, I'll wager," Lord said, and seemed to await her reaction with less than his customary stolid reserve.

A faint run of color laid its fleeting change across her face, and she gave a short laugh. "Thank you, kind sir," she said, and lowered her gaze to her hands, suddenly uncomfortable under his direct eyes. She shortened her reins and turned north, speaking over her shoulder. "If you'd care to see me to the hallowed and fiercely guarded borders of Star, I'll reveal my second sinister plot as we wend our way onward, m'Lord."

The word-play on his name was not lost on him, and she caught the brilliant flash of his smile and heard his hearty laugh ring out as he put the stallion alongside. "Shoot," he directed, and added quickly, "only in a manner of speaking, of course!"

"It's another lease arrangement I have in mind," Fresno told him, as they again moved out across the plain. "I'd like to use your stallion on some of my better mares."

She said it hesitantly, and his amusement at her self-consciousness was something he did not try to hide. He said drily, "So, you finally figured out how to latch onto him, I see."

Her laugh was a free and warm sound. "You never doubted I'd have my way in the end, did you?"

"About what?"

"The stallion, of course. That's what we're talking about, isn't it?"

Lord did not reply, but rode along in silence another little while. Suddenly he looked around, a half-smile creasing one corner of his mouth. "I'm not sure," he drawled. "Is it?"

Fresno's face flamed, and she dropped the looped reins to the mare's neck and ducked her head in a show of fastening her already securely anchored hat. She kept adjusting and readjusting the plumed headgear until she had regained her composure. But even when she picked up her reins again she would not look at him. "Well? Can I make a deal for the horse?"

"He's not leaving my place."

"All right. The mares will be brought to him."

"How many?"

"I'd thought twelve next spring."

"And I'm to get my pick of every third foal."

"That's fair enough."

"Done."

Fresno gave a sigh of relief. "That was too easy and too quick," she said then, turning suspicious. "What bonus are you thinking of this time?"

He did not look at her, but again his faint smile came and went. He said enigmatically, "Never mind for now. I'll come up with one," and once more smiled to himself. He drew up a dozen paces onward and sat looking around him. Something that was almost a scowl changed his expression, and when he looked at her his eyes were thoughtful. "This empire you rule, ma'am, how much does it mean to you?"

The question caught her off guard. "Why," she said slowly, "everything, I guess. Without it I wouldn't be me." She paused, then made a helpless gesture with her hands. "Why do you ask?"

"And if changes came, could you adjust, do you think?"

"Changes?"

"People coming in, roads cutting through here, miners and settlers throwing up cabins. Things like that."

"Why," Fresno mused, "I doubt I would like it much, but on the other hand it really wouldn't affect me. You see, you were wrong the other day. Star graze is all deeded land west of the river. Over thirty thousand acres." She broke off, realizing there was good reason for his curiosity. "Why do you ask?"

He shrugged. "It's just that I've been on the road for almost a year, looking the country over. Wherever I went, I found people moving west—streams of them. Nothing ever stays the same for long. I've a feeling you'll see some changes here before too long. There are too many hungry people headed this way."

Fresno threw her head back and laughed again, but this time there was a false ring to it. She sobered at once. "Mr. Lord, are you trying to frighten me?"

He shook his head. "Forewarned is forearmed," he said quietly, and put the stallion into motion.

They were nearing the lake now, and as they skirted it, Lord spied the cabin set back in the pines and once more halted. "Pretty," he murmured. "Is this on my land?"

In that moment Fresno realized for the first time that her personal retreat was in fact no longer hers. The discovery rendered her speechless, and she felt tears start to her eyes. "Yes," she managed to say. "Yes, it is. I'll move my things out tomorrow."

"Your things?" Lord turned surprised eyes on her. "You mean this is your *home*?

"My hideaway. Ever since I was a little girl it's been my private retreat."

He studied her soberly for a long moment, then slowly shook his head. "Keep it," he said curtly. "Some things aren't meant to be passed back and forth. A person's house is one of them."

She showed him a tremulous smile. "You're very kind. I'm sure you must think me a silly goose, but this spot has always been very special to me."

"Then let it stay that way, ma'am."

Quite suddenly they had nothing more to say to each other. It was a fact that came to them simultaneously and turned them awkward. Their glances met and fell away and they both turned and studiously examined the cabin and the surrounding area as if searching for something. It was one of the most unwieldy moments of Fresno's life, and in a blind attempt to shift it back into balance she rode into the shallows of the lake to let her mare drink. She said quite casually from her turned-away position, "I thank you for my retreat," and turned back to shore, her eyes going to him and holding his steadily. "You will be welcome, should you care to call."

"Do you come here often, ma'am?"

He said it idly, but there was a tentative, waiting note in his voice, as though he were expecting something unpleasant to happen and had prepared for it by assuming an air of indifference. It told her quite plainly that while he understood the meaning implicit in her statement, he would advance no further without additional reassurance from her. "Quite often," she said, and heard her voice come out unevenly. "As a matter of fact, I'll be spending the next few nights here. I sometimes do that when I'm working out a problem."

"You've one bothering you now, ma'am?"

She bent and readjusted the strap that held the lariat in place below her bent right knee. "I'm sure it will work itself out before long."

His next question issued from his dry lips in a thin, unsteady thread of sound. "Would the problem have anything to do with me, Mrs. Taggert?"

"It could have a great deal to do with you," Fresno murmured. "I mention it in case you were to ride this way and see a light."

"Mightn't someone else see your light?"

She shook her head. "It's forbidden ground. No one is allowed within a mile of it without my express permission."

When he spoke again, the same hesitant, waiting note was evident in his voice. "You make it sound almost like an invitation, Mrs. Taggert."

"You'll be welcome any time, Mr. Lord. Is that better?"

"You're sure?"

"Quite sure."

He took up his reins. "A strange woman," he said for the second time. "I've not met another like you."

A half smile lengthened her lips. "Does it bother you, my strangeness?"

"*Bother* me?"

"Disturb you, then."

"Yes," Lord murmured. "Yes, it disturbs me."

Fresno forced herself to go on looking into his enigmatic eyes. "In what way, Mr. Lord?"

"I'd better not say, ma'am."

"Do, please."

He started to speak, then firmed his lips and shook his head. "I wish I understood you better."

"That eventuality rests with you, Mr. Lord."

He gave a thoughtful nod, his gaze wandering over her gracefully erect body in its close-fitting riding habit. "Then, I'll see you again," he said, and went on studying her with an unmistakable purposefulness in his opaque eyes. "Soon," he added, and lifted the stallion with a feather-light hand in a pivot that set it squarely down on its backtrail. The powerful haunches bunched, and the grey surged into a run around the lake and out across the wind-ruffled grass.

But it was three days before Lord rode back up the valley. He sat straight in the saddle, pleasantly conscious of the feel of his relatively new doeskin pants and light blue linen shirt, and increasingly excited over the prospect of his rendezvous with the auburn-haired mistress of Star. Twice he had failed to appear, despite a conviction that she was waiting for him.

He circled the lake and entered the pines and felt the serenity of the setting at once soothe his tightly strung nerves. If Fresno Taggert had been seeking seclusion, she could not have made a happier choice, he mused as he drew up before the cabin. The area felt completely shut off from the rest of the valley.

He turned and looked back over the way he had come at the black line of hills to the east. Crouched in those wild and lonely hills, he knew, were the dwellings of those who had twice sought to invade Star Valley, and who would try again. Held at bay by Star's constant patrolling, the MacKays, the Shadleys, the Hallers, and others prowled incessantly, and watched and planned.

They were a shiftless breed of men he had studied all his life, and he knew their ways. Even in the east, they held to an unvarying outline, and he faced the discouraging fact that they always would. There would always be the few who dreamed and created, and the many who schemed to rape and destroy.

And this time he was a part of the savage pattern by virtue of his claim to the disputed territory. In taking over these twenty thousand acres of open graze, he had supplanted Star in the eyes of the hostile hill people. Nor would the legality of his rights serve to lessen that hostility one whit. Being what they were, those people would merely transfer their animosity to him.

All these musings created their counterweight to the excitement that had prompted him to don his best clothes and ride out eagerly to this secret trysting place. Not even his vivid recall of Fresno Taggert's flawless features and inviting body could wholly counter this sensation of being slowly and dangerously hemmed in by those forces that sooner or later would move down upon him out of the concealing hills. That they would come, he had no doubt. He felt it like the chill of winter. Whether their coming would find him competent to stand against them, he did not know. He knew only that he would stand. He had searched through too much emptiness, had reached too often for handholds that each time crumbled into nothingness under his touch, to have any illusions about a firmer security lying just beyond the forever-receding horizon.

Sitting the stallion there under the trees, he pulled himself away from these unwelcome thoughts, noting that dusk was piling thickly around him and rolling out over the valley below. He reined around the end of the cabin, dismounted, and turned the stallion into the corral that abutted the rear wall. He was fastening the gate when the grey loosed a sudden shrill neigh and wheeled to the far fence, there to stand avidly sifting the air with belled nostrils and busily working ears. A moment later he caught the sound of a horse taking the trail off the rim of the wall and knew that Fresno Taggert was once again coming to resume her vigil.

His frame stiffened as he stood in near-darkness listening to that distant horse come steadily down through the night. He waited until the sounds told him that the horse was almost to level ground, then went around to the door. A moment later he glimpsed the wide blaze of the mare emerge from the solid darkness under the trees. Then horse and rider were directly in front of him and the woman's low greeting came down to him through the gloom.

"Good evening, Mr. Lord."

"Evening, ma'am." He stepped close, arms lifted to assist her in dismounting, and heard the rustle of her skirts as she disengaged her right leg from the saddle's rest. She was then a tangible warmth swaying out and down into his hands.

She said, "Thank you," and retained her hold on the saddle, remaining half turned away from him. It was a moment of awkwardness that completely altered the tenor of this meeting, putting a silence and a distance between them, even while his hands still encircled her waist. "It was good of you to come," she murmured then, and slowly released her grip on the saddle.

She was free to turn toward him; but she did not, and this hesitancy on her part further deepened the strangeness of the meeting. He let his hands drop and swallowed audibly, and his voice sounded curiously hollow. "I meant to come that first night."

"But you didn't." She laughed self-consciously. "I really didn't intend my invitation as a command, you know."

"Oh," he said clumsily, "I didn't take it that way, I intended to come, all along."

His nearness inhibited her, and she attempted to speak lightly. "Shall we go in? There's a candle inside."

She went past him, then, leading the way into the utter blackness of the cabin's interior.

"The candle is on the mantle, I believe."

He crossed and touched a match to the wick and waited there with his back turned until the flickering light steadied. Dropping the match into the fireplace, he turned and saw her watching him from near the door. In the faint light her face showed starkly white under the cloud of glowing hair, and he was again struck by her beauty and by the slender reach of her full-bosomed body. Awareness of the purpose of this meeting pushed quickly through him and he became more and more conscious of the hard pounding of blood through his veins and of a simultaneous shortening of his breath. These same signs showed in her, turning her swiftly more exciting and challenging, and the effect of this on him was so immediate and so powerful that he was plunged into a purely sensual state of urgency, no longer objectively appraising her as a possible source of gratification but prematurely reveling in the feel of her flesh enclosing his. The realness of this lurid imagery fired the nerves and muscles in his groin and became a demanding pressure against the close confinement of his pants. He was aware of this involuntary arousal, knew that it must be unmistakably evident to the woman, and did not care.

On the point of going to her, he saw her eyes drop to that overt signaling of his readiness and immediately recoil with an expression of shock. Her gaze lifted to meet his aroused stare. Change went all through her, stiffening her and closing her away from him.

In growing puzzlement he watched her swing the door shut behind her and slowly pace down the room where deeper shadows lay. He heard her say, "I have selected the mares—" and suddenly laughed with a harshness that whirled her around. She said, "I—" and fell silent as he stepped to the table that occupied the center of the small room.

145

"Your pardon, ma'am," he said with cold formality. "I wasn't aware you'd invited me here to continue our little business discussion." He made a mocking bow and indicated the chair opposite him. "Shall we sit down and have a cup of tea—before we fuck?"

Her head snapped back as if he had slapped her. "Must you be so crude? There's—"

He threw his voice roughly at her. "Are you always so dishonest with yourself, Mrs. Taggert?"

The harshness of his voice knocked all composure out of her. She went deathly pale and half fell back against the wall, and pressed her hands flat against the logs to hold herself erect. Her eyes closed as they had in that moment of unbearable humiliation during their first meeting, and she rolled her head wordlessly back and forth. She said woodenly, "I'm so sorry. I thought I could—" and stopped, unable to force her voice from her constricted throat. She put a hand to her throat. The silence of the room became a cold and alien thing that clamped around them and held them helpless.

In this soundless void her voice, when it finally came, sounded shallow and toneless, as though she were merely saying meaningless words, with no hope of their being believed. "Until I met you, I felt no need of a man, Mr. Lord. Our meeting changed that. But it was not merely the animal part of me responding to the animal in you. I sensed so strongly something about you altogether different from any other man I've ever known."

Her voice grew weaker and weaker, and ceased altogether. She brushed her hand over her eyes, as if forcibly opening them, and was then looking straight at him. It required the greatest effort on her part to speak again.

"Whatever you may think of me, I am a chaste woman, Mr. Lord. I have never before invited a man ... led a man to think—" She could not finish. She breathed jerkily, and forced herself to go on. "I have never done this before. I always considered such a thing unthinkable, until I met you. I thought you could help me but I was wrong. I misjudged you even more badly than I misjudged myself. I think I am sorriest of all for that."

Lord leaned his weight on his arms, his big hands flat against the table top. "I am not a wild animal, Mrs. Taggert," he said in a suppressed voice.

She flinched, and her eyes closed again, but only for an instant. "Have I inferred that you were?"

"You have."

"Then I have put myself in that same class, have I not?"

He rejected this with a slow shake of the head. "You don't really believe that."

He was, she realized then, a man of far greater complexity than she had suspected, and he would never follow her along ways of her choosing. She said with more feeling than before, "I will not argue with you. You may be right. I will confess that at first I thought only of your body, which makes me the animal, not you. And I am deeply ashamed."

He was not satisfied with that. "Of what you felt? Or of what you are?"

"Both," she answered. "I find no cause for pride in letting myself be governed by lust, nor in seeking to use another's body for the sole purpose of satisfying my own."

In all this while she had not altered her taut stance. She remained pressed flat against the wall as Lord circled the table and crossed to her; but her eyes followed his every movement, and when he stopped within reach of her, she looked up at him with an expression of desperation.

"What do you want from me, Mrs. Taggert?" Lord asked quietly.

She strained back against the rough logs, the pulse at the base of her throat frantically beating. "Nothing," she whispered. "I can give you nothing, nor share anything with you."

"Why not?"

"Your contempt for me and for everything I stand for is something I cannot bear. I had not realized until now how much you hate what I stand for." Her voice sank to the thinnest thread of sound. "Please . . . please go."

She waited in an agony of suspense, but he did not move, and when she would have turned to the door, he placed a hand against the log on either side of her head, shutting off escape. "No," he murmured. "Not until I've had what I came for."

One of his hands brushed against her hair, and that infinitesimal contact acted as the catalyst that freed her from her state of near-hypnosis. Her rage was a holocaust sweeping up from deep inside her, ridding her of all fear, robbing her of all dignity. Her right hand flashed up and caught him a hard, open-handed blow across the face. "How dare you?" she blazed. "No man—"

Her words were cut off by his swift reaction. He seized her shoulders and shook her with a savagery that brought her hair whipping about her face and shoulders. He released one of her shoulders and slapped her with a strength that twisted her half around and sent her reeling along the wall. Blinded by her whipping cloud of hair, she brought up hard against the end wall and whirled to face him. She was genuinely afraid of him now, and would have fled; but he was on her like a great cat, throwing his arms wide to imprison her against the logs. His body was an ungiving barrier, pressing her back, its placement against her an unmistakable forewarning of his intent. In brightest panic she strained her head back and stared dumbly up into his aroused face.

"You wanted something from me," he said hoarsely. "Now, by God, you're going to have it."

He advanced his pelvis, deliberately letting her feel the hardness of his growing erection, and after a brief pause felt her almost imperceptible response. Knowing he could have his way with her here and now, he experienced a mighty upsurge of confidence such as he had never known—had never hoped to know. It altered his masklike expression and stretched his lips into a slow, knowing smile, and caused him to push his elongated hardness against her with a motion that was a blatant statement of intent.

A moan slid out of her and his smile became wider and more confident as her breathing took up a swifter in-and-out run. He was now rigidly erect against her, his need a tumulting pressure in his groin that verged on actual pain.

He moved his hands so that his palms rested nakedly against the slender column of her neck. His thumbs came together to form a V in the hollow below her throat where the pulse so swiftly beat. For a timeless moment she stared up at him, then lifted her hands and exerted a steady pressure against his chest; but when he slipped his hands down to her waist and swayed her closer, she came without resistance.

Their response to each other was now a definitely sexual thing that deepened their breathing and held them yearningly pressed together. She said tremulously, "Aaron?" and lifted her face more fully to him. His head came down, his mouth opened over hers, and she gave a low moan and lifted her arms to encircle his neck. Their breathing quickened still more and became a shallow, unsteady thing, and the slow movement of their hips set up a dreamlike motion of their shadows on the wall. Fresno whispered wonderingly, "You're like a great shadow engulfing me," and was silent, trying to pierce the depths of his gaze to find what lay hidden there. "Please be gentle. I am very afraid."

His answering whisper breathed past her ear. "Don't be afraid. I couldn't hurt you . . . not now."

Her bodice parted under his hands and hung free from her upraised arms, and then the voluminous skirts cascaded down and formed a shimmering pool of greenness about her feet. Under his deft fingers the corset strings slipped from their moorings. In the next moment she was fully disrobed.

He would have continued to caress her then, but in the impatience of her need she fumbled hastily at his shirt, and when it dropped to the floor she unbuckled his belt and worked at the buttons of his pants until they, too, slipped downward. He toed his moccasins off and was naked in front of her. Bending, he lifted her easily and carried her to the bunk at the far end of the room.

She was a trembling shape in the deeper darkness here, and he knelt and caressingly explored the rounded contours and the deep hollows of her body with knowing hands, and when this exploration continued to the point of unbearable desire, she clutched his arms and pulled him onto the bunk and over her, and grew motionless under him, waiting.

13

Lila MacKay was halfway up the side of the steep ridge when the cow's plaintive bawling came to her above the rush of her horse's labored breathing. She at once halted and waited. When it came a second time she fixed the source as immediately beyond the ridge she was climbing and continued at once upward, to top out on a narrow escarpment that dropped sheer to the floor of the box canyon a hundred feet below.

She was not surprised by the scene she viewed. An hour back she had read the fresh sign of cattle on the move and had followed it just long enough to ascertain the direction of movement before cutting across country to intercept it here.

She drifted in behind a clump of cedars and made her count and discovered that she had erred in her estimate of the herd by exactly twelve head. A hundred and fifty prime Star beef were bunched tiredly in the blind draw, gaunt flanks and slobber-trailing nostrils eloquent testimony of a fast, sustained drive through rough country.

The cow whose bawling had drawn Lila to the spot stood off to one side looking back over the way the herd had come, the while she repeatedly voiced her distress in sustained bursts of anguish. Somewhere along that backtrail, Lila knew, the brute's calf, unable to maintain the killing pace of the drive, had been abandoned, and the thread of motherhood ran strongly from this isolated canyon to that remembered place and held the cow facing that direction like a compass needle holding to its northern pole.

Listening to that stream of misery pouring endlessly through the hills, Lila experienced a profound disgust for the men responsible, and at once decided on a course of action. She rode along the hogback until she found a break in the wall's sheer face and sent her horse downward in a dangerous descent that laid her almost flat over its croup.

She struck level ground with a jolt that rocked her forward and ran in under the trees screening the canyon's lower end. Coming into the open, she saw, a hundred yards away, the three dismounted riders. They were between her and the herd, and they were facing toward her, alarm evident in their attitudes.

There was a brief run of time in which no one moved or spoke, and then one of the men lifted a hand in greeting while another, just beyond him, turned away and lifted his rifle. Lila saw the barrel swing up and steady on the distant bawling cow. She yelled, "Titus!" and jumped her horse into a run that took her past the first two men and around in front of the rifleman. She dragged her horse to a plunging halt and swung to face the nonplussed man. "Put it away, Titus," she said. "That's not called for."

Anger was a redness in the man's face. He took a step to one side, again bringing the gun up. He said, "Get the hell out of the way, Lila," and started to sight along the barrel, only to have her block his view a second time. He jerked the weapon down and laid his angry glance on the girl. "Now, goddammit," he said loudly, "you do that just once more, and I'll haul you off that goddamned horse and slap the shit out of you. Hear me?"

"You'll play hell," Lila told him, and rode over to the cow, keeping herself squarely in Titus Matlock's line of fire. She spooked the cow toward the tree-screened exit, and with the animal safely out of sight, wheeled and rode back to the three men, fully aware of the anger she had kindled in them. "Titus,"

151

she observed, drawing up and looking down at the man, "you're a cold-blooded bastard. You know that?"

"Who the hell are you?" Titus Matlock demanded. "Little Bo Peep, motherin' her sheep?"

"Lila," John Matlock broke in, "you ever try mindin' your own damned business—jest to find out what it's like?"

"Dry up," Lila told this one. "Every time you open your mouth, I get an earache."

The man thus addressed grinned and hitched up his pants. He came close and laid a hand on Lila's knee. "Speaking' o' aches," he drawled, "I got one right now; and it ain't in my ear." His hand slid upward, kneading the muscles of her thigh. "Why don't you climb down, an' the two of us take a little stroll over to that there clump o' sumac?"

Lila was smiling thoughtfully down at him, as if considering the proposition. "I have a better idea," she suggested pleasantly. "Why don't you lie down while I ride back and forth over the top of you?"

With the last word, she lifted her foot, placed it flat against the man's chest, and snapped her leg straight. John Matlock was propelled backward as if ejected from a catapult. He backpeddled frantically for a half-dozen steps, tripped on his spurs, and sprawled on his back. His yell was drowned out by the raucous hooting of his brothers, and before he could scramble up, Lila jumped her horse after him and brought it to a halt directly over him.

He yelled again and clawed his way into the clear, convinced that Lila meant to carry out her suggestion. But when she made no further move, he got to his feet, beating the dust from his clothes. He threw her a glowering look. "Damned she-wolf! What the hell's got into you, all of a sudden . . . pullin' a stunt like that?"

Lila sat there grinning down at him. "Next time, maybe you'll show a little more respect for a lady," she told him, and then could no longer suppress her mirth. She let her head fall back and loosed a shout of laughter that bounced back and forth between the walls of the narrow canyon.

She ignored him after that, reining around and winking at the two men whose amusement over their luckless brother's defeat had subsided from deafening guffaws to broad grins. All three of them were well known to her. All three had been recipients of her favors in the past, and her association with them often had been marked by just this kind of rough horseplay. Now it suddenly came to her that she was completely disinterested in them. For the first time she was seeing them for what they were—a trio of unshaven, unkempt, thoroughly disreputable riffraff with no single saving grace that she could put a name to. With something akin to shame she asked herself how she could ever have allowed herself to be physically involved with them.

But she let none of this show as she relaxed in her saddle and simulated the old air of casual camaraderie that had marked their former relationship. Her purpose in following them here was to discover the destination of this latest stolen herd. She said carelessly, "I'll give you a hand shoving this little gather onto the trail, as long as it doesn't take me out of my way," and alertly awaited their reply.

Titus Matlock nodded and squinted up at the sun. "Obliged," he grunted, and went to his horse. He took a moment to tighten the girth, then stepped aboard. "We could use another hand for a ways. Don't look like Balaam an' your old man's gonna show up like they said." He glanced impatiently around at his brothers. "Well, come alive, you two," he ordered. "Settin' here on our asses ain't gittin' us any closer to Silverton."

The three men were halfway to the bunched herd, with Lila following on their heels, when two riders burst through the trees at the lower end of the canyon and came pounding up.

Lila recognized her father and Balaam Shadley and knew from the way they were bearing directly down on her that she was in for it. Douglas MacKay rushed in and hauled his blowing horse to a halt, so close that Lila's own mount reared and plunged aside, while Balaam Shadley ranged up on her other side to neatly box her in. She put her level glance on her father and let a mild temper show in her words. "Why don't you just ride on over the top of me, for God's sake?"

MacKay had the ruddy color characteristic of redheads, and anger unfailingly turned his face a mottled crimson. He was a large, raw man who contained a wealth of power in his frame; but his pale green eyes had a way of sliding away from whomever he was talking to, and when he spoke, he invariably sounded a shade too purposeful to be convincing.

But now his gaze was fixed hard on Lila, and the anger in him came out and struck brutally at her. "All right, damn you. I'll hear about that little trip you made into town awhile back. *All* about it."

Lila could use her own voice unkindly when crossed. "You'll hear a hell of a lot of things you hadn't counted on me knowing anything about if you don't watch yourself!" she flared back at him, and dragged her horse away, deliberately ramming into Shadley. "Get the hell out of my way before I run you down!"

MacKay's eyes widened, and for an instant he was speechless in the face of the girl's blazing defiance. He went red with rage, then, and his voice came out in a shout. "God damn you! I'll learn you to talk back to me!" His arm swung out in a looping blow that would have knocked her out of the saddle, had it landed. But she swayed back out of reach, and the momentum of the swing pulled MacKay halfway around.

He was completely off balance and awkwardly striving to right himself atop his nervously plunging horse when Lila caught her own horse hard and unexpectedly with both spurs. It grunted and lunged forward, knocking MacKay's horse to its knees. She heard Shadley yell, "Close in here, boys! Head her off, dammit!" and out of the corner of her eye saw him haul his horse about and grab wildly for her reins. Her spurs stabbed again, and the gelding's powerful haunches propelled it forward, straight into MacKay's floundering mount. The luckless animal crashed over onto its side in a billowing cloud of dust as the sorrel gelding shot past, making for the lower end of the box canyon.

Flat along the neck of her racing horse, Lila threw a glance over her shoulder and saw the three Matlocks and Shadley fan wide of MacKay's downed horse and come streaking after her. She heard her father's strangled bellow of fury and glimpsed him staggering to his feet behind the curtain of dust, and then she faced forward and set herself to outrun her pursuers.

She was into the trees and through them before the three riders had covered half that distance. Once free of the canyon walls she gave all her attention to the trail which was boulder-strewn and occasionally half blocked by brush and deadfalls. But a lifetime of riding such trails had given her a faultless sense of timing and a judgment of distances that made her handling of her wildly running mount wholly automatic. In a race on open ground, she was a formidable opponent, over terrain such as this, she was matchless. Within a mile she had so hopelessly outdistanced her pursuers that they broke off the chase and glumly returned to the canyon and the profane beratings of Douglas MacKay.

Knowing herself safe, Lila eased the gelding down from its straining run and shortly dropped off the trail onto a timbered bench. Here she drew up to let the horse regain its wind, and thereafter made her leisurely way southward along a route that would bring her to the old Bland place.

She arrived just at sundown to find the house deserted and the stallion missing from its corral. The two dogs accompanied her as far as the stable with solemnly waving tails, then returned to their sentry posts on either side of the back porch. She spent awhile firming up her friendship with the filly, who had wandered up from the lower graze ahead of its dam, then crossed the yard and entered the house.

In the kitchen she noted the few dishes left to soak in the pan of water on the stove and absently tested the temperature of the water. It was still warm. The stove still radiated a faint heat.

This was the second time in five days she had found Lord absent, and, starting into the main room, she stopped and considered this fact carefully.

That there was a woman she did not for an instant doubt. Self-deception was so foreign to her that she did not even try to delude herself into believing Lord was in love with her. Nor did she consider herself a woman wronged. From the outset of their relationship she had taken the initiative.

Admitting all this, she admitted too that Lord had somehow

altered her. She had only to recall her recent confrontation with
the three Matlocks to be convinced of this. Whereas before, she
had regarded them as enjoyable partners in the ribald game of
sex, she had found herself looking at them this afternoon with
something bordering on contempt.

The barring of them from her sphere of activities occasioned
Lila no slightest regret, for no single one of them had ever
aroused any emotion in her other than one of transient physical
desire. Neither, for that matter, had any of the other men with
whom she had disported herself, with the possible exception of
Dave Moline. From the first, his overbearing arrogance had
posed a challenge. In him she saw a worthy opponent, as well as a
highly satisfactory sex partner, two necessary components in her
estimation. But the man's complete selfishness precluded any
possibility of the relationship's ever maturing beyond ephemeral
physical involvement.

She brought herself up short, mildly put out with Moline for
having intruded upon her thinking at this juncture. She returned
to Lord, and found herself wondering whether she were in love
with him. Almost immediately she ran into a blank wall. There
was no way of telling whether she loved him, because she had no
idea at all of what it meant to be in love. Whatever affection she
had felt for others had been wholly surface, wholly transitory.
She had been altogether truthful in telling her stepmother that
she had never really thought about her feelings for the woman.
For her father she felt only cold indifference tinged with contempt. Refusing to give herself to others, she had never experienced the joy of receiving. Hence, there was no criterion for
assessing the scope of her affection for the half-breed.

In the end she knew only that she felt curiously alone and
vaguely frightened at her discovery that Lord apparently had
found her lacking in some respect, and abandoned her for another.

She thought, *I'll have to find out who it is. Maybe then* . . . Her
glance took in the front window where red curtains now framed
a view of the yard. She was across the room in four long strides

and lifting one of the panels to examine the hem. A single look revealed a straight line of neat stitching which Lord's big fingers never could have mastered. Her eyes lost their focus; she became absolutely still, searching for the owner of the hands that had wielded the needle with such deftness.

She thought of Estelle Rogers, the town's seamstress, and rejected that possibility at once. The woman would have slashed her wattled throat rather than consent to touch material belonging to a half-breed. She mentally ticked off the names of the valley woman who might conceivably have done the work. Mary Gilstrap? Impossible. She was the wife of a Star man, as were Joyce Patton and Lorena Ranger. Those three made up the sum total of possible candidates for this bit of needlework.

"Except for Fresno Taggert, of course," Lila said, and laughed outright at the idea of the haughty beauty performing any such menial chore for the likes of Aaron Lord.

But no sooner had she thus summarily dismissed the idea than she snatched it back and examined it more closely. She said in a thoughtful murmur, "Or *would* she, now? I wonder," and at once summoned the woman before her mind's eye.

Fresno Taggert was all woman. Of that Lila was certain. All her life she had considered herself Fresno's inferior in every respect. She was, therefore, determined to discover at least one flaw in all that perfection. Yet, seemingly there was none to be found. Except for a studied air of indifference toward men, Star's mistress embodied everything that Lila deemed the epitome of grace, charm, beauty, position, and integrity—everything, indeed, that Lila was not and could never become.

And then she had discovered that that air of indifference was nothing more than a pose. To Lila's probing gaze the woman betrayed herself every time she was in the company of men, in ways so obvious that Lila marveled that others did not detect them.

A naked hunger shone in the violet eyes each time they flicked swiftly over a man before the heavy lashes modestly shuttered them. It swung the high-bosomed body instantly away whenever a man approached too closely. It constricted the slender throat and laid a chill over the normally warm voice each time the speaker addressed an arresting figure of a man.

And to Lila, the fact that Fresno, who until her husband's departure for war had reigned supreme as the belle of every ball, had absented herself from all such gatherings for six long years, told her all she needed to know about that seemingly cold woman. Despising her body for the threat it posed to her peace of mind, Fresno refused to expose it to temptation by steadfastly playing the role of a frigid recluse.

To Lila alone, whose deep sensuality rendered her so acutely sensitive to the subtlest of sexual responses in others, the haughty woman was an open book. Long ago she had pierced the smooth façade and glimpsed the unsated female crouched fearfully behind it.

But for some strange reason, Lila, whose spiteful tongue could wreak such havoc with the characters of those ill-advised enough to cross her, had revealed nothing of her findings to another living soul. One thing alone had preserved Fresno's character intact: her unwavering reserve. Had she slipped even once—had she given the tall hill girl any reason at all to suspect that she had slipped—she would have been destroyed without mercy, instantly and utterly. But this had not happened. Hence her secret had been safe—until now.

Somehow, Aaron Lord had made the selfsame discovery.

Standing at the window, clutching the curtain until her knuckles turned white under the tanned skin, she thought in an agony of desolation: *I'm not ready to give him up so soon. Not yet!* and heard a stifled and terrible weeping tremble the silence of the empty room.

14

At the moment Lila stepped from her horse and walked forward to greet the curious grey filly, Lord was dismounting in front of the lake cabin five miles away. He smiled at the woman framed in the doorway. "Hello, Fresno."

"Good evening, Aaron."

She took in the sight of man and horse, appreciating the little tableau they presented. "You suit each other," she said. "Completely." When he merely looked his puzzlement at the compliment, she smilingly explained. "You should always ride a stallion, and it should always be a grey."

He clearly had no experience at all with flattery and it embarrassed him. "Well," he replied awkwardly, "I guess we hit it off pretty well, at that," and was immediately called upon to justify the claim by disciplining the grey which chose that very moment to emit a piercing neigh and fidget around him in a nervous circle. He said, "Stand right there, sir," and reached up to unbuckle the throat strap.

The towering animal froze, but its eyes were rolling whitely, and its nostrils fluttered wide. A shiver racked the muscle-corded frame. To Lord the cause of the animal's agitation was at once apparent. He glanced around. "Is your mare in season?"

"Yes. She's in the corral. But I'll take her out, if you think—"

"No. Just so long as there's a fence between them." Lord grinned. "Unless you wouldn't mind your girl having a summer foal."

Fresno looked startled. "Why do you say that?"

He nodded toward the stallion. "You don't think he goes around in that condition all the time, do you?"

Fresno's face flamed. "Oh!" she gasped. "Oh, my goodness! What can we do?"

Lord was enjoying her embarrassment. "Well," he drawled, "I've an idea or two on that subject, now that you ask."

"You're incorrigible," Fresno informed him, and pointed commandingly at the stallion. "Tie him up. I definitely do not want a summer foal."

"The Emperor isn't one of your rank range studs," Lord replied defensively. "As far as he's concerned, that corral is solid brick and twenty feet high. All he'll do is talk dirty to your prissy miss for a while, then watch for a chance at her later on."

As if to emphasize his master's words, the stallion whirled and bolted around the cabin. An instant later the mare's shrill scream erupted, followed by the sharp cracking of iron-shod hoofs striking the poles of the fence.

"Aaron!" Fresno shouted, genuinely alarmed. "Go catch him and tie him up! He'll make matchsticks of that fence!"

"He'll do no such thing,"

She turned to him. "You're sure?"

His arms encircled her narrow waist and fitted her securely against him. "I know my boy pretty well."

She still was not convinced. "If he makes a liar out of you and gets Nut Maid with foal, I'll—" She paused, trying to think of a punishment sufficiently awful for such a crime. "I'll be mad," she said finally, and gave a shriek as Lord bent and swooped her up and whirled through the door with her.

He crossed the room in three long strides and deposited her on the bed. Whether from exertion or from swiftly risen passion, his voice came out in a breathless growl. "A minute ago you asked what we should do. Here's my answer."

He straightened, and with a dozen swift movements divested himself of his clothes and was stretched out beside her. His head came down, and the enveloping hotness of his seeking mouth closed over hers and sucked the breath out of her, while the knowing fingers of one hand undid the buttons of her confining waist.

Minutes later they were interlocked and breathlessly surrendered to a voracious hunger that found her as impatiently eager to receive him as he was determined to be received, and they merged and moved as one into an area made up solely of the senses—a timeless, mindless area of pure desire that knew no bounds and no reality other than its own.

To Lord, strongly inserting himself into that yielding warmth, it was a miracle of ever-expanding proportions—an ecstasy of self-awareness that forever increased his enjoyment even as it increased his resolve to lay hold on the intangible something hidden beyond the barrier of that welcoming flesh. He had told himself again and again that it was enough merely to possess her thus—to revel in his triumph over the thing that had symbolized his nonexistence as a man all his life. But it was not enough, and he knew it, just as he knew that though she seemed to find complete fulfillment in the act, she, too, sought something beyond his invading flesh—something more enduring than the all-too-transient joining of their two bodies.

He had no name for what he sought so feverishly, and at first he had thought the frustration would surely be laid to rest through possession of this body. But with each new indulgence of his passion it returned to taunt him with its elusive promise.

And so it was that each time he had positioned himself between her waiting thighs and exploringly lowered himself into the insoluble mystery, the act that had commenced as a leisurely probing of that mystery became a challenge against which he pitted himself with all his strength. He must discover it. He must have more of her than this brief, fiery response. And so he drove his formidable weapon into her with a remorselessness that rendered him breathless and empty, but did not satisfy the hunger he could not name.

And Fresno, thrilling anew to the sensations that poured ever more strongly through her each time he penetrated her being, felt it to be a miracle of incredible proportions working itself toward still more majestic wonders inside her—a consummation of all the yearning dreams she had dreamed through all the years of empty waiting. She felt a sense of awe at the realization that the agony of waiting had been in truth a period of preparation for this ultimate reward.

Her three years of marriage to Farley Taggert had offered no single instance that could remotely compare with the electrifying sensations touched off in her by this dark giant's artful lovemaking. Not once had she approached these dizzying heights under Taggert's pantingly futile exertions. Deluded and unfulfilled, she had eventually suppressed her sensuality; but in the intervening years that saw her progress into barren womanhood, it had risen again and again, cruelly reminding her that she was inwardly more wanton than any woman of the streets, for all her apparent chastity.

And then the day had come that had found her halfway across the bleak expanse of her thirtieth year and pausing, still-caught, to watch a dark and alien shape immerge into the reality which her long-denied hungers had led her to picture. In the instant Aaron Lord had first touched her she had known that she would be led by him into palpitant danger. It had been that definite.

Now, with the emptiness of those years so swiftly forgotten, she asked herself how she had sensed in that first fleeting instant that it had been this moody, withdrawn half-breed whose arrival she had awaited all this time. Everything in her aristocratic heritage cried out against it. The social mores of the time forbade it. Tradition, which had for generations seen the descendants of the first Star engraved on the scroll of the elect, could brook no such degrading act of miscegenation. And Christian dogma itself decreed that she must hold herself inviolate from males of Lord's caste. For while the bedding of females of inferior origin by men of her race was regarded as understandable, the white woman who cohabited with a male of that same lowly origin was guilty of sinning against both God and society.

All this she knew, and yet . . . something had passed from Lord to her, and she had willfully turned her back on it all to follow the unsuspected and wholly overpowering promptings of her deeper nature.

A dozen nights such as this had found them joined in passionate coupling, with only the briefest of respites. In breathless unison they had explored and discovered and explored anew, and briefly slept, only to pursue the search even in the depths of sleep.

And now another search was underway—another seeking out of the elusive mother lode—another series of titillating strikes which must surely culminate in the discovery of the richest and deepest-hidden treasure of them all—a treasure that encompassed more than mere animal desire.

They were almost upon the initial find, simultaneously sensing its nearness in the viscous warmth of the exploratory tunnel's close confines, and crying out as one as they reached for it, when the stallion's threatening rumble sounded beyond the thick logs. Helpless in the throes of simultaneous orgasm, they felt the cabin tremble as twelve hundred pounds of overcharged horseflesh came crashing down on the weathered poles of the corral. There was the rending sound of splintering wood, a piercing scream from the mare as she felt great yellow teeth sink into the muscles and nerves at the base of her neck, followed by the gusty grunting of the huge horse as it settled unerringly over its waiting target.

Fresno heard those sounds in the night as if from some far-off region of her imagining, and knew what was happening, and wanted to care, and could not because of the jettisoning flood being poured into her. The pulsations diminished, grew motionless in the depths of her soul, and she remembered then those sounds from beyond the walls. Wondering whether Lord, too, had been aware of what was happening out there, she heard him say in a voice of sincere regret: "Well, it's done, and I've only myself to blame. I'm sorry, Fresno."

She lay exhausted beneath him, wanting to cry. "I didn't want a summer foal," she said fretfully. "I wanted to watch it discover the great big world of spring when everything is new and fresh and so full of promise it hurts to look at it."

He sighed heavily and stroked her damp temples. "I know."

"Maybe," she said hopefully, "Nut Maid won't catch, after all."

"She caught."

She pushed him off. "Aren't you the reassuring soul!" she exclaimed impatiently, and sat up. A moment later she gave a sharp gasp. "I forgot about the pie!"

He lifted himself on his elbows. "What are you talking about?"

"I baked a pie for you and carried it all the way over here balanced in one hand. When Nut Maid shied at a jackrabbit I came close to dumping it upside down in my lap." She swung her legs over the edge of the bed and stood up. "So get up and put your pants on. It's apple, and I even brought cream to go with it."

In the darkness she bent, found her dress, and slipped it over her head. "Shoot!" she muttered a moment later. "I've got it on wrong side out!"

He reached out and tugged at her skirts, preventing her from lifting them. "Why bother?" he teased. "You'll not be needing it."

"I am not in the habit of dining in a state of nudity," she retorted primly.

"Always the proper lady."

"Well, I wouldn't say that, exactly," Fresno replied drily. "Threshing around in the dark, trying to get my dress on straight, while my naked lover lies and watches me is hardly the act of a proper lady."

"I'm not watching you."

"Only because you can't see."

It was the measure of Fresno's growing sense of freedom that she could engage in light banter of this kind with him now. From the first, his half-serious, half-teasing attacks on her modesty had wrought havoc with her time-honored inhibitions. In his opinion, no subject was taboo, no word indelicate, no act offensive, so long as it was rooted in sincerity. Nor was she unaware of the irony in their reversed positions. He, who had so hesitantly entered into the relationship of her devising, had from the outset assumed the role of tutor with an aplomb completely at variance with his initial attitude. And the confidence with which he played the challenging role never ceased to amaze her.

But not yet could she bring herself to exhibit her naked body for his admiring gaze, nor could she look at his nakedness without embarrassment.

Her mind filled with these thoughts, she finished hooking her bodice, made her way to the fireplace, and felt along the mantle for the matches. She had brought a lamp from the ranch to replace the candle, and in its light the room took on a warm glow. She spoke without looking around. "Get dressed now. I'll cut the pie."

His drawling response came to her like a searching hand. "If you're in such a hurry to get back to bed, we can forget the pie."

In the act of opening the cupboard door, she straightened and came about to face him. "Your durability is unsurpassed," she said with lofty dignity. "Unfortunately, the same cannot be said of your delicacy." With that she reached out, took the dipper from its nail above the water bucket, and filled it. Holding it out at arm's length, she advanced a step toward the bed. "Are you going to get up, sir?"

"Yes, ma'am!" he shouted, and flung the blankets aside. He was on his feet and grabbing for his trousers as Fresno laughingly emptied the dipper into the bucket and returned it to its nail. By the time she had cut the pie and served it, he was seated at the table, minus his shirt, but decently covered from the waist down. He ignored his plate, however, and sat regarding her steadily as she took her place opposite him. "Fresno," he said sternly, "tell me something: are you ashamed of what you're doing? Be honest."

Her eyes mirrored her distress. "Don't be angry with me, Aaron, please. I'm sorry if—"

But he would not be sidetracked. "Answer me."

She flushed, and lowered her gaze to her plate. For a little while she was wholly still, fighting down her embarrassment. Her eyes came up, then, and she was again the self-possessed woman he had met three weeks ago. "I am two women." she said quietly. "One lives at Star and is embarrassed at the very mention of anything having to do with . . . the intimate relationship between man and woman. The other counts the hours between visits to this cabin and is an utter stranger to shame."

He was not satisfied with that. "You've not answered my question."

"No, I haven't," she confessed with a wry little smile. "The mistress of Star insists on meddling, I guess." She put her elbows on the table and laced her fingers together. With her chin resting on her interlocked hands, she faced him, her gaze as direct as his. "No, I am not ashamed, but my social conscience keeps insisting I should be. It's not easy to suddenly throw all trace of modesty out the window."

"Not modesty," he corrected her, "prudishness. In bed, you act as if it were the most natural thing in the world to give yourself to me. But the minute the lamp is lit, you grab the bedclothes up around your neck like a damned caterpillar winding itself up in a cocoon. It doesn't make sense."

He paused and leaned back, calmly studying her. "Does the fact that I'm a half-breed bother you?" he asked levelly. "Is that why you can't stand the light?"

She shook her head vehemently. "No! Even my husband never saw me undressed."

"Well, by God!" Lord exclaimed. "No wonder he got himself shot! He must have been the most frustrated man in the world!" He saw this strike home and was at once contrite. "Sorry. I'd no business saying a thing like that." He got up suddenly, took a match from the mantle, and knelt to light the shavings under the firewood Fresno had laid there earlier.

Fresno looked down at the wedge of pie and pushed it aside, her appetite gone. She spoke to Lord's naked back. "You're right, of course. I shall try to overcome it."

Hitching around on the hearth, Lord gave her a slow smile. "And I'll try to keep my mouth shut in the future."

He continued to squat there while she rose and crossed to the bench under the room's single window and picked up a bundle of blue cloth. His eyes followed her graceful movements as she came to the fire, sat down in the rocker there, and unfolded the material preparatory to hemming one of the lengths. He smiled again, struck by the naturalness of this scene. He said, half in jest, half in earnest, "All the comforts of home," and went on smiling when she showed him a quick, pleased look. "When all's said and

166

done," he went on, quite serious now, "people could make do with a lot less than they think they could. Why do we spend our life grabbing for things that aren't really important? Can you tell me?"

Fresno shook her head, frowning slightly as she threaded her needle. "No, I can't." She knotted the thread and let her hands fall to her lap, her gaze on the flames that were now hungrily lapping at the logs. "It occurs to me that I'm happier right now than I've ever been in my life. I can't think of another single thing I need or want." She broke off with a little laugh. "Does that sound silly?"

"Should it?"

"Well, when you think of all I've had handed to me on a silver platter, so to speak, it's a pretty condescending attitude for me to assume—or it *could* be."

"That all depends," Lord murmured.

"On what?"

"On whether it's true—whether the things you wanted or needed were on that platter. Were they?"

"Why, no," she answered slowly. "None of them were. Those things don't come on silver platters, do they? Either they come of their own accord, or not at all."

"What happens if they come and you don't have sense enough to recognize them, or to accept them?"

"They'll go away." She sounded very sure about this. "If I knew that I was what someone needed, but was rejected, I'd leave. Wouldn't you?"

Lord did not answer immediately. A log broke through the smaller lengths of wood supporting it and rolled out onto the hearth, and he turned, reaching for the poker. When he had the several pieces replaced he set the poker aside and squatted there gazing into the fire. "I can't say," he murmured finally. "I've no way of knowing what I'd do, because it's never happened to me. I doubt I ever will."

"You would not stay," Fresno said quietly. "Not you."

A short, dry laugh came from him and he swiveled around to

face her. "As a matter of fact, you're wrong there," he told her. "I found out I wasn't wanted in Star Valley, but I stayed."

"That's not the same thing at all. I was talking about being rejected personally. There was never any question of that where you were concerned." She saw his expression change, and leaned forward, her hand going out to his knee. "You know that, don't you?"

He did not respond to her touch, nor to her words, and his eyes narrowed slightly. "Fresno," he said in a changed tone, "this is dangerous—what you're doing. Is it worth it?"

She deliberately read her own meaning into the question. "It's worth everything to me."

"You said that without thinking."

"I've thought of little else from the moment I first met you."

"But if we're found out?"

"Star writes its own law," she said matter-of-factly. "I am Star."

Lord nodded gravely. "For now, yes. But there's a change in the wind. More and more people are flocking out here. I saw it happening all the way from St. Louis. Before the year's out, there'll be a dozen new families in the Basin. When it's filled up, they'll start spilling over into this valley."

"No," Fresno stated quietly. "They will not." When he said nothing, she sat a trifle straighter in her chair. "At least, not the part that is deeded Star range."

Lord understood her unasked question and gave his head another purposeful shake. "All right, nor in my third either. But we don't own the country around here. In time, the squatters will fill every square inch of it. You've had it all to yourself for so long, you can't picture its ever changing; but it will—in ways you can't imagine, and faster."

"Granted all this were to take place overnight," Fresno retorted impatiently, "what does it have to do with us?"

"Fresno, Fresno," he murmured, "you're a grown woman living in a child's dreamworld. You've no acquaintance with blind hatred, or ugliness, or reality."

168

"That's not fair!" Fresno replied hotly, stung to defensive anger. "I've lived with reality all my life! If you think it's been child's play running this—"

"You're talking about the reality of being an absolute power in a powerless community," Lord broke in gently. "I'm talking about the reality of men blindly hating other men and wishing them dead because of the color of their skin." He broke off, staring unseeingly at the floor. "Why is it," he asked, "that the only way a man can be right in his own eyes is by making all others out to be wrong? If you're not white, you're just so much dirt to be trod underfoot. Why is that, Fresno?"

"Aaron!" Fresno cried in a distressed voice, "you can't mean that! It may be true to some degree—I can't speak for the whole world, of course. But I can swear that I've not once thought of you as anything other than a man—a man who inspires in me a self-pride I've never known before." She thrust the heap of material off her lap and went to her knees in front of him, her eyes looking levelly into his. She reached out and took his head between her hands, as if to insure his continued attention. "I won't say you're being unfair in accusing white people of having a superior attitude. Unfortunately most of them do, though I'm not certain why. I suspect it might be rooted in a guilt they either won't or can't admit, even to themselves. I also suspect that the majority never reason why they think the way they do. It's what they've been taught; they accept it as gospel. To say I'm sorry for what you've suffered all these years sounds terribly condescending—as though that holy, elevated position affords me the right to bestow pity on a lesser being. But that's not true. I sympathize with you and pity you exactly as I would sympathize with and pity anyone charged with a crime of which they were innocent." She gave his head a little shake. "Do you believe me, Aaron? *Do* you?"

He raised his hands and took her wrists and lowered them gently. "I believe you," he said. "Unfortunately, your lone vote isn't going to reverse the verdict."

Still on her knees she watched him rise and turn to stare down into the fire. Distress turned her weak and helpless. He was going away from her, shutting her out, retreating into the unrelieved darkness of his thoughts, where she could not follow. Determined to break through that barrier, she rose and turned him toward her.

"Kiss me, then we'll eat."

For a long moment he stood looking intently down at her, then slowly grinned. He put his hands on her hips and swayed her close against him and bent his head. His lips brushed her ear. "I'd rather go back to bed," he whispered.

"But *I* would rather eat," she said tartly, and stepped out of his arms. Taking her place at the table, she said without looking up, "We'll have our pie: *then* we'll go to bed," and knew that she had surprised him.

He sat down opposite her, took a bite of the pie, and chewed reflectively. "Good! It's *good!*"

"You sound surprised. Didn't you think I knew how to cook?"

"Considering your *other* accomplishments," he replied pointedly, "I'd not have thought you'd ever taken the time to learn your way around a kitchen." He put his amused glance on her and could not quite keep his face straight when she turned a bright red. He helped himself to another mouthful, swallowed, and was suddenly grave. "It's just now occurred to me—except for my father's housekeeper, I've never sat at a table with a white woman before."

Fresno kept her gaze on her plate. She said casually, "Is that so?" and took another bite. When she had swallowed she went on in the same indifferent tone, knowing that this moment must be handled carefully. "Now that you mention it, I can't remember ever having baked a pie for a half-breed before . . . or a miner, or a grocery clerk, or a senator, or a judge, or even my father, for that matter." She looked up, then, showing him an utter lack of interest in the subject. "I'll tell you something I've never told another soul," she went on. "In all my life I've never dared give anything I've made to anyone."

Lord frowned. "Why should you be afraid?"

"It's very simple, really. I've never been allowed to forget I was Fresno Star, the untouchable. Who would believe *she* would go to the trouble of knitting a pair of stockings for Grandma Taylor? Or make a batch of cookies for the church bazaar? Or cook strawberry preserves for old Uncle Lafe?" She paused and gave a sigh. "So . . . I never did."

"You must have felt pretty unnecessary."

"Completely."

"Do you still feel that way?"

"Of course not," Fresno replied. "But thanks to my father, who mistrusted everyone's motives and taught me to do the same, I spent half my life holding perfectly innocent people at a safe distance without ever giving them a chance to prove themselves either human or humane. Suspicion is the most foolproof guarantee for loneliness that I know of."

He had a brain as agile as hers, and a pair of eyes that missed nothing, and he was not fooled for an instant. His slow smile drew little wrinkles in the corner of his eyes. "You'd make a fortune running a gambling boat," he told her. "You never overlook a bet, do you?"

"Not when I'm playing for high stakes," she retorted. "I never bluff, either, nor do I ever place a bet I'm not able to cover."

He gave a sudden laugh, pushed back his chair, and reached for her. But she eluded his hands, swinging away from the table and gaining the safety of her rocker in front of the hearth before he could read her intent. Taking up her sewing again, she bent over it. "I've another pair of curtains hemmed for you," she said. "If you'll move the lamp closer, I'll finish these for the kitchen."

He reached over, slid the lamp close to her, then swung his chair around and sat down facing her. He was perfectly well aware of the little game she was playing, and willing to go along with it for a time. But he could not resist a sudden impulse to prick her seeming calm. "Better be quicker than that," he warned. "I'm starting to get sleepy again, and you know what that means."

Fresno bent lower over her work, her lips firming in a straight line. "You may go to bed whenever you feel like it," she told him primly. "I have work to do."

He leaned back and sat regarding her out of dark, amused eyes. He was aware of the picture the two of them made, seated thus before the fire, and the novelty of it impressed him profoundly.

But the very peacefulness of the setting conspired against him. He had no way of fitting into the pattern so quickly, knew no guidelines for conduct or speech, and so he sat bolt upright in his chair, staring fixedly at the fire, his hands tightly gripping his thighs.

"Am I just supposed to *sit* here?" he demanded suddenly.

She started and looked up. The picture he made, sitting there, tensed as if ready to spring into action, was so ludicrous that she very nearly burst out laughing. She quickly bent her head and resumed her meticulous stitching. "I believe," she said carefully, "it's a custom of long standing the world over—people taking their ease in front of the fire of an evening."

"But aren't we supposed to *do* something?"

"The rules aren't very specific," Fresno said, straight-faced. "I believe, however, that it's rather common practice for people to do little odd jobs, such as mending, or knitting, or repairing harness, or shoes—things like that." She glanced up again, eyes twinkling. "I imagine that if two people felt so disposed, they even might bring themselves to visit a bit."

"Visit? About what?"

Laughter almost overcame her a second time, but she caught herself in time. He was clearly serious. The idea of participating in a casual, undirected conversation was totally foreign to him. With surprise she realized that she actually knew very little about him, beyond the fact of his presence here in the valley.

Knowing that getting the desired information out of him would be like pulling teeth, she set about it with a determination that was wholly belied by her casual manner. Returning her attention to her work, she spoke off-handedly. "Where were you born, Aaron? You've never said."

"In a teepee."

"I hardly thought it was the governor's mansion," she said drily. "Kindly be a little more explicit."

"It was my Uncle Tall Bull's tepee, and it was situated about a hundred yards back from the Yellowstone River," Lord told her. "In case you never heard of Tall Bull, he was quite a big man among—"

"I know who he was," Fresno interrupted smoothly. "That is, if his was *the* Tall Bull of the Northern Cheyenne." She caught Lord's confirming nod and went on. "He's long had quite a reputation, even this far south, and ranks, I believe, with such prominent tribal leaders as Dull Knife, Little Wolf, Standing Elk, and several others I could name. Was your mother his sister?"

"Yes."

"What was her name?"

"My father called her Mary," Lord said, and laughed. "Her real name was White Buffalo Robe Woman." He laughed again, and Fresno looked over at him quizzically. He was genuinely amused about something.

"What is so funny?"

"It might not be funny at all to you," Lord told her, "but the name 'Bull' was very popular in my family. Just about everybody was a bull of one kind or another . . . Three Bulls, Two Bulls, Short Bull, Tall Bull, Big Bull, Old Bull, and so on. Well, when my grandmother married into the family, she got completely carried away with the glamor of belonging to such a prominent family and entered into the spirit of the thing with a vengeance. She named her first son Tall Bull, her second Standing Bull, and when my mother came along, she was all for naming her She Bull, until my grandfather put his foot down. He pointed out that such a name would be a bad thing because it canceled itself out, and would result in the child's becoming a nobody. My grandmother gave in and did the next best thing, by naming her daughter White Buffalo Robe, the buffalo, of course, being a bull, as far as she was concerned.

"My mother used to laugh about it, and say that my grandmother was forever giving herself away by slipping in the name she *really* meant."

"You mean, 'Bull'?" Fresno asked.

Lord nodded, his shoulders shaking with mirth. "Right! She'd stick her head out of the tepee and yell, 'Hi! White Bull Buffalo Robe! Run bring me some wood!' or 'Hi! White Bull Buffalo Robe! Where'd you hide my needle?' and then swear by all the gods she'd said no such thing whenever anyone caught her up. In the end she won out, because people nicknamed my mother Bull Cow, and it stuck to her all her life. Everybody thought it was funny, except my grandfather. To get even, he gave my grandmother a nickname that took about five minutes to say in Cheyenne, and meant, 'The - Woman - Who - Can - Never - Remember - the - Name - of - Her - Daughter - Because - Her - Thoughts - Are - Always - With - the - Bulls.' "

It was the first time Fresno had ever known him to be actually lighthearted, much less talkative, and the change in him was amazing. He was an altogether different person from the dour stranger who had so coldly turned her threats aside that first day, and she could not blend the two disparate personalities into one. "I suspect," she mused, smiling, "that Indians aren't always as humorless as they're made out to be."

"Only around whites," Lord replied, sobering. "I don't know much about other Indians, but the Cheyennes come pretty close to being human, in the matter of giggling, and playing dumb jokes on each other, and telling tall stories. Even their religion is funny to them. I mean, half the stories are about the crazy things the gods do to each other and to men. Which isn't to say they aren't really serious about it, even when they're laughing. Maybe that's the way a religion should be, so it can fit in with everything else in life. Does that sound crazy?"

Fresno shook her head. "I wouldn't say so. Personally, I've always found it rather tiresome trying to work up a deep sense of guilt over having been born, as most ministers insist I should. It's never quite made sense to me." She took another half-dozen stitches, then returned to the original subject. "How long did you live with your mother's people?"

"Until I was five."

The answer was curt, and Fresno glanced over at him from beneath lowered lashes and saw that all humor had fled from his dark face. "What happened?"

"My father came out from St. Louis on an inspection trip of his trading posts. He took me home with him."

"But not your mother?"

"No," Lord said tonelessly, "not my mother."

Fresno stitched on, acutely aware that the talk had gotten onto dangerous ground. On the point of shifting the topic to safer footing, she knew suddenly, without knowing how, that the man sitting close to her had never before spoken of that time to another. She said very quietly, "Did you miss her very much?" and caught the faint sound of his hard indrawn breath.

"I can't answer that."

She looked up then. "I wish you would, Aaron."

His eyes were two mirrors of misery. "I can't answer your question," he said in that same toneless voice, "because the white half of me never learned the words that would let you understand even a tenth of it. The only way I could tell you would be by crying, and the Indian half of me never learned to cry."

Fresno reached out and pressed the big hand so tightly gripping the thigh. "You have answered my question, my dear. I really needn't have asked, but I think that talking about something that hurts can be like lancing a boil. It lets the poison out." She moved her hand, lifting the splayed, stiff fingers and enclosing them in her cool palm. "Please tell me something about your childhood in St. Louis. I'd like to see you as a little boy."

But he seemed not to have heard her. He was staring into the fire, far from her. She took her hand away and sat back, resuming her sewing. "Did you love your father?" she asked.

"No."

If she was surprised by the blunt truth, she gave no sign. "Not at all?"

"I tried to." His voice had become hoarse. "He wouldn't let me."

"Did you know why?"

"Not for a long time. By then it was too late."

"What was the reason?"

Lord's chest rose with a long intake of air that trembled his long frame. "Shame," he said. "All kinds. He was a very proud man. He was ashamed of having slept with a squaw and gotten her with child, and of having disgraced himself by marrying her . . . he *did* marry her, in case you wondered. Then there was the shame he felt for abandoning her, and for taking me away from her, and for bringing me into his world where I didn't belong, and for letting her die at Sand Creek, and for keeping me in a hell of his choosing, even when the failure of his plan to raise me as a white boy so that I could be a worthy heir to his fortune was evident."

He closed his eyes and let his head fall back until it rested against the back of his chair. He said in a stifled voice, "I used to wonder why he always looked away whenever I'd catch his eyes on me. I finally came to know, but there wasn't anything I could do about it."

"And you never talked to him about it?" Fresno queried softly.

His head moved in negation. "I had been taught never to ask personal questions of adults. Nor was Angus Lord the kind of man who invited personal relationships."

"Why do you think he refused to meet your eyes, Aaron?"

"Well," Lord said drily, "even when I was a child, it wasn't easy to mistake me for a pale, freckle-faced, red-haired Scotsman. Knowing Angus Lord, I'd say the sight of a skinny little black-haired, black-eyed, copper-skinned offspring wasn't the most pleasant reminder."

Fresno folded her hands on her sewing and looked into the flames. "I think," she said, low-voiced, "Angus Lord was not a man I would have liked." She turned and saw Lord watching her from beneath lowered lids. For a moment she studied him in silence, noting the broad expanse of the forehead; the black-lashed, hooded eyes with their strongly arched brows; the narrow, straight nose; the wide mouth; and the square, almost-heavy jaws; and framing it all, the thick, faintly waving hair that reached to the shoulders. It was a face at once arrestingly bold and wholly noncommittal. It demanded attention; it gave away nothing at all. She spoke before she thought. "Have you any idea how unbelievably handsome you are?"

The words made him self-conscious, and he shifted his feet and sat forward in his chair, again fixing his gaze on the fire. "I guess I was around ten when I looked in the mirror one day and saw myself as my father had always seen me. I knew then why he always looked away whenever I caught him watching me."

There was a burning ache in Fresno's throat. She was like someone feeling her way along a narrow path in complete darkness—a path that ran through a region recently devastated by fire. And behind her, he was following, unwilling but trusting. She knew where safety lay, but not how to reach it. A single misstep, a single error in judgment, and they would be off the path among the blackened skeletons of the fire-swept forest where a wrong turning would find the earth caving in under them. For here the fires still burned, devouring the forest's root system and hollowing out a vast network of fiery caverns with overheads that collapsed without warning under the slightest weight.

Sensing the danger in probing further into the father-son relationship, she changed topics. "You're obviously well educated. Your father must have sent you to quite a good school."

Lord laughed mirthlessly. "Why, yes, he did . . . for three whole weeks."

"Three weeks?" Fresno echoed. "Why did he take you out?"

"Because the head of the school asked him to."

"Oh, no!" Fresno exclaimed involuntarily. "Surely not!"

A sardonic smile thinned Lord's lips. "Oh, *yes*," he corrected her. "You see, it was one of those exclusive academies for the sons of well-to-do people, and when those nice people found out that their children were sitting in the same room with a half-breed, they kept them at home." Again he gave that humorless laugh, as if trying to turn the whole thing into a harmless, amusing incident. "I remember the first time I ever had the word "breed" applied to me. I was seven, and it was my third day at school. At

177

recess I ran outside to play with the other boys and found them all lined up in the yard waiting for me. I went running up to them, yelling, 'What'll we play this time?' and one of them yelled back, '*We're* playing goose base, but *you* can't, because you're a damned breed. My Dad said so. So go on away.' I said, 'I'm not either a breed! I'm Aaron Lord!' and someone else yelled, 'Dummy! You don't even know what you are! You're a *breed*. It's got something to do with your blood, my Dad says . . . something bad. So just go on!'

"Well, I was so scared at finding there was something wrong with my blood that I ran all the way home and asked my father if I was going to die from it."

He stopped, and he was no longer smiling. Fresno found it harder and harder to meet his gaze. "And what did he tell you?"

"He said, 'No, boy. Not in the way you think, at least.' "

"Did you understand what he meant?"

"Not at the time. But from the way he said it, I knew I shouldn't ask any more questions."

Fresno drew an unsteady breath. "Those boys!" she said furiously. "How you must have hated them!"

"No," Lord contradicted. "When you're that age, you can only *try* to hate. It never quite comes off. Real, lasting hatred comes only with practice. Which isn't to say I didn't give it a good try; but even though they'd kicked me out, I kept remembering that they had only said what they'd heard their parents say. I did better in the hate department where those parents were concerned. It wasn't until later that the sons came in for their share."

Listening to that deep monotone revealing the pain that had seared that long-ago child, Fresno felt the ground once more caving away underfoot and again sidestepped quickly. "Then where did you receive your education?"

"From my father's housekeeper. She'd been a schoolteacher when she was young."

"Was she good to you?"

"She tried to be. But before very long I noticed that she had the

178

same habit of looking away every time I'd catch her eye . . . exactly like my father."

Looking into his eyes, Fresno voiced the thought that came to her then. "Maybe nobody ever told you," she said in her old, direct way, "but you're not the easiest person to face eye-to-eye. You don't just look *at* a person; you look *into* him. Did you know that?"

Lord was mildly surprised, but after a moment he nodded. "I've never thought about it, but now that you mention it, I remember Tall Bull planting me between his knees and making me stand for what seemed like hours, staring into his eyes. If I blinked, he'd touch my eyelids with his fingers and say, 'No. Don't hide your thoughts behind these. They are meant only for watering the eyes, not for hiding behind. Now, once again, try to find my thoughts.' Maybe he taught me better than he knew." He shook his head, fondly remembering those long-ago sessions and the man who had conducted them. "But you're right: nobody ever mentioned it to me before."

"I suspect," Fresno murmured, "there are a good many things nobody ever mentioned to you."

"And I," Lord soberly conceded, "suspect you're right about that, too."

For a long moment they remained like that, looking at each other, half smiling. And then, in response to a signal that struck silently but imperatively, they rose. Fresno's sewing fell to the floor unheeded as she moved into his lifting arms.

It was over for now, the painful probing into a bleak and chilling past. There was now only the undeniable reawakening of their need for each other. His arms tightened, drawing her harder against him with a pressure that was almost painful. His slowly flexing hips woke a response in her, and his mouth was over hers like an open furnace with a tongue of flame flicking out to light its answering fire deep inside her. And with this kiss of unbridled passion bearing them irrevocably beyond all restraint, he bent and caught her up and carried her into the deeper shadow at the far end of the room and the waiting bed.

15

While the sinuous shadows stirred on the wall of the lake cabin, Lila MacKay rode from the pitch blackness of the canyon's floor along the steep trail to the bench, and so arrived home. Lamplight, spearing through the open door of the cabin, lay like a yellow lance on the ground as she unsaddled and turned her horse into the corral. Walking tiredly toward that narrow shaft, she dimly glimpsed her father's bulk seated on the porch to one side of the open door. She passed without speaking.

Nor did he give her any greeting, but as she entered the cabin, she felt him rise and follow. She was instantly on guard, remembering that he was supposed to be hazing the stolen Star cattle north toward Silverton. She heard him say, "Set down," and turned to see him standing wide-braced in the middle of the room, his pale eyes boring into her like an unkind hand. He pointed to the table. "I said fer you to set down."

She knew then that she was in for a rough time and characteristically readied herself for what was to come by blanking everything from her mind while she took stock of her surroundings. The door had been left open, the fire replenished, and as she turned the chair slightly and lowered herself onto it, she saw Carla rise soundlessly from her customary place in the shadows at the end of the fireplace and stand motionless against the wall. Putting up both hands to lift her hair back over her shoulder, she turned her head and gave the woman a closer look and saw the Comanche mask settle over the handsome features. But there was a tautness to the strong frame that told her the woman was attuned to this threatening situation.

Her father's boots struck dull echoes from the plank flooring, and she turned to watch him come into the lamp's stronger light and sit at the table opposite her. The pressure of his stare was like an unpleasant weight against her. She placed both hands on the table and intertwined her fingers. Her voice was deliberately bland, almost careless.

"Well? Let's hear the piece you've been practicing."

MacKay tilted his chair back and hooked his thumbs in the armholes of his vest. "I'm speakin' no piece. *You* got somethin' to tell *me*, so start talkin'."

"About my trip into town?" Lila asked. "Is that what I'm going to tell you?"

MacKay nodded. "And the rest of it. The whole goddamned stinkin' story."

A slow smile stretched Lila's lips thin, but her eyes glittered with a cold light. "Shall I give you all the facts?" she asked. "Or would you just as soon I left out the part about town and got to what really interests you—the breed-fucking part?"

MacKay rocked forward and brought his hands crashing down on the table with a violence that jarred the chimney off the lamp. It struck the table and shattered, and in the abruptly lessened light Carla stepped across the hearth and spoke loudly to Lila in sibilant Comanche. "Watch him, daughter. This is getting bad." She made a point of glaring at the girl to mislead MacKay, who had never bothered to learn the complex language, into thinking she was angry over the broken chimney.

The warning so surprised Lila that she momentarily forgot her own danger. She said in that same tongue, "You will be made to suffer, not I. Stay out of this, my mother," and kept all expression out of her face as she continued to meet her father's aroused stare.

"Shut up that goddamned Comanche jabberin'!" MacKay commanded. His fury tore through him, shutting off his breath. He started to speak again, choked, and gulped down spittle and air. He leaned across the table. "You worthless slut!" he shouted deafeningly. "You goddamned trashy whore!"

Before he could move, Lila reached out and slapped him full across the face. Her chair scraped back and she was on her feet, her eyes glittering with the light of battle. "Who the hell are you to point your filthy finger at me and call me names, you cattle-rustling, back-shooting, child-robbing son of a bitch?"

Now MacKay's chair went over with a crash as he lunged erect.

"Oh, yes." Lila came to her feet. "Do you think I don't know about those trips of yours up north? And the ones down south? Do you think I can't name every single one of the six miners you shot and robbed last year? And the Fargo agent you shot between the eyes while he was handing you two sacks of new-minted currency eight miles north of Denver last year?" She let this tear through him. "And as for the children you've robbed: four of those miners had families. That Fargo agent had six children and no wife to take care of them when you killed him for no reason at all. Oh, yes!" she told him with a chill smile, "I even know the amounts of your takes. In fact, I know a hell of a lot more about *you* than you do about *me*, dear father!"

Her contempt washed over him in a chilling torrent. Their entire relationship had been one of mutual avoidance. This personal, vindictive confrontation was without precedent, and because MacKay so little understood the tall, uninhibited girl he had sired, he was completely taken aback by her explosive reaction. A man wholly lacking in pride or personal integrity, he did not expect to find them in this daughter, whose licentious conduct he had never checked. Now he found himself face to face with a girl he had never met—a hard-eyed stranger with a tongue like a skinning knife, whose knowledge of his activities stunned him. He felt those green eyes stabbing into him and realized how dangerous she could be. Fear touched him; and he hit back at her in the only way he knew, clumsily and defensively.

"We're not talkin' about *me!*" he shouted. "We're talkin' about *you,* an' what you been up to lately. Now—"

"No!" Lila shouted back, her aroused voice overriding his. "We'll talk about *you,* and what you've been up to all your goddamned life! My doings don't concern you. They never have. You've never been a father to me. The only decent thing you ever did for me was to give me Carla for a stepmother, and even that was sheer luck. God knows you weren't thinking of what kind of a mother she'd make when you bought her!"

Her strident outburst ceased. She stood in the wavering light of the guttering wick with all her deep-rooted dislike for the man opposite her showing through at last. She was closer to losing control of herself than she had ever been in her life, and the fact that she had revealed her vulnerability made her want to kill this callous man.

She took a long, slow breath to steady herself, and spoke in a low, controlled voice. But every word came out and found its mark with the exactitude of an artfully aimed dagger.

"A whore takes money for what she does, Douglas. Which one of us does that? Whatever I've done was done because it pleasured me and cost no one else a goddamned thing. Now you think about that. And then you think about this: the next time you start to throw the word 'whore' at me, you'd better hang onto it. Because if you ever hit me with it again, it'll be the last time. You'd goddamned well better believe that."

MacKay turned dead white. For an endless moment he stood staring dumbly at the cold-eyed girl, his senses shocked by the lethal hatred in her face. And then his face was suffused with crimson and he opened and closed his mouth, as if strangling. He said with no inflection at all, "I'll kill you. So help me God, I'll kill you for that," and started around the table for her.

Carla's voice got in front of him and turned him halfway around. "Husband," she said in her cumbersome English, "tell me. I don't know what this is about. None."

"Stay out of this!" MacKay said roughly. "It's no concern of yours!"

"I think maybe so." Carla surprisingly contradicted him. "I think you better quit this."

"I told you to stay out of it!" MacKay roared.

Never before had the Indian woman presumed to pit her will against that of the bullish man whose bed she had shared for over twenty years. That she dared do so now shocked her almost as much as it did MacKay. Her eyes were flat and still, and her voice as devoid of resonance as a drum struck with the flat of the hand. "If you touch her," she said in English, "I will kill you. I will do it."

The very fact that she had intruded herself into his pathway served to make MacKay veer aside from his initial goal. He hunched his shoulders forward and peered more closely at her. "Did you know about Lila lettin' this half-breed Injun buck straddle her?" he demanded suspiciously. "Did you?"

"Ah, hell!" Lila spat disgustedly, purposely drawing his attention back to herself. "If shit was brains, you could rule the world, Douglas!" In the moment it took the man to rally for another attack, she crossed to the hearth and took her place at Carla's side. "God knows you've got barely enough sense to bring you in out of the rain; but even that ought to be enough to tell you Carla had nothing to do with this thing that's got you so all-fired hot and bothered."

"You shut up and answer me!" MacKay yelled.

Lila's lips twitched. "Well, make up your feeble mind," she drawled. "I can't very well do both, now, can I?"

MacKay would have hit her then, had he dared. His hands balled into fists. "Answer me! Did she know about you and that Injun buck?"

"Of course she knew!" Lila suddenly yelled at the top of her voice. *"I told her!"*

MacKay swung on Carla. "And you said nothin' about it."

"How the hell could she?" Lila demanded in the same deafening yell. "You been down at Durango for the last two weeks, you ass! What was she supposed to do, send up smoke signals, for Christ's sake?"

"All right!" MacKay ground out. "But that don't wash the stink outa *your* skirts. What the hell am I supposed to say when folks ask me is my daughter spreadin' her legs for some god-damned Injun?"

Lila threw back her head and loosed a whoop of derision at the ceiling. "Why, tell them the same thing you tell them when they ask you is your daughter spreading her legs for anyone!" she instructed him. "I doubt it'll come as any great shock to any-body." She saw the muscles along his jaw round into hard knots, and could not resist letting him see her deep-seated contempt. "Don't tell me you've been suffering from disgrace over what I've been up to all these years, Douglas," she said scathingly. "You never could lie any better than you could use the few scrambled brains you lay claim to."

She watched him, grimly amused, knowing she had him on the run now. But she was not through yet. "It's a little late in the day for you to come around and start playing Daddy, don't you think?" she said coldly. "You've known all along what I've been doing, and it never mattered a good God damn to you, until now." She paused and cocked her head to one side. "Why all this sudden ruckus over my good name, Douglas?"

"This is different," MacKay said tightly. "Mighty goddamned different, and you know it."

"Different?" Lila queried. "How?"

"You're white!" MacKay bellowed. "An' he's a stinkin' *Injun!* There's the difference!"

Lila spoke to the woman beside her without looking around. "Carla, how come you've been pretending to be a Comanche all these years? Why didn't you tell me you were white?"

Something that may have been amusement flickered in Carla's opaque eyes. "I forget," she said, straight-faced. "I mean to, only I keep forgetting."

The man in front of them sensed he was being made the butt of some joke whose subtlety escaped him. "What the hell's that supposed to mean?" he demanded. "What the hell's this shit about her bein' white?"

"Why," Lila replied innocently, "she *has* to be white, Doug-las. No fine, self-respecting, upstanding gentleman like you would soil himself by sleeping with a dirty Comanche, now would he?"

It clearly required all MacKay's self-restraint to refrain from knocking her down. "You've got a mind like a goddamned snake," he said through clenched teeth. "It ain't nowise the same

185

thing with a man an' a squaw as it is with a white woman an' a half-breed buck, an' you know it."

"I'm afraid you'll have to clear that up a little better, Douglas. I guess I'm too dumb to catch it on the first go-around." Lila again cocked her head to one side, put a finger to her lips, and became the personification of puzzlement. She said thoughtfully, "Now, let's see . . . if a white man humps an Indian squaw, that's all right . . . even if he gets a baby by her. Is that the way of it?"

"That's right," MacKay stated.

"But," Lila went on, frowning as she worked it out, "if this baby grows up and humps a white girl, that's all wrong."

"You're damned right, it's wrong."

The tall girl was proving herself to be a consummate actress. "But you just got through saying it was all right for the white man to make that baby!" she protested. "Now you turn around and say it's wrong for his son to go through the same motions. Why?"

"He'd be a breed, that's why."

"Is there a law against breeds?"

"You damned right they is! Even if it ain't writ down in no book."

"Then there must be a law against *making* breeds," Lila said in that same innocent tone. "Even if it's not written down. Is there, Douglas?"

"Hell, no, they ain't!" MacKay snapped. "It ain't noways the same—" He stopped, realizing that his kind of logic could not extricate him from the morass into which the girl's feigned naïveté had led him. He said violently, "It ain't the same thing! Injun blood's Injun blood! They's no gittin' rid o' the stain!"

Lila was suddenly out of patience with the senseless exchange. "That's pure horseshit, Douglas, and you know it!" she said disgustedly. "If fucking a half-breed can stain *me*, then *you're* twice as dirty as I am. So just where in hell do you get off playing it so high and mighty?"

MacKay abandoned what passed with him as reasoning and fell back on authority. "I'm still your Paw," he bellowed, "and by God I'll have your respect!"

"You're an addle-brained fool," Lila corrected him. "And you'll have nothing but grief if you try to mess around in my business. Is that plain?"

MacKay was lifting his hand to knock her down when Carla again spoke.

"You see this man, husband?"

MacKay's attention was diverted. "No, I ain't; but I don't need to. He's a dirty, stinkin' breed. That's all I need to know."

"What difference?" Carla asked stubbornly. "What's wrong with Indian? I Comanche. I no can change that. You no can change. Everybody what he made. Why your blood better as mine? Both red."

"You shut up!" MacKay ordered. "You don't know what you're talkin' about, so shut up. The difference is that mixed blood is bad blood."

Carla's eyes widened with what seemed sudden understanding. "Aaaah!" she exclaimed. "That make difference, all right!" She gave Lila a sidelong, worried glance. "That man bleed inside you, daughter?"

Only Lila saw the amusement flickering in the obsidian eyes. "No, Carla," she replied straight-faced. "I'm still as pure as I was."

"Ah!" Carla sighed in relief. She nodded to MacKay. "You hear?" He not put bad blood in her, so everything fine."

MacKay glowered at her. His mind was a cumbersome thing, incapable of grasping subtleties; but he suspected the two women were making fun of him. "You tryin' t'be smart with me?"

"I not smart," Carla protested; then could not resist a final summing up of the situation as she saw it. She moved her hands in a gesture that included the three of them. "I think nobody here smarter as me, and I dumb as hell."

The man jabbed a forefinger at her. "Now, I've heard all I want t'hear outa' you! The only rights you got is them I give you, an' that don't include buttin' your damned Injun nose into business you don't know nothin' about, an' bad-mouthin' your betters!"

"Aaaaah!" Carla shouted, and paused, blindly reaching for some word that would convey her complete disgust. Of the great wealth of swear words she had accumulated during her years with MacKay, she had never used more than a few, for the simple reason that they invariably made her scanty English even more unwieldy. Now, acutely needing a specific one, the sheer enormity of that carefully hoarded backlog only confused her. In desperation she snatched up one at random and flung it into the stunned silence.

"Bullshit!" she yelled deafeningly.

Its effect on her listeners was even more rewarding than she had dared hope. It brought a giggle from Lila. It took all the color out of MacKay's face and snapped his head back, and this so delighted her that she snatched up a whole handful and threw them out broadcast. "God the hell damn whore my bare ass!" she shouted, and swept past MacKay on her way to the door.

"Carla!" MacKay's voice hit her like a blow between the shoulder blades. It halted her and brought her half around. She said, "Well?" and stood there, a strong, full-bodied woman pulled out of herself by a situation unsought and unwelcome.

"I'll have none of that talk from the likes of you!" MacKay shouted at her. "You get one thing clear right here and now. This is my house, and by God, in my house—"

"*Your house!*" Carla yelled furiously. "*Your house!* You keep it all then! You do that! God damn!" She turned, snatched up two blankets from the bench near the door, and was halfway through that door when MacKay caught her and hauled her around.

"Jest where you figure you're goin'?"

She looked down at the hand gripping her wrist. "Get away," she said quietly.

MacKay's eyes were alight with a desire to physically hurt her. "Don't tell me what to do! Don't *ever* tell me what to do!"

"Get away," Carla repeated in that same flat voice. She was deadly calm, knowing what was coming and setting herself for it. When he lifted his hand to hit her, she freed herself with a sudden wrench and gave back into the room a short step, dropping the blankets. She was a powerful woman, and when her backward movement stopped she was firmly braced. Her looping fist caught MacKay flush on the point of the chin with all the weight of her body behind it. The blow whipped him halfway around and sent him reeling sideways across the room. He crashed into a chair, went to his knees, and knelt there, dazedly shaking his head. His blank eyes came up, stared uncomprehendingly at her for an instant, then went cold with the backwash of reason. "Why, damn you," he whispered in a shaking voice. "I'll beat your brains out for that." He was on his feet and lunging for her when Lila's voice stopped him.

"Douglas. Hold it right there."

He swiveled his head around and saw her standing in front of the fireplace, the heavy rifle in her hands centered on him. She had lifted it from its pegs above the mantle, and he had no doubt at all that she would kill him. It was in her voice and in the unwinking gaze that never left his face. Silence closed in, so complete that when a limb on the fire burned through and fell into the bed of coals, its faint noise was a loud explosion in the room.

This sound acted as a catalyst on the three still-caught figures. Carla bent to retrieve the blankets. Lila came away from the fireplace, moving sideways toward Carla, all the while holding the rifle steady on MacKay. And MacKay abruptly wheeled and tramped over to the hearth. He gripped the rough surface of the log mantlepiece and levered himself around to face the two women. "Get out," he said. "Both o' you. They's no place under this roof fer the likes o' you."

"We'll be back," Lila told him, "to take what belongs to us."

MacKay shook his head. "The door'll be locked. You'll take not one damned thing." He glared into her cold green eyes and realized with shock that she was still on the verge of killing him. In that moment he grasped for the first time the full scope of her contempt for him. It was boundless and unchangeable, too complete to allow any vestige of mere hatred or even dislike to disturb its fathomless depths. It placed him beneath consideration as a human. It could see him obliterated with no shade of remorse. Terror clamped icy fingers around his throat, pinching off his voice so that it came out thin and hesitant. "Where'll you go? You'll find no door open to you."

Lila said to her mother in Comanche, not taking her eyes off MacKay, "Where will we go this night, my mother?"

"Anyplace away from here," Carla replied in the same harsh tongue. "The house that belonged to those people who left two seasons ago is empty. Let us go there; but don't tell this mad son of a wolf."

"We'll be at the old Sandrin place," Lila told MacKay. "To-morrow we'll come for our stuff."

MacKay shook his head, trying without success to rid himself of the conviction that he still stood in imminent danger of his life. "I told you the door'll be locked."

"Then you'd better be gone," Lila warned him in the same level voice. "If it's locked, I'll shoot the lock off. If you get in my way, I'll shoot you. I mean that."

It was no idle threat. The very absence of anger told MacKay she meant it, and he knew then he had lost. The knowledge was a corrosive acid inside him. It burned his vitals and bent him forward in a half crouch. It was a pain that fed upon itself and spread all through him, making him want to hurt her for what she had done to his pride this night.

He had a single weapon at hand, and he brought it up from that burning acid pit and poured it over her in a stream of filth. For a full minute his cursing went on, and when it finally ceased he stared fixedly at her, vainly waiting for some break in her ex-pressionless face. But there was no change at all in the steady look she showed him, and in the end it was he who turned away. "I'll not be here tomorrow," he muttered. "You can take what you want. Now get the hell out of here before I puke."

He stood there, his heavy shoulders hunched, staring sight-lessly into the fire until their footsteps faded away in the direction of ths corral. After what seemed a long time he heard two horses cross the bench and take the trail down to the canyon floor.

Silence came into the room, then, strange and unwanted. It filled all the house and piled up thickly in the dark corners and flowed around him like a disquieting noise, turning him edgy and vaguely uneasy. When he turned and looked around him at the familiar furnishings in the room he found them utterly unfamiliar.

In an excess of sudden self-pity he muttered, "But for that goddamned half-breed, none o' this would o' happened, God damn him t'hell!" and felt a burning desire to see the man dead at his feet. As the picture flashed before his mind's eye he experienced an uplift of spirit.

He was building the framework of a plan that would see him avenged on the unknown stranger who was responsible for this night's doings. But with the plan only beginning to form in his mind, a rare insight brought his thoughts to a grinding halt, and he knew that even were he to succeed, nothing would be changed. He shook his head and slumped back against the mantle, staring hopelessly out across a bleak, dismal expanse of unloveliness that stretched on and on and ended at last on the edge of nothingness.

"So be it," he whispered. "All the same, we'll see who has the last word, by God. We'll just see."

16

Jesse Whitehead drew up under the trees to watch the distant figure atop the stable lever a newly peeled pole into position and nail it securely in place with four well-aimed strokes of the hammer. He drifted in so quietly then that he was halfway across the yard before the two dogs became aware of his approach.

They lunged up in raging embarrassment and came streaking toward him to abruptly veer away at Lord's whistle.

Jesse let the little dun amble to a halt and sat looking up at the half-naked man silently regarding him from that eight-foot elevation. He said, "Howdy, Lord," and reached into his pocket for a chew. He caught the low rejoinder that came down to him, and had his envious look at the massive reach of that bared torso and knew a fleeting regret for the ruin the years had worked in his own gaunt frame. He shaved off a liberal jawful of the leaf, tucked it securely between gum and cheek, and dropped the plug back to its resting place. "Hot," he observed, then added pointedly. "An' hungry."

Lord inclined his head briefly. "Step down. I was just about to go in and fix myself a bite. Care to join me?"

"That was the gen'rl idee," Jesse stated and eased himself out of the saddle. "My belly's been slappin' hell outa my backbone fer the last hour."

Lord leaned down to grasp the rafter he was standing on, swung out of sight behind the wall, and reappeared a moment later in the doorway swatting dust from his pants. He wiped his dripping chest with his wadded up shirt, then shook out the shirt and slipped it on. "When does summer break in this country?"

"Gener'ly sometime along in September. This year it's apt t'be some later." The old man squatted on his hunkers in the strip of shade against the stable and gave Lord a bright look. "Thought you said somethin' about stirrin' up some grub."

His air of being wholly at home here on this his second visit brought Lord's slow smile. "Put your horse up," he said. "I'll go get busy on it."

He had two venison steaks in the skillet and was dropping biscuits into a pan when his guest sauntered in.

"I'll jest have a look around," Jesse announced, drifting through the kitchen and on into the main room. He paused in the doorway and made a little humming sound in his throat at sight of the changes. " 'Pears like you done a mite o' straightenin' up, fer sure," he observed, and moved on across the room in that easy, silent way he had.

His prying glance kept darting around the room. At the window he paused again and absently fingered one of the red curtains. He looked down, saw the fine stitching of the hem, and said murmuringly, "Well, now!" and went on humming tunelessly while his eyes got narrower and sharper.

He returned to the kitchen and sat down at the table. He was loosely arranged in his chair and he seemed old and tired and indifferent; but one of his fingers kept up a slow, thoughtful tapping on the green-and-white-checkered oilcloth, and he noted the newly hung green curtains at the window and was more and more curious. He said carelessly, "Them red curtains in that there front room sure enough dress it up," and caught the almost imperceptible hesitation of Lord's hand as it moved to turn one of the steaks.

"The window needs glass," Lord said. "I should run into town, but I keep putting it off."

"Lila run 'em up fer you?"

"Lila?"

Jesse sounded mildly reproving. "Don't tell me you done fergot her name already." He saw the big man's eyes narrow ever so slightly, and went on in the same idle tone. "Damn fine girl, Lila. Knowed her since she was ass-high to a ant." He paused, then added, as if it were an afterthought, "Last time I seen her, I was headin' over t' Perce Downey's . . . he's over in the Basin . . . t'shoot me some cats. She damn near run over the top o' me on that long-legged jackrabbit she rides. We set an' jawed quite a spell." Again he paused, and again he appended an idle afterthought. "That was maybe a quarter mile east o' here . . . long 'bout two in the mornin'."

"I see," Lord said noncommittally, and busied himself with setting the table.

Jesse took his hand off the oilcloth, tilted his chair back against the wall and idly rocked to and fro. "Never figgered Lila t' be much of a hand with a needle."

Lord emitted a brief laugh. "I doubt she could even manage the knot in the thread."

Jesse chose to ignore the slip. "Now, they's some women jest

natcherly have a knack fer needlework, seems like. Allus stitchin'
away on one thing or t'other. Ever notice that? You take Fresno
Taggert, fer example. Now, how come you t' fork that piece o'
meat clean over the plate onto the stove like that, boy?"

Lord cursed under his breath and speared the errant steak back
onto the plate, then brought the plate to the table. His lips were
set in a grim line and he would not look at the old man.

"Like I was sayin'," Jesse went on imperturbably, "There
Fresno is, ferever sewin' away. An' neat stitches? I never seen
anythin' could match 'em . . . 'ceptin' maybe them in them there
curtains o' your'n. It do beat—"

Lord was gripping the back of his chair in his big hands, and his
unwinking stare was fixed on the seated man. "Old-timer," he
said evenly, "say what you're trying to say."

"All right," Jesse agreed, and rocked his chair forward. "*Did*
she make them curtains fer you?"

"Why would she do that?"

"Well, now, knowin' Fresno like I do, I'd say she'd do it fer
jest one reason . . . because she felt like it."

"And why would she feel like it?"

Jesse glanced down at the food before him. "That there meat's
gettin' cold."

"Let it," Lord said curtly. "I'm waiting for your answer."

Jesse shook his head, picked up knife and fork, and cut the steak
into sections. "I ain't sayin' another damned word 'til after I wrap
my insides around this here grub," he stated, and proceeded to
suit action to words.

Lord grinned in spite of himself and followed the other's lead.
Before he was well underway, his guest was mopping up a last
pool of gravy with a biscuit.

Finished, Jesse leaned back, gave a resounding belch, and then
sat there studying Lord with the frank attention he would have
given a curiously wrought piece of furniture. He held his peace
until his host laid knife and fork aside, then crossed his arms on
the table and stared intently into the dark face opposite him.
"You want me to talk plain, son?" he inquired.

194

Lord's lips quirked. "I doubt I could stop you."

Jesse nodded. "Y'ain't as dumb as you make out to be," he stated, and then made a seemingly irrelevant remark. "You must sleep sound o' nights."

"Why is that?"

"Well, they's two possible reasons, but you ain't no half-wit, so that narrers it down t' one. You're a feller that don't spend much time worryin' about things that'r headed his way, sure as judgment day's a'comin'. That makes fer sound sleepin'."

Lord did not change his relaxed position, but suddenly he was tense. "Should I be worrying?" he asked casually.

"Not if you was that half-wit I jest now said you wasn't," Jesse replied tartly. "Bein's you're you, though, I'd say yes, you damned well ought'a be doin' some honest t'god worryin' fer a change."

"Why?"

"It damned well might *stop* a couple o' things," Jesse corrected him. He watched the big man turn the warning aside, and decided he had been using the wrong kind of words long enough. "Boy," he said, and concern was strong in his voice, "that big stick you got between yer legs is in a fair way o' stirrin' up a mess o' trouble around here, whether you want to face the truth or not!" He saw Lord open his mouth to speak, but he pressed on in the same lecturing tone. "The personal right 'er wrong o' this question don't make me no never mind. Other people's business is their business, as far as I'm concerned. But that's only what *I* think, an' nobody in his right mind ever accused me o' thinkin' like anybody else. So what I'm sayin' is you'd maybe best slow down an' admit that your big hard-on ain't the most important thing around here. They's two women goin' to have t'do some painful payin' fer all the pleasurin' they're gittin' off 'n you. An' not only them, neither. If 'n you don't start lookin' a little farther ahead than the next tumble on the bed, *you're* apt t'open a letter one o' these days an' find a bill inside marked 'due, as of this date.' Y' give that any thought?"

Lord's head went up, and the cold mask dropped over his

features. His eyes, looking out from between their thick fringes, were hard and flat and completely unreadable. "I've asked them for nothing," he said. "Nothing."

"That ain't the point, an' you know it."

"What is, then?"

Jesse looked pained. "You want I should say it right out?" He caught the other's faint nod, and inclined his own head in turn. "All right then. So be it."

He put his gaze on his empty plate, stared hard at it for a long moment, and finally heaved a sigh. When he looked up he found the black, inscrutable eyes on him, and was suddenly indignant. "Why the hell should I?" he demanded. "You goddamned well already know the answer!" He slammed a hand down on the table and swiveled around in his chair. "What the hell am I doin' here?" he asked of the room at large. "What the hell good is my settin' here wastin' my breath on some damned fool that'd play deef t' th' blowin' o' Gabriel's own horn, I'd like t' know? I'm goin' home, by God!"

He heaved himself to his feet and glowered down at Lord, in a show of disgust. He said complainingly to an invisible third party, "Well, at least y'can't say I didn't offer him a hand," and turned to the door, a lean wraith of a man, smarting under the rejection of his proffered friendship. He was halfway through the doorway when he heard Lord say something which he did not catch. He stopped short and turned. "How's that?"

"I said I apologize."

"What's that supposed t' mean, anyhow?" Jesse wanted to know. "All yer sayin' is that you wisht you hadn't said what you did. It don't mean you figger you're wrong about anythin'."

Lord came about in his chair and his eyes speared up from beneath the black brows. "The thing that's wrong," he said levelly, "is my color. That's what we're talking about, isn't it, Jesse?"

For a long moment the old man in the doorway faced that naked look, wanting to deny the words. His chest rose and fell with his inaudible sigh. "I reckon it is," he muttered finally.

"Well," Lord returned drily, "there's not much I can do about righting that particular wrong. So where does that leave me?"

"Betwixt a rock an' a damned hard place, I reckon."

Sarcasm twisted Lord's full lips. "Thanks for the help."

Two strides brought Jesse around the table. He grabbed the back of his chair and flung it aside, helpless anger turning his movements jerky. "Don't come that smart-alecky bull on me!" he said violently. "You act like I made the rules. Well, that ain't fair, an' you know it! The fact is I don't cotton to 'em any more'n you do. Why else d'y reckon I stay t'hell an' gone up in the hills? 'Cause the sight an' sound o' most o' the jackasses that call theirselves human bein's is a heap more'n I kin stand, that's why! Most o' what they say an' think an' do is what some other jackasses decided on for 'em, an' they accept it all as gospel 'cause they ain't got sense enough t' pour piss out'n a boot afore pullin' it on. So, I jest keep clear of 'em an' git along fine.

"Well, I don't reckon I need t'tell you 'bout people, considerin' who you are. But it do strike me as powerful queer that after all you bin through, you figger them same kind o' folks is gonna all at once start thinkin' o' you as just a ordnary feller with a perfect right to breathe the same air as them. It jest ain't so."

The rasping voice subsided, and the gaunt old man stood there hunched over the table, glaring down at the still-faced Lord. All his life he had studiously avoided close association with others. And now, for some reason that he could not readily understand, he was actually forcing his concern upon another, with no assurance that his intentions would either be understood or appreciated. This latter possibility struck unkindly at him and made him momentarily unsure of himself. But, on the point of abandoning his hard-hitting attack, he remembered Lila's supplication on behalf of this dour man, and knew that he would do as she had asked at whatever cost to his own dignity.

"Now, then," he went on in the same emphatic tone, "I'll git down to what this little visit is all about." He dragged the chair around and sat down, hating this moment, hating the words he was going to say, hating himself for being the one to broach a subject whose very nature forbade its being discussed by a third party. It was this last which prompted him to say in an altered voice, "I got no right a'tall to meddle in your private business, son. Say the word and I'll go back t' mindin' my own business."

"No," Lord said quietly. "That would leave it nowhere. Go on."

Jesse took a deep breath. "Things ain't the same as they was," he began lamely.

"They never were," Lord said drily.

Jesse grunted. "An' that's God's truth, ain't it? But what I mean is, this country around here is startin' t' fill up. I mind a few years back, when I come down here, they wasn't more'n a handful o' folks down in the Basin. Old Ewing Star an' his wife an' girl an' his hands was the only ones in this here valley. Now, overnight, seems like, the whole damn country's fillin' up. Anymore, a man ain't got room t' swing a cat without hittin' somebody alongside the head.'" He paused, shaking his head in regret for a time long gone. He brought himself to with an impatient jerk of his shoulders and returned to the task he had set himself.

"The point is, folks settin' out to start over in a new place don't seem t'be able t' leave their old wore-out notions behind. They got t'bring 'em along. They want somethin' new—a fresh start in a new place—an' right away they start makin' it into somethin' as near like what they left behind as they kin. Ever notice that?"

"A thousand times," Lord murmured.

"Like a British feller come out to the Yellerstone country a few years back. One o' them lords, he was. Had a flock o' servants trailin' after him y' wouldn't believe. Couldn't open his mouth 'thout spoutin' off about the untouched beauty o' the wilderness. Meant it, too. Never seen nobody more took with the great outdoors, as he called it. 'God's second Garden o' Eden', he was forever sayin'. An' Injuns? He was like a kid turned loose in a candy store whenever he'd find hisself in a village. 'Children o' nature,' he called 'em.

"Well, y'know what that lord feller done? Soon's he found

hisself in what he thought was the middle o' the Garden o' Eden, he had them servants o' his'n run up a big stone house you wouldn't believe, moved in, and invites the Injuns t' come live close by. An' as soon as the first dozen 'er so families come in an' pitched their teepees, he calls 'em together an' starts holdin' school. Only trouble was, he couldn't make hisself understood, not knowin' no Cheyenne—yeah, they was yer mamma's folks, son. Matter o' fact, your Uncle Tall Bull was in the bunch, I mind—so you know what he done? Set out t' learn 'em English! Damned if he didn't!

"Well, old Dull Knife didn't cotton too much to the idee, an' pointed out that since they was a hunnert 'er so o' them, an' only one o' him, it'd make a heap more sense fer *him* t'learn Cheyenne, 'stead o' t'other way around. But that lord feller wouldn't have none o' that a'tall, an' when old Dull Knife stuck to his guns, the honeymoon came to a sudden-like stop. The lord feller told 'em they was nothin' but a pack o' thievin', ignorant heathens, an' packed up bag n' baggage an' headed back where he come from, madder'n a wet hen."

Jesse shook his head dolefully. "Never could figger that feller's way o' thinkin'. Woulda' even felt sorry for him, if 'n he hadn't been sech a damned fool." He gave Lord a bright look. "Get my point, son? He come accrost somethin' new; then set about tryin' t'fit it into a old pattern, so's it'd come out as near like him as he could make it. Well, he was no better ner no worse than any o' his kind, an' he run true t' form.

"Which is by way o' sayin' that all these people that've come out here from back East, an' is still comin', has their minds already made up 'bout most things, an' nothin' ain't gonna change their way o' thinkin', not quick, anyways."

Lord shifted his weight in his chair and showed his companion a sardonic grin. "You can make it plainer than that, Jesse."

His very composure touched off Jesse's temper. "All right, then, dammit! I will! They figger a half-breed fer a damned Injun."

Lord gave a slow inclination of his head. "So?"

"So, what you aim t'do about Fresno an' Lila, dammit?"

"Nothing."

While Jesse was no more enlightened than before, he was considerably more put-out with his impassive host. "You figger t'go on like you have been with the both o' them, is that it?"

"I haven't seen Lila for two weeks."

The information took Jesse unawares. He said thoughtfully, "I see," and absently stroked his bearded chin. "Then that takes care o' that," he finally said. "Now, what're yer intentions t'ords Fresno?"

"Intentions?"

Jesse dipped his head. "That's what I said. You figger t' marry her?"

Lord's features became cold. "Are you trying to be funny?"

A knowing gleam appeared in Jesse's pale eyes. "How come you all of a sudden taken t' twisten' an' dodgin' around my questions, when a simple, straight-out 'yes,' 'r 'no' would do a heap better?" He sat there waiting for some response from the still-faced Lord, but none was forthcoming. The man had retreated from the moment, and nothing could compel him to commit himself. It was a conscious manipulation of the mind Jesse had often observed during his long association with Indians. It rendered a person impervious to any outside influence, and it could be as complete and could last as long as the person willed. More than once Jesse had used the trick himself. Now he felt only resentment at its being used against him, a resentment compounded by frustration. For he knew all too well that until such time as Lord voluntarily consented to resume the former open association, nothing on earth could breach the mental defenses he had erected.

When occasion warranted, however, Jesse could be as passively patient as any Indian. So, now, with a final glowering look at the inscrutable visage across the table, he blanked out his own thoughts and subsided into his own motionless, soundless, timeless void.

A minute passed—or an hour. At the time, Jesse had no idea

which, although later he estimated the time lost at less than fifteen minutes, before Lord shifted in his chair and spoke.

"I'm sorry."

"'Pears you got more sorrow than brains in that head o' your'n," Jesse said bitterly. "Pretendin' it's night don't knock the sun out'n the sky."

"Meaning?"

Jesse hunched forward and tapped a long forefinger on the table for emphasis. "Meanin' the sun's still up there in the middle o' the sky, an' its broad daylight down here. In daylight a man orta keep his eyes open an' see things as they is, not as he'd druther see 'em. You ain't no damned yearlin'. You bin up the trail an' over the mountain fur enough t'know what'll happen if 'n the news gits out that you bin messin' around with them two women. No!" He lifted his hand and waggled it in a denying gesture. "I ain't sayin' you run 'em to ground an' raped 'em. I know Lila well enough t' figger out who beat who t' th' ground. An' I know Fresno well enough t' know that if 'n she wasn't agreeable t' th' idee, ain't no man alive could talk her into it. So, layin' the blame on you fer what's happened I ain't. Howsom-ever, if 'n it goes on, they won't be no question in my mind as to who's t' take the blame." He paused, then added in a lower tone, "It could be you jest plain don't give a damn about anythin' besides satisfyin' yer needs; but somehow I don't figger you fer that kind o' man."

"You could be wrong, you know."

Jesse reacted as if he had been slapped. He stiffened, and slowly straightened, his weathered face turning dead white. The scraping of his chair was loud in the silence as he slid it back and stood up. "If it turns out I'm wrong," he said softly, "I'll waste little time makin' it right."

Lord was looking steadily up at him. "And how will you do that?"

"Why," Jesse murmured gently, "by killin' you. An' I'll make sure you're a long time dyin'."

Lord cocked his head to one side, carefully studying the old mountain man as if seeing him for the first time. "You'd do it, too," he said. "At least, you'd try."

"Oh, no," Jesse said with a wintry smile. "They won't be no *tryin'*, boy. I'll *do* it, an' you'll likely never know, fer I don't fool around with no rules o' fair play. When I figger somethin' needs killin', I kill it, an' it makes me no never mind how." He moved toward the door, then turned for a final word. "An' if yer thinkin' the Injun half o' you will stand you in good stead, don't. I'm more Injun than any buck o' yer mamma's people. I lived amongst 'em when that weren't easy t'do, an' I'm still here. A lot o' them ain't."

Lord slowly rose. "Why?" he asked quietly. "What has any of this to do with you?"

"A heap," Jesse stated. "I ain't too troubled 'bout Lila. She's as tough as you 'er me, an' she's bin caught in gullywashers before this an' lived to laugh about it. But Fresno's somethin' else again. She's waited around too long fer the right man t' show up. If 'n she figgers yer him, I'll go along with that . . . all the way. But if 'n she's figgered wrong, I'll go only fur enough t' see you dead. A minute ago I ast you what yer intentions t'ords her was, an' you said nothin'. You *could* have said sumpin', an' you *should* have, but you didn't. All right. I'll not ast agin. I'll wait an' see . . . not too long, mind. But I'll wait."

With that he turned and went through the door. He was across the porch and stepping to the ground when Lord's voice stopped him and again turned him.

"Jesse, I can't."

"Can't *what*, son?"

"Marry her. Can't you see that?"

"I cain't see usin' a good woman t' pleasure yerself . . . draggin' her good name in the mud, an' leavin' her t' be called 'whore,' an' 'half-breed's slut,' *that's* what I cain't see. How you set about keepin' that from happenin' is up t' you. But you best git at it. An' that's all I got t' say on the subject."

He wheeled and was gone, then, moving across the yard with the gliding, slack-kneed action of one accustomed to covering long distances with the barest expenditure of energy. He disappeared around the corner of the stable and reappeared a moment later astride his tough little dun.

17

Jesse climbed into the higher hills by leisurely stages, letting the dun pick its own way for the most part. Here and there he reined wide of an unnecessarily steep climb, out of consideration for the horse. The moment the timbered terrain and rocky outcropping closed in on him he became sharply attuned to his surroundings, and his head took up its customary incessant turning as he sent his prying gaze skittering hither and yon in suspicious searching.

This was his country, this confusion of upthrust ridges, criss-crossing canyons and draws, long-sighing pines, rioting streams and long slopes steeply falling into hidden draws and meadows. Had he been an artist, he could have painted every detail of this widely sprawling landscape, and could have sketched in similar detail every reptile, rodent, predator, and cloven-hoofed creature that lived here. He could mimic to perfection the song of any bird. The way a deer bounded through the underbrush or rushed panic-stricken along a trail told him what had prompted its flight.

All this had for so long been a part of him that he was no longer conscious of the formidable storehouse of knowledge to which he held the key. He sometimes yearned for the old days. More often, he reluctantly admitted that the present was kinder to his old bones. He was seldom lonely.

This day he was not at ease. The trees stood motionless, and the leaves of the chokecherry and vine maple hung quiet on their boughs; yet a curious, unremitting suction kept pulling him off course toward the east.

At first he was only mildly nettled to find himself repeatedly drifting in that direction; and each time, he veered back and bore stubbornly ahead on a line for his distant cabin. But that subtle pull became a nagging irritation in the obscure recesses of his brain, prompting him to give to the right, then impatiently straighten as he alternately gave way and resisted it. In the end, he came sharply about and went coursing eastward in search of its source, for he was disturbed by this vague pull. It had happened too many times in the past to allow for any doubt as to its realness. From the moment he had left the old Bland place and begun his ascent into the broken high country he had sensed something wrong about the afternoon. It was in the very air he breathed.

That the cause of his uneasiness lay to the eastward he knew as instinctively as he knew when a cougar he was stalking would circle around and attempt to come up on him from the rear. It was something he could not have explained; but he seldom questioned it, and he never ignored it.

He was traveling faster now, as the summons came more and more strongly to him. He sent the little dun over the lip of a near-perpendicular drop and swayed far back to balance the wildly scrambling animal as it took the dangerous decline in a series of furious backpeddling lunges. They rode the talus slide the last hundred feet; then the dun was free of the suction of the rotten sandstone and ran through the shafts of green-yellow sunlight spearing through the trees. The only sounds were the rhythmic breathing of the speeding horse, and the muffled *tunk-a-tunk-tunk-a-tunk* of its hoofs on the deep-cushioning humus.

This was a long, flat tableland stretching straight east and bisected at three places by energetic, spring-fed streams. Nearing the first of these he murmured, "Watch where yer goin' now," jiggled the reins, and felt the dun gather itself and arc up and across the ten-foot expanse of rolling water and rush on without breaking stride.

The sameness of the shadowy vistas down which they ran so steadily contradicted the speed of the industriously working little dun and made it seem that they were passing across the afternoon in slow motion.

The sun was bright in the overhead greenness. Another mile onward the second stream cut across the bench. It was wider than the first, and the effort of clearing it brought a grunt from the dun; it was this straining sound that reminded Jesse Whitehead that the tough little animal had run full tilt for better than two miles. He at once drew up and swung down and ran ahead on foot with the blowing dun dogging his steps. When, after a half mile of this kind of travel, the horse's breathing steadied, he mounted again and continued onward at a steady gallop. Reaching the third and last creek, he put the dun into the water. It wanted to stop and drink its fill, but he said, "Jest a swaller 'er two, now. We're not done runnin' quite yet," and sent it scrambling up the far bank.

He rode more and more cautiously now as the table narrowed to a point. He did not like this place at all. On his left a sheer wall reared a hundred feet into the air, and to his right the rim of the table marked a fall of nearly twice that distance, thus making of this long and flat expanse a gigantic stairstep carved into the side of the mountain.

He arrived at the farthest point of the step and spent a quarter hour working his way through a jumble of boulders. Once free of this, he was in a land of towering ponderosa pines and dense undergrowth, whereupon he breathed easier, for this was his kind of hunting ground; horse and rider drifted through it with almost no sound at all.

The feeling that had brought him this far so swiftly became stronger and stronger, and he went ever more carefully, pausing often to examine the long vistas ahead, and occasionally holding the dun motionless against a tree until he was satisfied by his findings. He was conscious of leisurely movement all around him, and of the steady downpouring of bird songs, though these things registered on his senses without involving his thoughts in any way. But when he saw a doe with a fawn glued fast to either flank run straight down to him and on past him at a distance of less than ten feet, he at once put his thoughts on her and mentally back-tracked her. And when several minutes later a bluejay erupted into furious cursing he went out of the saddle, pulled the dun into the shelter of a thicket, and stood carefully listening to that cursing rend the afternoon in a continuous burst of sound that left him in no doubt at all as to its cause.

Motionless as the trees around him, he waited for the second warning, and when it came in the form of a concerted outburst of profanity from a dozen jays, he abandoned his place of conceal-ment for a second, denser thicket fifty feet to his left.

Then he settled himself to wait. His knowledge of the country was so detailed that he could reckon to the half mile the distance between any two given points, and envision every main and connecting trail between those points. At the moment he was exactly one mile from the Matlock place and something better than two miles from Rob Haller's cabin. Less than three miles to the north lay the Shadley place, and two miles of downfalling terrain lay between him and the rounded foot of the hill marking the lowermost point of the eastern valley's outspreading arms. It was fifteen miles to Star headquarters, directly northwest, and six miles to the Bland place by crow's flight.

All this became a mathematically perfect diorama in his mind's eye, complete with each and every possible interconnecting route. And all this he kept in mind as he tied the dun's reins to a maple sapling and moved soundlessly around the thicket to scan the long vista between the close-ranked giant pines. He felt no surprise when he saw a rider come into view at the far end of that avenue, but he became more worried when he saw a second and then third, to the count of nine, riding single file toward him. At this distance of a hundred yards he had no difficulty identifying each in turn as they approached. Douglas MacKay was in the van, with Rob Haller closely following. A little way back the five Matlocks—John, Luke, Titus, Mark, and Matthew—formed their close-knit group, easily talking back and forth as they rode in and out through the trees and undergrowth. Last in line were Balaam and Newt Shadley.

They passed within a hundred feet of Jesse Whitehead, who watched this procession with narrowed eyes, and who long after they were gone remained wholly motionless at the dun's head, absently stroking its velvety muzzle while he sent his thoughts racing out in wider and wider circles. When five minutes of this silent communing brought him no satisfactory solution, he untied the dun, stepped up, and jogged along the party's backtrail. Ten minutes later he rode into the Matlock yard, saw Luke's slatternly wife indifferently draping wet clothes across a sagging wire, and reined over to her. He said, "Howdy, Idy," and made himself smile when the woman looked around.

At twenty-five, Ida Matlock looked twice her age. Her eyes stared dully out of puffy sockets, and her sallow skin sagged into deepening creases around her mouth and along her fleshy chin. She looked like what she was—a worn-down prostitute fallen on evil days—and he felt only the faintest pity for her, knowing it to be a quality quite wasted.

This he carefully kept out of his voice, which came out, he was pleased to note, amazingly hearty and casual. "How's life treatin' you these days, Idy?" he asked, and kept the smile on his face while she stooped to retrieve a fallen pair of pants from the dirt.

"Same as usual, I guess. Could be worse, though I ain't none too sure about that."

"Hopin' I'd find Luke t'home," Jesse announced. "He around, by any chance?"

Ida reached up a soap-bleached hand and pushed at her stringy hair. "You just missed him," she said. "Him and the rest of the boys, and Rob and old man MacKay and them two Shadleys rode off west less than twenty minutes ago."

"The hell!" said Jesse disappointedly. "If that don't beat all!" He seemed grievously downcast, but suddenly brightened. "Now, maybe I could ketch up to them! Did they by any chance say where they was headin', Idy?"

Ida was so clearly unused to being asked anything, that she was momentarily confused as to whether she actually knew anything worthwhile, although she had been present in the cabin throughout the laying of plans less than a half hour ago. "Well," she said doubtfully, "I heard them talkin' about payin' a visit to some feller I never heard of before. Can't call his name to mind right now, but I think he lives on the old Bland place down valley." She paused, casting around in her mind for something more interesting to impart. "I dunno," she said finally. "They kept sayin' they was gonna pay this feller a *visit,* but from the way they was laughin' it didn't sound none too friendly to me. Who is this feller, anyway?"

Jesse Whitehead picked up his reins. "Never heard o' any such feller," he lied, and turned the dun. "Well," he said, "if I don't ketch up to them, I'll likely see Luke another time." He waggled his hand in farewell and rode across the yard. "Thanks, Idy. Take care o' yerself, hear?"

He kept to a leisurely jog until he dipped from sight on the trail running down the long slope to the valley. He said then to the little dun, "Told you we wasn't through runnin' yet, didn't I? Scat now!" and threw it into a straining run along the falling trail. This day was wrong—all wrong. He felt it like a chill in his bones, and, lying low along the racing horse's neck, he knew that it would get worse.

18

Aaron Lord fitted the last notched rafter in place, nailed it securely, and, with a final bang of the hammer to emphasize the end of this part of the job, sat back to congratulate himself on his progress.

Another day should see the roofing boards nailed on and covered with a layer of turf. The restoration of the stable would be complete. Looking down through the rafters, he could visualize the four horses snugly housed against the winter. He was impatient to complete the present job and get at the haying.

This called to mind the necessity for fashioning new handles for the scythe and pitchfork he had unearthed in the rubble of the collapsed roof. Then there was the matter of repairing the wagon and building a hayrack, tasks which could be done while the hay was curing.

All these jobs piled up in his mind until they assumed formidable proportions, whereupon he summarily dismissed them. The winter was still far distant; the tasks would get done.

A gusty expulsion of breath from the edge of the grove brought him around and he saw a pronghorn antelope buck staring at him, defiance in every line of its lightly poised body. The buck released a second blast, stamped to emphasize its disapproval of this invasion of its domain, and whirled back through the trees with a white signaling of its rump hairs.

The reverberating challenge and noisy retreat brought the two dogs roaringly awake from their afternoon sleep in the shade of the stable. Like twin juggernauts they shot across the yard and through the grove in hot and hopeless pursuit. With his lips pursed to whistle them back, Lord decided to let them go. The chase would end, he knew, as all such similar ones had ended—with the ever-optimistic pursuers eventually conceding victory to the pursued miles from home. They would be lucky if they managed to make it back by dark.

Immediately below Lord, the stallion emitted a shattering snort and wheeled out into the center of the corral. Lord looked around and saw it frozen at attention down there, its eyes angrily searching the benchland beyond the falls; but when he followed the direction of its gaze he saw only the empty timbered step on the hillside.

And then, some flash of light, or some bit of motion on the edge of that timber, caused him to stand up. Searching the edge of that thick screen, he saw, perhaps two hundred yards distant, the head of a horse slide glancingly across his sight. He thought at once of

Jesse Whitehead and wondered at the old man's return; then realized his error when that distant, briefly glimpsed motion was repeated eight more times. He was frowning puzzledly now. Holding himself carefully balanced on the rafters, he went on watching while the file of riders came into view and wound swiftly down off the bench, bearing off on a line that would bring them to level ground at the yard's far edge.

Uneasiness touched him as he watched them descend, and the feeling mounted until he was consciously afraid. Momentarily he succeeded in halting the unmanning encirclement of his mind, but in the instant of victory he heard Jesse Whitehead say, "Maybe y'oughta' do some good honest worryin'," and felt his insides hotly quiver.

The foremost rider was almost to the edge of the yard now, less than a hundred yards away, with the rest closely following. The fact that there seemed to be no talking at all among them struck Lord. He saw the leader move his head back and forth to scan the yard, then halt as his eyes touched the stable. The man half turned in the saddle and spoke to those behind him, and immediately all nine of them were staring across the distance at the lone figure atop the stable. They struck level ground in a loose phalanx and came on, the horses' hoofs making no sound in the sand, and this silent advance gave the whole scene an air of unreality that came to Lord like a numbing coldness rising from the ground and working its way all through him.

It occurred to him that some one of them ought to have signaled some sort of greeting by now, even as he admitted with ever-darkening dismay that he had known from the first that an evil thing was coming upon him . . . that there was no hope at all that this strengthening terror would dissipate under the warmth of a friendly hail from that steadily advancing line.

He saw the sun strike against the foremost rider's florid face and glimpsed a fringe of red hair under that one's hatbrim and knew at once the identity of the man. And now Jesse Whitehead's pointed warning assumed even darker significance, and he dropped his hand to his right hip, only to remember that he had left the gun in the house. Numbed, he took a wider stance on the two walls where they joined at a corner, and from this high and exposed outpost watched the riders as they passed the house and drew up at the stable in a single line. The red-faced leader squinted against the strike of the setting sun, and Lord realized that he himself showed only as a featureless silhouette against the sky. This man said, "Git down from there, redskin," and made a beckoning motion with one hand.

Lord made no reply. He bent, grasped the nearest rafter, and swung down into the stable. Stepping through the doorway, he stopped, and for a wordless run of time narrowly surveyed the nine men ranked before him. These were the hill people, then . . . the land-hungry interlopers whose attempts to invade the valley had been balked repeatedly by Star . . . these the night-riding predators who slunk around the edges of Star's lands, watching for an opportunity to make off with bunches of prime stock, stubbornly hoping for some miracle that would see them gaining ascendancy over the embattled ranch. He had heard of them almost from the moment of his arrival, had been acutely aware of their presence without having seen them, and now they were here.

His initial impression of them . . . one that flitted glancingly across his mind . . . was that they all looked alike. Despite a divergency in ages and physical makeup, each had the same dirt-encrusted, unkempt look, and every face seemed set in a sour, hangdog cast.

The thought occurred to him that but for his being a breed they might well have come to enlist his support in their endeavors against Star. But the idea died aborning. There was no friendliness in their manner, no curiosity, even. And Jesse Whitehead's warning sounded again in the farther recesses of his brain, and he fixed his gaze on the red-haired spokesman, knowing why that one had come. He spoke then, realizing even as he heard the sound of his own voice, how completely inane the words were. "I'm Aaron Lord."

One of the riders laughed, the sound crude and out of place in all that stillness. "First I ever knowed about the Lord bein' a Injun!" He was so pleased with his own wit that he felt constrained to make certain the others appreciated it. "Git it? This breed says he's the Lord; so that makes—"

"Mark," said the red-haired man, never taking his pale-green eyes off Lord, "shut up." He lifted his left hand and absently scratched his ear. "You ain't no full-blood. Half, maybe?"

Lord's answer came out hoarse with impotent rage. "My father was white."

"That a fact, now? A white daddy, an' a good supply o' cash, like I hear tell you got, prob'ly sets you up higher'n yer red mamma's own sin, in your eyes. Likely y'even consider yerself a sure enough man, jest like anybody else. That right?"

Lord shook his head. "Not like you," he replied quietly, knowing it was wrong to do this. "I'd rather be dead."

The man's face flushed, but he checked his fury and showed Lord a tight smile. "Oh, you will be, Injun," he said softly. "You *will* be."

The heat of the dying day still was cupped here in this sheltered amphitheater, but a cold wind was blowing against Lord. It poured over him and through him in a chill tide, faster and stronger with each passing moment. Its pressure made him instinctively brace himself wider on his legs, and it set up a hollow booming in his ears so that the red-haired man's voice sounded very far away. He said tonelessly, "That will be nothing new," and felt the chill and dismally howling wind sweep ever more strongly over the crumbling walls of his defenses. Alone and naked inside those disintegrating walls, he dumbly crouched and waited and heard quite distinctly the stallion stamp the ground behind him and breathily mutter to a mare in that motionless line of horses. Directly above him, a bird alighted on one of the rafters and loosed a single brief trilling measure of its song, took wing again, and coasted away on a whisper.

And then there was only the rush of air around him again, freezing in his brain the memory of a thousand other moments that found him helplessly gazing into the face of unreasoning hatred. Above the bone-chilling scream of the wind he heard the man say, "Let's have your rope, Titus," and thought once more of the gun so far away in the house.

With no telltale gathering of his muscles he flung himself suddenly straight at the line of horses and loosed a wordless, piercing shout as he charged. He threw his arms wide and saw the line erupt into a blurring melee of rearing horses and swaying, cursing men, and then he was beyond them and racing across the yard. He was halfway to the house and increasingly certain that he was going to reach it, when a horse ran in behind him from the farthest point of the line. A loop appeared directly ahead of him. With unbelievable slowness it widened and hung suspended in the air, and he ran headlong into it and felt it clamp his upper arms to his sides in a vise-like grip. His breath went out in a grunting rush and he was suddenly, helplessly, and endlessly falling backward out of a red and wholly empty sky.

Under the bloody wash of that same darkening sky Lila MacKay looked beyond the foam-flecked ears of her laboring sorrel and glimpsed the road directly ahead. She struck the dusty track, reined south, and whipped the flagging animal on.

The terror that had sent her racing down out of the hills and across the valley struck at her again as she felt the gelding's action roughen to a jarring gallop. Driven beyond the limits of its endurance, it was dying under her, and she was still some three miles short of her goal. Too late she realized that, for the first time in her life, she had surrendered to panic at the sight of her father leading the file of riders valleyward. Instead of heading for the Bland place, she had raced toward town, thinking to summon help from God alone knew what source, for no amount of frenzied mind-searching brought forth the name of a single man who would lift a finger for the big half-breed. It was this utterly wrong decision of hers that now turned her sick with hopelessness as she brought the blood-soaked quirt down once more across the sorrel's pounding shoulders.

The sound of the lashes striking the streaming hide turned her sick, for never before had she abused a horse thus. The sorrel was as hard as iron. More than once it had run five miles at top speed. But it had traveled more than three times that distance today. Its once glossy hide was mantled by a blanket of blood-flecked lather, and bloody froth exploded from its distended nostrils with every blasting burst of air. Gone completely was the lifting glide that had for three years seen it hailed as the unbeatable racer in the Territory.

But this day's run had marked the end of its brilliant career. For the last three miles it had been a ruined horse, running on heart alone. Now, even that great heart was faltering. The knowledge of this was now borne home to Lila with shocking clarity, for even as she sought to assay its remaining reserves she heard the heavy in-and-out rush of its breathing thin to a frantic shallow gasping that had no relationship to the rhythm of its strides. The head became an insupportable weight dragging lead-enly against the sweat-sodden reins in her hands. By main strength alone she held it to its shambling gallop; but she had no doubt at all that it was a dead horse she was riding.

They passed from dusk into the darkness of the narrow pass, with the roar of the river overriding all too briefly the sorrel's agonized breathing. And then the lane through the orchards fell slowly to the rear. The ford was just ahead. But a hundred yards short of it, the utter futility of her mission pressed in on Lila with a weight she could not dispel. There would be no help at all in town. The handful of men with whom Aaron Lord had had any contact had suffered humiliation at his hands. They would not only refuse their help but rejoice at his undoing. And foremost among them would be the one man who, by virtue of his office, constituted an authority against which the hill people might have hesitated to act. Out of spite for his lost dignity, the sheriff would not budge from his armchair; there was no one who could urge him to move.

One tensile thread of hope remained, and Lila seized it: Martha's Mission. Even as the idea occurred to her, she reined the sorrel left at the ford and went pounding down the wagon road toward the bridge that spanned the river directly opposite Martha Bland's establishment.

One last endless sweep of empty road, and then the bridge planking was dully echoing to the leaden strike of the sorrel's hoofs. The thunder ceased, and Lila looked ahead and saw Martha Bland step from her chicken house with a basket of eggs on her arm. She called out and rode ever slower toward the woman as the sorrel dropped from a gallop to a trot and finally to a shambling walk.

19

At the moment Jesse Whitehead spoke his greeting to Ida Matlock, Dave Moline let the screen door slam shut behind him and hobbled out onto Martha's back porch. Bracing himself on the stout staff he used as a crutch, he dragged his splinted leg into position and turned his face up to the sky. He sighed in deepest pleasure as the lowering sun poured its welcome warmth over the soreness of his face.

Yesterday Doc Bolter had removed the last of the sutures, and with the worst of the swelling now gone, the mirror was no longer anathema to him.

This was the first time he had consented to abandon his room, despite Martha's repeated urgings to go outside, for he would not risk having his whereabouts discovered by some chance rider, or by the men who patronized Martha's Mission. Indeed, such was his aversion to being viewed in his humiliating condition that not once had he availed himself of the willing services of any of the four girls in the house

But physical activity was as necessary to the big man as breathing, and the two weeks he had spent in the little room had drawn his nerves to the snapping point.

Now, in the drowsy hush of late afternoon, he felt the tension drain from him like water. With his face still turned to the sky he hitched his splinted leg around until he could lower himself onto the top step. He heard someone cross the kitchen, and turned to see Martha smiling from the doorway.

"Congratulations."

"It was either get out or go out of my mind."

Martha gave a light laugh and, reaching out, touched his shoulder gently. "Time to get the eggs," she said and went swiftly across the yard, swinging her basket in long loops, like a young, carefree child.

Moline watched her disappear inside the chicken house, and wondered that people could fail to see her for what she so clearly was, a beautiful and warm human being.

The chicken house door opened again and Martha was just stepping out, carefully handling her basket now, as a horse ran heavily across the bridge fifty yards away. The booming of the planks beat at the softness of the late day with a hurtful hand, the sound so sudden and out of place in all that silence that Moline frowned.

There was a screen of willows between him and the bridge; but, glancing at Martha, who had an uninterrupted view of the oncoming rider, he saw her stop midway across the yard and suddenly stoop and set her basket down. Her voice came to him across the distance, sharp with alarm.

"David, it's Lila! Something's wrong!"

Moline grasped his staff and lurched to his feet just as Lila rode into the yard. In one hard-hitting look he took in the sorrel's ruined condition. In the same instant he caught the sound of its agonized breathing, recalled so vividly the girl's oft-voiced pride in the unbeatable racer, and realized the truth of Martha's warning. Something was indeed wrong. The girl was far too canny a horsewoman to heedlessly run a horse off its legs, her beloved Ridgerunner least of all.

Halfway across the yard the lathered horse took four staggering steps, and stopped. It was shuddering throughout its length, and its head drooped almost to the ground. The noise of its breathing was an unbroken sob pouring endlessly into the shocked silence. Moline heard Martha cry out, "Oh, God! Oh, dear God!" and out of the corner of his eye glimpsed her running forward, and then he was hobbling down the steps and through the dust as Lila slipped to the ground and sagged weakly against the shaking sorrel.

It took him a dozen lurching, dragging steps to reach the girl, and he grabbed her by the arm and jerked her clear just as the horse went down. She tripped on the heavy staff as he flung her past him, and fell loosely to her knees. He said without looking around, "Martha, undo that horse's cinch and try to get him up," and bent to grasp Lila's heaving shoulder. "What is it? What's happened?"

Lila was fighting for breath, and the muscles of her shoulder were rigid under Moline's touch. She said in a harsh croak, "I've got to get help," and bent sharply forward to relieve the stitch in her side.

"Help for who?" Moline demanded. "What the hell's happened?" He tightened his grip, forcing her around.

"Aaron," Lila rasped, still in that bent-over position. "Aaron Lord . . . they're going to kill him."

"Who is?"

She sucked in a longer, fuller breath and painfully straightened. "Douglas," she got out. "And the Matlocks and the rest of the hill bunch."

"But why?" Moline shouted. "Why are they going to kill him, for Christ's sake? What's he to them?"

Lila's head dropped back and she took three deep breaths before answering. "They found out about him and me. This afternoon I saw them heading for his place, and I came down here. I ought to have gone and warned him, but I came here."

"Why the hell would they want to kill—" Moline began, and stopped as the meaning of her words hit him. "What do you mean, they found out about you and him?" he said harshly. He bent and thrust his face close to hers. "Are you saying you been pleasuring that damned breed? Is that what you're saying?"

Lila's breathing was steadier now. She twisted under his clamping hand and jerked free. In swift anger she stood up. "Hell, yes!" she said violently. "Why shouldn't I?"

"Why *shouldn't* you?" he echoed blankly. "Why, goddammit, he's a *breed!*"

Lila's reaction was wholly unlike her. She closed her eyes and lifted her hands in a vague denying gesture. Her voice came out woodenly. "You're as worthless as the bastards with my father. I didn't believe that until this minute; but you are." She opened her eyes and looked at him without seeing him, and her question was a numbed admission of her helplessness, rather than a plea for direction. "What can I do now? I thought you'd tell me where I could find somebody who'd help. That's why I came to you."

Behind Moline, Martha spoke. "The horse is dead."

The quiet words hit Lila like a body blow, bending her sharply forward. She gave a little moan and crouched there for what seemed a long time. At length she sighed and straightened. She threw her hair out of her face with that familiar impatient jerking motion of her head and turned to look down at the dead sorrel. She looked very tall and unutterably lonely as she stood outlined against the darkening sky, and Moline, closely watching her, was touched by the realization that she was vulnerable, for all her habitual air of self-sufficiency.

For a full minute Lila gazed down at the horse, and because she made no sound, it was some time before either the watching man or the woman realized that she was crying. There was no contortion of the sun-tanned face, no quivering of the full lips, only a soundless outpouring of bottomless grief from the green eyes. "And all for nothing," she said hoarsely.

All at once she went into action. Stepping to the saddle Martha had dragged free of the foundered sorrel, she bent and drew the rifle from its scabbard, then turned to Moline. "I'm taking your bay." She caught his beginning refusal and eared the hammer back with her thumb. "You can't stop me, you know. If you're fool enough to try it, I'll break your other leg."

Martha moved in between the two of them. "Where are you going, Lila?"

"To help Aaron Lord . . . or at least try."

"But what can you do against all those men?"

"Not much. But I can kill Douglas MacKay, and I can bury Aaron Lord."

Seeing the iron determination in that set face, Martha knew the futility of argument. She said quietly, "I'll get the saddle and bridle," and went swiftly toward the stable.

Moline hitched around and hobbled after her, and Lila, running, was almost past him when he reached out and caught her by the wrist. Her momentum swung her around in front of him, and she stumbled, off balance. "You're staying right here," he said harshly. "Right *here.*"

Surprisingly, Lila made no effort to break his hold. "I warned you, Dave," she said levelly. "Don't play the fool."

"You're not going up there."

"You watch me."

"But why? Why the hell should you?"

"It's my fault he's in this trouble. I'll not stand by and see him killed for something that was none of his making."

Mistakenly, or out of a desire to hear a truth denied, Moline chose to misread her meaning. "You saying there wasn't nothing between the two of you, after all?"

With a sudden hard jerk that came close to capsizing him Lila tore her wrist free. "You damned fool!" she said furiously. "Of course there was something between us! And you know me well enough to know who started it. All I wanted from you was the name of maybe one man with guts enough to go up there with me. But I had you figured wrong; that's plain to see."

Moline's protest was wrung out of him against his will. "I don't know anybody!" he shouted. "Goddammit! I don't know of a single damned soul that'd go. If I did—"

His voice trailed off, and change came into Lila's face. "You'd what?"

"I'd tell you! By God, I would!"

Lila crooked the rifle in her arm, her eyes closely studying him. She said, more to herself than to him, "Maybe you would, at that," then turned and ran toward the corral where Martha was vainly striving to hoist the heavy saddle onto the bay's back. She caught the saddle, swung it into place, and cinched it tight in a half-dozen swift motions. Tossing the reins over the bay's restlessly turning head, she vaulted up and went racing out of the yard. A moment later the bridge sent up a furious dull bellow under the punishing drive of the iron-shod hoofs. The sound ceased abruptly, and there was then only the fading beat of those hoofs washing back on the evening air.

Into that heavy silence Martha dropped her voice. "She meant what she said, you know . . . about killing her father."

"I know it!" Moline replied furiously. "Hell, yes, I know it! But what was I supposed to do? I've no part in this."

"Haven't you?"

"Hell no, I haven't! Where in hell does she get off . . . asking me for help for this damned breed, after what the two of them's been up to?"

"She came to you."

"She would of come to anybody. I just happened to be here."

Martha shook her head. "She knew you were here. It's closer to town from the ford, but she came to you. Doesn't that tell you something?"

"No," he said. "It don't tell me a damn thing." He gave her a sharper look in the gloom. "What're you getting at, Martha?"

But she was turning away toward the stable. "Nothing," she flung over her shoulder, and broke into a run. She snatched a bridle off a peg, opened the corral gate, and quickly bridled the mare that had all this while stood at the fence staring in the direction the bay had taken. Leading it into the stable, she strapped on the light buggy harness and was backing the mare between the shafts of the trim, yellow-wheeled vehicle when Moline staggered awkwardly through the doorway and halted.

"What are you fixing to do, Martha?"

For all their long, tapering fineness, Martha's hands worked with the competence of a farm woman's as they wrapped the straps about the shafts and snapped the two metal catches into the rings. She caught up a trailing tug and hooked its metal ring to one end of the singletree, then went around to the other side and did likewise with the other tug. Going to the mare's head, she took hold of the bit and was leading it outside when Moline put out a hand, barring her way.

"I asked you what you was fixing to do?"

Martha looked up at him out of cold eyes. "To help a friend," she said levelly. "Obviously the term means nothing to you. To me it means a great deal. Now step aside."

His arm was still held out at a right angle from his body, and the mare would not advance. "Not alone. You ain't going up there alone."

Anger flared in her eyes, but her voice was deceptively calm. "David, I'm not going to argue with you. I'm going to lead this mare to the house for some medicines I'll be taking along. If you don't *step* aside, you'll *fall* aside, because in your condition I can put you flat on your back with one hand. Now, are you going to be sensible?"

Moline moved with amazing suddenness and agility. Keeping his splinted leg clear of the ground, he hopped to the mare's head, swept Martha aside with a shove of his sound arm, and caught the leather ribbons in his grasp. Three more hops took him to the buggy. But here he turned and gave Martha a rueful grin. "This may take a little doing," he admitted, "so you get over to the house and collect your gear while I figure out how the hell I'm going to get myself up there from down here."

"You're not going!" Martha said sternly. "You'll never man-

221

age to climb into that rig and you know it!"

"You watch my smoke!" Moline retorted. "Get a move on, woman!"

There was no arguing with that tone. Without a word, she caught up her skirts and sped across the yard. When she reappeared on the porch a few minutes later, under a load of hastily collected supplies, Moline was waiting for her, his splinted leg propped up on the dashboard, the lines firmly held in his left hand. His features were set in a fixed smile, but the deathly pallor of his skin told her all too clearly what this victory had cost him.

20

Against the great red wash of wheeling sky, Aaron Lord glimpsed a horse rear high and swing away. Dull blows struck the sand, and then the encircling rope clamped tighter about his chest as the horse dragged him across the yard and into the trees.

With his arms pinioned, he made no attempt to struggle; but when the horse stopped, he rolled over onto his stomach and lunged up. He had the loop loose and was jerking it up over his head when more horses ran into the grove behind him to ring him solidly in. He retained his hold on the rope, and when the horses slid to a halt around him, he used it like a flail, lashing out at the lunging, wheeling shapes until they momentarily fell back. Whirling, he caught one of them a slashing blow across the forelegs that sent it to its knees, and with grim satisfaction heard the rider give a shout of alarm as the horse went heavily down onto its side. From behind him someone yelled, "Jerk that damned rope outa' his hands, Matt!" and he felt the hemp burn his palm as it was torn from his grasp.

He was now defenseless, but his darting glance caught the dull gleam of a saddlegun's stock protruding from the scabbard of the downed horse; he dove for it in the instant the horse lunged up and spun away in terror, and then the riders were no longer above him, but on the ground and weavingly closing in. Hands clawed at him and struck him, and this wild confusion of grunting, shouting, struggling men swirled blindly back and forth under the trees, gouging up the brown leafy mold and stumblingly falling over limbs that cracked and snapped underfoot. He glimpsed a scarlet face immediately in front of him, and saw MacKay mouthing orders which he could not hear above the roaring in his ears. He drove a fist squarely into that convulsed face and felt the shock of the blow travel the length of his arm and saw blankness overlay the fury in those pale eyes as the man went reeling back. Someone yelled, "Git away from him! Git away from the son of a bitch!" and the shapes leaped clear, leaving him suddenly alone. He caught the metallic snick of a hammer snapping back and pivoted around to see MacKay crouched on one knee off to one side, a cocked pistol leveled on him.

"Stand quiet, Injun," the man panted through the bloody lips Lord's fist had ruined. "Stand right still, or I'll blow a hole clean through your stinkin' red belly."

Lord dragged air into his burning lungs with a gulping sound. "You crazy bastard," he said. "You expect me to stand here, so you can hogtie me before hanging me?" He ran out of air, gulped again, and could not refill his aching lungs. He yelled, "Pull that trigger, God damn you!" and lunged at the man without any hope of reaching him, certain of death now, and wanting it to come quickly.

To his vast surprise, he saw the gun directly under his outreaching hand; but in the instant his fingers closed around the barrel he was buried under an avalanche of striking, kicking men. Heaving and bucking, he spilled them away and beat them off, and had one leg bent under him, striving to lever himself erect, when a shadow glancingly fell from the trees behind him and struck him just above the left ear. He distinctly heard the sound made by the pistol barrel crashing against his skull. He stumbled over a buried limb and fell through a great hole. The strange thing was that he never struck the ground, but fell on and on through endless space into a place of utter blackness.

It was the fire blazing across his back that hauled him up from the depths of that darkness. He moaned under its bite and heard the sibilant rush of the rope as it came down across his back like a white flame; he grunted under its searing pain and lunged up, feeling the bark of the tree rip into his cheek as he jerked his head around. When he sought to throw himself away from the tree something bit into his wrists and he then numbly sensed that he was bound to it and that no amount of frenzied struggling could free him. From close behind him he caught the labored breathing of the man wielding the rope, and the breathy hiss of the rope slicing through the air again. With the blow his entire back was enveloped in a sheet of white hot agony that brought his voice tearing up from deep inside him. Hearing the sound erupting in his ears so appallingly, he clenched his teeth and strangled it even as it was forming.

There was a deepening gloom here under the trees. He closed his eyes and saw pinpoints of lights dance crazily around behind the tightly shuttered lids as the rope sent flames of pain writhing across his back. The enveloping heat of this serpent-fire now wholly engulfed him, spreading through his brain to fill the corridors one by one until his tortured nerves snapped under the strain and could no longer relay the message of unremitting terror to the vital center. He opened his eyes and saw the trees wavering, dancing, swaying, and dizzily tipping end over end around him and thought, *I cannot bear this.* The trees whirled ever slower and slower and the raging flames sank to a warm and comforting glow, and he thought, *I am dying. I wanted to live and to love a woman. I wish . . .*

From somewhere in the darkness a voice said, "He's either fainted, or up an' died on us a'ready, Douglas," and from farther away another voice replied, "Dead 'er alive, I'll castrate the red fucker. Stand him up an' tie him with his back to that there tree, then git his pants off."

He felt his wrists come free, and again fell helplessly into space as his weight carried him over onto his back. Hands grasped his arms and turned and supported him while ropes again encircled his wrists and held him saggingly against the tree. He tried to lift his head, but it was a ponderous weight that he could not control. Standing thus, with his chin resting against his collarbone, he stared dully at the ground and dimly saw hands working at his belt buckle. It came free, and the hands undid the buttons and stripped the pants away, pulling his boots with them.

And then there was only one hand down there, lifting the symbols of his manhood which had betrayed him to this final indignity and displaying them for the benefit of the audience so closely watching. A voice in that press said suddenly, "Damn me! I've saw stud horses that was lighter hung!" and after the laughter had died, another said, "Cut 'em off, Douglas. Geld the fucker so's he'll tear down no more fences," and then the owner of the hand said from directly beside him, "Rob, loan me yer knife. I done lost mine in the ruckus."

Boots rustled the leaves and when they stopped there was a deep and complete stillness. And then a horse ran in through the trees with a sound like a stray gust of wind roughly scattering the leaves. It stopped abruptly, and the leaves drifted whisperingly down, and there was then only the frantic blowing of a run-out horse whistling through the gloom, and a rusty voice saying so softly, "Slide that blade right back where it come from, Douglas, before this thing in my hand goes off an' turns your head into a smashed punkin'."

That voice was like a bucket of water flung in Lord's face. His head jerked up and he saw Jesse Whitehead sitting on his dripping dun thirty feet away. The rifle in the old man's hands centered hungrily on Douglas McKay.

For the space of a dozen slow heartbeats he stared disbelievingly at that gaunt figure, not knowing that tears gushed from his eyes and mixed with the blood mantling his torn cheeks.

There was a tension here like a far-running shout of warning, a breathless waiting space in time in which no man facing the mounted figure moved or spoke. Across that finely drawn still-ness Jesse Whitehead eased his paper-dry voice. "Before you put that blade away, Douglas, reach out nice an' easy an' cut them ropes." When the order was not obeyed at once, he jiggled the rifle suggestively. "Mind me now, Douglas. I'm not a patient man."

Douglas MacKay was no coward, neither was he a fool. He knew Jesse Whitehead, and so knew that he was standing on the very edge of death. But an inborn streak of perversity held him where he was. "Stay out of this, Jesse," he said thinly. "You don't know what this Injun's been up to."

"I know," Jesse told him. "I know all about it. Cut him loose."

"Comin' in here rapin' white women. You know about that?"

Jesse emitted a short, barking laugh. "Shit!" he said contemptuously. "Tell that to the boys behind the barn."

MacKay pointed a shaking forefinger at Jesse. "You interfere here," he said stridently, "an' you'll not live out the day. I'm warnin' you!"

"I'm countin' to three, Douglas. If that feller ain't cut loose by the time I hit three, you're dead. One . . . two . . ."

There was a tug on the rope binding Lord's wrists and his hands dropped limply to his sides. He swayed forward, put out a foot to brace himself, and fell back against the tree.

"What's ailin' you, son?" Jesse demanded roughly. "You ain't hurt none. Git aholt o' yerself now an' slip Douglas' gun out'n the holster."

Lord closed his eyes and fought down the waves of nausea roiling upward into his throat.

Jesse was thoroughly put out, but immediately his suspicious mind caught at something and pulled him up short. "Turn around, son," he ordered. When Lord slowly complied, he sat there as though riveted to the saddle. His mouth dropped open and all the color drained out of his leathery face. He said in a

226

wintery voice, "Who done this?" and sent his glance striking among the faces turned to him. "Which one o' you done this?" No one answered; but something he saw in one of those faces gave that man away, and he said in a gently questioning tone, "You, Titus? Was it you handled the rope?"

Titus Matlock looked at the ground. "Yeah. I done it, an—"

He never finished. The heavy gun in Jesse's hands swung six inches to the left, and the detonation of the shot ran crashingly into the hills and bounced never-endingly from peak to peak on its way to the far-gleaming snowfields. Titus Matlock took one long and sudden step backward, tripped on nothing, and dropped loosely into the brown leaves. Quite by accident his right hand flew up as he fell, as if to hide the unsightly black spot that had appeared suddenly in the exact center of his forehead.

In the stunned aftermath, Jesse drew his pistol and slipped the rifle back into its boot. He thumbed back the hammer and looked coldly down into the shocked faces. "That's one," he murmured. "I'll try fer six more, if 'n you don't unbuckle them gunbelts real slow an' easy."

From the edge of that carefully watching group, a man threw his voice high. "Jesse, hold on! I had no hand in this!"

A white and shaken youth took three long sidesteps away from the others. His hat was gone and his shock of hair was a thing of brightness wholly out of place here in this increasingly dim light where night was thickening. "Jest where *was* yer hand all the time this was goin' on, Newt?" Jesse asked. "In yer pocket?"

Newt Shadley shook his bright head and made a crossing, wide-swinging motion of rejection with his hands. "I come on account o' my old man done made me," he said, and threw a look of pure hatred at the astonished Balaam Shadley. "There wasn't nothin' I coulda' done to stop 'em. But I swear before God a'mighty I took no part in it. I swear that, Jesse!"

For a long moment the old man on the horse hesitated, reading the youth, weighing him for the truth. He nodded finally. "Climb on yer hoss, boy," he said. "You could do with more backbone, an' might be you'll find it some'ers else. Move now." He watched young Shadley turn away to locate his horse, and had another thought. "Newt."

The man with the bright hair halted and came about, his face betraying the nakedness of his shame. "Yeah, Jesse?"

"I don't wanta see you around here no more . . . not fer a year. But along about this time next year, you git back here an' look me up an' tell me how it feels to be a man. You do that?"

"I'll do it, Jesse. I will."

"All right, then," Jesse said gently. "Scat now."

Newt Shadley went to his horse, swung up, and reined away. Without looking back he put the horse to a climbing run away from the condemnation written so clearly across the face of Balaam Shadley.

And then the feeling of hate and terror clamped down again around the seven men frozen under the trees, now black in the downfalling night. From the edge of that group a shadow voiced its hollow sound of revelation. "Jesse is lyin'! They's seven of us, an' he's got jest one shot in that handgun! Fan out! He can't watch all of us 't once!"

Jesse shook his head. "Yer wrong there, Mark, boy," he warned. "I got *six* shots in my hand. Ain't you never heerd o' that new gun a feller named Colt has put out? It can spit six bullets as fast as you kin pull the trigger. You take a close look at this thing in my hand, an' you'll maybe notice the little cylinder jest in front o' my finger. That's where them six bullets is tucked away. Now, you set tight."

Mark Matlock could not see the gun in the dusk; but he had heard of it. He gave back a step and started to unbuckle his gunbelt; but the man next to him yelled, "I don't believe him!" and leaped forward, dragging at the gun on his hip. In that same instant Lord shoved away from the tree, driving into MacKay from behind. He wrenched the man's half-drawn gun out of his hand and dodged back to the tree and halfway around it, seeking a target. Out of the corner of his eye he saw smoke blossom from the barrel of Jesse's big pistol and heard the report of the shot.

Simultaneously Mark Matlock cried out, spun halfway around, and sprawled lifelessly on the thick mat of leaves.

And then the grove was alive with dodging, running shapes, and the sound of gunfire rolled up in a single, furious burst. Something struck Lord a staggering blow in his left side. He was thrown away from the tree, and he clamped a hand to the place, and felt blood pouring through his fingers. He glimpsed MacKay frantically trying to shove a cartridge into the firing chamber of a gun and realized that the man had been wearing two handguns. As MacKay snapped the breech shut and brought the gun into line for another shot, Lord lunged behind the cottonwood, threw up his gun and fired. Two explosions rent the night. Splinters stung Lord's face and he distinctly heard the impact of MacKay's bullet ripping through the bark inches from his head, even as MacKay gave a choking scream and collapsed with both hands clamped to his left thigh.

With his single shot expended, Lord was defenseless. He made for the writhing, shouting MacKay as a third burst of firing rocketed up to his left. It was almost dark under the trees now, and he stumbled over a limb and crashed headlong, the gun flying out of his hand and skittering away through the leaves. On hands and knees he reached the downed MacKay and clawed a handful of cartridges from the man's belt, then began desperately beating the leaves for the redhead's gun. He found it less than a foot from MacKay's shoulder, reloaded it, and hitched himself around, peering through the gloom for a target.

Thirty paces distant, Jesse was hunched over the pommel of his saddle, clumsily trying to reload his pistol with one hand. His other arm hung useless, and Lord knew that the old man had taken a bullet. He shouted, "Jesse! Hey, Jesse! Get down!" and lunged to his feet and raced that way. He was halfway there when Jesse looked up and yelled, "Behind you, boy! *Behind you!*" He dodged to the right, wheeled, and saw a shape detach itself from a tree trunk; he fired without taking time to aim. He heard the man's wild cry and knew that he had hit him; but his concern was for Jesse, and he turned and ran on. It was growing darker here and he could only dimly make out the old man's slumping silhouette.

He reached him just as Jesse fell sideways. The descending weight bore him down beneath the old man, and for a moment he was helplessly pinned there. Close by, someone called out, "John? Hey, John!" and from farther back in the trees a voice painfully answered, "Over here, Luke. I got one in the chest." A third voice called from the near-darkness off to Lord's right, "I've got the horses. Let's git the hell out o' here. How many o' us is left, anyhow?" There was the papery rustle of leaves, and the first voice said, "I dunno, but I seen Rob git it jest now, an' I seen Jesse nail old Balaam square in the mouth right after he downed Mark. Good Christ a'mighty! How'd it all happen so fast? I didn't hit nothin' but the trees!"

In this gloom Lord could not detect any visible movement at all, but from four widely spaced points came telltale rustling noises and the dry snapping of twigs. He reached around and levered Jesse's slack weight off him and heard the old man's whispered, "Lay still! They's pullin' out," and became wholly motionless against the ground.

There was a slow and steady stirring through the grove and someone said in a pain-wrenched groan, "Douglas? Goddammit t'hell! You'll have to git up by yerself, fer I sure as hell cain't help you." A moment later MacKay's voice pantingly sounded. "Luke? Y'gotta help me onto my horse. I caught one in my thigh. I think I'm bleedin' t'death. Lord God! What a hell of a stinkin' mess this turned into!" Long minutes later, horses moved away through the trees, the noises growing fainter and fainter until at last they ceased altogether.

Into this silence the two dogs tiredly trotted, questing through the overturned leaves. The sound of their sniffing came clearly to Lord, and he heard them stop four times and knew that they were examining the dead men. The odor of blood was a vibrant thing in the night, rising thickly and turning them savagely suspicious, and when they circled close and sensed his unidentified presence their sucking snarling began to rise and fall, louder and more dangerous. He said sharply, "Leopold! Elizabeth! Cut that out!" and felt their astonishment and relief come through the darkness to him like a tangible thing. He heaved his left leg out from under Jesse's collapsed weight. "Jesse," he said, feeling for the man's face. "Jesse, are you hurt bad?"

Jesse's reply came in a strained growl. "Ain't hurt a'tall. It's my damned left arm that's doin' all the complainin'." There was a brief silence, followed by a stirring of leaves as he sat up. "How the hell did it git dark so quick?" he demanded peevishly. "Jest before I blinked my eyes that last time, it was jest comin' on dusk. Reckon maybe I passed out, son?"

"I'd guess you did," Lord replied, and bit off a scream as he rolled onto his side. Dry twigs and leaves had stuck to his lacerated back and the act of turning over tore them loose and jerked every outraged nerve in his back into violently protesting life. His left side felt as though someone were methodically and sadistically drawing a saw through tissue and bone, and he could not wholly stifle a groan as his flayed flesh awoke, screaming. He got his right elbow under him and succeeded in hauling himself to a sitting position. He said in profound apology, "Jesse, I can't help you," and felt cold sweat pour down his face and drip onto his naked thighs. He began to shudder uncontrollably and knew he had to get to his feet. He was appalled at how weak he was and at how the slightest and most careful movement resulted in instant, sickening pain. He thought, *I can't stand much more of this,* and became more and more certain that if he did not get up now, he never would.

Jesse all at once grunted and lurched to his feet. "Hoss," he said to the little dun that had never moved out of its tracks, "you step around here, real easy-like, so's this here feller can grab a stirrup. Watch where you're puttin' yer feet now." He drew the horse around until it was directly in front of the kneeling Lord. "Find the stirrup, son?" he asked, and felt along the saddle fender until his hand touched Lord's. He said, "Now then, I'll ketch holt o' yer left arm an' prize up on that side, while'st you heave on the stirrup. C'mon now. Cain't squat nekked under these trees all night, y'know. Ketch the rheumatiz, certain sure." He started to lift, came against Lord's unresponsive weight, and drove his voice harder at him. "Now, Goddammit, you gotta do some o' the work, boy! You don't git up, I'll wrap a rope around you an' drag you to the house. I'll count three. On the last one, we both take a deep breath, an' then I pull an' you push, an' you'll likely go floatin' right on up through them trees. Ready? One . . . two . . . *three!*"

On the third count, Lord inhaled deeply and pushed with his legs and was astonishingly upright. Immediately, dizziness threatened to capsize him again; but he snared the saddlehorn and pulled himself weakly against the horse.

"How's it goin'?" Jesse wanted to know. "Kin you manage now, y'reckon?"

"In a minute," Lord panted. "I'm a little lightheaded."

Jesse stepped to the dun's head. "Wouldn't wonder," he said matter-of-factly. "Sing out when ye'r ready. We'll move along slow an' easy."

Lord waited until the world ceased to roll and pitch under him and said tightly, "All right," and felt the little dun move forward, taking him with it. With that first step, he emitted a gasp, but when Jesse at once halted, he muttered, "Go on. Go on. It can't get any worse," and was amazed to discover that this was true. The very fact that he was forced to center all his attention on the almost insurmountable task of staying on his feet rendered him less subject to the anguished throbbing of his lacerated back and the gaping wound in his side.

In this slow way they left the utter blackness of the grove and immerged into the lesser darkness of the yard, the horse carefully lifting its feet and putting them down so that there was almost no movement of the saddle Lord so tightly grasped. He heard Jesse say, "Now I know how it feels to be blind," and almost in the same breath swiftly warn him, "Stand right still, son. They's somebody a'comin'."

Lying slackly against the patient little horse, Lord caught the

232

faint pulsations of a fast-running horse come through the night and knew a moment of utter desolation when he realized that neither he nor Jesse had any defense against this new danger.

Fresno arrived at the lake cabin earlier than usual to meet Lord. It lacked an hour of sunset and the heat of the day still lay full in the valley. Circling the lake, she looked longingly out over the shimmering surface and quickly made up her mind. She turned the mare into the corral and crossed to the lake, unfastening her shirtwaist as she went. Two minutes later, poised on a boulder in the shallows, she launched herself outward in a clean, arching dive. The waters closed over her, and she swam beneath the surface for fifty feet, emerging suddenly in mid-lake with hair streaming on the surface of the water. She slid onto her back and floated leisurely, at one with the peaceful setting, her thoughts going easily and naturally to Aaron Lord. With an effortless gesture of the will, Fresno summoned him before her. His face hung there so vivid in its nearness that she clearly saw the thick-lashed eyes, the sensual lips slowly framing words she could not understand. Suddenly she was seized by inexplicable panic. She put her hands down and caught at the gravel to hold herself still in the water, willing her mind to retain the image. She had the sensation of floating not in water but in a soundless vacuum, where far below, pinpoints of fire like tiny night flowers blossomed in the darkness all at once; and then, a long time later, the sound of gunfire.

"Aaron!" she cried out. "Aaron, what's happening?" His face appeared again, and the lips again framed words.

"What is it?" she whispered. "Tell me." And then, quite clearly, she heard him say, "Help me, Fresno. I'm dying."

In terror she struck her feet against the gravelly bottom and lunged upright, wildly staring around. She made herself remain motionless then, trying to convince herself that she was acting foolishly. But the sensation of drifting out over that dark void returned to fill her with a sense of foreboding that would not be willed away. She thought: *What can I do? I don't know where he is.*

Turning, she gazed out over the valley in the direction from which he always came. Nothing moved on all that wide expanse of wind-tossed grass.

Her growing fear took her out of the water at a run and around the shore to her clothes, then running for the corral, donning her shirtwaist as she went. At the corral she stamped into her boots and jerked the gate wide. The big chestnut mare shied away to the far side of the corral, made uneasy by the tension in the woman; but when Fresno flung herself into the saddle, the mare reared and went skittering sideways through the pines. The bit came firmly against her lips, a heel touched her side, and she half squatted on her powerful haunches and launched herself into thundering flight away from the cabin, her body stretching longer and lower to the ground with every giant stride.

Even in her near panic, Fresno realized the folly of letting the mare run herself out at the start of the five mile ride, and after a mile she shortened rein and carefully rated the animal.

For what seemed like hours, the rhythmic beat of hoofs were the only sounds in the night. They rounded the headland and started up along the edge of the green sward below the grove of cottonwoods. Nut Maid, tiring badly, made no effort to jump the stream that cut across her route, but bulled through it. She stumbled on the far bank, but caught herself and ran heavily on toward the trees. She was almost to the yard when she released a shattering snort and shied so violently that Fresno grabbed at the saddle to keep from being thrown.

She brought her quirt down hard on the horse's lathered shoulder and was at once fighting the mare through the trees, handling her roughly in an attempt to bring her to her senses. And then suddenly they were in the clear. But the mare's terror did not abate. Held under a cramping rein, she plunged uncontrollably, fighting to wheel away, and releasing snort after violent snort through widely flaring nostrils. When Fresno would have entered the blackness under the trees again, knowing she must investigate the cause of her mount's fear, Nut Maid gave a savage jerk with her head that tore the reins from Fresno's grasp, spun

234

and bolted into the clear again. And all at once in this windless clearing Fresno caught the faint but unmistakable odor of burnt gunpowder, and heard the oncoming roaring of the two giant dogs, and waited in vain for the familiar whistle that would recall them. But that sound did not come, and the terror that had seized the mare and turned her wild took hold of Fresno now and shook her, and she shouted into the downpressing darkness that was threatening to suffocate her, "Aaron? Aaron? It's Fresno!"

From so near at hand that she could almost have reached out and touched him, Jesse Whitehead said roughly, "Fresno, git over here, quick. They's been all hell to pay."

Fresno's startled scream died in her throat. She freed her right leg from the saddle, kicked her left foot out of the stirrup, and jumped down. But there was nothing at all to be seen in the darkness. "Jesse, where are you?"

"Right here, girl. C'mon."

His voice sounded thin and pinched and she sensed that he was hurt. She took three steps, arms outstretched in front of her, and touched the old man's shoulder. "Where's Aaron? What happened?"

"He's here, an' he's bad off. Give him a hand while I toll him along."

Fresno touched the dun's neck and felt along its side until her hand came into contact with a naked shoulder that cringed away. A shuddering cry went up, and she jumped back. When she clenched her hands, they were wet and sticky, and awareness of what this meant turned her cold. She stood quite still then, willing herself to act calmly. "Aaron," she said, "I can't see you at all. Tell me where you're hurt."

Lord's reply was an indistinguishable mumble, but Jesse said from his place at the dun's head, "His whole back's been cut to shreds, an' he's got a bullet hole in his side some'ers. Jest wrap his left arm around yer neck an' ease him along while'st I lead the hoss. Hurry now, girl. He'll likely go down any minute, an' God only knows how we'd ever move his carcass then."

"All right." Fresno found Lord's arm. "Just hold onto the horn

235

with your right hand," she instructed him. "Put your other arm around my neck. All right, Jesse."

Step after slow step they made their way across the yard until, on the outermost edge of eternity, Jesse said, "We're here," and Fresno looked up to see the house as a more solid part of the darkness directly in front of her. The horse moved turningly against her, and she gave way, and in this fashion was positioned within reach of one of the posts of the porch. She heard Jesse Whitehead say, "Hold him up 'til I can git a light lit inside," and waited there while he went away, feeling Lord's weight bearing down heavier and heavier. She said sharply, "Stand up, Aaron! You've got to stay on your feet until we get you inside." Lamp-light blossomed through the open door, and a moment later Jesse Whitehead returned.

"You'll have to let me take the left side," he told her. "My own left arm ain't no good."

She glanced at him, saw the welter of blood blackly shining on his left sleeve in the light, and knew that it was serious. "We've got to stop that bleeding," she said. "You've had an artery cut."

But Jesse Whitehead pushed his voice unkindly at her. "Git around on his other side, Goddammit! I kin still navigate by myself, which he cain't."

In silence she slipped around behind Lord and grasped his shaking upper arm. "Just turn loose now," she ordered. "We've got you." When he still retained his vise-like grip on the horn, she reached up and forcibly bent his fingers away, and staggered almost to her knees when all his weight came crushingly against her. She clenched her teeth and strained to push herself up and realized in growing panic that she was incapable of lifting him. Holding onto the stirrup with all her strength, she sagged help-lessly under her burden. She gasped, "Jesse, I can't—" and was shocked into silence by the old man's voice.

"Now, listen here, you goddamned lazy Breed! We ain't gonna fart aroun' here all the goddamned night, damn you! Either you straighten up an' act like a goddamned man, or we'll by God leave you stretched out birth-nekked right here! Y'hear me, now?"

The harshness of that voice slapped Lord across the face. It penetrated to his flagging consciousness and momentarily stung him to life. His whisper seemed to die on its way past his lips, so that Fresno barely heard his, "All right . . . let's go." Expecting to maneuver him carefully across the porch and through the door, she was wholly unprepared for what happened. Hauling himself upright, Lord gained the porch's slight elevation, reeled across it, and went staggering through the door, heedlessly dragging Jesse and her with him. Fresno cried out as her hip struck the door-frame with a force that fired numbing pain all along that side, and Jesse Whitehead's tortured yell rocketed out as he was thrown hard against the other side of the doorway. And then they were inside and reeling across the front room toward the bedroom, with Fresno running crashingly into the wall and going to her knees as Lord's shoulder struck the side of the doorway. The impact knocked him sideways into Jesse Whitehead, who gave way yelling, "Watch it, Goddammit! Watch it!" Miraculously he managed to keep his feet and shove the weaving giant in the other direction so that when Lord went down, he fell face-down on the bed. Fresno regained her feet and rushed through the door in time to glimpse the finish of this macabre dance. She shouted, "Oh, my God! Aaron!" and staggered forward, trying to reach him before he fell, knowing that she could not.

Only the faintest light came from the lamp Jesse Whitehead had placed on the mantle in the front room, but even in that dimness Fresno could see the blood glistening wetly on Lord's back from neck to buttocks. She felt her stomach heave and shut her eyes, fighting down a surge of nausea. Behind her something thudded dully to the floor, and she whirled and saw Jesse White-head sprawled loosely in the doorway. She was starting toward him when the dogs' clamoring uproar spilled in through the front door, and this so startled her that she stopped in mid-stride, her glance striking toward that opening. In this pose of arrested motion she caught the distant beat of running hoofs and heard Jesse Whitehead's faint, "Douse the lamp! Quick!"

She leaped across the fallen man and raced for the fireplace. She snatched the lamp down, extinguished it with a swift breath, and stood frozen in her tracks, hearing the running horse come on, and knowing a terror beyond anything she had ever experienced.

21

The big bay under Lila was full of run after its long lay-off, but after that initial burst of speed she shortened rein and held it to a measured gallop. A full brother to her own beloved Ridgerunner, the powerful gelding was so like the latter in action and temperament that tears unexpectedly sprang to her eyes as she thought of the game sorrel now rigid in death in the yard behind her.

Running up the lane between the fruit trees, whose low-hanging branches set up a rustling whisper in the wind of her passing, she smelled the ripening fruit thick in the night and found it incongruous that so sweet a thing could fill an air of blind hatred and death.

And then the scent of sun-warmed fruit was gone, and she was breasting the chill air that poured steadily out of the narrow pass ahead. The scent of wet moss and ferns was like a draught of cool water soothing her parched and aching throat as she plunged into the roaring pass. Traversing the deep cut, she had the sensation of riding a flying mount, for the bellowing river drowned out all sound of the bay's pounding hoofs, and so effortless was the horse's action that there was almost no suggestion of movement under her.

Free of the pass, the bay would have continued along the river road to Star out of lifelong habit, but Lila reined right onto the overgrown trace leading to Lord's place. Her night vision was sharpened to a fine degree, and she could clearly make out the bulk of the hills as she ran steadily toward them across the outwinging base of the great leaf.

She felt the night breath of those hills warning her away from their unkind darkness. It began as a faint wind, partook of the elements angrily swirling through the blackness of that falling country, and sucked ever greedily as it rushed on toward the valley below. It struck shatteringly at the ground fronting the hills' abrupt rise where a line of cottonwoods stood ranked before its spearheading attack, and the force of its attack set off a string of explosions as though a carelessly laid minefield had blown up under the trees. For an uncertain moment it wavered there, then rolled crushingly over the trees and struck on southward, spilling out over the uneasy nightland in a solid flood.

Coming up against it, Lila felt that overpowering weight of horror like a striking fist and cried out against the reality of knowing, dragging her horse to a stop. *I'm too late,* she thought. *It's happened.*

For an endless run of time she sat there taking in the knowledge that her ill-conceived plan of rescue had resulted in the very tragedy she had sought to avert. Trying to foresee what future action she might follow, she made no progress at all into the unknown, and at length closed her mind against all further thoughts but one. Douglas MacKay would pay for this day's work. However far he might run, wherever he might hide, she would find him. Her contempt for him gave way to a feeling of such implacable hatred that droplets of sweat broke out on her forehead and made her gasp for air.

And then the momentary hotness died and left her chilled to the marrow, and she spoke to the bay, loosened the reins, and was once more advancing on the hills at a steady run.

So riding, she came at length to the grove. Fifty feet into the trees she found herself suddenly and roughly handling the wildly snorting, terrified bay to keep it from bolting. She gasped as it shied into a tree with a violence that sent pain shooting up her wrenched right leg from knee to hip. It stumbled, and only Lila's instinctive shifting of her weight in the saddle and her powerful hands on the reins held it up. In this utterly black confusion it went lunging and bucking through the noise of snapping twigs and rattling leaves, and the snarling and roaring of the two giant dogs who came racing in to lay their challenge over all this other noise, so that the night was rendered wholly crazy and wild.

Lila threw her voice at the dogs, and their bellowing at once ceased. She fought the bay out into the clear and wheeled toward the house just in time to see the distant yellow eye of the window wink shut.

She hauled the bay around and ran that way, sending out a call as she rushed up. "Hello, house! Hello, house!"

Directly in front of her, two horses uneasily shifted, swinging around on their ground-anchored reins; Lila, peering at them, dimly saw a wide blaze swimmingly appear on the surface of the darkness. She was out of the saddle and feeling along the side of the blazed-face horse for the brand. Her searching fingers found the off shoulder and slid downward to trace the five-pointed star, even as her other hand reached up and identified the sidesaddle. She straightened then and lifted her call more strongly against the solid bulk of the stone house. "Fresno? Fresno Taggert? Are you in there? This is Lila MacKay!"

There was a sound behind the thick wall as someone hurried forward. The door swung partly open, and Fresno's voice reached tentatively through the night. "Lila?"

"Goddammit! I said so, didn't I?" Lila swore impatiently. "What the hell's going on here? Get that lamp lit in there, for God's sake! Where's Lord? Is he dead?"

All this came out in a single, continuing rush, and Lila was across the porch without giving the other woman a chance to answer. Taking a match from her pocket, she bent and struck it on the floor, caught the gleam of the lamp on the mantle, and crossed to light it. Turning, she saw Jesse Whitehead sprawled in the bedroom doorway. She said blankly, "What's he doing here?" and in two long strides crossed to the motionless figure and knelt. "Jesse, are you dead?"

Two eyes glared up at her from behind the tangle of yellow-gray hair. "Hell, no, I ain't dead!" the old man said waspishly. "I'm jest restin' here whilst I bleed t'death, you damned fool!"

Lila saw the blood-soaked sleeve, and heedless of the man's gasping outcry, seized the coat and divested him of it in one swift, continuing motion. At sight of the blood welling thickly from the inside of the arm just above the elbow, she took him by the shoulders, rolled him onto his back, then guided his right hand to the wound. "Clamp down on that artery," she commanded. "I'll get something to tie it with as soon as—"

She broke off as, turning, she caught sight of the shadowy form on the bed six feet away. Instantly she was on her feet and over to the mantle. She seized the lamp and stepped across Jesse Whitehead's inert form into the bedroom. At the bedside she stopped, bending over to study the bloody welter of crisscrossing cuts on Lord's back. "Good God Almighty!" she whispered in a stricken voice.

Without taking her gaze off the sickening sight, she set the lamp down on the trunk at the head of the bed. She laid a hand on the back of Lord's thigh, but could feel no warmth through the blood crusted there. She felt Fresno move into the room and halt beside her. "Is he dead?" she asked, and reached for Lord's wrist.

"No," said Fresno in a choked voice. "Jesse says he's badly hurt . . . he's been shot in the side . . . but he's still alive."

Lila caught the faint flutter in the limp wrist she held. Not liking what she discovered, she willed herself to think clearly. "Go get a fire started," she ordered the white-faced woman who was staring transfixed at the grisly sight on the bed. When the words went unheeded, she used her voice roughly on the woman. "Dammit, Fresno! Get a hold on yourself! You're no good to him or anybody else, getting yourself set to faint! Go get a fire started!"

Her deliberate harshness jerked Fresno upright. "Yes. Of course!" But instead of going, she stood and stared blankly around the room for a long moment, as if trying to orient herself. She turned and started away, but the stillness of the figure on the bed caught at her and pulled her back. She bent over Lord and gently turned his head until the skinned side of his face was exposed to the light. Her fingers tremblingly touched these slightest of all his wounds; it was this glancing contact with the fact she had come to know so well that cracked her composure. "I've seen cruelty before," she said in a shaking voice, "but God in heaven! I never dreamed that men could be such beasts!" Quite suddenly she was soundlessly and helplessly crying.

This silent agony was something Lila could not endure. She put out a hand and turned Fresno away from the bed. "Go on, now," she said in a voice that threatened to betray her. "Tears aren't going to help him." She accompanied her as far as the door and dropped to her knees beside Jesse. "You damned old fool," she said disgustedly, smoothing the tangled hair back from the clammy forehead. "All the bragging you've done about taking on bears single-handed, and lifting hair off Injuns, and you've not got sense enough to jump behind a tree when the shooting starts!"

Her taunting produced the desired results. Jesse's dull gaze brightened and the set features twisted into a scowl. "And your mouth was allus twice as big as your brain," he retorted with a hint of the old asperity. "Jest what tree would you figger to be the right one, with seven crazy bastards fannin' out on all sides? You'd been in that little free-fer-all, you wouldn't be talkin' so damned smart!"

"Pretty bad, was it?"

Jesse snorted. "Oh, hell, no! Jest a tame little game o' Drop the Handkerchief!"

Lila remembered the bay's insane terror coming through the grove. "Who all's out there, Jesse?"

"Ain't sure. Light wuz poorly, an' everybody jumpin' aroun'

like they'd knocked over a beehive. But I figger I downed Titus an' Mark an' Balaam. An' I recollect hearin' John let out a squall when I cut loose on him, but I don't figger I quite got the job done there. Later, I heard one o' 'em say Rob Haller swallered one o' Lord's bullets. Come t' think of it, right after I come to, I heerd yer old man bellyachin' about catchin' one in the leg. But I figger the bastard's still kickin'."

Lila's face was unreadable. "That's good," she murmured. "I hope he's still alive when I find him."

The look in the green eyes sent a chill through Jesse. "You figger to run him out'n the country," he said, very low. "That it, girl?"

Lila's head moved from side to side. "Is that what you'd do?"

"That's different. He ain't my pappy."

"He was never my father. He only sired me."

"Girl," Jesse said tightly, "you're tough. But you ain't *that* tough. Leave him be. Sooner 'er later, he'll git what's comin' t' him. His kind allus does."

The plea fell on deaf ears. "You kill your snakes, Jesse," Lila said, and leaned over to inspect the wound in his upper arm. "I'll kill mine." She went to her feet. "I'll find some rags and tie that thing up for you. The bleeding's almost stopped."

She was turning away when Jesse's voice stopped her. "Lila?"

She bent over him. "Yes?"

"Did you know about Fresno an' Lord?"

"I knew."

"I'm sorry as hell, girl. This must be rough on you."

Lila gave her head a quick shake. "Not as rough as you think, Jesse. Like you said, I'm pretty tough."

Jesse tried to pierce the surface of those inscrutable eyes, and was again defeated. "That's good t'hear," he said without conviction.

She went away then, to return moments later with a towel which she proceeded to tear into strips. Laying the strips on his chest, she went about bandaging the bloody wound with a competence born of long practice. Finished, she went into the bedroom, lifted the lamp from the trunk, and took out two folded blankets. One she spread on the floor near Jesse, then straddled him, and in two lifting movements moved him onto it. The second blanket, she shook out and spread over him. This done, she moved around to his head, grasped the two corners of the blanket, and, walking backward, dragged him across the front room and into the kitchen. When she had him positioned along the wall near the stove, she straightened, breathing hard from her exertions.

"For a dried up old prune, you weigh enough," she told him, and reached for the dipper above the water bucket near the door. "Thirsty?"

Jesse gave her a dour grin. "Spittin' cotton."

Lila filled the dipper and knelt to lift his head. She had the dipper to his lips and was turning to speak to Fresno, who was swiftly tearing more towels into strips at the table, when the dogs' sudden outcry near the back porch caused her to freeze in a listening attitude. From out in the grove came the sound of voices, lifted commandingly above the dogs' bellowings. Lila said, "Jesus God!" and threw the dipper aside as she went to her feet. Reaching the table, she swung a hand over the lamp chimney, plunging the room into blackness, then whirled and bent over Jesse. She snatched his gun free of its holster and was out the door and starting around the house when the sound of the on-coming buggy reached her, simultaneously with Martha's call. Relief washed over her, and she came to a halt. Above the roaring of the dogs she could hear the frightened snorting of the horse, and she sent a piercing whistle through the darkness, trying to emulate Lord's note of recall. To her surprise, the uproar ceased at once, and the two shaggy brutes came loping up to take station on either side of her as she went forward.

"Martha? Is that you?"

"Yes!" came the woman's reply. "What on earth were those . . . wolves?"

"Dogs," Lila told her, and caught the oncoming horse by the bridle as it came within reach. She guided it to the porch and was moving back to help Martha alight when the murmur of a man's voice brought her up short. "Who's with you?" she demanded. "Did you bring Doc Bolter?"

Martha gasped. "Oh, my God! Brainless fool that I am, I never once thought to send for him!"

"Then who the hell is it?"

"It's me," Moline stated belligerently. "You got anything to say about that?"

Lila was at the front wheel in two strides. "You're goddamned right I've got something to say about it," she informed him angrily. "But it can wait." She reached up and caught Martha's groping hand. "Come on, Martha. Step down. I'll keep you from falling."

They were on the porch when Moline spoke quarrelsomely from his invisible perch above them. "What about me? Do I just set out here and twiddle my thumbs all night?"

"You got up there," Lila threw back over her shoulder. "You can damned well get down." She led Martha into the front room and sent her call toward the kitchen. "Fresno, you can light that lamp again. We've got help."

Light bloomed in the distant room, and the two women moved that way. "I brought some things I thought we might need," Martha said. "Unless—" She stopped, not sure how to phrase it. She stopped and looked fully at Lila. "Are we too late? I mean . . . Is the man dead?"

"Four men are dead," Lila informed her. "But Aaron Lord is still alive . . . barely. Jesse got shot in the arm, but he's all right."

Martha glanced into the kitchen, saw Jesse Whitehead against the far wall, and hurried forward. "Jesse!" she exclaimed, kneeling beside him. "How on earth did you get mixed up in this mess?"

Jesse grinned wryly. "Got bored fightin' b'ars 'n catamounts," he said. "Sure proud t'see you—"

"Martha," Lila interrupted from the doorway. "This is Mrs. Taggert." As the kneeling woman started and rose slowly to her feet, Lila swung her gaze to Fresno. "Mrs. Taggert," she said deliberately, "this is Martha Bland. She owns Martha's Mission, down by the bridge."

If she had thought to disconcert the red-haired woman at the table, she was disappointed. Fresno laid down the section of towel she was tearing and stepped across the room, her right hand going out to a thoroughly shocked Martha. "Bless you for an angel of mercy!" she said. She seized one of Martha's half-lifted hands and pressed it between both of hers. "I heard you say you brought some things. Can you get them, please? I've looked everywhere, and there's nothing here in the way of medicines . . . nothing!"

"In the buggy," Martha replied. "If you'll bring the lamp—"

She turned and left the kitchen, and Fresno caught up the lamp and hurried after her.

In the diminished light, Lila glanced over at Jesse Whitehead. "Well, I'll be damned!" she stated blankly. "You'd think they were old girlhood chums!"

From his makeshift pallet Jesse peered slyly up at her. "Yer shot went a mite wide o' the mark that time, girl," he chuckled. "Could be there's a thing 'er two even you don't know about."

Lila took a step toward him. "What do you know that I don't?" she demanded. "Come on. What?"

Hurried footsteps approached, cutting off Jesse's reply, and Martha re-entered the kitchen with a basket that she placed on the table. Going to the stove, she tested the pan of water, and handed it to Lila. "Would you take this to Fresno? I've got to warm the salve."

22

Alone with Lord, Fresno turned to inspect the sickening mass of lacerations and wondered whether she were equal to the task. She was no stranger to the sickroom. Often she had dressed the wounds of her injured men. But never had she beheld such a grisly mutilation of human flesh.

"Don't think!" she told herself sternly. "Just do what must be done." And so resolved, she fought down the wave of hopelessness that threatened to overcome her and set to work.

There was a steady seeping of blood from the deep furrow in Lord's side where the bullet had channeled deep between two ribs. Folding a cloth, she laid it against the wound and wedged it securely in place with bunched-up bedding.

She turned her attention then to the welter of bloody debris coating Lord from neck to buttocks, and immediately suffered another attack of rising panic. Reflecting despairingly that the most efficient method of cleansing the wounds, and the swiftest, would be to submerge Lord bodily in a tub of warm, soapy water, she decided to experiment with the grossly inadequate means at hand. She wet a towel in the basin and transferred it still dripping to Lord's back. When she removed it, it was coated with a layer of the debris.

With this gratifying result spurring her on, she repeated the process again and again, each time bringing away more caked blood and leaves and twigs, until a final compress drew away only a half-dozen small particles. Abandoning that technique, then, she set about the final stage with her fingers. So completely absorbed in her task had she become that she was unaware of Martha entering the room until the latter spoke.

"I've heated the salve so it will spread easier."

Placing the supplies she had brought with her on the trunk, the fair-haired woman, who once had occupied this room, spread out a clean towel and proceeded to coat it with a thick layer of pungent salve heated to a viscous consistency.

From her bent-over position Fresno asked a quiet question. "Is this the first time you've come back here, Martha?"

The older woman's hand hesitated in the act of spreading the salve, then continued its careful motion. "Yes, it is."

"You took nothing with you that night. I've often wondered at your not coming back for your things. Surely, not even Ewing Star would have begrudged you that."

"You don't carry things from one life into another life, Mrs. Taggert," Martha said, her words barely audible. "I thought it best to leave them here . . . along with the rest of it."

Fresno painstakingly snared a last particle of twig between thumb and forefinger, rinsed her fingers in the basin, and turned. She said very quietly, "You've been on my conscience ever since I came back and learned what had happened here. I asked you then to let me right the wrong my father did you. I'm asking—"

"Don't," Martha broke in gently. "I believe you, and I'm grateful. But there's no going back, you know."

"But it's all so wrong!" Fresno protested. "You've no business running a . . . house! Why not come to Star? You can keep house for me. Please, Martha!"

Martha had lifted the poultice and was holding it carefully in front of her. She gave the taller woman a smile and shook her pale head quickly. "One scarlet woman in the valley is quite enough, my dear. I'll not stain you with my color."

Fresno recognized a will as strong as her own, but she was driven to make one more offer. "Then let me build you a place of your own. Anywhere in Star Valley."

"The color would still rub off on you, Mrs. Taggert." Martha nodded toward the unconscious Lord. "Shouldn't we get this on him before he regains consciousness?"

Without a word Fresno took two corners of the towel and, with Martha assisting, laid it over Lord's back. Taking up a thick square of sheeting, Martha placed it over the poultice, and proceeded to bind it in place with long lengths of bandages which she passed under the recumbent figure and tied securely. "There," she said, tying the final knot and straightening. "Now it only remains to hope and pray that infection doesn't set in."

Despite her overpowering concern for Lord, Fresno was determined to make one final effort to rectify the wrong done this woman who so ill fitted the role she had assumed ten years before. Moving to the foot of the bed, she faced Martha and spoke in a voice which she had difficulty controlling. "Your reason for refusing my offer is hardly valid anymore, Martha, if it ever was." She caught the other's look of perplexity and went on in the same definite tone. "Hasn't it occurred to you to wonder what I am doing here in this man's house?"

Martha shook her head. "Why, no," she said slowly. "It hasn't. Should it?"

"*Shouldn't* it?" Fresno parried. She watched the other turn this over in her mind, and when the meaning of her question struck home, she nodded. "Aaron Lord and I are lovers. That's why I'm here. We were to meet at my lake cabin tonight. When he didn't come, I came looking for him. I thought no one knew, but I was wrong. The scum in the hills found out, and before long, everyone in the Territory will know." She stopped, and then asked very quietly, "Now who's the scarlet woman, Martha?"

Martha surprised her by smiling. "It's trite to say so," she said, "but isn't the world full of surprises!" She gave Lord a long, slow look. "You've waited a long time for him, haven't you?"

"He's a half-breed, you know." Fresno stated defiantly.

The older woman gave no sign that she had heard. "Even with that face all skinned, he's handsome as sin." She turned and gave Fresno an amused look. "He's already gotten himself quite a reputation in the Basin. They say he came into town, raised hell, and put a chunk under it. People have been expecting sparks to fly in Star Valley when the two of you met."

"We met," Fresno stated drily, "and they flew. Now they'll really have something to gloat about."

Martha moved to the trunk, picked up the basin of bloody water and emptied it out the paneless window. "Well," she said comfortably, "I wouldn't let it bother me very much, if I were you. That hill crowd has never been any too popular with Basin folk. I'd guess this latest trashy bit of work on their part will pretty well cook their goose. And if you marry Mr. Lord, here, soon, I don't—"

Fresno was drawing a blanket over Lord. "If wishes were horses, beggars would ride," she quoted.

Martha paused in the act of folding the unused bandages. When she looked around at Fresno, her expression conveyed only mild perplexity. "I know the old saw," she said carefully. "I don't know why you quoted it just now."

Fresno straightened and faced her. "It was by way of saying he hasn't asked me to marry him."

"Oh . . . Would you, if he did?"

"Tonight, tomorrow, any day, any hour."

"I see," Martha said slowly, and knew a swift pity for this tall woman whose heritage and air of self-sufficiency had walled her off from any close personal contact with others. She had no doubt at all that this was the first time the heir to Star had ever permitted herself the luxury of indulging in a personal confidence of the kind so much taken for granted by women the world over. She said meaningly, "I suggest you correct the oversight on his part," and saw confusion change the set of that aristocratic face. "I mean it."

"How?" Fresno asked. She gestured to the silent Lord. "Those cuts on his back only drew blood. In time, they will heal. The other beatings he's taken all his life left wounds that go a lot deeper. I doubt they will ever heal."

Martha nodded her understanding; but above all she was a woman who dealt in practicalities. "Does he love you?" When Fresno inclined her head, she went on. "Well, then, it only remains for you to bring him to his senses."

"But how?" Fresno almost cried. "How do I do that?"

Martha's reply held no hint of sarcasm. "You've something of a

250

reputation for getting your way, my dear. If this is as important to you as I think, I've no doubt at all you'll think of a way to make it come out right." With that she abruptly terminated the talk. Gathering up the supplies from the trunk, she placed them in the basin and started out. She paused in passing Fresno and laid a hand on the other's rigid shoulder. "Don't wear yourself out beating at the wall," she admonished her. "Step back and look for an opening. You'll find one, my dear. And now I'll go fix us something to eat. It's been a long, hard day . . . for all of us."

She gave the shoulder a gentle pat and went away then, leaving Fresno alone with Lord, and her lonely thoughts.

23

All the time Fresno sat beside the bed waiting for Lord to regain consciousness, disjointed thoughts kept coming and going in her mind so that she found it impossible to hold any one for any length of time. She noted how slowly Lord breathed, and for a time concentrated on pacing her own breathing with his, but discovered that she could not take in sufficient air that way, and fell to puzzling over this. At one point, she mentally looked in through the window from outside, saw herself sitting there, and thought: *What an odd place for Fresno Taggert to be!*

For all she had assisted in caring for injured men at the ranch, and had alone delivered two of Joyce Patton's babies, this was her first night vigil at a sickbed, and she found it more and more difficult to endure the interminable waiting.

She was a woman who consciously prided herself on her ability to cope with any situation, and she felt that in the main she had conducted herself with a fair amount of competence tonight. But now she had no foe with which to contend save the passage of time, and this lack of anything to do lowered her deeper and deeper into a pit of depressed loneliness. She thought of summoning Martha to keep her company, but resisted the impulse, for the woman doubtlessly was worn out with all she had done.

From Martha, her thoughts went directly to Lila MacKay, and she wondered how the girl had happened by here tonight. But Lila's restless roamings were so well known as to make her turning up almost anywhere at any time a thing to be expected, or at least not questioned. She thought closely about the girl, feeling as she did each time she encountered her, the blatant sensuality that so strongly ruled her. She was, Fresno realized, one of those rare free spirits who could not abide restrictions of any kind—a spirit as ungovernable as the winds from the high snowfields, and as intangible. She thought suddenly: *I can learn something from her,* and with the thought admitted that her own lofty position in the Territory would no longer be impregnable once the tide of social opinion turned against her.

That it would turn she did not doubt. She was no cynic, but she knew human nature and the way the mercilessly disciplined human mind reacted to anything outside its scope of experience and hence outside its ability to comprehend. Because she had seen that intolerance manifest itself tonight with such incredible savagery, she was for a moment unsure of her ability to cope with it. This self-doubt was so foreign to her that she at once was repelled by it, and in sharp self-disgust she rose and restlessly paced the silent room, determinedly bringing her emotions to heel again.

Turning to the bed, she looked down at Lord, detected no sign of his rousing, and decided to go to the kitchen for a cup of coffee. She found Jesse Whitehead drowsing on his makeshift pallet beside the stove, but no one else was in the room.

Jesse answered her unspoken question. "They're outside gettin' them other springs out'n the wagon."

Fresno knew only that Moline had accompanied Martha from

town. His presence here, after what had transpired between them, was something that puzzled her. "Why did Dave come with Martha?" she asked.

"To quarrel with Lila, looks like," Jesse said disgustedly. "Leastwise that's what the two o' them's been doin' ever since him an' Martha drove in. If'n he don't watch his mouth, he's apt to find his other leg an' arm busted."

"What are you talking about? Has he been hurt?"

"I reckon y' could call it that," Jesse grunted. "From experience I'd say busted arms an' legs generally hurts."

Fresno looked her astonishment. "When did all this happen? And how?"

"The damned fool jumped his horse off a cutbank into a patch o' boulders. He's been holed up down to Martha's ever since."

"For the love of heaven!" Fresno exclaimed. "That's not like Dave at all! Whatever got into the man, I wonder?"

Jesse's chuckle was paper-dry. "Your tongue-lashin' I'd guess. From what I know o' him, he don't generally make a habit of ridin' crazy-blind: so I'd say whatever happened 'twixt the two o' you musta sure enough got under his hide."

"And still he came here tonight," Fresno said wonderingly. "I can't think why."

"Lila's why," Jesse informed her. "From what I gathered, she run that sorrel hoss o' hers plumb t'death, gettin' t' him this evenin', after she spotted her old man bringin' that hill bunch thisaway. They had words down t' Martha's; then he clumb in the buggy with Martha an' follered her up here."

But Fresno did not hear the last part. "Then, she knew this was going to happen," she said slowly, her brows knitted as she worked at the puzzle. "How do you suppose she found out?"

All at once Jesse became evasive. "Hell, you know Lila! Ain't nobody ever figgered out how she latches onto things. But, as usual, she caught onto what Douglas was up to, and made a beeline fer town." He broke off and chuckled again. "Right now, it's hard to make out who's the maddest at her—Moline, fer reasons o' his own, or herself fer makin' the mistake o' headin' fer town, 'stead of comin' straight here an' warnin' Lord so's he could run."

"He wouldn't have run," Fresno said quietly. She sounded very sure about this. "Even had he been warned, he would have stayed."

"Yeah," Jesse agreed, "I don't reckon they's any question about that."

Fresno's glance sharpened. "I didn't realize you knew him. Were you here when the hill bunch arrived?"

"Had dinner with him earlier. I come back jest as they was settin' to carve him up."

Fresno's face went white, and she put out a hand to the table to steady herself. "Are you saying they were going to knife him?"

Jesse was suddenly embarrassed, but he felt constrained to enlighten her. "You bin around brandin' camps enough to know how a bull's turned into a steer. That's what they was fixin' to do to Lord."

"Dear God in heaven!" Fresno said in a stricken voice, and slumped weakly into the chair beside her. She lowered her head and stared unseeingly at the floor, then looked up, dragging her hands through her hair. "The filthy, cowardly animals!" she said in a shaking voice. "They will die for that . . . every last man of them! I have held off running them out of the country. Now I won't let them go. Not if they crawl to me on their bellies, like the snakes they are, and beg to leave."

In the glow of the lamp, her features showed as hard and cold as stone. Only the great eyes burning in the bloodless face gave it life, and Jesse, closely watching her, knew beyond any shadow of a doubt that she was capable of personally supervising the execution of the men who had incurred her wrath this day.

From the front room came the sound of low voices, and Fresno turned to see Martha and Lila staggering toward the second bedroom under the cumbersome burden of a set of bedsprings, while Moline sought to light their way with the lantern. A moment later they filed into the kitchen. Fresno turned with a cup of coffee in her hand. She said, "I'd like to ask a favor of you," and looked squarely at Moline.

The man halted on the threshold and leaned against the doorframe for support. His surprise and puzzlement were evident as he returned Fresno's look. "All right," he said. "Let's hear it."

"I'd like you to resume your place as foreman at Star."

Shock held her listeners motionless. It was an axiom in the Territory that Fresno Taggert never changed her mind, once it was made up. Yet, here she was, revoking a sentence of her own pronouncement with no hint of hesitancy or self-consciousness. For a long moment Moline stood there in stunned silence, trying to grasp the full significance of what he had just heard. And then, his mind made up, he nodded. "I'm obliged to you, Mrs. Taggert," he stated, then ruefully indicated his condition with a glance at his splinted arm and leg. "But I can't see how I'd be much use to you for a while."

"You can sit a buggy seat, can't you?"

"Well, sure. But—"

"That will be sufficient, for the time being. In the morning, I'd like you to go to Star and bring back Gil Hodspeth, Sol Davis, Henry Hanks, Will Brody, and Artie Stevens." She paused, as if undecided about something, then nodded. "That ought to be enough," she said then, more to herself than to Moline.

"For what?" Moline queried. "Enough for what?"

"For a ride into the hills," Fresno stated. "That scum up there has been warned for the last time. Today they overdrew their account. Tomorrow they pay up."

From the door leading onto the porch Lila spoke, "Make your count seven. I'm going along."

Fresno at once put her glance on the still-faced girl. "Your father will be one of those we're after, Lila."

"That's right," Lila replied. "But don't let it trouble you. I'd already made up my mind to kill him."

She said it so matter-of-factly that for a moment the full import of her words failed to register. When it did, Fresno put her cup down on the stove in obvious agitation. "Others will see to it, Lila."

"No," Lila contradicted her. "Nobody else."

Fresno took a step toward her. "But why? I don't understand!"

For a brief run of time Lila looked fully at her, then shrugged and turned in the doorway and leaned back, gazing through the darkness toward the corrals. "That's right, you don't understand. I doubt you ever would. So just leave it alone."

There was something here which Fresno could not grasp. It was doubly puzzling because the silence of the others told her quite clearly that they fully understood. Why she was being excluded, she had no idea; but because she knew so well the nature of these people, she admitted the futility of trying to probe any deeper. Watching Lila's profile, she saw it locked in a stony expression that gave nothing away, and she realized with shock that the girl was perfectly capable of committing patricide. She said tonelessly, "All right, Lila. I'll stay out of it," and turned back to conclude her business with Moline.

"We need supplies here, but I'll leave the choosing to you." She turned to Martha. "You'll be staying?"

"As long as you need me."

"My mother will be here, soon as I get word to her," Lila spoke up. "She's good with her Comanche cures. I'll go fetch her pretty soon."

"Thank you," Fresno said, and returned her attention to Moline. "I'll give you a note for Hod, so there'll be no question of your being in charge." She picked up her cup, then remembered something. "The bodies out in the grove: what's to be done with them?"

"Why," Moline replied, "we'll take them along with us when we make our call on the Matlocks tomorrow."

"Someone should see to their horses. They shouldn't stand ground-tied out there all night."

Lila said without turning around, "I already tended to them."

Fresno returned to the bedroom to find Lord dully watching

the doorway. She hurried to the bed and set her cup on the trunk. "Thank God you're awake!"

He made a vague nodding gesture and started to roll over onto his side. A startled grunt of incomprehension burst from him as pain lashed through him, and he shot Fresno a puzzled look. "What's wrong?" he whispered through clenched teeth. "What in hell is wrong with me?"

"You've been hurt," Fresno told him. She went to her knees and put her hand to his forehead. "You must lie still. Don't try to roll onto your back."

He shut his eyes, concentrating on remembering. "Where's Jesse?" he asked finally. "He was shot in the arm."

"He's in the kitchen. He's doing fine."

Lord's brows drew down. "I wonder why he came back?"

"Because he wanted to. It's all the reason Jesse would need."

He looked at her for a while in silence, and finally mumbled something which she did not catch. When she leaned closer, he repeated it. "I said you've got to get out of here. Why did you come?"

"Never mind. I'm here, and I'm not leaving."

"It'll put you in a bad position, if word gets around. You know that."

She turned it aside with a shrug of her shoulders. "I'm not concerned."

"Don't get mixed up in my life, Fresno. You'll only be dragged down to my level. You've got to see that."

Fresno smoothed the matted hair away from his temple. "I knew the risk I was running from the start, Aaron, or thought I did. It never occurred to me you'd be the one to suffer. You're here because of me. Don't try to make me leave, because I won't."

Again his brows came down in a scowl. "What are you talking about? You had nothing to do with what went on here. Where did you get an idea like that?"

Her ignorance of the true state of things was evident in her frank gaze. "Don't be gallant, Aaron. Someone in the hill bunch

257

found out about us and passed the word. They chose this way of getting at me."

He tried to shake his head, but even that small gesture sent tendrils of pain shooting all through him. He broke out in a sweat and lay there panting. "You're wrong," he said after a moment. "It was—" And then he stopped, unable to voice the truth that would bring her world crashing down about her ears. He said lamely, "It wasn't that at all," and closed his eyes, unable to meet her gaze. But his hand closed over hers on the blanket, and after a moment he looked thoughtfully at it. He closed his fingers, exerting a steady pressure. "Just by taking hold of you, I could break you," he muttered.

"I'm tougher than you think."

He shook his head and was again silent, following his thoughts along ways she could not follow. But that he was sinking lower and lower into that inner darkness where he had for so long lived alone she knew all too well. A sense of helplessness threatened to destroy her composure. She was as full of pain as he, and because she could not endure it in silence, she said the only thing she could think of—the only thing that had any meaning for her in this endless moment of loneliness.

"I love you, Aaron. You know that, don't you?"

His dark gaze lifted to her face. He stared gravely at her for a long moment, then let his hard-held breath out like a sigh. "Yes," he said. "I'm afraid I do."

"Never be afraid of love, Aaron. I'm not."

His hold tightened painfully. "Not for myself: for you. You're lost."

"That's not true at all. I am following a different path now. But I know where I'm going, and I expect the journey to be most rewarding. I mean that, my dear."

"The old path was safer."

She shook her head. "It led in an endless, meaningless circle."

"But it was safe," Lord insisted more urgently.

"So is a virgin's bed. But it's also cold. I don't like being cold."

That brought a slow smile to his lips and kindled little fires in his eyes. He said drawlingly, "You've no cause for fear in that quarter," and became openly amused at the run of color in her face. "You're even prettier when you're embarrassed," he said, and lay there smiling at her.

Some too-long inactive muscle in his body signaled for relief, and he started to alter his position on the bed. But at the first tentative movement he sucked in his breath with a loud, raw sound and went rigid as pain solidly encased him and squeezed water from his pores like a sponge.

Fresno slipped to her knees beside him, wanting to cry. She pressed her hand against the side of his neck and felt the rattling clamor of his pulse under the clammy skin and knew a feeling of utter helplessness. She said, "Is it so very bad, Aaron?" and gripped his cold hand with all her strength.

"It'll pass," he whispered thinly.

"I wish I could take at least a part of it away. I wish it were I instead of you. You could give me so much more than I'm able to give you."

The pain gradually eased, and he lay watching her disapprovingly. "That's not true. Why did you say it?"

But she didn't answer and he didn't repeat the question. Her face came closer and she gently laid her cheek against his, not speaking. She was a fair and complex woman, hard to know. She did not reveal herself readily as a rule, and she never spoke except directly. But he felt somehow she was terribly involved, and he tried to think—when the pulsing waves of pain let him alone—that it was strange he knew so little of her. Her hand was cool and soothing against his neck; her nearness comforted him. There was a depth to her, very real and very profound. It was a stillness, a reservoir of latent power. He could not find quite the word he wanted, but he had the meaning. It was as though she possessed qualities beyond her own understanding which were all the greater and more real because of her unawareness of them. When she drew back and looked at him now, he saw this unplumbed depth of her reserves in her eyes, its clear and change-less reflection. It made him say, "I don't know much about you. What made you what you are?"

She showed him a faint smile. "My father and my mother working at cross purposes, I suppose. My father was a law unto himself—always taking, never giving. My mother was, like Mary, 'full of grace and blessed among women.' I was in awe of him, but I loved her."

"If she came into this room now," Lord said quietly, "what would she say, Fresno?"

Fresno was still-caught, picturing the scene in her mind. Her features softened as she looked into a remembered face and heard a remembered voice. "She would say, 'Be very sure and very honest with yourselves and with each other.' "

"Nothing else?"

Fresno shook her head, quite certain on this point. "No. Nothing else. She wouldn't judge another . . . ever. That was why my father was afraid of her. He could never make her follow him. He said, 'A thing is this, or a thing is that, because I see it that way.' She said, 'I see what looks like a weed, but it might very well turn out to be a flower, so I will leave it alone.' "

For a time he studied her, his big hand maintaining its pressure. "Your father undoubtedly won a battle or two," he said then, very low, "but your mother won the war. I wish I'd known her. I would have liked her."

Fresno nodded, blinking back the tears. "Yes," she whispered, "you would have. And she would have loved you."

He started to shift his position again, and again the slight movement brought a look of acutest distress to his face, and he caught his breath and held it while he waited out the pain. It took its toll of his scant reserves, and he seemed to sink deeper into the bed. He lay with his eyes closed, breathing shallowly in the backwash of pain, and his hand went lax and fell away from hers.

"Try to sleep a little," she said. "I'll be here."

"This is too much for you," he said on the drowsy edge of sleep. "You can't look out for two helpless men alone."

"I'm not alone, dear. Lila MacKay and Martha Bland and Moline arrived soon after I did."

That roused him to full wakefulness. "Lila MacKay?" he echoed. "What's she doing here? And how come Martha Bland and Moline showed up?"

"Lila saw her father leading the hill people in this direction and went for help. She killed a horse getting to Martha's place. After she left, Martha and Moline followed in the buggy. I don't know what I'd have done without them."

"Where are they now?"

"In the kitchen, or were when I left. They've brought that old pair of springs in for somebody to use."

Lord grinned wryly. "Sorry I'm not fixed up for overnight guests."

"We'll make out," Fresno assured him, and picked up her cup. When she started for the kitchen, she glanced back and saw that he was asleep again.

Back at her post a few minutes later, her feeling of temporary encouragement took a downward turn when she noted the reluctant way Lord breathed. Not even sleep could wholly quiet his flayed nerves. The slight expansion of his chest with each indrawn breath brought a rhythmic play of the back muscles, which in turn set up a rising and falling graph of pain in his subconscious. Each high point was marked by a momentary catch in his breath, with its following faint moan. It was a steady, hurtful sound in the room, and it would not subside into monotony but worked more and more unkindly on her nerves until she found herself tensely waiting for each slow breath to catch and hold and slide away on that note of suffering. She got up and paced the floor, but even that did not free her from tension, and after two hours she was too exhausted to leave her chair.

In this ragged frame of mind she searched for something that would make the time pass more quickly, but there was simply nothing to do. She spent fifteen minutes braiding her hair into a thick plait, and when that was done, she again sat and followed the nerve-wracked graph of pain with a helpless concentration that held her rigid in her chair. With a slow turning over of her mind she became aware that Lord's eyes were open again, and she realized that he had been silently watching her for some time. His lips moved, but she could not catch what he was saying. She leaned down, and this slight motion caused the room to tilt crazily so that she grabbed the edge of the bed to keep from toppling to the floor. "I can't hear you," she said.

He waited for another ripple of pain to flatten out, and ran his tongue over his dry lips. "I said there's no sense in your sitting there like that all night. There's room on the other side of me. Lie down and get some sleep."

"I might not wake in case you needed me."

His words thickened and ran together as sleep dragged him downward again. "I'll yell loud enough to be heard. Lie down, now."

"All right."

She got up and moved stiffly around the foot of the bed, shocked at how heavy her body felt. She had not thought it possible to be this tired. She seemed to be moving with the leaden-footed sluggishness of a dream figure. Letting herself down carefully to avoid jarring Lord, she stretched out beside him and groaned aloud with the blessed relief of easing muscles. Her last thought was that she had never felt such a wonderfully soft mattress.

24

The odor of frying bacon pulled Lord up from the uneasy depths of half-wakefulness. He lay there savoring this smell and laboriously trudged back through drifting layers of memory in search of the time he had last eaten. The present flavor dominated his thoughts so strongly that it kept getting between him and his object, but he was quite certain the meal had not been breakfast. He turned and plodded forward and heard a voice say, "My belly's been slappin' hell out o' my backbone for the last hour 'er better," and glimpsed a worn old face somewhere below him in the mists, and tried to put a name to it. After what seemed like hours of this kind of labor, he said, "Jesse Whitehead. He ate with me. Venison." With this much accomplished, he worked at affixing the time of day, and at long last hazily recalled seeing the old man go jouncing away on the little dun. It was quite light and quite warm, with the shadows lengthening, and he gave a satisfied grunt. "That would make it after noon," he decided.

Feeling more sure of his ground now, he moved forward again and got as far as the roof of the stable, when a curtain abruptly dropped down out of the darkness and left him stranded above the ground.

In rising panic he tried to peer through the curtain, but it was an impenetrable mass of cloying terror before him. Turning on the precarious footing of his aloneness, he discovered that he could see behind him quite clearly, but when he faced around again, the curtain was still there, hanging solidly down into a lower darkness, and he dared not descend from his present position because of the awful something he sensed lurking below. In mounting horror he felt it come closer, to the bottom of his lookout, and there stop and coil in upon itself and expectantly wait. He could not see it, but he definitely could feel its gradual, remorseless swelling. Panic tore at him, and then his whole body contracted and became tinier and tinier until it was nothing but a minute nodule perched precariously on the knife edge of the wall above that swelling danger. And then the wall beneath him started to tremble, and he gave a single, soundless scream and reached out both hands to save himself. He toppled over the edge and plummeted heavily downward into the expanding coils of darkness. He screamed again and would have flung himself away, but from somewhere just beyond the edge of darkness a strong hand grasped him and roughly drew him back to safety. The movement sent bright rivulets of pain streaming all down his back and around and across his left side, and he whimpered before this overwashing torture that threatened to fling him headlong into that feared darkness again. And then he heard Lila sternly say, "Dammit, Aaron! Cut out that bawling and wake up!"

He opened his eyes to find her bending over him, her eyes sharply examining him. He said in the unwieldy voice of intense sickness, "What's wrong? What happened?" and was more relieved to find her there than he would have thought possible.

"You were having a nightmare."

"Oh."

"What was it about?"

He started to describe it, then caught himself. "I don't remember." He breathed slowly and deeply and felt the taste of bacon on his tongue, thicker and stronger, and saw the plate on the trunk close to his head. "I'm starved."

"You can eat after I've washed some of that dirt off you. I've already had my breakfast, but I'm apt to lose it if I have to look at you much longer."

So saying, she wrung out a cloth in the basin she had brought, and proceeded to swab his face. "Now you listen to me," she commanded in a low voice. "Fresno's eating now, but she's apt to be back any minute, so pay attention." She made a final swipe at his face, then drew his left arm straight and set to work scrubbing the crusting of caked blood and dirt from it. "She knows nothing, and won't, as long as you and me keep our stories straight. She thinks the whole damned thing is her fault, and that's the way we'll leave it."

"But she had nothing to do with it!"

"You don't say!" Lila drawled sarcastically. "No wonder you two got together so quick. Neither one of you has sense enough to pour sand out of a boot!"

Her careless washing, and her taunting words, touched off Lord's temper. "Of course you don't figure in this at all!"

"You've got the point," Lila told him. "As far as Mrs. Star Taggert is concerned, I don't. She's done a lot of thinking, and though I'm damned if I know how she managed to do it, she's come up with just about all the wrong answers there are. And that's fine. I'm out of the picture. Understand?"

"No," Lord murmured, "I don't."

"Oh, hell!" Lila said disgustedly. "I'll put it plainer. As far as she knows, last night was the first time I ever laid eyes on you. If she was to find out that you and me . . . Well, even you've got brains enough to see that her and me aren't exactly cut out of the same bolt of goods. You let her find out that her great, sacred knight in shining armor wasn't all that pure and noble when it came to blanket-wrestling a piece of trash like Lila MacKay, and she'd fly apart like a jar of fruit dropped on the floor."

"She's not made of glass!" Lord said defensively. "I won't lie—"

"*God damn you, listen to me!*" Lila hissed furiously. "If you think I'm doing this for you—or just to keep my own skirts clean—you've got less brains than I gave you credit for! I don't give a damn what she thinks of *me*, but, and so help me God, I don't know why, I *do* care what she thinks of *you!* Will you get that into your thick head?"

She dropped the cloth into the basin, and reached for the plate. Hitching her chair forward, she broke off a piece of bacon and thrust it into his mouth. "Chew on that, and on the rest of what I've got to say," she ordered. "Fresno's in love with you, the poor little fool. She never could stand Farley Taggert, from the day she married him. But for years she's given every man that came sniffing around her the cold shoulder. Then you show up, and for reasons I'll not go into, she decided you were something special. Well, that's her business . . . and yours. Nobody else's. And it should stay that way. Is that plain?"

Lord swallowed and nodded. "I guess so."

"Well, see that you bear it in mind," Lila ordered. She watched him accept another bite and slowly chew it, and noted how carefully he worked his jaws, as if even that slight motion might jar loose more pain. She said suddenly, "How do you feel about all this?" and saw his face darken with the sudden surge of passion.

"Somebody is going to pay."

Lila inclined her head. "Four already have. The rest will have their accounts totted up today."

Lord's eyes struck up at her. "What are you talking about?"

"I'm talking about the Star hands that are on their way over here by now, probably. Fresno's put Dave Moline back on the payroll, and he's taking some men into the hills on a little business call this afternoon."

Lord swore under his breath. "This is no affair of hers! I'll not have her fighting my battles for me!"

Lila was not at all concerned with his show of temper. "This was her fight long before you ever showed up, my friend," she told him. "You just happened along in time to touch the match to the powder keg. So, you can rave and rear around all you want, it won't stop Star from stomping a few snakes into the ground. Feel better now?"

This last referred to the final section of bacon she placed between his lips, but he deliberately chose to misinterpret it.

"No, dammit. I feel like a helpless invalid that somebody else has got to take care of . . . even to doing my fighting for me!"

Lila emitted her explosive, barking laugh. "God! What a self-pitying bastard you are! There's no doing the right thing for you!" She stopped, took up the basin, and went to her feet. For a moment she stood over him, a tall, grave girl who would not let

266

her gentler feelings show. "Get that sour-apple look off your face, and concentrate on getting well," she ordered him. "Things aren't as rotten as they smell sometimes."

And so saying, she turned and strode out of the room, leaving him staring after her and pondering her parting words.

25

Shortly before noon, Moline returned from Star with four mounted men following the buggy. Some distance back, the fifth man, long and solemn Harry Hanks, drove a big wagon piled high with the supplies Fresno had requested.

Drawing up at the front porch, Moline laboriously lowered himself from the buggy, caught a porch support, and levered himself around. "You can get down," he told them. "Mrs. Taggert will want to see you before we go."

He opened the door to find Fresno crossing toward him. He said, "They're waiting, ma'am," and watched the effect this had on her. She could not have failed to hear the rattle of the approaching wagon, nor the loud challenge from Leopold; yet at his words she stopped, all color draining out of her face. Knowing full well what the next few minutes might do to her, he felt quick compassion for her, and spoke gently. "Don't underrate them, ma'am. They're good men, and you stand pretty tall in their eyes."

She drew herself straight. "Thank you, Dave. Will you ask them to come in, please?"

A moment later the five trooped in, at once doffing their hats as they straggled into a line down the room. They clearly were puzzled by this situation, but long association with the cool and competent woman in front of them had taught them that she was not given to empty theatrics. They had been apprised of the task outlined for them this day. They were, however, mystified over being summoned into this room.

Their unquestioning loyalty touched Fresno as she stood in front of the fireplace and looked directly at each man in turn. For a moment she was reassured.

"You are undoubtedly wondering why I asked you to come in," she said. "By way of explaining, I'd like you all to step into the next room. There's something I want you to see."

Gil Hodspeth, with more than twenty years experience as a Star hand, acted as spokesman. "Jest lead the way, ma'am."

She turned and entered the bedroom. Bending over the sleeping Lord, she lifted the two lower corners of the salve bandage and held it away to reveal the deeply scored back. She said nothing as each of the five men stepped cautiously forward and looked at the revolting sight. But her gaze studied each of those well-known faces, and she saw the shock and revulsion visible there. She saw Sol Davis close his eyes and turn a sickly grey under his leathery brown skin, and she saw Will Brody swiftly step back after one brief glance and clutch Henry Hanks' arm to steady himself. And she heard the low murmur of curses that ran through the group.

When the last man had had his look, she replaced the bandage and led the way back into the front room. At the fireplace again, she swung around. "That," she told them, "is the work of the hill bunch. Yesterday they rode down here and caught Mr. Lord alone. Four of them are lying out under the cottonwoods. Dave has volunteered to return them to their relatives with Star's compliments. Do the rest of you agree it's the fitting thing to do?"

Artie Stevens, eldest of the group and never a patient man, sought to put an end to what he considered a waste of words. "What're we standin' around here for?" he demanded of no one in particular. "I thought it was all settled."

"It's been too long comin'," seconded Will Brady, and glared about, as if daring anyone to contradict him. "'Way too long," he added emphatically.

Fresno reached out and grasped the corner of the mantle, seeking to draw strength from the unyielding wood. "Hear me out," she said, and was surprised that her voice did not betray her inner turmoil. "The reason behind this is something you will learn, sooner or later. I prefer that it come from me."

Her words brought them up short and at once fixed their attention on her more closely than before. The strained look on her face caused Gil Hodspeth to search his mind for something he had sensed for some time now without being able to put a name to it. "Whatever you have to say, we'll listen to, ma'am," he stated quietly, and nodded his encouragement to her.

"Thank you, Hod," Fresno replied. On the point of going on, she hesitated, wondering whether she actually were capable of going through with it. Weakness trembled her legs under her, and she spoke quickly, almost roughly, to mask her mounting panic. "It happened because the hill bunch found out about Mr. Lord and me . . . that we are lovers."

Shocked silence greeted her confession as the five riders vainly sought to take it in. Three of them had been present in this very yard on the occasion of the meeting between their employer and the half-breed. All had known the truth about the shooting incident that had left one of their number dead. None had been proud of his silence in the face of Moline's lie regarding that shooting. They had their code which accorded every man the right to defend himself, and the fact that they had betrayed that code by their silence was a source of shame to them all.

But this was something outside their experience . . . outside their ability to imagine, even. This was covered by another code which had never before affected them personally, but which had been ingrained in them from birth as an unbreachable commandment. And here was this woman, whose every action and word had to them embodied the very essence of integrity and morality, openly stating that she had transgressed that commandment by giving herself to a man of inferior blood.

"You mean—" Will Brody began, and could not go on—not because of the delicacy of the subject, but because the idea of this stately woman having committed such a heinous crime was utterly intolerable to him. He dropped his gaze to the floor and tried again. "You mean to say that you and this breed—" He gave up, unable to put a name to it.

"Yes, Will," Fresno said levelly, "we have been lovers for some time now."

Brody lifted stricken eyes. "That just can't be, Mrs. Taggert!" he burst out, and it was as though he were pleading with her to deny it. "That man in there's a *breed!* You can't tell me you'd—" He stood there, shaking his head miserably. "Not *you!*"

Fresno's face stiffened. "That man in there is a *man,* Will."

Brody changed then. He took a deep breath and slowly exhaled, and in that moment he shut her out as completely as though he had closed a door in her face. He said heavily, "I can't accept that, Mrs. Taggert. Not any of it."

Fresno was gripping the mantle so tightly her arm shook. Now that the horror was upon her, she realized how unprepared she had been for this . . . how defenseless. Searching numbly for words to lay across the widening chasm, she heard Moline's quiet voice reach past her from his position on her left.

"I seem to recollect your saying on the way over here that you'd never known Mrs. Taggert to play the fool, Will. You wouldn't be saying now that this is an exception, would you?"

Brody shifted his aroused stare to Moline. "That was somethin' altogether different, an' you know it," he said harshly. "You never said nothin' to me, or the rest of the boys here, about these goin's on, else I'd never of come over here in the first place!"

Moline hitched himself forward a step so that he was positioned squarely in front of the furious man. "That being the case," he said softly, "maybe you'd best leave." He waited, and when Brody remained stubbornly in place, he said, with a dangerous lift to his voice, *"Now,* Will. Don't wait any longer."

For a moment, Brody sought to face the big man down, but the silence grew thinner and colder, and all at once he said, "Aaaah!" in a tone of deepest disgust and wheeled for the door. He hauled it violently back on its hinges and let it slam against the wall.

Swiveling his head around on his heavy shoulders, he fixed a look of open revulsion on the woman staring at him out of stricken eyes. "You need some good clean air in this room," he said wickedly. "They's a Injun stink to it." With that, he tramped outside to his horse, hauled himself aboard, and reined out of the yard.

In the backwash of silence, Moline's matter-of-fact question was almost laughable. "Well, now, who else thinks Aaron Lord has got smallpox?"

"*Smallpox?*" Sol Davis echoed blankly, his cumbersome way of thinking badly affected by the scene. "I never heard nobody say he had them, too!"

He was a leathery, stringbean figure of a man with an Adam's apple that leaped and cavorted seemingly with a life of its own whenever he was agitated. It gave a spasmodic jump now as he spoke, and the planes of his homely face had a worried look.

On this distressed individual Moline placed his sardonic gaze. "Judging from the way Will lit out, Lord must have *something* mighty catching, wouldn't you say?"

"No," Sol contradicted him, his thinking once again safely on its plodding way. "It ain't fair to be too hard on old Will, not considerin' what Mrs. Taggert done said jest now."

"Oh," Moline murmured, "I see." He stood there awkwardly off balance with his splinted leg angled stiffly out, a half smile pulling his lips thin. He was by nature intolerant of indecision in another, but his knowledge of these men and of their importance to Star and its vulnerable owner prompted him to hold his temper. A summary command, issued by him now, would doubtlessly be obeyed, if only from fear. It would not resolve the issue.

For perhaps the first time in his life, Moline was aware of deliberately controlling his impatience, and even in the tension of the moment felt a twinge of satisfaction that he could do so without fear for his image. He let the silence build up, then eased his voice into the waiting void. "Funny thing just occurred to me, Sol. I always figured I'd been hired on to do a job I was equipped to handle—like break horses, or mend fences, or doctor wormy cows. Isn't that sort of the way you figured, too?"

"Well, yeah," Sol admitted, "but this throws a different light on things, Dave. Makes a hell of a difference. You know that!"

"Why, no," Moline disagreed. "I don't know anything of the kind. About the only thing I do know for sure, right now, is that Mrs. Taggert has hired me on again . . . to do the same job I've always been well-paid for, and for the life of me I can't recall that job ever including having to mind Mrs. Taggert's personal business for her."

The lank rider's Adam's apple gave another convulsive jump. "Now then, that ain't the point, Dave, an' you know it!" he protested. "It ain't as if they was alike—the two of them." He tried to meet Fresno's gaze, but could not. "I mean, that feller in there ain't her kind. What's it goin' t'look like t'anybody that don't know her like we do? I mean, it jest ain't somethin' a white woman'd do. Anybody knows that!"

Moline's expression was a study in innocence. "I didn't realize you knew Lord, Sol."

"Hell, I *don't* know him! Not a'tall. Only other time I seen him was the day we come over to run him out'n the valley."

"You mean the day Mrs. Taggert fired me for lying about Lord shooting Frank in the back?" Moline said it deliberately, knowing his man, and seeing this frank admission of his own wrongdoing throw Sol into deeper confusion.

All at once Sol was openly angry. "T'hell with the whole sorry thing!" he said loudly. "I ain't gonna git me no headache tryin' to figger out no more riddles! I got work waitin' for me back to the ranch; so if we ain't goin' after that crowd up there, I'm goin' home an' git back to work on them corral posts."

On the point of turning away, he glimpsed Fresno's face, and realized there was an apology owing her. "As for what I said about you, ma'am . . . I started talkin' before I started thinkin', I reckon. You ain't never come nosin' around, tryin' t'tell me how to do my job; so it sure ain't for me to tell you how to do yours." He ran out of breath, gulped, and jammed his battered old hat down around his ears. "Now then," he stated belligerently to the others, "I'm goin' outside, an' I'm waitin' fer maybe five minutes or so. An' then, if we don't head fer the hills, *I'm* headin' fer home."

His boot heels struck emphatic echoes from the floor as he stalked out onto the porch.

Moline glanced at Gil Hodspeth. "Well, Hod?"

The stocky rider was Sol Davis' partner and as unlike him as a man could be. He was quick to react to any given situation, and as quick to speak his mind. Having come to Star with his parents as a boy of ten some twenty-five years ago, he regarded the ranch, its mistress, and his own position in the hierarchy from a wholly personal and protective viewpoint. Better than anyone here, he knew what was going on and what might result from a tragic division of loyalty in the ranks of Star employees. In the controversy over Frank Wheeler's death he had, by his initial silence, bartered his honor for the welfare of the ranch on the grounds that the ends justified the means. That he had disavowed that premise under pressure from the woman who stood now so white-faced and alone before him still did not rid him of the feeling of guilt he had experienced from the first. That, coupled with a militantly protective attitude toward Fresno, now prompted him to shift the problem around so that he could regard it as a pure and simple case of Star's reputation being at stake, which was definitely sufficient to make him bristle.

"Ain't nobody going to come in and tell us how to run our business," he snapped. "Mrs. Taggert, you do whatever you want about that feller in the next room. I'm like Sol: I got other things to worry about. I'll be waiting outside, too."

"Henry?" Moline asked of the fourth rider, a tall man molded along Sol Davis' lean lines.

Henry Hanks resembled his fellow crew member in ways other than mere looks. He took a moment to scratch thoughtfully for just the right words that apparently were concealed somewhere under his untrimmed thatch of roan hair. When he finally unearthed them, he brought them slowly and carefully forth. "Sol an' me generally think pretty much alike. I don't recollect jest what-all he said a minute ago, but I remember thinkin' at the time that he pretty well summed it up fer me, too. So, I'll jest mosey out an' wait along with him an Hod."

Moline's eyes crinkled at the corners. "All right, Henry. You go along while Artie finishes making up his mind." His glance narrowed as he fixed it on the only man remaining. He kept his voice even, but there was an unmistakable edge to it now. "You seem to be having a little trouble getting the job done, Artie."

The man shook his head. "No. No trouble a'tall. I'll be catchin' up with Will."

"Get at it, then," Moline instructed. "But send somebody to Star to collect your gear and wages. I just now took a strong dislike to the color of your shirt."

"What's that supposed to mean, anyhow?"

"It's bright yellow all down the back," Moline said softly.

Steven's face went white, then red. "A man's got a right to his own opinion, by God!"

"Watch your tongue," Moline warned. "As for your opinion, you've got none—only a mess of crazy ideas about Indian blood that you drank in, along with your mama's milk. The milk helped you grow up to *look* like a sure-enough man, but inside you're still as little and no-account as you were while you was still nursing. Now, get out of here."

"You can talk all you want!" Stevens shouted. "It still won't take the Injun stink out o' here! Maybe I'm not so much, but by . . . I'm still a *white* man, not a damn . . . not some Injun-lovin' son of a—"

That was as far as he got. Without warning, Moline drove his fist straight into Stevens' mouth, then lurched forward on his sound leg and caught Stevens by the shoulder as the latter fell back. With his good arm, he whirled the dazed man around and with a hard shove propelled him through the door and out into the dust squarely in front of the three startled men waiting there.

Stevens tripped on the edge of the porch, sprawled, and rolled over twice. He struggled to his knees, blinking and spitting sand out of eyes and mouth. Through streaming eyes he glared wildly up at Moline, who had followed to the edge of the porch. "By God, I'll kill you for that!" he raged, and clawed at his gun.

From six feet away Moline swung his left arm forward, the gun in his hand centered on Stevens' forehead. "Try it," he urged. "Go ahead, try it."

Stevens froze, his boundless fury pushing him to the narrow edge of rashness. But even as he started to draw his gun, he read the wild hunger in the tall man's eyes and knew he would be dead the instant his hand made the fatal move. Through the swirling mists that blanketed his brain, he dimly heard Moline's hard voice come down to him.

"Unbuckle your gunbelt, Artie."

Three paces off to the side, Hodspeth looked on and voiced his puzzlement. "What the hell's comin' off here, Dave? What brought this on?"

Moline said without looking up, "Artie's leaving, that's all."

"Well," Hodspeth observed skeptically, "he ain't apt to git very far—on his knees thataway." He sounded far less concerned than he actually was. One look at Moline's face told him the man was a hair's breadth away from pulling the trigger, even now. "Artie," he suggested, "if you're figgerin' on doin' any ridin', you'd best be about it. I would, if I was you."

"Shut up, Hod," the kneeling man said in a shaking voice. "I know what I'm doin'!"

"Then go an' *do* it!" Hodspeth snapped. "But don't figger on me buryin' you, fer I'll not!"

Sol Davis inserted himself into the scene. "Here now, you fellers," he said placatingly. "Ain't this gone about fur enough?" He stepped over on his stilt-like legs and bent to unfasten Stevens' gunbelt. He lifted it and looped it over a long forearm. "Your hoss is right behind you, Artie," he suggested. "Was I you, I'd haul my ass outa here while'st I still had a ass to haul."

Stevens got slowly to his feet, his gaze still locked with Moline's. He needed no one to tell him how close he had come to dying, and the reaction which had set in turned his movements jerky as he stumped over to his horse, beating the dust from his clothes. He grasped the horn and rose to the saddle and from that elevation looked down at Moline. He said hoarsely, "Best o' luck, Injun lover," pivoted his horse, and threw it into a run across the yard.

Behind Moline, Fresno stood rooted in her tracks, weakened and shaken by the scene. This hour had seen her stripped of every vestige of her former power, leaving her for the first time in her life dependent upon the goodwill of those who served her. Had these men elected to desert her as a unit, all hope of regaining her seat of authority would have vanished. Nor would it have ended there. Their departure would have been a signal for the dozen remaining hands, now in isolated camps across the valley, to desert Star also. And with news of that wholesale abandonment of the valley bruited abroad would have come the ultimate fall of Star.

She had always known that men as a whole were pitifully subject to frailties of the spirit and fearful of straying from the body elect. Few indeed possessed sufficient force of character to shunt this fear aside and stand firmly against popular opinion. That three out of five of her men had displayed that rare moral fiber just now appeared to her an act of such rare fidelity that she was humbled by it.

There would be others among the two remaining crews who would follow Hodspeth and Stevens, she had no doubt. But so long as a hard core remained, the gaps in the ranks would be filled by others who possessed a similar independence of spirit, and Star would emerge from this trial more strongly tempered than before. It required the heat of the furnace to rid the metal of its dross, and she had knowingly laid Star on the fire.

26

Fresno had just finished feeding Lord some thin broth when she heard Leopold rush full-throatedly away from the back porch and make for the grove where Moline and the three hands had disappeared two hours before. She set the bowl on the trunk and went to the window as a rider entered the yard. "It's a woman," she informed Lord. "Lila's mother, I guess. She's alone."

She turned out of the room and was waiting on the back porch when the Comanche woman rode up. "You must be Carla," she smiled. "I'm glad you're here. I'm Fresno Taggert."

There was no overt change in the woman's expression, only a faint turn of the full lips, and a direct and deliberate movement of the black eyes over Fresno's face and figure as she swung her leg over the cantle and stepped down.

"Lila say I come help."

She had a thick roll lashed behind her saddle, which she untied and lowered to the ground before unsaddling and depositing the tack on the porch. She carried the packroll into the kitchen and lowered it to the floor with an almost imperceptible nod to Martha, who was at the table kneading bread.

Carla was an arresting figure, with her jet black hair worn loose down her back in the Comanche fashion, and her superb body colorfully garbed in a man's shirt with the tails tucked into a full, tightly belted skirt of red gingham. But her strong symmetrical features were curiously expressionless. It was the same mask Lord wore whenever he was determined to keep his thoughts hidden, and Fresno tried to imagine what the woman would look like were she to smile.

"We're very grateful to you," she said. "I'm afraid neither

Martha nor I know too much about treating wounds." She paused, waiting for some response, but when the woman merely stared back at her she grew slightly embarrassed. "I was going to send for Doctor Bolter this morning," she continued, "but Lila said you'd be better with your herbs."

On his pallet of saddle blankets Jesse Whitehead woke from his nap. "Well, howdy there, Carla!" he said, frankly pleased to see her. "Where's that daughter o' yours?"

Carla turned her head and looked down at him. "She see men go into hills. She go along, damn her."

Jesse's eyes laughed up at her. "Well, why didn't you make her stay with you?"

Carla said without any amusement at all, "You funny," and turned back to Fresno. "Where this man?"

Fresno led the way to Lord's bedroom and stood aside while Carla, oblivious to Lord's quizzical look, bent and lifted a corner of the salve bandage. She studied the swollen wounds, then leaned closer and sniffed. Straightening, she continued to study the deeply scored back, then replaced the bandage. She was directly above Lord, and when she finally consented to address him, she showed him the same closed expression she had shown Fresno. "Hurt bad?"

"Bad enough," Lord admitted.

Carla uttered a short, grunting sound, and bent over again, this time to peel back a section of the bandage covering the wound in his side. "Not bad," she decided. "No worry about this one."

Fresno had never ceased to watch the dark face, hoping to catch some unguarded break in it that would tell her something of the woman's private opinion. But when Carla at length finished her examination and stepped back, Fresno knew no more than she had in the beginning. "The salve was all we had," she said.

"I brought things. I fix."

Carla left the room, and Fresno saw that Lord was soundlessly laughing. "What's so funny?"

"It's just that she's so Indian, you're surprised to find out she can say something besides, 'Ugh!' "

"You're an ungrateful wretch," Fresno told him. "I think she's quite handsome, and probably is very friendly, once you get to know her."

"That might take some doing. I can't picture her sitting and gabbing about babies and recipes over a cup of tea. Can you?"

Fresno was looking through the doorway after the tall woman. "Yes," she mused. "I can."

"Well, you watch her," Lord said darkly. "If she slaps a lot of stinking witch's brew on me, I'll scalp her."

Fresno gave him a quick smile. "I'll watch her," she assured him, and went out.

In the kitchen she found Carla pulverizing some dried leaves, which she then added to a pan of water steaming on the stove. Apparently the leaves were not the first ingredients to have gone into the pan, because the contents already gave off a pungent odor. Fresno went over and looked on while Carla slowly stirred the concoction. "What is it?" she asked.

Carla stooped and sniffed critically, then continued stirring. "Things," she said enigmatically. "Things I know."

Fresno said, "Oh," and turned to Martha. "Do you know?"

"No, and neither will you apparently," Martha replied, clearly amused by the Comanche woman's utter indifference to her surroundings. "But I've heard too many stories of miraculous cures from Indian potions to doubt that she knows precisely what she's doing."

Fresno went to the door. "I'm going to the pool," she said over her shoulder. "Maybe a bath will clear the cobwebs out of my brain."

Carla said, without looking up from the simmering pot, "Bring water," and nodded at the empty bucket on the bench by the door.

Taking the bucket, Fresno crossed the yard, undressed beside the pool, and lowered herself into the water, shuddering at its chill bite but feeling immediately more alive. She spent the better part of an hour alternately paddling about and stretching out on the sand to watch the clouds drift slowly across the endless expanse of blue above.

The steady beat of water pouring down the shoulder of the hill was a sound that blotted out all others and worked its gentle healing on her frayed nerves and tired muscles. It produced a soporific effect so strong that for the time being she found all worry held in abeyance. The events of the past night and of this morning faded further and further into the past, and the fear of what might be happening in the hills to the east at this very moment was kept just beyond reach of her consciousness as the downroaring water laid its impenetrable barrier around her.

At the end of an hour she reluctantly returned to the house with the bucket of water. She set it down on the bench and went on through the kitchen without speaking to either Jesse or Martha. In the bedroom she found Carla straightening a new square of clean sheeting over Lord's wounds. The bandage gave off a bitingly spicy smell which was not at all unpleasant. From the foot of the bed she smiled at Lord. "How does it feel?"

"Good," he grunted. He slewed his head around and looked up at Carla. "You're a fine doctor. I'm obliged."

Carla shrugged this off. "Tonight you be sicker. I fix something for that." She turned and would have left, but Fresno moved to intercept her.

"What do you mean, sick?"

"He get hot inside. Burn up, maybe."

"But he seems so much better."

"I don't know about seems," the dark woman replied indifferently. "He get hot tonight."

"You mean fever?" Fresno glanced around at Lord, then back to the woman. "You're very sure?"

Carla was not accustomed to having her word questioned. Displeasure tightened the skin of her lower lids, narrowing her obsidian eyes. "Wait and see," she snapped.

Fresno made a quick turn and went to kneel beside the bed, one hand going out to touch Lord's forehead. "You've no fever at all," she said, and looked around accusingly; but Carla was gone. "No sign of a fever," she said emphatically. "She must be mistaken."

"She could be," Lord conceded, "but I doubt it." He saw her

distress and moved his hand across the blanket until he could encircle her wrist with his fingers. "Don't be upset, Fresno."

"But I feel so useless! I don't seem to do anything right. What sort of a woman am I, anyhow?"

He smiled, his eyes briefly caressing her. "A pretty good sort. As to the doctoring: you'll do just fine until somebody better comes along."

"She already has."

"That's a different kind of doctoring from the one I meant," he said quietly. "Your kind works on another wound. Who knows? If I had you around long enough, I might get cured altogether."

"As long as you want me around, I'll be here, Aaron."

There was no longer any amusement in his look. "That's a big statement, little lady."

She leaned down, meaning to kiss him on the temple, but he rolled his head so that her lips found his mouth instead, and the gesture that was meant to be a fleeting caress became something entirely different. Despite his helplessness and the awkwardness of his position on the bed, the reflexive movement of his lips against hers produced a violent reaction in her. She gave a little gasp and drew back. It occurred to her now, as it had on countless other occasions, that his latent sensuousness was so vital a part of him that it served him as his vision or his hearing or any of his other senses—automatically. It lay in his hand that firmly held hers. It called to her from the smooth line of his neck that swelled into the heavy muscles of his shoulder. It lay nestled in the blackness of his heavy lashes, and was a slow and unabating caress in his eyes. Even the faint pulsing of the vein in his temple had its disquieting effect on her. His physical appeal was working on her now, and her awareness of what was going on inside her turned her uneasy. She thought: *Is this all it is?* and did not know the answer.

"You're bothered about something."

She flushed guiltily. "Am I so transparent?"

"To me you are. That kiss set you to wondering about yourself . . . and me "

His ability to read her so easily shocked her. "How could you know that?"

"It was pretty plain on your face," Lord said, then added quietly, "You felt nothing I didn't."

"It does bother me," Fresno admitted. "I can't seem to separate your body from you."

"Have you got to do that?"

"Shouldn't I know which affects me more?" she countered.

"Maybe *you* have to," Lord told her. "Personally, I've no wish at all to divide you into sections. I might not be able to put you back together as you are." He shook his head solemnly. "I wouldn't like that to happen."

She sank back on her heels. "Tell me, how do I affect you?"

"I can't answer that."

"Can't? Or won't?"

"Oh," said Lord, "I would, if I could. But how do you describe a thought, or a feeling? Where's a word to tell exactly how you feel about the sky? Or the wind in your face? Or some new taste in your mouth? What's the word for knowing you're alive? What, exactly, does 'happiness' mean? Or, 'love'? Or—" He grinned. "Your old standby, 'make love'? I could use them all, and when I was through, I'd still end up saying, 'I don't know.' "

Fresno asked softly, "Shouldn't there be something said about giving?"

He shook his head slowly and she saw that closing-in look pull all feeling out of his face. "There should be, yes," he said tonelessly. "But I can't say it, Fresno. Not to you. Of all people, not to you."

"Why?" she cried in a low voice. "Aaron . . . I need to hear it!"

"Not from me."

"But *why?*"

Even his voice was closing her out. "You want me to answer, so you can say it's not true; when all the time you know it is. Don't, Fresno. Don't do this."

282

"If you loved me as I love you, then you'd *want* to give. You couldn't *not* give."

He was wholly beyond her reach. His eyes would not let her in, and his voice came from behind a door she could not find. He said, "If you can believe that, it'll make it easier . . . for both of us," and closed his eyes, refusing to look at her.

"What else can I believe?" Fresno asked miserably.

"Nothing, I hope."

All at once she was crying. Seldom in her life had she resorted to tears, either for comfort or to win a point. It was a weakness she had always abhorred in others of her sex. And now that it had come so suddenly upon her, she was too stunned by its outpouring to stem its flow. She slumped forward and put her hands over her face, not wanting him to see her helplessness. "What do you want me to do?" she finally asked.

"I want you to go away."

She shook her head. "No. I won't do that."

He lay and watched the bowed head move dumbly from side to side, "I thought not," he said heavily, and lay there unhappily watching her.

The silence ran on, with Fresno sinking deeper into her own private misery. He tried to think of words that would summon her back, but he would not use the ones that came to him, and in the end he knew he could do nothing. He tried to slide his arm across the blanket and reach her, but even this effort was beyond him. He felt his hand drop through space, and its weight pulled him over the edge of unconsciousness into yielding darkness.

Through the concealing thickness of her wet lashes Fresno glimpsed the shadowy movement of the dark hand limply falling, and she reached out and grasped it. A low whimpering sound escaped her. She moved his hand until it rested on the edge of the mattress, then laid her cheek against it and felt it grow damp with the tears she could not contain. She said in a lost voice, "Oh, Aaron, what are we going to do?" and continued to crouch there, staring hopelessly out over a landscape devoid of all life and color.

283

The sound of someone entering the room roused her, and she looked around to see Carla approaching the bed with a cup in her hand. She shook her head to clear it, and winced as pinpricks of pain lanced down her neck and all along her right side. She knew then that she had been asleep for some time, and started guiltily to her feet, only to discover that her right leg was useless. Grasping the chair, she dragged herself to her knees and gritted her teeth while she waited for the blood to resume its flow through her legs. By the time she had regained her feet, Carla had administered her steaming potion to a helplessly gasping Lord and had taken her departure without once having spoken to either of them.

She felt as if she had been physically mauled. She said, "I'll be back after a while," and moved stiffly to the door. Instead of going through the kitchen, she left the house by the front door and continued on to the pool undetected. Here she dropped to her knees and scooped water onto her tear-swollen face. At length, feeling somewhat revived, she fumbled around in the pocket of her skirt and found two sections of the comb that had been broken when Lord's lunge through the door last night had flung her into the doorframe. Taking the larger section out, she set about trying to put her hair in order; but without a mirror, and with such an unsatisfactory tool, the task seemed hopeless, and in the end she took the thong and tied the rebellious mass at the base of her neck.

Returning to the house, she noticed that she was walking in the shadow of the hill; she looked to the west and saw that the sun was almost gone behind the high range. She thought with surprise: *Why, I've slept the afternoon away!* and quickened her steps.

She went through the kitchen without speaking to either Carla or Jesse Whitehead. Lord's breathing, when she bent over him, was noticeably heavier and faster and the heat of his body came through the sheet Carla had spread over him. "Aaron," she said, "how do you feel?" There was no answer. He kept rolling uneasily on his stomach, and his breathing was a nerve-racking noise in the room. She could not help him, and knowledge of this

284

brought her to her feet. What if the fever got worse? What if Carla's medicines had no effect? What if he died? Standing there in the fading light, she felt fear strike all through her and turn her weak. She grasped the chair, trying to squeeze strength back into herself, trying to regain control of her nerves. When she felt quite steady on her feet, she turned out of the room and went in search of Martha.

"Martha," she said to the woman at the stove, "he's worse. He's burning up with fever."

Martha turned and nodded gravely. "I know. We can only wait and hope."

"Isn't there something we can do?"

Carla's voice came in through the open doorway from where she sat on the edge of the porch. "He hot, all right, but he not burn up."

"He's becoming delirious!" Fresno said, half angrily. She was being foolish, she knew, but she could not seem to get ahold of herself. She felt as though she were on the verge of flying apart. "What if it gets worse? He can't take much more!"

Jesse was sitting propped up against the wall. "I wouldn't worry too much," he told Fresno. "He's a mighty tough feller." He saw that this was not enough and spoke more sharply. "Now use your head, girl! You been around long enough to know that a thing o' this kind generally brings on a fever. Hell, I been havin' all kinds o' crazy dreams all day, off an' on; but I ain't kicked the bucket yet, have I? An' your man's a hell of a lot tougher an' a hell of a lot younger than I be! He ain't a'gonna die, I tell you. But if you're so all-fired set on drivin' yourself crazy worryin' about him, go ahead an' worry."

"You sound very sure."

"Hell, I *am* sure!" Jesse retorted peevishly, then softened his tone. "Jest try to git aholt o' yerself, Fresno. I know it ain't easy. But you'll be no good to him, if 'n you git all weak-kneed and teary."

Martha stepped close and laid a hand on Fresno's arm. "He's

285

right, you know. I don't know how, but in some way the sick draw strength from the strong. It would be wrong for you to let Mr. Lord feel your fear and your doubt."

Fresno nodded like a chastened girl. "I'm sorry," she said meekly. "It's just that all this waiting without being able to do anything is getting on my nerves."

"It's perfectly natural," Martha said gently.

Heavy dusk had come in, and Carla entered and lit the lamp above the stove. She had prepared a thin soup for Lord which Fresno took to him. But when she lit the lamp and settled herself in the chair to feed him, she could not get him to taste it. Each time the spoon touched his lips, he rolled his head away and made impatient muttering sounds, and he never ceased that aimless turning from side to side on his stomach. As darkness became complete outside, she continued to sit there, willing herself to a patience utterly foreign to her, and feeling more useless than she had ever felt in her life.

The minutes piled slowly one on top of the other to constitute an hour, then dissolved and started the laborious process all over again, and all the while the sound of Lord's breathing ran up and down a monotonous scale, measure after measure, phrase after phrase.

At first Fresno closely followed this endless quest for relief with a conscious attention, as if by so following she might some-how hit upon a means of altering its line of progress. But as time moved ponderously onward, she found herself faltering in her attempts to retain this close contact. The first few times this happened, she felt acutely guilty, but after a while she gradually succumbed to the unrecognized need for self-preservation and at last surrendered all contact with Lord and simply sat beside him and let sickness have its way with him.

Her bones ached; she had no appetite; and odd thoughts born of this lonely waiting began to drift through her mind.

She remembered a Fourth of July celebration long ago and herself drifting out onto the dance floor on the arm of Farley

Taggert—a fair and stately girl aware of her beauty and made even more beautiful by her ready acceptance of it.

Slumped in her chair beside Lord, she became momentarily aware of the helpless turning of that body under the sheet and felt guilt and anger thicken inside her and destroy the fleeting peace her aimless remembering had brought her. All this had happened because of her—all of it. Yet she was not enough to fill the big man's heart. She had asked him for his body, and he had obligingly complied with that request. But his compliance had engendered a wholly unexpected feeling of obligation in both of them. Rising during the initial sex act itself, it had made of that act a disconcertingly spiritual thing. She hesitated over the term, briefly wondering if it were too extreme, then accepted it without argument. It was of the spirit, quite separate from the undeniable sexual responses aroused in each other. Yet, perhaps it was the success of the act from its beginning that had served immediately to free them to explore other regions in hopes of finding a second miracle—one not of the flesh.

From the first she had so clearly sensed in him a need beyond her comprehension, just as she had found in herself a desire to fulfill that need. She did not think it was based entirely on pity, albeit pity undoubtedly played its part. Until then she had allowed that emotion scant play in her associations with others, lest it weaken her hard-held position as a woman among men. But in the final analysis, the element of pity had done no more than let her see Lord as he truly was: an introspective person of great compassion and understanding whose humiliating origin tragically blinded him to his true potential.

And nothing would ever change: he was convinced of this. She reached out and laid her hand over his, catching the heavy slugging of his pulse, and becoming frighteningly aware of the heat raging in him, and of his complete surrender to the pain encasing him. She spoke against the impenetrable wall of heat barring her way to him, knowing he wouldn't hear. "I can have you now, my dear. More of you than I'll ever have again. Though I'll never stop trying to win you away from yourself."

Sometime afterward, she fell asleep, still holding his hand, and woke suddenly to the sound of voices in the kitchen. She recognized Moline's deep-chested baritone, and Lila's explosive laugh, and, with a quick glance at the fever-ridden Lord, rose and hurried out.

Her legs felt unaccountably weak as she went through the front room, though whether from having remained too long in a sitting position or from fear, she did not know. It came to her that something had happened to her own body during her sojourn with Lord's agony. She had always been proud of its abiding strength, and now it was trying to betray her; she would not tolerate it. She went into the kitchen and stopped. Lila and Moline, alone, stood near the door. "Where are the others?" she demanded swiftly. "Where are Sol and—"

Moline cut her off. "Home by now," he assured her. "Or on the way." He saw relief flood her face and realized how great had been her anxiety for her men.

"And the hill bunch?"

"They're gone," answered Moline levelly. "They won't be back. Except," he added, "that the Shadley woman begged to stay in town, so's to be there when Newt comes back. I said that was all right."

"Yes, of course," murmured Fresno. Strangely she felt no triumph, but only deep, swelling relief. It was broken when Jesse Whitehead spoke from the corner. "That leaves jest one o' them up there."

Moline kept his eyes on his cup. "Luke says he rode out this morning. Out of the country, Luke says."

"You believe that?"

Lila strode to the door and stood looking into the darkness. Fresno glanced at Jesse and shook her head. "Leave it alone, Jesse," she ordered quietly. "There's been enough hate here."

Jesse Whitehead read something in her voice which no one else quite fully grasped. He said, "For the time bein', then, Fresno. Jest for the time bein'," and subsided into silence.

288

Fresno remembered Lord and rose quickly. She looked directly at Moline then, saying quietly, "Thank you, Dave," and went back across the front room, more relieved than she had thought possible.

By daylight Lord was a little less feverish, and Fresno would have stayed with him but for Lila's stern handling of the situation. Entering shortly after dawn, the tall girl took one look at her and hauled her to her feet. "Off you go," she ordered. "Get yourself something to eat, then get into that bed in the next room. You look like hell warmed over."

Fresno shook her head perplexedly. "He's no better," she said dully. "What if he doesn't get better? I mustn't leave him. I mustn't."

Lila had no intention of engaging in a senseless argument. "Come along," she said, and with an arm looped about Fresno's waist, escorted her to the door and through it. In the kitchen she deposited her on a chair near the table and spoke three brief words to Martha. "Keep her here." With that she went back to watch over Lord.

When Moline came in from looking after the horses, Fresno was listlessly toying with the food Martha had set before her. Suddenly she went deathly pale, pressed her lips tightly together, and rushed outside.

When she returned, she looked wrung out, and could hardly make it to her chair. She slumped into it, braced her elbows on the table, and held her face in her hands, panting quickly. The floor was rolling and pitching crazily under her. Dimly she heard Martha calling out to Lila, and then she was being lifted by the two women and carried through the house. The last thing she remembered was the feel of the bed sinking away under her and someone drawing off her boots.

27

The hoofs of Carla's horse knocked heavy echoes from the stony floor of the canyon, then loosed a rattling barrage as the horse took the trail up to the bench at a rush.

With her sudden appearance, the six bloodhounds erupted into loud greeting from over by the cabin, then rushed forward in a delirium of joy at her return. Carla spoke to them, and the outpouring of noise at once ceased. She saw a slack-flanked bitch wheel and go hurrying around the cabin and thought, *Belle has had her pups, then.*

Fifty yards away, the cabin door stood open, and she kept her gaze on it as she rode forward and stepped down. She left the horse ground-tied, slid the rifle out of the boot, and went inside, pausing on the threshhold to let her eyes adjust to the sudden dimness.

Dirty dishes and pans littered the work counter and the table. Cupboard doors swung wide on empty shelves and dirt crunched underfoot as she moved farther into this scene of disorder. She looked at the fireplace, saw the ashes spilling out over the hearth, and noted that no fire had been kindled there for some time. Her thigh struck the corner of the table, setting up a rattling of dishes piled there, and at once Douglas McKay's voice called from the room beyond, "Who's there?"

She crossed to the bedroom and halted in the doorway, surveying the same disorder; the stench of human sweat and sickness thickened in her mouth. In the faint light from the room's single window Douglas MacKay showed as an indistinct shape on the bed against the wall.

Looking closely at the man, Carla noted the sickly pallor that had replaced his habitual high color, and the sheen of fever that glazed his pale eyes. In this short time, all the flesh seemed to have melted away. It was all there, nakedly exposed now—the ruinous brutality, the crude hungers, and the ungiving hardness—like a curse sharply carved in perishable wax.

The shock of unkempt hair was a mass of red against the grey pillow, the sole patch of color in all this dismal colorlessness. In stolid silence Carla stood there watching the ruined man as she would have watched an utter stranger. She saw recognition come belatedly to him through the layers of pain dulling his senses, and heard his voice strike roughly at her across the six feet of space separating them.

"What the hell do you want here?"

Carla had the rifle cradled in the crook of her arm. She shifted its weight and stared steadily into the ravaged face. "Nothing," she said in her heavily plodding English. "I come to kill you, but you already dead."

"Like hell I am! You hear me talkin', don't you?"

Carla shook her head. "All the same, you dead."

"A fine way for a wife to talk!" MacKay lurched up onto his elbow. Agony shot its fiery bolt from the wound in his inner thigh all through his big frame, and he gasped and gritted his teeth, waiting out its shock.

Looking at that leg, exposed from the hip down, where the pant's leg had been cut away, Carla saw that it was swollen to more than twice its normal size. It had turned a sickening blue, and she caught an unmistakable fetid odor that rose from the filthy bandage. She said, "You never leave that bed, you know that?" and saw the words turn him wild.

"God damn you! Ain't you gonna help me? Did you jest come to watch me die? What kind of a woman are you?"

"I come to kill you," Carla corrected him. "But you dead, so I go."

"Ain't you got no feelin's a'tall?"

"For you, no."

MacKay sagged back. He rolled his head from side to side,

then roused and shot her a look of pure hatred. "You won't lift a hand to help me . . . is that it?"

Carla again shook her head. "You ever help anybody?"

MacKay fought down his fury, realizing that the cold-faced woman constituted his single hope. "Send Lila then," he said urgently. "She's duty bound to help her Pa. Will you do that much?"

"She not come, 'cept same as me. She not help."

"You're lying!"

"Not lie," Carla stated. "We talk before I come. She say if I want, I come first. She come later make sure."

In growing horror MacKay heard her out, knowing she was speaking the truth, knowing there was no hope now. He fought his rage in a shaking voice. "Goddamned savage bitches, the both o' you! Come to laugh at a dyin' man!"

"I not laughing," Carla denied. "I just glad you die."

MacKay would have killed her then had he been able to reach her. He clawed at the bedding and dragged himself to the edge of the bed and there collapsed, weakly panting. "I'll put a curse on you from my grave," he whispered. "You'll wish to God you'd never come here like this, you dirty Comanche bitch!"

Carla lowered the rifle until its stock rested on the floor between her feet. "You no can make curse," she said in her inflectionless voice. "To make curse, you got to believe in something. You no believe in nothing, because you nothing. You so much nothing, nobody remember you when you die, 'cept like bad dream, maybe."

The truth of this hit MacKay crushingly. It turned him absolutely still. He said thinly, "I'll make it up to you, Carla . . . all of it! Only help me, Carla! My Christ a'mighty . . . you *got* to help me!"

"No," Carla said coldly. "You no make anything up. It too much, what you already make. They no good in you. You talk nice now, 'cause you afraid. That's all."

She paused and stood looking down into his tortured face for a long moment, feeling again that she had never seen him before.

292

She lifted the rifle and cradled it in her arm again and went on in the same flat tone. "If you get well, you be mad dog again. You not change." She straightened and shifted the rifle into her right hand, holding it ready for instant use. "I put your gun where you get it when pain get too bad. After you shoot yourself, I come back and burn cabin. I do that much."

She stepped over to the bed, bent and retrieved MacKay's holstered gun from the floor where he had dropped it, and removed the cartridge from the chamber, knowing he would shoot her the instant she turned her back on him. Placing gun and cartridge on the bed where he could reach them, she turned and left.

She was at the top of the trail leading off the bench when a flat, unechoing sound came from inside the cabin and she drew up and sat there thinking: *He had to have someone know,* and felt no briefest twinge of pity for the dead man.

She stayed on the ledge, looking out over the wild hills she had known for twenty years, not wanting to return to the cabin. From somewhere in the trees behind her a bird sent up its brief lament for a day too swiftly gone; the four-note trill thinly rose and dissolved in the air. From the lower hills an eagle beat its slow way upward, passing finally so close overhead that she caught the whispery wash of its great wings churning the air. A narrow line of sunlight lay precariously close to the edge of the bench where she sat her horse, and the shadow of the upswimming eagle ran out of the canyon's darkness across this last bright remnant of the day and crossed into the deep-piling darkness behind her. Far below, night began to roll its dark bulk along the outflung arm of Star Valley, and she thought of the big man lying on his bed of pain in the long-abandoned Bland house, and of the other people there. And then she thought of Lila and the few moments of warmth that had briefly touched them after so much silence.

When she laid the rein against the side of the horse's neck, it obediently went about, and she let her gaze make one final glancing run from one end of the narrow shelf to the other, knowing she would never return. Back at the dark and silent cabin she carefully noted that it stood safely away from any brush that might spread the fire into the higher timber.

Dismounting, she became aware of the bloodhounds silently gathered around her and noted that one was missing, and remembered the pups. She said, "Belle? Show me where you hide babies," and caught the faint slapping of the bitch's tail against the cabin wall off to her right. She followed the bloodhound around to the lean-to shed behind the cabin and stooped and went in under the sloping roof to find the mother and her softly grunting family of six pups on a pallet of old grain sacks. Searching through the refuse in the shed, she unearthed a battered old willow basket she had woven long ago and lined it with a discarded skirt before transferring the pups to it. She carried them outside and around to the horse, who bent its head and sent its warm breath washing down over them in vast wonderment.

The hounds circled her, looking up and wagging their tails and thinly whining, and she realized suddenly that they probably had not been fed for a long time. She stood there, pondering this problem until she remembered the venison she had cleaned and hung in the shed near the corral. She said to the dogs, "Come. We find something," and led the way across the yard. The side of venison still hung from a rafter, and she took it down and swiftly cut it up with the knife she carried in her belt. With the hounds noisily tearing at the meat, she opened the corral gate and turned out the two horses, who immediately trotted over to the spring midway between shed and cabin.

Inside the cabin again, she took the lamp from the cluttered table, unscrewed the wick, and spilled a line of coal oil along the base of the walls. When the lamp was empty, she set it down, took a match from the mantle and struck it against the fireplace. She dropped it flaring into the line of oil and watched the flames spring up and run brightly around the room. A moment later, a faint crackling sounded as the fire bit into the logs, whereupon she went outside, picked up the basket, and rose to the saddle.

She sent her call across the yard to the dogs, who obeyed the summons with their unfinished meal clenched in their jaws.

294

"Come," she commanded, and turned across the bench toward the trail. The mother of the pups trotted directly alongside the horse, staring worriedly up at the basket, and Carla spoke soothingly to her. "It all right, Belle. Pretty soon I stop so you see they safe."

Just before she dropped out of sight off the bench, Carla looked back and saw the whole area hotly lighted by the flames from the burning cabin. Hoofs rattled across the flinty shelf, and the two horses she had turned out came between her and the light, determined not to be left behind.

An hour later she splashed across the creek and halted in front of the long-abandoned cabin she and Lila now occupied and spoke to the figure who rose from the step and came forward. "Take this basket, and be careful. It is full of Belle's children."

With an exclamation of delight, Lila took the basket and rushed inside with it. A light bloomed, and when Carla entered a moment later she found the girl sitting on the floor, her lap filled with squirming, whimpering puppies.

But the smile on Lila's face disappeared when she looked up. "How is it with you, mother?" she asked in Comanche. "Is your heart heavy inside you?"

Carla's shoulders lifted and fell. "It is not fitting for us to talk about him. It is finished. Now I will go away."

Lila's face mirrored her astonishment. "Why? You are my mother. My home is your home."

"Your people are not my people. Tomorrow I am going back to my own kind."

Lila gently removed the pups to the floor and stood up. "All right. We will go."

"Not you," Carla said shortly. "I go alone." When Lila would have touched her, she moved away. "We will not talk about it. The path divides . . . now."

For a long time they silently faced each other, with Lila vainly trying to find words that would fill the void now steadily widening between them. Too late it came to her how every much she would miss this silent woman whose affection she had so tardily recognized. Knowing so little about Carla, she was certain of one thing: nothing she might do or say would sway her from her course. She felt tears burn her eyes, and after a long look at Carla, she turned abruptly and went to the door and stood staring out into the night. She said in a voice that shook despite all she could do to control it, "I will not wait for you to go. I will leave and come back after you have gone." She stepped to the ground, and spoke again, still without turning around. The sibilant Comanche words barely reached the woman standing so alone in the flickering light of the globeless lamp. "Carry my heart in your hand carefully, my mother. Let it warm you . . . always. And do you give me yours?"

Carla's lips moved in the traditional response. "I give you my heart, my daughter. Hold it carefully, that it may warm you."

Meaning to adhere to the accepted mode of leave-taking, Lila started to walk away; but suddenly she turned, tears streaming down her cheeks, and stared at Carla for one brief instant, as if to carve on her memory forever the features she would never see again. One final look, and then she whirled and ran toward the corral. Moments later her running horse struck dull echoes through the darkness. As the measured beat faded in the distance, it was replaced by a low keening wail from the cabin where Carla knelt and poured her wordless grief into the night.

28

On the third morning Lord drifted up from the suffocating pit and saw a pale-haired, middle-aged woman occupying the chair near the bed. "Who are you?" he demanded. "Where's Fresno?"

Startled by the suddenness of the voice, and the clarity of the words, Martha jumped to her feet and peered intently down at him. Whiskers roughened his jaws, his lips were cracked and peeling, and there were deep caverns under his high cheekbones. But his eyes were clear, and he definitely was aware of his surroundings. She put a hand against his neck and discovered that the fever had gone out of him. He said again, "Who are you? Where's Fresno?" and weakly attempted to lift himself onto his elbows.

"I'm Martha Bland," she told him. "And Fresno is asleep, or at least I hope she is. She's fainted twice in the last two days."

Concern showed in his dark eyes. "Why? What's wrong with her?"

"Mostly nerves, I should imagine. The poor soul is worn out from looking after you." Martha was touching him on the shoulder, then on the forehead, as if unable to believe the fever actually was gone. "How do you feel?"

"Weak as a newborn kitten, but my back doesn't hurt as much as it did."

Martha slipped the blanket down around his hips and lifted the bandage to inspect the lacerations. "I don't believe it!" she exclaimed, and lifted the bandage higher, exposing more of the wounds. "I've never in my life seen anything like it!"

Lord made as if to roll over, but her hand on his shoulder held him where he was. "What's wrong?" he demanded. "What is it?"

"A miracle!" Martha told him. "In three days, that concoction Carla put on you has all but closed the cuts! Why, you'll be on your feet in no time at all, Mr. Lord!" She replaced the bandage and drew the blanket back over him. "Are you hungry?"

"I could eat a cow."

Martha smiled. "I'll go cook you one," she said, and hurried out.

She found Lila stirring soiled bandages in a boiler of soapy water on the stove. "He's awake and hungry," she announced. "I think I'll give him some of the stew left over from last night."

Jesse was sitting up to the table, busily eating his breakfast. He spoke through a mouthful of bacon. "You mean he's finally out o' the woods?"

297

"Far enough to be cross as a bear and aware that he's hungry."

Bare feet ran across the front room, and Fresno burst through the doorway. "He's awake!" she stated happily. "And his fever's gone!"

Lila looked around at her, stirring stick suspended over the boiler. "What are you doing out of bed, anyhow?" she asked bluntly.

"I feel fine," Fresno protested. "Just fine."

"Well, you look like hell," Lila said, and glumly resumed her stirring. She scowled at the steaming cloths, and gave them a sudden, hard jab with the stick, sending water sloshing over onto the stove. "I'm so damned sick of looking at puny people, I could throw up!"

The statement was so unexpected that all three turned as one and stared at her. It was Jesse who first found his tongue.

"Somethin's eatin' you, girl. What's happened?"

"Nothing," Lila muttered, then was immediately ashamed. "Yes. Carla's gone."

"Gone?" Fresno echoed. "You mean she went home?"

"Yeah," Lila said, "home . . . back to Texas, or wherever the hell her people happen to be this time of year."

There was another silence, then Jesse voiced the question in all their minds. "What brought this on, girl?"

Lila dropped her stirring stick into the woodbox, and leaned back against the windowsill, arms folded across her chest. "She went up to kill Douglas. Whether she shot him or he was already dead, I don't know. Anyway, she burned the cabin and headed south."

"Well, I'll be damned!" Jesse murmured. "She's quite a woman." He looked around at the others, as though defying them to contradict him, then put his gaze back on Lila. "Where you fixin' to hang out now?"

Lila shrugged.

Fresno went over to her. "Come to Star, Lila. Please come."

Lila would not look at her. "No," she said. "I guess not. I'll make out." An idea struck her, and she looked at Jesse. "How about cutting me in on your hunting?" she asked. "I've got those hounds, you know. Together we could clean out every cat, wolf, and bear from here to Denver inside of a year."

Jesse's features were suddenly wreathed in a radiant smile. "Done an' done!" he chortled. "How soon you movin' in?"

"Today," Lila said, an answering smile turning her at once girlish and more appealing than any of them had ever seen her. "I'll get my gear and go up and have your pigsty swamped out by the time you drag your old bones home."

Jesse slapped the table top with his good hand and rocked back in his chair. "Damned if this ain't my lucky day!" he chortled. "Fallin' heir to a daughter an' the best pack o' bloodhounds this side o' Georgia all to once't! *Girl, git goin'!*"

"I'm gone!" Lila laughed, and in a confusion of shouted thanks and orders to hurry back she ran out to saddle Moline's bay. Going past the house at a gallop, she yelled, "Tell Dave I'll bring his horse down as soon as I get my stuff moved," and was gone.

When Fresno entered Lord's room with the bowl of stew, she was delighted to see that he had managed to roll over onto his right side. He lifted himself on his elbow as she sat down and reached for the bowl.

"Is your hand steady enough, do you think?"

"I'll not be spoon-fed like a baby anymore." He set the bowl gingerly on the sheet directly under his chin, then frowned disapprovingly at her. "You're supposed to be in bed. How come you're up?"

Fresno shrugged this aside. "I had nothing but a little stomach upset. I feel fine."

He was not convinced. "You still looked pretty peaked. Why don't you go back to bed? I can handle this all right."

But, appearances to the contrary, she indeed felt fully recovered, albeit a trifle shaky in the knees. "I want to sit here and watch you spill your breakfast all over yourself and the bed," she smiled, and sat back to observe his initial attempt to handle the spoon with his left hand. When he had emptied the bowl, with only minor dribblings down his chin, and handed it to her with a curt, "More," she shook her head. "That's all you get this first time," she informed him, and rose to take the bowl back to the kitchen. When she returned with a basin and cloth and set about sponging his face and arms, she found him morose. He kept readjusting his length on the bed.

"I'm going crazy, lying flat on my stomach like this!" he grumbled. "I don't really hurt . . . just ache all over. But I can't sit up for fear of tearing everything loose. I can't even get onto my left side and eat with my right hand. Why doesn't somebody fetch the doctor from town?"

It was the first time he had evinced any impatience, and Fresno knew then that he was going to be all right. "If you want Doc Bolter, why, we'll get him," she said reasonably. "But all he'll do is look at you and tell us to keep right on with what we're doing. I'm sure of that."

"How do you know?" Lord demanded. "He might have something better than this sagebrush tea Carla has you pour down me, and this damned pine pitch she smeared on the cuts!"

Fresno laughed outright. "It's not sagebrush tea nor pine pitch, and you know it. Just try to be patient a little longer, for heaven's sake! If you could only see the way your wounds are healing, you'd get down on your knees and thank Carla, instead of grousing about her cures."

He muttered unintelligibly under his breath, but he could not wholly conceal the lift her encouraging news had given him. As she took up the broom and started sweeping the floor, his glance followed her, and some pleasant thought brought a half smile to his face and kept it there. By the time she had finished, he was in another sound sleep.

Relief made her feel let down, suddenly tired and inexplicably irritable. She had been conscious of his eyes following her and she became more and more bothered about her looks. She went into the kitchen, took warm water and soap, and thoroughly scrubbed her face. Then, aided by a shard of mirror propped in the window, she made a determined effort to rearrange her hair. But the piecemeal picture she viewed in the murky glass depressed her more. In this half-quarrelsome mood she went back to Lord's room and sat down near the bed. She was gazing moodily out the window when he woke.

"What's the matter, Fresno?"

She started and turned quickly away. "Don't look at me! I'm the tackiest-looking woman in the world. I haven't had a good bath for a thousand years. I can't do anything with this damned head of frayed hemp. My clothes—"

He was smiling openly, which made her unreasonably irritated. "What's so funny? Stop looking at me!"

"If you're feeling all that put-out about your looks, things must be improving all around. The only thing wrong with you is you're worn out. You've spread yourself too thin looking after me."

"The only thing wrong with me is that I feel as dirty as a coal miner on Saturday night!"

"Then take a bath, Fresno," he said calmly. "There's a tub in the barn. Take it into the other bedroom and soak until your skin dissolves, if you feel like it. Speaking of looks, I imagine there's considerable evidence I wasn't molded in God's perfect image, after all." He reached his hand around and scrubbed the stubble on his chin. "Feels like wire. I was thinking just before I dozed off that maybe I'd grow a beard . . . one of those great, bushy things. It'd give me lots of dignity. That's better, Fresno. You're much more beautiful when you smile. Did you know that?"

Her smile faded and her eyes darkened. "Is the beard all you thought about, Aaron?"

The thing he read in her gaze turned him sober. "No. But there's no point in talking about it," he said, and let his glance fall away.

"Isn't there?"

"No."

It got between them again, destroying the feeling of ease that had come to them all too briefly. She got up and left, and he followed her with his troubled gaze. He was still looking at the doorway when she returned some minutes later, and she knew that he had been lost in his thoughts. He said in an obvious attempt to make conversation: "Did you put water on to heat?"

She went to the window and stood looking up at the green, shadowy hills. "No. After a while, maybe."

That was all. Something had left them so suddenly, so definitely, that there was an emptiness in the room. In the warm afternoon air the beat of the distant falls sounded unnaturally loud, and the loneliness of this place was something Fresno clearly felt. What, she asked herself, had so unexpectedly happened? She had never felt so unwanted and useless—so canceled out. Wanting to banish this sensation of aloneness, she continued to stand there, no longer seeing the hills, strongly feeling Lord's presence behind her, like a compelling force dragging at her, and willing herself not to turn and look at him. Sometime later his voice came quietly to her.

"Thinking about it will do no good, Fresno. You should get some rest."

She went out without a word. Lying on the bed in the next room, she felt almost afraid to stir, lest he hear her. It was a strange emotion, after all that had happened between them—after the close, abandoned passion they had known so recently. Their distance was a reaction to an intimacy that would never be again. Of this she was dismally certain. Desire had thrown them together. Tragedy had rendered him helpless and had given her strength enough for two. Now she felt rejected. She thought of the last words he had said just now, and to her it was as though her very presence irritated a wound inside him that would not heal. Would it always be this way? She thought: *Perhaps my leaving will do more than my staying. If I matter to him at all, he will have to admit it sooner or later.*

Then she thought of the big, silent, empty house at Star, and of the isolated lake cabin, and of the people who now knew about Aaron Lord and her, and of all the others who would come to know. She turned onto her side and closed her eyes and willed sleep to come and blot it all out.

29

Three days later, Lord sat at the table sharing a farewell cup of coffee with Martha. He said for the second time, "Don't go back to town. Stay. You can keep house for me," and for the second time watched her shake her head in refusal.

"Please don't tempt me, Mr. Lord. I've a business to run. I should have left days ago . . . Ruby's probably turned the place into a charity hotel by now . . . but it was so restful here I kept putting it off."

Lord reached for the coffee pot and refilled their cups. "You've no business managing a whore—" He caught himself and changed the wording. "You don't look, act, nor talk like any madam I ever knew."

She looked up at him, eyes twinkling. "And how many madams have you known, Mr. Lord?" The question brought a dark flush to his face, and she burst out laughing. "The witness need not answer. All the same, I am a madam, and duty calls."

"If you decide to change your mind, my offer stands."

"Thank you. I might take you up on it." Martha pushed her chair back and stood up, her gaze traveling around the room. "Suddenly the place seems so empty, with everybody gone. I cried like a little girl when Jesse rode off this morning. And ever since David went back to Star there's been a big, empty hole where he used to sit with his leg propped up on the table." She bent and picked up the valise containing her medical supplies. "I forgot to tell you . . . after you'd gone to bed last night, Lila stopped by for a few minutes. She looked like the cat that had just swallowed the canary. And she was still riding David's big bay."

"You mean he's lent it to her awhile longer?"

"I mean he *gave* her that horse. If you ask me, it's a lover's token."

Lord's brows went up. "Lover's token? Well, I'll be damned! Nothing will ever surprise me again!"

Martha shot him an arch look. "I wouldn't be too sure."

He caught the irony in her tone, but not its implication. "Well, I am."

Martha's lips quirked. " 'Experience keeps a dear school: a fool will learn in no other,' " she quoted. "That's your thought for the day, courtesy of a Mr. Benjamin Franklin. No doubt you've heard of him."

She shifted her bag to the other hand and was turning to the door when Fresno's sudden entrance stopped her. In a single glance she took in the other's drawn expression and the way she held onto the doorframe. "Mrs. Taggert, are you all right?"

Fresno nodded. "I hitched your mare to the buggy for you. You'll be home—" Suddenly her head dropped back, and with a little gasp she crumpled to the floor before either Martha or Lord could catch her.

She came to in the room she had slept in during her stay and for a while lay staring uncomprehendingly at the ceiling. *This is the third time in less than a week,* she thought, *what on earth is the matter with me?* Someone spoke nearby and she moved her head to see Martha sitting on the edge of the bed. "What?"

"I asked if you were feeling better?"

"No," Fresno said. "I feel an utter fool! What in heaven's name happened?"

Martha took one of the lax hands and patted it. "You fainted, that's all." She paused, then asked very gently, "Were you sick to your stomach again, while you were outside?"

"Yes! And it's all so silly! I can't remember throwing up since I had the measles at the age of seven. I can digest nails!"

Martha patted the hand again, a troubled look on her face. "It's been happening every morning lately, hasn't it?"

"Every single day for the last two weeks!" Fresno stated

angrily. "The minute I get out of bed I have to dash outdoors. Anyone would think I was—" She stopped abruptly as the full implication of it hit her. She lay rigid and her eyes got wider and wider in her bloodless face. "Martha," she said tonelessly, "I just now realized . . . my time should have started long ago. I've always been absolutely regular. *Always!*"

Martha spoke with a confidence she did not feel. "Sometimes nervous strain can throw us off, you know. Hasn't that ever happened to you?"

"I've never missed before in my life."

Leaning forward, Martha smoothed the tangled red hair back from the pallid forehead. "Don't take it too hard. I'm very sure that as soon as you've told Mr. Lord—"

"No!" It burst from Fresno in a shout. She grasped Martha by the upper arms and pulled herself up right. "He's not to know! Promise you'll say nothing! *Promise!*"

"Child," Martha began, but Fresno shook her roughly.

"Promise!"

"All right, my dear. I promise. But that isn't the answer, you know. It's only a matter of time until he finds out."

Fresno drew her knees up and locked her arms around them. She turned her head and stared dully out the window. "He'll never know," she said in a low voice. "Never."

"How on earth can he *not* know?"

Fresno was silent a moment. "I'll not be here," she said at length. "I'll go away until it's over."

Martha could not conceal her dismay. "You'll give the child away?"

"Wouldn't you, in my place?"

"I think that's something no woman could answer without having been in your place."

Fresno was still staring out the window. She said slowly, feeling her way, "I'd not want the child to know its father didn't want it. I couldn't bear to look into its eyes and see the question written there, and know I was to blame. I am an intelligent person, but I can think of no way to make a child understand why it may claim only half its rightful heritage of love." She turned and looked at Martha. "Can you?"

"No," Martha admitted reluctantly. "I don't think there is a way."

"So, you see, there's nothing else I can do."

Martha sighed and absently pleated and repleated a fold in her skirt. "It's not my place to advise you, Mrs. Taggert," she said quietly. "But isn't there a possibility you don't know Aaron Lord as thoroughly as you think you do? Do you have the right to keep this from him?"

"I know him," Fresno replied, and added so low that the words were barely distinguishable, "and I love him. That is why I can't . . . obligate him. He knows I would marry him the moment he asked, but he won't ask. Perhaps he never will."

Martha was closely studying the chiseled profile. "You're very sure he doesn't love you?"

"No. I'm very sure he *does* . . . but not enough to make him forget the price I'd have to pay if I married him. The fact that he is half Indian has twisted his thinking until everything starts and ends with that."

Such reasoning was beyond Martha's understanding. "But that makes no sense! By now, everyone in the Territory must know about you and him. How could his marrying you possibly be more ruinous to your reputation than his sharing your bed out of wedlock? A child reasons better than that!"

"I know him," Fresno repeated dully. "If I told him about the child, he would marry me, but he would still think it wrong. If people turned against us, he would feel that he was wholly to blame. In time he would cease to love me. That is a risk I cannot face. You see, I was married to a man I didn't love, but who loved me. I could never endure that kind of hell, Martha. I'm not strong enough to be that weak."

Without understanding how, Martha was convinced that this woman's reasoning was somehow faulty. But she would not presume to force her convictions on another. She sighed. "If you're quite certain, then of course you must do as you think best. But I will say this: if you give the child away without having offered Lord a chance to claim both it and you, only to discover later that there was more to his love than you believed, you'll know hell as long as you live. Of that I'm very sure."

"That may happen," Fresno conceded, "but now is now. I will not risk his hatred or contempt by resorting to blackmail."

Martha rose, smoothing her dress. She was a strong and open woman who could not hide her feelings, and her fine eyes misted as she looked down at the younger woman. "I'll say one more thing before I leave, and you will remember it, my dear. I gave birth to three babies, and I buried them all. I am a barren woman now, and a fallen one, in society's eyes. But I have known motherhood, and I know what happens when you look for the first time into the face of your child. When it happens to you, it may be you'll discover you *are* strong enough to be weak, after all."

She was at the door when Fresno slipped off of the bed and hurried to her. "I want you to know how very grateful I am, Martha. I'd like us to be friends."

Martha smiled to soften her answer. "A close-range friendship would pose its difficulties, wouldn't it?"

"Difficulty and I are old companions," Fresno said. "I should be proud to call you my friend."

Martha's answering smile was completely genuine. "Then by all means, you must call me that. And you must remember that 'friend' is something more than a title. Will you do that . . . my friend?"

"Yes," Fresno said levelly. "I will do that." She turned the knob and pushed the door open. "I mustn't keep you any longer. Good-bye for now, and don't worry about me. I will be fine."

Martha looked once more into the violet eyes. "Yes," she said very softly. "You will always be fine. You could be nothing else. But I want you to be happy, as well." She encircled Fresno's waist, gave her a quick, firm hug, and walked swiftly across the front room to retrieve the bag she had left in the kitchen.

Alone, Fresno paced restlessly back and forth, in a fever to be gone from this place. She found her hat and put it on. Her brain seemed to be aimlessly whirling, spinning fragments of thought into space as fast as they formed. And in this terrifying state of confusion, she knew only that she could not look Lord in the face without breaking down. But the mere thought of leaving left her trembling, so that she was obliged to sit on the bed and concentrate on breathing deeply and regularly to keep from fainting again. Straining to catch the sound of Martha's buggy leaving, she heard nothing until Lord's footsteps sounded in the kitchen. They stopped there a moment, then grew louder, crossing the front room. Before they halted in front of the door, she was across the bed, out the window, and fleeing around the corner of the house on legs that threatened to buckle at every stride.

At the corral she snatched up her bridle, calling the mare to her as she opened the gate. With hands that shook uncontrollably she slipped the bridle on, led the mare out, and flung the saddle into place. She was reaching under for the cinch when Lord spoke from directly behind her.

"Going for a ride?"

She started violently and almost cried out, then sought to cover her agitation by settling her hat more firmly and drawing the thong tight under her jaw. "Home," she said without looking around.

When she bent for the cinch again, Lord said, "Let me do that," and stepped over to finish saddling for her.

His back was to her and she found herself staring dumbly at the thick mass of faintly curling hair that brushed his bandaged shoulders. Suddenly she had an almost irresistible impulse to reach out and bury her fingers in that glossy mane. But with her hand lifting, she caught herself and stepped back, forcing her gaze to wander out over the empty yard now bathed in new sunlight. When Lord spoke she started again, and turned to find him quizzically staring at her. She saw the reins he was extending toward her, and nodded jerkily. "Thank you."

She was in the saddle and reining the mare around when Lord

spoke again. "Mind if I throw a saddle on the Emperor and ride part way with you?"

"Do you feel up to it?"

He tried to smile, but it was merely a meaningless flexing of his facial muscles. "I've been cooped up long enough. The horse could do with a little exercise, too. Be with you in a minute."

Side by side they rode through the grove and down the green sward toward the headland jutting out into the plain. Unspoken in both their minds was the thought that this was the route Lord had so often taken on his way to the isolated cabin, and it put a constraint on them that was hard to break through. They were almost at the crest of the hill when Fresno broke the silence.

"There's a feeling of fall in the air."

Lord held the strutting stallion safely away from the mare as they rounded the point and breasted the billowing sea of grass on a direct line with the distant lake cabin. "Are the autumns long here?" he asked. "I'm looking forward—" He stopped, as if he had forgotten what it was he had started to say.

There was an awkward silence, unrelieved save for the rhythmic thud of trotting hoofs and the sibilant rush of the horses' legs through the grass. Again it was Fresno who broke the tension. "I've always loved this side valley. It has a special feel to it . . . friendlier, somehow, than the rest of the valley." She gave a little laugh. "I imagine that sounds silly."

He turned and looked gravely at her. "You never sound silly, Fresno."

She felt a frantic need to lighten the mood, but nothing lighthearted occurred to her, and in the end she was obliged to reply to his statement. "Unfortunately you're right. I somehow never acquired the knack of saying gay, clever things. I've always suspected I've missed out on a lot by being created so infernally sober."

Lord's attention was taken up by the stallion, who sought to crowd too close to the mare. He rode less relaxed than customarily, held stiffly erect in the saddle by his wounds, which were still only partially healed. When he glanced over at Fresno, he moved only his head, and the stiffness of the movement lent him an austerity which further compounded his remoteness in her eyes.

"Would you like to be like other women?"

Fresno forced another laugh from her aching throat. "It might be more restful . . . certainly safer."

He was still watching her. "Aren't you safe, Fresno?"

The very quietness of his voice put her instantly on guard. He sounded altogether too curious, too deliberate, as though he suspected something. "Of course I am! It was merely a figure of speech to describe the type of woman who occupies her time and her thoughts with little, everyday problems, such as what dress to wear to the sewing circle and what to fix for supper—not exactly the kind of problems I deal with." She gave another short laugh, and glanced sideways at him. "Why do you ask?"

"No reason," he said slowly. "Or at least I didn't think so. Now I'm beginning to wonder." He let the stallion edge closer. "What's worrying you, Fresno?"

Once again she forced a laugh from her dry throat and was appalled at how false it sounded. She saw his frown deepen and took refuge in a show of sarcasm. "Aren't you the inquisitive soul today! Do you always show your gratitude to your nurses by cross-examining them?"

"I've not had a nurse before," he retorted, and withdrew into silence.

She at once regretted the gibe. "Forgive me. I've abominable manners sometimes."

"Your manners aren't what's troubling me," he told her seriously. "It's *you*. You're not yourself." Again he reined closer. "Are you feeling all right? Martha said you'd had more than one fainting spell lately. What's wrong?"

Fresno felt her cheeks grow hot, and she spoke impatiently to mask her alarm. "Don't be ridiculous! All ladies faint! Didn't you know that?"

"*Some* do. You're not the type."

"Am I not? Tell me, sir, what type am I? I should like your opinion on it."

"You're not the type to faint," Lord said doggedly. "What's gotten into you all of a sudden?"

The irony of this brought a harsh laugh from her. She willed herself to sound matter-of-fact. "I'm a little tense from being shut up so long, that's all. Surely you can understand that. You voiced the same complaint a few minutes ago."

"It was an excuse. You knew that."

"Did you need one?"

"I'm not so sure anymore."

"If you'd rather go back," she said cuttingly, "you needn't feel duty bound to escort me any farther."

He reined in with an air of finality. "Do you want me to go back?"

"I didn't say that!"

"*Do* you?"

She had stopped a little distance beyond him and swung her mare around. They were close to quarreling and the knowledge that she had willfully brought it on made her miserable and even more unfair. "Apparently your nerves are as frayed as mine. Perhaps we should say good-bye right here and now."

He walked the stallion over to her. "Fresno," he said in a troubled voice, "I don't know what this is all about—why you're bent on hitting at me like this. I came along because I wanted to. I still want to. But if you'd rather be alone, why then, I'll go back. All you have to do is say so. But don't do it this way—like a silly girl hiding behind meaningless words. Is my company offensive to you?"

She sat there with her cloud of hair tumbling about her face in the warm run of the morning wind and stared back at him for an endless, empty moment, knowing she had handled the thing badly, knowing she could not keep up the pretense any longer. "Your company could never be offensive to me, Aaron," she told him, unable to keep the quaver out of her voice. "If you believe nothing else, believe that. I admit I've been acting the fool. It was my cowardly way of trying to tear myself away from you. You see—" Suddenly she could not find breath to go on and was forced to wait until she could master her voice again. "You see, I'm going away. I was trying to avoid a 'good-bye'."

"Going away?" he echoed blankly. "Where are you going? When will you come back?"

She looked down at her reins. "I don't know."

"But you *must* know!"

She gave a little shrug. "I haven't decided for certain where I'm going."

"Then why? At least tell me when you'll be back."

Her shoulders lifted and fell again. "In the spring. Perhaps."

He was utterly baffled. "Will you write to me?"

She shook her head, still not looking up. "No," she said very low.

"But for God's sake, *why?*" he burst out. "I'll go crazy, not having any word from you!" In his agitation he leaned forward, unmindful of his wounds. "Why are you doing this to me, Fresno?"

Her head came up then, her eyes enormous in her drawn face. "I might ask you the same question!" she cried. "But I won't, because I know the answer. You will have to find your own!" Her voice broke and she put up a hand to shield her eyes as tears threatened to betray her. She drew a ragged breath, let her hand fall, and looked out across the restless grass. "And now, will you please go, Aaron?" she asked hoarsely. "You will have to be the one who turns away, for I cannot."

"I don't understand any of this."

He came close alongside and would have reached out and taken hold of her; but she shook her head quickly and went rigid in a way that stopped his gesture in midair. "But I do," she whispered tightly. "Now go. Please!"

He stared at her and after a long time slowly nodded. "I'll find out," he said, and he was not speaking to her, but to himself. He shortened his reins, inclined his head, and without further words turned the stallion and pointed it back the way they had come.

30

Summer retreated reluctantly down the valley, lingering on the thick blanket of grass to soak up the last comfort of warmth during the day, stealing ever closer to the outer edge of the outflung leaf at night. And then one day there was a chill in the air that sent the last remnant of the dying season hurrying from the valley.

When Lord stepped from his back porch the next morning, the distant grove of aspen shone yellow in the rising sun, like a handful of new-minted coins flung down on the carpet of the hills. He felt that slow turning of the year and yielded to the half-mournful feeling that always comes at autumn.

That morning he hauled in the last load of hay and added it to the lesser of the two stacks near the stable, which now boasted a thick roof of sod, and a partition dividing it into two stalls, one for the stallion, the other for the two mares and the filly. Lord had no intention of leaving his precious, thin-skinned thoroughbreds to fend for themselves during this, their first winter in an alien clime. There remained only the hauling and stacking of firewood, and a trip into town for supplies, and he would be ready for the winter.

Beset by loneliness, he had turned to the two dogs for companionship, keeping them with him wherever he went and inviting them into the house at night. Aloof and self-sufficient as they might be, he nonetheless drew comfort from their nearness.

By the end of the third day of wood cutting he had a shoulder-high double rick of cedar and pine stacked along the back of the house from the porch to the corner. In cold dawn on the fourth he started the jolting trip to town in the wagon. By noon he was fording the river on his way home, the wagon creaking and groaning under its high-piled load.

Midway along the lane leading to the pass he turned in at a house and bought three boxes of apples, smiling down into the faces of the three children who gaped in open-mouthed astonishment at this great bronze giant come suddenly to their doorstep.

He traveled up the valley beside the busy stream, feeling the sharpness of autumn in the air. A deeper silence had settled over the land, isolating the calls of the few birds still remaining and giving a hollow ring to the air.

It was a feeling that got into Lord as the wagon rocked steadily across the brown sea, making him lonely and turning his thoughts inward. He went back to the day that Fresno Taggert had ridden to his house, and felt once again her difference from all other women—her boundless pride, the steadiness of her will, and the deep-rooted integrity. And once again he felt himself involuntarily responding to her womanliness and her startling beauty.

He was not naïve enough to believe in love at first sight. It could not flower until the seed had been fertilized with understanding and nurtured by acceptance. He was a man of strong animal hungers, but he did not regard this physical element as the foundation stone of love.

What was perhaps even more important—and he thought very carefully about this now—was that he had almost from the first felt a need to help her. Once begun, their affair had seemed the most natural thing in the world to him, and he knew now that this feeling was owing to her immediate and complete acceptance of him as a man altogether worthy of her respect. That he could so readily and so easily accept that generous outpouring of passion, with no hint of servility, he regarded as a sign of growth on his own part. In this newfound pride he had reveled, until the hill riffraff had apprised him of the heinous wrong of miscegenation.

That the actual cause of the attack on him had been his brief coupling with Lila MacKay was not important in the final analysis. One dismal truth alone had significance—that his mixed blood could destroy Fresno Taggert as surely as if he had murdered her with his own hands.

Later, with the lamp extinguished, he lay awake, feeling the cold sheets and wryly reflecting that there was more than a modicum of truth in the adage having to do with unwisdom of man's living alone.

Day followed day with monotonous regularity. He laid in a supply of meat, shooting an antelope buck less than fifty yards from the back porch, and one day in the hills he brought down a young bull elk with one well-placed shot. After that, he took to riding the stallion almost daily on extended forays through the region, getting a surer feel of the country as it changed to a grimmer, less hospitable host.

Happening upon the deserted Matlock clearing on one such ride, he heard a cow's mournful lowing and found in a pasture beyond the barn an abandoned brindle cow with her day-old calf at her side. He noted the state of her painfully swollen udder, drove her to the barn, and milked the pain from her. About to turn her out to shift for herself in the timberland, he hesitated, weighing her chances of surviving. And then he realized the foolishness of passing up an abundant milk supply that could be his for the taking, and happily captured the loudly bawling calf and draped it across the pommel of his saddle. The next two days were spent building a lean-to at one end of the stable to shelter the cow and calf.

Whiteness overlaid the blue of the far mountains, moving lower as winter tightened its grip ever more strongly, and one night he woke to a different wind and knew that the valley would be white when dawn came. Going out to milk that morning, he found the snow trampled around the haystacks where deer and

315

antelope had slipped in to feed during the night, and in a nest flush against one of the stacks, a late-born sickly antelope fawn lay curled in shivering sleep.

It was Elizabeth who discovered its resting place, and at her full-throated roar the little thing staggered up in purest terror and sought to flee. Lord's shout clamped the dog's jaws shut before they could close on the slender throat, but it was borne to the snow by the hurtling weight of its attacker. Lord hurried over and cradled it against his chest, pressing his face against the frantically palpitating body and crooning wordless comfort into the rigid ears.

The stricken look in its great eyes touched him, and without pausing to deliberate he hurried into the kitchen and deposited the fawn in the corner near the stove, then left to milk. Returning with a bucket of steaming milk, he fashioned a makeshift nipple out of a piece of deerskin and tied it to the top of a bottle. Thus armed, he took the trembling creature onto his lap and set about the frustrating business of teaching it to drink. Eventually, with his entire front soaking wet, he accomplished the miracle, and laughed as the tiny brush of a tail waggled frantically in time with the energetic sucking sounds. ·

Twice more that morning the battle of the bottle was reenacted; but the fourth feeding saw all opposition vanish. By suppertime the minute creature had abandoned its corner and was following him about the kitchen on stilt-like legs, its tiny, needle-sharp hoofs rattling on the floor as it trotted back and forth at his heels.

Its terror of the two huge dogs likewise evaporated, and when a timorous investigation of Elizabeth revealed a remembered warmth, it forthwith attached itself to that astonished giant with a perserverance that left the dog no recourse other than to submit. When Lord rose from his chair in front of the fireplace to go to bed, the two were curled up near the hearth, the fawn nestled like a spotted ball against the coarse hair of Elizabeth's chest, the bitch's chin resting on the fawn's shoulder.

"Talk about the lamb and the lion bedding down together," he chuckled.

A week later Jesse and Lila came sliding down off the bench bearing a magnificent silver wolfskin coat which Lila had made. Whatever misgivings Lord had entertained about the girl's ability to adjust to her new mode of life as Jesse's hunting partner were immediately dispelled at the sight of her glowing countenance. The restlessness had gone out of her, and her laugh no longer exploded disconcertingly but came out full-throated and warm. They stayed for an early supper which Lila insisted on cooking as she regaled Lord with hair-raising accounts of her hunting.

Supper over, Lord seized on the few minutes that saw Jesse out saddling up for the trip home to voice the question that lay forever on his mind now, like an insupportable weight.

"Lila, do you know where Fresno is?"

She was belting her bulky bearskin coat about her lithe waist. At his question, all friendliness went out of her. "Why should you care?" she demanded.

"I've got to know."

She put her green eyes on him, letting nothing at all show beneath their impenetrable surface. "You've taken your own sweet time about deciding that, seems to me," she told him levelly, and drew on a fur-lined gauntlet. "Why so concerned all of a sudden?"

"It's not sudden, Lila. I was afraid you wouldn't tell me."

"Well, for once in your life you were right about something."

"I don't understand you," he began heatedly. "I don't—"

Lila leaned forward and placed her hands flat against the checkered oilcloth. "There's a hell of a lot you don't understand," she stated bluntly, and went on before he could interrupt. "Let me make this short and sweet. I like you. Dave Moline likes you, and so do Sol and Henry and Will—the whole damned Star outfit, in fact. In one way or another, we all make you out to be quite a man in one sense, but pretty much of a sorry shit in another."

She let that sink in, then hit him again with her punishing voice. "For what it's worth, I think you ought to know that, except for me, you're the only other living soul Jesse Whitehead ever gave a single damned thing to. It was his idea that I make that wolfskin coat for you. But you don't find the Star boys or Dave Moline visiting, do you? Ever wonder why?"

She straightened, folded her arms across her chest, and stood there gazing down at him, a vibrant, impulsive girl turned brutal and cold by something she could not make come out right. "When you've figured that one out," she said in the same unfriendly tone, "see how you can do with this one: everyone I named loves Fresno. In their eyes she can do no wrong—and that includes tumbling in bed with a dumb bastard named Aaron Lord. Now she's gone. When they look at you, they see the reason for her leaving. They may still *like* you, but they don't respect you. Why? Well, mister, that's something you can figure out while you're sitting here alone on your lonely backside." She stopped, then added with a hint of her old drollery, "Anything else I can do to cheer you up before I go, friend?"

Lord went to his feet, no longer trying to salvage this visit which was ending so badly. "You won't tell me where she is?"

"I wouldn't tell you which way to jump, if you were stone-blind and about to get bit by a rattlesnake."

He looked into her aroused eyes and read the animosity there. "You really despise me, don't you?"

"Not at all . . . just your damned bullheadedness." She caught the sound of Jesse approaching with the horses and reached out to grip Lord's shoulder. She gave it a firm shake. "Wake up, Aaron!" she said, suddenly gentle with her voice. "It's broad daylight, and you've overslept."

She opened the door and stepped out onto the porch. When Jesse would have gone in, she barred his way. "Let's go."

"I aimed to warm up a minute before we started," he complained. "It's colder'n hell out here."

"It's colder than hell in there, right now," Lila told him, low-voiced. "I've just spread a layer of ice over our big friend. Let's go."

Once again the days formed their long procession, with Lord

vainly trying to fill them with meaningful accomplishments. He
brought in pine saplings and made a settee and covered it with the
magnificent jet-black hide of a bear he had surprised prowling
around the stable one bright moonlit night. Two matching chairs
he upholstered with lynx pelts of a texture so luxurious it seemed
almost sacrilegious to sit on them. Immediately he had finished
the second one, he regretted his choice of fur, for he could not
look at them without recalling the lease agreement he had made
with Fresno, and the bonus he had laughingly demanded and
which had been so readily promised. With masochistic determination he placed one at either side of the hearth, then studiously avoided sitting on them. Nightly thereafter, he per-
formed a ritual that was a deliberately contrived torture. Seated
on the settee, he would stare at one or the other of the chairs until
he was again riding up the sun-drenched valley with Fresno
beside him, vividly alive with the blue of her riding habit echoed
in her eyes and her wealth of copper hair cascading down her
back to catch the sunlight and ignite it in a blaze of glory. And
then the quick warmth of her voice would fill the empty room,
and he would find himself smiling, remembering.

But in the darkness of his room there was neither sunlight on
waving hair nor a remembered voice to blot out the sound of the
wind prowling about the house—only an empty, dull ache that
spread all through him until it occupied every finely drawn nerve
in his body and held him helpless until fitful sleep eventually
overcame him.

He came to dread the dawn, for then the greyness of his world
must be faced and the empty gestures of living gone through once
again. But, unrewarding as the days were, the long evenings by
the fire were even worse. In time, he discontinued the mem-
ory-evoking ritual with the lynx-covered chairs because he
found that it destroyed all hope of winning forgetful sleep.

Except when observing the rapidly growing fawn, which he
named Winter Star, he never smiled. The fawn trailed after him
wherever he went, now, and he never ceased to marvel at the
resilience of the minute body and the incredible speed in the

319

reed-like legs. So apparent was the little waif's contentment with her lot as a privileged member of the household, so complete her indifference to her own kind, who often grazed within a stone's throw of the grove, that he had long since lost all feelings of guilt over having adopted her.

Christmas came, and with it Lila and Jesse, the latter bearing a wild turkey which he had neatly decapitated with one well-placed shot from his Springfield. Throughout the day, Lord made sporadic attempts to rise to the festive occasion, only to find himself repeatedly submerged in gloom. More than once he surprised Lila regarding him with penetrating, amused eyes. Finally his patience gave out, and he glared angrily at her.

"Am I really all that funny-looking?"

Her amusement deepened. "Frankly, you look like hell."

"Then why all the giggling behind your hand?"

She had been holding the fawn on her lap, fondling the velvety ears. Now she rose to her feet and tucked it under her arm. "Let's say my middle name is Daisy," she drawled, starting for the kitchen. "I'll never tell."

"Nettleweed would be a more apt name," Lord retorted. "You never miss a chance to sting."

Lila paused and stood over him, meeting his aroused gaze with a studied calm. "Don't blame your itching on me," she stated pointedly. "If you're in all that much misery, do something about it, why don't you?" She took the fawn from under her arm, draped it, unresisting, around her neck like a furpiece, and rubbed her cheek against one of the lax ears. "Come on, little sister. Let's you and me go see if that old turkey's done yet."

The meal itself was enjoyable enough, but long after the two guests had ridden away, the girl's enigmatic remark lingered to irritate Lord. Sleep, that night, was long in coming.

31

For seven days Lord did not stir beyond the yard. He spent hours brooding into the flames in the fireplace. He attended to the stock out of habit, and occasionally roused himself to eat a little food, but after a few bites his throat constricted and the food became repellent to him.

In appearance he had become a mere caricature of the man who had ridden into Star Valley seven months before. He was gaunt almost beyond recognition. And his unkempt mane straggled well below his shoulders. His eyes stared dully out from dark, sunken caverns, making his cheekbones appear even higher and sharper. There were deep hollows beneath his cheeks, and his skin had taken on an unhealthy pallor. Whereas before he had moved with a cat-like, gliding grace, he now trudged heavy-footed, with a foreshortened, slack-kneed action. On the last morning of December he willed himself to shave, and when he washed the lather from his face and glimpsed his reflection in the mirror, he was appalled at what he saw.

Momentarily shaken out of his despondency, he threw on the wolfskin coat, and with his trio of four-legged companions trailing in his wake, set off on a hike that took him far up the valley, thence into the hills, and finally home by way of the benchland behind the house.

But even this self-enforced exercise did little to revive his flagging spirits, for the day was bleak and overcast, with no hint of warmth breaking through the depressing pall. The timbered hills showed black in the muted light, and the valley was a blank expanse of white under its mantle of snow.

Reentering the house, he kindled the fire into new life and was on the point of taking up his customary vigil in front of it when he loosed a violent string of oaths and jumped to his feet. In the kitchen he snatched up the milk bucket and went out, slamming the door behind him. Ignoring the fact that it was a good two hours short of milking time, he called the surprised cow into the lean-to and filled the bucket to the halfway mark, afterward turning the calf in for its share.

He returned to the house, strained the milk into a crock, then fed the dogs and the fawn. After banking the fire in the fireplace, he went back to the barn, grained the two mares and the filly, then saddled the stallion.

The big grey was beside itself with excitement over the unexpected outing and cavorted about the yard like an unbroken colt, forcing Lord to employ all his skill to avoid being thrown. When he succeeded in pointing it toward the lower valley, it grabbed the bit and shot away through the grove like a cavalry charger spearheading an attack.

Two bone-chilling hours later he rode into Martha's backyard, tied the stallion in the stable, and after throwing a rug over it, stumped to the house on feet that felt like solid chunks of ice. Night had overtaken him a mile back, and lamplight glowed through the window as he knocked on the kitchen door. A voice bade him enter, and he lifted the latch and stepped inside to see Martha replacing the chimney of a second lamp she had just lit.

She started in surprise, then she was smiling and coming forward to greet him, hands outstretched in welcome. "Mr. Lord! It's good to see—" Her voice died as she took in his ravaged face. "Mr. Lord . . . are you all right? Here, come sit by the stove and let me help you off with your coat. You must be frozen!"

Her concern came out in a rush as she deposited him in a chair, opened the oven door, and started to undo the rawhide lacings of his coat. Dropping the coat to the floor, she whisked a cup off a shelf and poured him a cup of coffee.

"Drink that down," she ordered. "We call it Ruby's Black Thunder, and it's guaranteed to cure any ailment known to mankind, providing your insides are acid-proof." She drew up a second chair and sat down facing him. "What on earth brings you out on such a bitter night?"

Lord took a long swallow of the virulent coffee and grimaced. "If Ruby's one of your girls," he choked, "tell her to stick to her trade. She'll never make it as a cook!"

"I heard that, and it's not funny," said a voice behind him, and he quickly turned to see the redhead scowling at him.

"You must be Ruby," he said lamely. "I apologize."

"And you," she returned, "must be that wild Indian I've been hearin' about. Tell me, Mister," she said, sauntering to the stove, "is it true your kind never attacks at night?"

Lord saw the eyes laughing at him. "That's purely an old wives' tale," he told her soberly. "We'll attack at any hour of the day *or* night . . . just so long as there's no danger of the victim shooting back."

"I *never* shoot back," Ruby drawled, "but I moan a lot if the pain gets too bad."

Martha decided this had gone on long enough. "All right, Ruby," she said. "That will do. I'm sure you've demonstrated that you're the world's greatest temptress, so you can get back to the parlor now." Clearly Ruby would be delighted to take Lord by the hand and lead him upstairs, given any encouragement at all. "Mr. Lord is a friend of mine," she added pointedly.

Ruby picked up her cup. "And a happy New Year to you, too, Madame," she retorted drily. Passing Lord, she let her free hand trail over his head, her long fingers running through the heavy hair with a gesture outrageously familiar. On Martha she fixed the pained look of a mother faced with irrefutable proof of her daughter's waywardness. "And I always thought you was such a *good* girl," she said reprovingly, then closed one eye in a conspiratorial wink. "Remember, it's more blessed to give than to receive. So, when you're done with this one, point him toward my room. I'll damn sure receive him in the proper spirit."

When she had gone, Martha looked at Lord and gave in to laughter. "She's impossible!"

"She ought to be on the stage."

"She was. But according to her, she had so many offers from gentlemen admirers that she decided to capitalize on her other talents."

Now Martha refilled his cup and settled comfortably into her chair again. "Why *did* you make the long, cold ride down here tonight?"

"Well, it's New Year's Eve, isn't it?" he replied blandly. "Isn't Martha's Mission the logical place to see it ushered in?"

"You didn't come here to wallow in sin," Martha stated. "You came to see *me*. Why?"

Lord made a gesture of resignation and sank back in his chair. "All right." But he did not enlighten her immediately. His eyes gazed out at her from their deep caverns with a curiously lost look in them, fixed on her, but not seeing her. For some time he regarded her thus, a big man rendered helpless by thoughts which could not find utterance. He looked down at his hands lying loosely on his thighs. "Yes," he said abruptly, going back to the moment of their meeting, "I *am* sick . . . in the head. I think I'm going crazy."

"You don't mean that!"

"But I do. Look at me, Martha. Do I look like a man in command of his faculties? I used to weigh a hundred and eighty; now I doubt I'd tip the scales at one forty. I used to sleep like a log; now I stare at the ceiling half the night, and toss and turn the other half. I can't think of any one thing for more than five minutes at a time, or, if I do manage to hold onto a thought that long, my brain just keeps grinding around and around in an endless circle." He hunched forward and seized Martha's wrist in a grip that made her wince. "Martha, you've got to help me! Please!"

His desperation lifted his voice until Martha was alarmed lest it be overheard in the distant parlor. Martha's Mission was doing a brisk business tonight, and there was every likelihood customers would be waiting there. She got up hurriedly and closed the hall door, then resumed her seat. "I'll do anything I can," she assured him. "Anything. You know that."

"Do you mean it?"

"Of course I do!"

He looked closely at her, his lips pressed into a thin line. "Where is Fresno?"

If he had reached out and slapped her, she would not have been more hurt. She shook her head sadly. "I was hoping you would not ask that, Mr. Lord."

"You said you'd help," he retorted accusingly.

"I said I would do anything I could," she corrected him. At the look of despair on his face, her tone softened. "You couldn't know, of course, but I gave my word that I would say nothing to you about her leaving."

"Did she specify *me?* She made you promise not to tell *me?*"

"Yes, Mr. Lord. But take care how you interpret that. She had her reasons, and to her they were sound."

Something in her tone aroused his suspicion. "You said that as though you might not altogether agree with her."

All at once Martha realized that she was no match for him in a duel of wits. He was like a stalking cat, tensed to spring the instant she was off guard. "I will not discuss it any further," she said coldly. "And I must say, I consider it unworthy of you to attempt to make me betray a solemn trust."

He made his quick judgment of her and knew that she was as strong as he. Still, he could not accept this abrupt collapse of his hopes. He said accusingly, "But you know where she is," and saw her lips thin to a grim line.

"Whether I do or not makes no difference."

He slumped back then. "As Ruby put it," he said drily, " 'And a happy New Year to you, too, Mrs. Bland.' "

"That's unfair!" Martha said indignantly. "My personal opinion doesn't come into this at all. I am abiding by the wishes of someone who needs my support right now. Even if it had been left up to me to decide, I'm not sure I'd tell you where she is," she stated, then seemingly contradicted herself. "Though I think you should be with her now."

"Well, that makes two of us, at least."

"Then, why aren't you?"

Lord was completely mystified by the irrationality of her thinking. "My God, woman! If I knew where she was, would I be asking you?"

His sincerity was unmistakable, but Martha refused to be moved by it. "Your concern comes a bit late in the day," she said coolly. "Nor does it explain why you're here and Fresno is somewhere else, does it?"

Lord lifted his hands chest high and banged them down on his thighs. "Was there ever before such a damnfool conversation between two supposedly sane people?" he asked of the room at large. He put his gaze back on Martha and addressed her with exaggerated patience. "I am not with Fresno for the simple reason I don't know where she is. Is that quite clear, Mrs. Bland?"

"It *sounds* clear enough, Mr. Lord. But it doesn't *think* clear, if you understand what I'm saying."

"Frankly, I've no idea what you're saying."

She leaned forward slightly and spoke with a deliberation that matched his. "Then I will put it simply and bluntly. You *should* be with Fresno—not in London or Paris or New York, or wherever else she happens to be at the moment, but *here*. Right here in Star Valley, because *she* should be here, and *would* be, but for one simple reason: she was given no reason to stay."

"That's not true! I asked her not to go! I swear it!"

"I didn't say she wasn't *asked*. I said she was given no *reason*," Martha reminded him. "There's a vast difference."

"What do you mean?"

"You know perfectly well what I mean, Mr. Lord."

Lord's gaze wavered and fell to the floor. "If you mean, I should have asked her to marry me, you're wrong. I couldn't do that."

"Why not?"

His eyes lifted accusingly. "You know why not!" All at once he was on his feet, his whole frame shaking. "I wanted to!" he burst out. "My God, how I wanted to! If I could believe there was any chance it might not ruin her . . . any thread of hope it wouldn't kill her in the end . . . I'd marry her the minute I found her! I've thought about it until I'm half out of my mind . . . trying to convince myself it wouldn't destroy her. But I *can't!* I love her too much to drag her down to my level."

He fell loosely into his chair again, his hands covering his face. A single, choked sob tore through his throat. And then he became utterly still, fighting the emotions that unmanned him.

Looking at that bowed shape, Martha felt an impulse to draw his head onto her lap and soothe away the torment raging within. But she stifled the urge and went on with her unwelcome task. "Since it's Fresno's reputation that's uppermost in your thoughts, I wonder you can't see that you've already destroyed it, according to your lights. Personally, I don't agree with you at all. Altered the symbol of untouchability that was Fresno Star Taggert? Very definitely. Proved her to be a mortal woman with certain of the failings the term implies? Again, yes. The two of you very neatly managed to outrage peoples' sense of propriety with your carryings-on. Of her own volition, Fresno willfully flouted the taboos, and will, as a consequence, be snubbed by any number of former so-called friends."

She paused, sensing she had his attention now, and for the first time dared to hope she might somehow shake him from his rigid conviction. "All the things I mentioned are undeniable," she went on. "But you're forgetting a very, very important additional one, when you speak of ruining her: she isn't some little, feather-brained nobody. She is Fresno Star Taggert, heir to one of the richest cattle and mining empires west of the Mississippi, and one of the best-known and most influential figures in the Territory. If she were not, there would have been raiding parties stripping the valley of every head of stock the day her fall from grace became known. Her headquarters would have been burned to the ground, and she would have been run out of the valley. But has any of this happened? Who has tried to take a single calf wearing the Star brand? Who has tried to stake out a claim in Star Valley? Who has been heard to refer to her aloud as 'that breed's woman,' even behind her back? *No one!* So, kindly tell me how Fresno has been made to suffer for her misstep—aside from being rejected by the man she loved?"

She sank back, as if finished. But when he would have spoken, she silenced him with a gesture. "And please spare me that overworked excuse of yours—that it was the color of your skin, your blood, that caused all the damage. If she'd been found in bed with any man, be he white as snow, the dirt would have been thrown just as quickly. Don't think it wouldn't."

"It wouldn't have been the same," Lord stubbornly protested. "If I were white, they'd forget, in time. They'd lie themselves into believing the whole thing was a rumor."

A laugh of derision burst from Martha. "My God above! One day you'll find out what a stupid thing you've just said! *Rumor?* You poor, ignorant man!" She started to laugh again, then caught herself, warned by the speculative look in the narrowed eyes fixed on her. Realizing that she had very nearly blundered, she spoke swiftly and vehemently. "If you think the color of a man's skin determines how quickly people forget a scandal, you've a lot to learn about your fellow man. I know whereof I speak. I was raped by six *white* men. No one believed their story; but the Basin buried me just as fast and just as deep as if I'd been guilty. It was easy, because I was a nobody. I couldn't fight back. But Fresno isn't a nobody, and that makes all the difference in the world." She pointed a forefinger at him. "Think about that for the rest of the winter, and who knows? Come spring, you may have your thoughts lined out straight."

Lord stared unseeingly at the ceiling. After a long while he spoke in a thoughtful, searching voice, as if he were quite alone. "If only I could believe that!"

And now Martha did what she had wanted to do long minutes before. She rose and took his head in her hands and pressed it to her chest. "You will in time, my dear. You will."

He reached up his long arms and encircled her waist, exerting a strong pressure. For that unmeasured run of time they were very close, and then he spoke without moving his head from the reassuring warmth of its resting place. "But you still won't tell me where she is, will you."

It was a statement, not a question; but Martha answered it. "I don't know where she is. I only know she will be back."

He was on his feet in the instant, his eyes alight in his drawn face. "When?"

328

"I can't tell you that. It was part of my promise."

Reading her inflexibility, he sighed. "All right," he said, and bent to pick up his coat. "I guess I can wait awhile longer." He shrugged into the coat and grinned lopsidedly. "It's all I *can* do, isn't it?"

Her answer was barely audible. "It's all any of us can do." She stood close to him, looking up into his face with a half smile that failed to belie the soberness of her words. "If you have any prayers tucked away, take them out and put them to work while you're waiting. Maybe they'll help cut down the odds."

32

Exhausted by the scene in Martha's kitchen and the subsequent freezing ride home, Lord fell into bed long after midnight and immediately plummeted into a deep and dreamless sleep. When he woke at dawn, he was acutely aware of being clear-headed for the first time in months. Dressing hurriedly, he shooed the dogs outside, kindled the fires, and set the coffee pot on to boil before going out to feed and milk.

After a hastily downed breakfast, he returned to the stable and threw himself into the task of putting the long-neglected stalls and the cowbarn to rights. During his protracted seige of self-pity he had let them fall into a disgraceful state, contenting himself with dumping in new bedding without removing the old. As a result, stalls and stanchion contained a deep matting of muck that exuded a choking cloud of ammonia as he bared layer after layer with his fork.

He commenced by adding it to the pile behind the stable, then suddenly broke off and laid his fork aside as an idea struck him.

Fifty feet up the creek he found the ideal location for the vegetable garden in an area slightly lower than the creek—one which could be easily irrigated.

With the team hitched to the wagon, he backed up to the stable door and started loading the fermenting bedding. By noon he had both stalls cleaned to the bare ground and their contents spread in a steaming carpet over his garden plot. Deciding to leave the cowbarn until later, he went to the house and ate his first hearty meal of the winter.

Throughout the rest of the day he drove himself without letup, and by nightfall congratulated himself on a job well done as he set the milking stool in place and inhaled the fragrance of the fresh wild hay underfoot. Later, when he rose from in front of the fire to undress for bed, it seemed the most natural thing in the world to turn the two giant dogs out for the night. They would return to their long-abandoned cavern in the larger of the haystacks, but only after they had completed their customary patrol of the perimeter of the yard to assure themselves that no alien beings had invaded their domain during their stay indoors. Listening to their blood-curdling challenges reverberating on the still night air, he smiled. Things were back to normal again.

A week later Lord shouldered his axe, climbed to the bench behind the house, and started cutting pine saplings for the fence he proposed to build around his garden plot. He was about to knock off for noon when the sound of riders descending the timbered slope above turned him that way. At sight of Lila and Jesse, he loosed a welcoming hail and hurried to meet them.

Lila, riding in the lead, negotiated the final steep drop at a rush and drew up. "Well!" she exclaimed, taking in Lord's broad smile, "if it isn't Lazarus himself, come back from the grave!" She turned in her saddle, hand extended palm up, as Jesse ranged alongside. "You owe me five dollars. He's not a corpse after all."

"What is this?" Lord demanded, more pleased to see them than he would have thought possible. "You mean you've been making bets on whether I was still alive?"

Jesse leaned down to grasp Lord's lifted hand. "Figgered I stood a fair chance o' gittin' some o' my money back, considerin' the way you was turnin' into a shadder awhile back," he grinned. "This damned girl has well nigh cleaned me outa my life savins' bettin' on which one o' us is the best shot. And since we was headin' fer town, we swung around to see if you was still among the livin'!"

"You say you're headed for town?"

"Yep. Lila, here, is fixin' t'do a pile o' sewin', an' wants t' lay in a stock o' gewgaws, so's—"

"Jesse!" Lila cut in warningly. "You shut up! You said I could do the telling."

Lord shot her a quizzical look. "Telling?" he repeated. When she flushed guiltily, his gaze narrowed. "Well, do it, then. What's the big mystery?"

Lila kneed her big bay toward the road leading off the bench. "I'm telling nothing until I get a cup of hot coffee inside me," she said over her shoulder, and dropped out of sight.

Two cups of coffee later, she rose from the table, which movement plainly was a prearranged signal for Jesse to make himself scarce, for he immediately clapped his hat on his head and went outside, mumbling about bringing the horses around.

Lila waited until the latch clicked, then nailed Lord with a suspicious look. "What have you heard?" she demanded.

Lord was wholly unprepared for this sudden change in her manner. "I don't know what you're talking about!" he protested. "What do you mean—"

"Don't lie to me!" Lila snapped. "It's written all over your damned face! Now answer me!"

Lord was too taken aback to be angry. "So help me, God, Lila, I don't know what you mean! I've been holed up here all winter. How could I hear anything about anything? What are you getting at?"

"The *truth,* damn you!" She took a step toward him, eyes blazing. "You've managed to find out where she is, haven't you?"

"Look," Lord said patiently, pushing himself to his feet. He stopped as the meaning of Lila's accusation dawned on him. "You mean Fresno?" he asked quietly.

"Yes, I mean Fresno, dammit! How'd you find out?"

Lord threw back his head and loosed a howl of laughter at the ceiling. But with his mouth open, all humor deserted him, and instead of laughing, he merely made a sound that was half grunt, half sigh. "As God is my witness," he said, looking Lila in the eye and speaking slowly and carefully, "I have found out nothing of Fresno Taggert's whereabouts. If I had, I would be there with her. I went down and tried to get Martha to tell me where she was. Whether she wouldn't or couldn't, I'm not sure; but she *didn't.* And that is still the truth."

His sincerity was unmistakable, but the puzzle still remained. "Then how come this sudden change in you?" Lila wanted to know. "Two weeks ago you looked like hell warmed over, and had the disposition of a rattler shedding his skin. How come the sudden change?"

"Let's just say it's something personal that I'd rather not discuss, Lila," Lord replied quietly. He caught the flicker of hurt in her eyes before she could mask it, and realized he had no right to shut her out with that brief reply. He closed the distance separating them and took one of her hands before she could withdraw it. Looking down at her, with a half smile, he gave it a little squeeze, then released it and stepped back.

"What was that for?"

"For you being you, that's all," Lord grinned. "Lila's don't happen along very often. When they do, I always make it a point to shake their hand."

It was one of the few times in her life that Lila was embarrassed. She looked down at the floor, then out the window. "You're a crazy man," she said, and reached out to the shelf for her gauntlets.

"A little over a week ago I wouldn't have argued the point."

The soberness of his words brought her around. "But now you would. Why?"

"Martha didn't tell me where to find Fresno, but she told me a few other things."

"Such as?"

"Such as how people who walk in circles seldom get anywhere, and that while a person may think he's pretty smart, there may still be one or two things he could learn, and that while a magnifying glass enlarges the thing you're looking at, it leaves everything all around it blurred. Things like that."

Lila cocked a quizzical brow. "And it made sense to you?"

"It did."

She began pulling her gauntlets on, gravely studying him. What she saw apparently satisfied her, for she at length nodded in her abrupt way. "Then, I guess that takes care of Mr. Lord, for the time being. Which brings us back to the reason behind this little tea party."

"You were going to tell me something."

"I came by to invite you to my wedding next month."

"Your *wedding?*"

Lila turned her head as if addressing a third party. "We seem to have an echo in here, don't we? Or am I just repeating myself?"

"But who?" Lord asked blankly. "Who's the man?"

"Guess."

"I've no idea."

"Dave Moline!"

"Do you mean—? When was this decided?"

Lila grinned. "About a month before he got around to asking me. Don't look so boggle-eyed. I've known Dave for five years. The wedding's set for one o'clock, first of February. You'll be there?"

"With bells on!"

Lila opened the door and stepped out onto the porch, then stuck her head back in. Her green eyes conducted a very leisurely, very personal survey of Lord's buckskin-clad figure and stopped finally on his flushed face. "Never mind the bells," she drawled. "Just remember to wear some clothes. They may help keep you decent . . . for a change."

Before he could think of a suitable retort, the latch clicked and footsteps bounded away in the direction of the corrals.

He arrived at Star headquarters on the appointed day, attired in a dove-grey suit, tailored to his exact measurements in St.

Louis, and boots of finest Spanish leather. With his hair once again neatly trimmed to shoulder length, and mounted on the proudly strutting grey stallion, he made a picture the assembled guests would long remember. Moreover, he was aware of it, and as he drew up before the hitching rail in front of the mess hall where those guests waited, he kneed the stallion to a rock-like stand and posed there for a carefully calculated moment.

He was known by sight to only a handful of those watchers; but that he had long been the subject of conversation throughout the region he had no doubt at all. Nor did he doubt that any slightest detail of the picture he presented escaped the notice of the eyes trained on him. Willing himself to endure that barrage of stares with all the feigned assurance of a veteran performer, he reflected that no power on earth could have induced him to do this six months ago, and he wondered at his newfound assurance.

Some minutes later, standing alone just inside the door of the mess hall, which had been lavishly hung with evergreen boughs to transform it into a bower for the occasion, he inwardly cursed himself for having come; for his presence here was no favor to the couple standing so attentively at the far end of the room before the solemn Methodist minister from Valley Junction. Faultless as his grooming might be, and impeccable as his manner, he still riveted the attention of the assembled guests.

His affair with the mistress of this ranch, with all its titillating tales, had long since been accepted as fact; but until this moment he had existed in the minds of most of these people as something not quite real—a disembodied presence that had drastically altered all their lives in ways they still did not fully comprehend.

The day of his arrival had marked the beginning of a chain of events which, while hardly involving them personally, had included each in turn until, collectively and singly, each had come to regard him as some mysterious force whose influence over them was as undeniable and as ungovernable as a phenomenon of nature.

The bloody ordeal which had transpired at the old Bland place last fall had taken them completely unawares. Consternation had rendered them dumb when Fresno Taggert had unabashedly revealed herself as a voluntary participant in what could only be described as lustful goings-on in that isolated lake cabin retreat. Disbelief, indignation, outrage, and eventual reluctant acceptance had followed on the heels of that revelation. And then a deep-rooted sense of loyalty to the woman, who all her life had exemplified everything that was honorable and fair, had assumed dominance over all else. Waiving personal and racial prejudices in the face of public censure, they had rallied to the defense of their mistress in an upsurge of fidelity as feudal in nature as the unreasoning loyalty that had for centuries welded the Highland clans of Scotland into unbreachable rings of steel about their chieftans.

But the expected attack had never materialized, and in the end the long-vaunted impregnability of their mountain bastion was seen by them to be an actuality. Having survived what might very well have been a holocaust, these Star people now regarded themselves as beings set apart and dedicated to a higher cause.

This, Lord sensed. Without being able to put a name to it, he felt that the oneness of purpose binding these people together was that which prompted his mother's people to refer to themselves exclusively as *the humans*. And he knew that while no individual here would openly confess to considering himself a superior being, the conviction that he was such lay in each and every one of them, as deeply fixed and as unshakable as the conviction of the true zealot whose deafness to reason is in direct proportion to the narrowness of his vision.

And with that same awareness, Lord sensed that by some unique manipulation of the mind this exclusive gathering of Star adherents had elected to include him. It was a paradox. He, an outsider of alien blood, had defied social mores in a way never before dreamed of in this convention-bound society. In so doing he had placed Star in the untenable position not only of having to countenance his conduct out of loyalty to Fresno Taggert but of having to sanction that conduct publically.

Not that they freely accorded him all rights and privileges owing to one truly of their kind, Lord knew. For all their outward acceptance of him, they actually regarded him with the jaundiced eye of the close-knit family forced to make room for an unexpected and unwanted stepbrother.

Quite unexpectedly, Fresno was in his thoughts, vibrantly real and disturbing, and even while he wondered at her sudden emergence, the reason was known to him. Quite simply, she was present in the mind of everyone else here as well; it was disconcerting. He sensed the silent crowd in front of him thinking of her collectively, regretting her absence, and wondering just how responsible he himself was for that absence.

The certainty of these soundings sent a chill through him, and though he sought to put it down to an oversensitivity on his part, he knew that it was not imagined. A moment later his fears were confirmed. In one of those inexplicable happenings that sometimes sees an entire gathering acting on a common impulse, every eye in the mess hall turned and centered on him simultaneously with the minister's closing words. As clearly as though the words were spoken aloud, Lord heard the accusation reverberate through his shocked brain: *You are the reason she is gone!*

For what seemed an eternity the battery of accusing stares remained centered on him. And then, with senses reeling, he heard the close-packed room erupt in shouts of traditional well-wishing and advice as the crowd surged around the bride and groom. On wooden legs, he made his way through the press to grasp Moline's outstretched hand. He felt himself smiling, heard himself congratulating the man. But when he would have done likewise with Lila, the bride decided otherwise.

Before he knew it, she had seized his head in her hands and drawn it down to plant a resounding kiss squarely on his mouth. In the same instant her voice sounded in his ear, purposely loud and carefree, but with a meaning for him alone. "Keep it up, sonny: you're doing fine." He flushed to the roots of his hair, then burst out laughing. He should have known: nothing escaped those piercing green eyes. They had read his play-acting for what it was. But, more importantly, she approved.

Awareness of this steadied him, and on the instant, he decided to remain for the wedding feast that was already being hurriedly set out on the long trestle tables by the half-dozen women present.

He gauged the proper moment to leave, down to the instant, and before anyone else had moved in the direction of the waiting horses and buggies, he said his good-byes and went to the stallion. Slipping the reins free, he flipped them over the high-held head and stepped into the saddle. No watching eye could detect the signal that suddenly lifted the giant grey onto its hind legs and held it suspended there like a statue for five slow counts, nor the one that sent it forward in an airy leap that flowed into an effortless canter down the drive leading to the river road beyond.

33

Throughout February the valley lay clamped in the frigid grip of winter, with the temperature dropping well below zero at night and seldom rising above freezing during the day. But by mid-March drastic changes were everywhere in evidence. Sudden winds caught up curtains of snow from the floor of the valley and whipped them back and forth between the hills. Tiny trickles of water sneaked from hiding, flashed brief signals to the sun, then dodged back out of sight under the glassy surface of the stream beds and continued their tentative journey toward the distant river. And the side valley above Lord's place where the Star herds wintered reverberated to the ceaseless lowing of cows and the bawling of newborn calves.

In the blackest hour of a night toward the end of the month, Lord was jerked out of a sound sleep by the loud trumpeting of the stallion. Throwing on his clothes, he lit the lantern and raced to the stable. And there, in the deep hay of the section of the stall he had partitioned off for her, was the bay mare standing over her glistening-wet foal. Taking a clean grain sack, Lord slipped through the poles, knelt beside the shivering foal, and proceeded to rub it dry, while the mare snuffled soothingly to it, and the stallion peered intently through a crack in the partition, rumblingly boasting of this latest evidence of its immortality. In the light of the lantern, the foal's coat appeared dark red, like its dam's, but a close inspection of its face revealed a faint sprinkling of white hairs around the eyelids and the tiny muzzle—a sure sign that it would eventually be a grey. When, after a half-dozen abortive attempts, it gained its feet and went careening around the stall on its long and wholly unmanageable stilts, Lord ascertained that it was a colt and relayed this information to the half-delirious sire. "I guess we picked the right name, after all, your Majesty. Say hello to the Archduke."

Two days later Moline appeared, accompanied by Lila, to discuss the settlement of the winter lease. "We can cut your stuff out anytime, of course. But the sooner we do it, the less trouble you'll have holding them on your own range. With new calves at their side, they'll do a lot less straying back to their old range."

"Good enough," Lord agreed. "When do you want to do it?"

"Today's as good as any." Moline glanced at Lord's hands. "Ever done any ropin'?"

Lord grinned. "Not much. But I've been practicing. I've gotten so I can lasso that corral post one time out of ten . . . sometimes."

"My God!" Lila put in, "at that rate, you'll be 'til next Christmas getting your stuff branded!"

Dave turned to her. "Lila, let's rope off the herd and charge admission to the show. We could make a killing!"

Both men laughed, and Lord suddenly found himself liking the tawny-eyed rider.

Now Moline thumbed his hat off his forehead and dispensed with Lord's shortcomings with a rope. "The idea's temptin'," he admitted. "Only trouble is, I got to move those cattle back acrosst the river this spring. So I'll tell you what: you come on up and point out the stuff you want, and the boys will slap your brand on 'em for you this first time. That suit you?"

"Bet five dollars he hasn't even decided on a brand yet," Lila put in. "How about it, Aaron?"

Lord would not give her the satisfaction of knowing he had

been caught flat-footed. Hunkering down, he traced the outline of a star in the sand, and above it a crescent moon. "There's my brand."

"A half moon and a star," Lila mused. "Not bad. What do you call it?"

"Moonstar, of course."

"Got your iron made yet?" Moline inquired.

"No," Lord admitted, then decided to confess his shortsightedness. "As a matter of fact, I just now thought of the brand."

Again Moline brushed difficulty aside. "No hurry. The boys can easy enough trace that crescent with a runnin' iron. Get your horse and we'll get at it."

For no reason other than that it gave him a feeling of satisfaction, Lord daily rode up the valley to inspect the five hundred head of cows and their calves that now ranged his land. With the dogs and the fawn bounding through the grass flushing birds and rodents, and the strengthening sun of April spreading greenness ever more thickly over the land, he told himself that he was happier than he had ever been and knew that this was true.

But only to a degree, for no matter how often he repeated it, no matter how vehemently he mentally underlined the words, he knew that he was only marking time. Nothing was settled. Nothing was complete. Nothing really mattered, save the passage of time—time that would stop and stand forever still with Fresno's return to Star Valley.

34

The news, when it finally came, caught him completely unprepared. Shirtless, arms submerged to the elbows in the washtub, and with but half the wash hung up in the mid-June sun, he heard the dogs rush bellowing across the yard toward the grove. He glimpsed movement through the trees and caught the faint jingle of trace chains as the dogs' clamor abruptly ceased. The next instant he was sprinting across the yard. He reached the edge of the trees just as Martha drove into the clearing and drew up.

"Is she back?"

Martha nodded. "She's back." She sat looking down at him, her expression vaguely troubled. "She's back," she repeated, "but—"

"When?" Lord demanded. "When did she get here?"

"A few hours ago. She stopped at my—"

"Is she still there . . . at your place?"

"No. I imagine she's home by now. I had to wait until they were far enough ahead not to see me following them to the turnoff."

Lord's face took on a questioning look. "They? Who's with her?"

"Did I say, 'they?' " Martha asked, startled. She dabbed her neck with a handkerchief. "Well," she explained quickly, "she's in that heavy coach of hers, so of course she has a driver on the box." All at once she scowled down at him. "I feel like a traitor!" she burst out. "I promised her I wouldn't tell you, and the minute she drove off, I practically broke my neck getting hitched up." She sank back against the seat and mopped her face, clearly put out with the whole situation. "At least I kept my promise to *you*," she said defensively.

"She asked you not to tell me?"

Martha nodded, and when he merely stood there staring questioningly at her, she became openly impatient. "Well, what did you expect, for heaven's sake?" she demanded. "A gold-engraved invitation to a reception in your honor? She's not about to advertise her homecoming in this section of the valley! Would *you*, in her place?"

Lord's teeth suddenly flashed in a broad smile, and he reached up to squeeze her clenched hands. "Thanks, Martha! Go water your mare, then help yourself to a cup of coffee, or whatever else you can find. You'll have to excuse me while I saddle up. There's someone I've got to see, and if I don't do it now, I might lose what little courage I've got."

"Mr. Lord." Martha sat straighter, her expression again troubled. For a moment she seemed to have difficulty in finding words. In the end she shook her head and spoke with a curtness wholly unlike her. "Don't expect to find the same Fresno who left here last fall. She's changed."

"So have I, Martha."

"No, that's not what I mean. She's *very* changed. She's not the same woman who left here."

He had started to turn away. Now he came close and gripped the rim of the wheel in both hands. "Martha," he said quietly, "are you trying to warn me that I shouldn't go over there?"

"No . . . oh, no! Nothing like that! It's just that . . . Oh! I wish I'd never come up here! If I'd had any sense, I'd have sent someone with a note, and let you find out for yourself! I've no business being mixed up in this!"

"What are you talking about? Find out *what?*"

"Nothing!" Martha said violently. "I'm not going to say any more, except this . . . if you're not more sure of yourself than you were last fall, don't go over there." She again sat back on the seat, her lips firming to a grim line. "And that's *all* I'm going to say."

Lord looked at her closely for a long moment. "But I *am* sure, Martha."

"Then don't waste time standing here talking to a fool like me!" she snapped. "Get your horse and go!"

When Lord led the saddled stallion around to the back porch a few minutes later and dashed inside for his shirt, she had returned from watering her horse. They almost collided in the doorway, and he quickly stepped back into the kitchen to allow her to enter. "I'm sorry to rush off like—" he began, but she cut him off.

"Just take yourself out of my sight," she ordered. "I'm so rattled I'd just as soon beat you over the head with a skillet as not. So get out and leave me alone."

Gravel geysered under the stallion's hoofs as it skidded to a stop before the walk leading up to the front door of the stone mansion. Lord swung down, saw Lila spurring toward him from

341

the corrals a hundred yards away, and ran to meet her, hauling the stallion in his wake. He tossed the reins to her. "Cool him out for me, will you?" he said, and was sprinting across the lawn before the surprised girl could do more than catch the reins and nod.

With his hand on the ornate latch of the massive door, the courage that had brought him this far suddenly deserted him and he stood there, reaching deeply for wind, his heart hammering, his legs trembling as though he had run a mile instead of a scant fifty yards. He swallowed once, wiped his sweating palms on his thighs, and knocked on the door. When it did not instantly open, he knocked again, harder and longer. His fist was poised to bang out a third summons when the latch clicked. The next instant he was looking down into Fresno's displeased eyes.

"Must you beat this door," she began impatiently, and ended in a falling whisper, "off its hinges?" and stood there as if paralyzed, all color draining out of her face.

His gaze fixed on that white face, Lord felt his mind grind to a halt. The silence that enveloped them was so complete that he could hear Lila's voice fifty yards away sternly ordering the stallion to behave as she ponied it alongside her bay. Every word was as distinct as though she were speaking from ten feet away. Into that continuing stillness, he dropped his voice and did not recognize it as his own.

"Hello, Fresno. Welcome home."

Her frozen lips scarcely moved. "Good . . . afternoon, Mr. Lord."

The icy formality of her tone locked his throat against further speech. He swallowed, then coughed, and the sound was harsh and crude in his ears. "I came over as soon as I heard you were back."

She had not fully opened the door, but had merely swung it wide enough to permit her to look out. Now she reached out her other hand and gripped the casing, making of her high, taut shape a barrier across the narrow opening. "Who told you?" she asked woodenly.

"Martha. She promised to let me know the minute you returned."

"I see."

Again his throat constricted, and again he swallowed audibly. He put up a hand and raked the hair back from his right temple, and forced his lips to smile. "You haven't invited me in, Fresno."

"No."

He stood there at a complete loss. In all his countless imaginings of this moment, he had never pictured one remotely resembling this. The pale woman before him was an utter stranger—an alien being carved in ice. In the great violet eyes he could detect no faintest warmth, nor even recognition. They were fixed on him in an ungiving stare that transmitted such coldness that he felt his entire being congeal, his thinking rendered ponderous and unwieldy. In a desperate attempt to free himself from the paralysis creeping over him, he forced his voice past the stifling stricture in his throat and was mortified to discover that his superhuman effort had produced only a hoarse, rasping whisper.

"I came over here to tell you—" he began, and in a kind of horror felt his throat close completely.

"Yes?"

Her voice was as clear and as utterly detached as the single strike of a bell. She gave him no help at all.

"—that I love you and to ask you to marry me," he got out in a breathless rush.

"You love—?" Her lips moved stiffly, as a thin wail sounded in the room behind her; and on the instant her expression changed to one of sheer terror. Before Lord could equate the sound with its effect on her, she had slammed the door shut in his face.

The heavy key was grating in the lock when his striking hand knocked the door wide. He leaped across the threshold as a second door swung shut directly across the wide foyer. It, too, gave to his thrusting hand, and he was then inside a high-vaulted, shadowy room which he recognized as a library. He abruptly halted to watch Fresno bending protectingly over something which at first glance he mistook for a bundle of clothing on the leather couch by the fireplace. But even as he strode forward, he realized that the wailing sound was issuing from that bundle. Three more long strides place him alongside the couch, and he was staring down in shock at a baby's contorted, reddened face. Seemingly of their own volition his legs folded, lowering him to

343

his knees. He reached out a long forefinger and tentatively touched the wrinkled forehead.

"What is his name?" he breathed.

"What makes you think it's a boy?"

"It's a boy." He could not take his gaze off that tiny face. "What is his name?"

"Saul."

He made a thoughtful, humming sound, and tried the name on his tongue. "Saul . . . Saul . . . Israel's first king. Quite a name to live up to, isn't it?"

"It means, 'the desired one,' " she said faintly, and sat down on the edge of the couch, as though her legs would no longer support her.

He found himself looking directly into her eyes when he glanced up. She was within easy reach, but he made no attempt to touch her. He asked very quietly, "Why didn't you tell me?" and watched her gaze fall away and become fixed on her clenched hands in her lap. "Did it never occur to you that I had a right to know?"

She gave her head a tight, quick shake and would not look at him. There was a wide spill of frothy lace down the front of her close-fitting bodice. It sank slightly with the faint outrun of her breath, started to lift, and caught. "I intended to give him away . . . at first," she said, the words sounding as though they were being dragged out of her against her will. "I meant for you never to see him . . . never to know."

"Why?"

"For fear you would turn away from him as your father turned away from you. I was determined to spare him the hell you knew . . . the hell of knowing he was not wanted by *his* father."

"But you didn't," Lord said. "Why?"

The froth of lace again sank, started to lift, and again caught and held. She started to reply, but the trembling of her lips rendered speech impossible. Suddenly and terribly she was weeping. She put a shaking hand over her eyes and bent forward to hide her humiliation from him. A single harsh sob escaped her, and then she was speaking in a hollow voice.

"Long before he came I knew I could not do it! May God

344

forgive me if I've done wrong by him! But even if it is wrong, I don't care! He is all I have left to me out of the wreck of years, and I will never give him up . . . *never!* Somehow I will make it up to him. *I will! I will!*"

He touched her now, taking her hand from her eyes, and very gently and very firmly laying hold of the fist tightly clenched in her lap and forcing it open so that the warmth of his brown flesh enveloped the icy palm. He said so softly, "Fresno, look at me," but she would not. He said then in deepest contrition, "You must believe me: I never meant to shame you."

Her head lifted as though jerked by invisible wires. "I have felt no shame! None! Nor have I ever regretted giving myself to you. I regret one thing only: that my love was not enough for you. I had thought . . . *hoped* . . . it might be . . . *would* be . . . but when—"

"Fresno," he ordered, "be quiet."

"No, I will not be quiet! I will tell you now—"

"I said, *be quiet*, Fresno."

"No! Now I will tell you—" She stopped, thunderstruck by the expression of amusement that had come into his face.

"I was blind," Lord stated. "Apparently you are becoming deaf."

"Deaf?" she echoed blankly. "Aaron, what are you—?"

There could be no doubt about it: he was openly laughing at her, for all he made no sound. "Either that, or else you have become mentally deranged to the point of being unable to remember from one minute to the next what someone has said to you."

"Aaron, please! This is hardly the time—"

"Otherwise," he went on imperturbably, "you would have remembered what I said to you out on the terrace just now. *Do* you remember?"

She was utterly confused by this unexpected line of questioning. "Not exactly. I think you said something like, 'Welcome back,' but—"

"Good," he said gravely. "Your condition may not be altogether hopeless, after all. What I actually said was not only, 'Welcome back,' but also, 'I love you and want you to marry me.' Will you?"

345

For a long moment she stared at him, watching his amused expression change to one of utter seriousness. On the point of answering him, she let her glance fall to the sleeping Saul and felt doubt touch her. "Did you know about him?" she asked. "Did Martha tell you?"

"She told me only that you were home again."

The dark lashes lifted, and the great eyes were again holding him, searching deep inside him for the truth she must find. "Then . . . you actually came here to say what you just said you said?"

The way in which she jumbled her grammar, who had never been known to permit either her grammar or her thoughts to become jumbled, brought that look of amusement back into his face. "If your question means what I think it does, then my answer is yes, that is why I came. But I also want you to forgive me, as well as marry me. Will you?"

"What?"

The very realness of her confusion served to heighten his amusement. "*Forgive* me and *marry* me," he said.

"The answer is yes and no."

His left eyebrow drew down; the right lifted quizzically. "Yes *and* no?"

Fresno kept her face smoothly noncommittal. "To your request for my hand," she said with immense dignity, "I return a most emphatic '*Yes!*' To the other I must reply, 'No, I will *not* forgive you . . . *ever!*' "

In setting herself to play out the little scene, she had sadly overestimated her ability to resist the powerful influence his nearness exerted over her. Feeling that resistance beginning to crumble with alarming suddenness, she spoke swiftly.

"The explanation is very simple, my dear. There is nothing to forgive. Nothing at all." And having said that, her composure deserted her without warning and she cried, "Oh, Aaron! Please hold me, and quickly! I'll not believe this is true until you do!"

It was a thing she need not have asked, for even before the words were out his hard arms were encircling her and drawing her close against the hunger that trembled in his big frame and told her all she needed to know.

346